CONTENTS

THE AFFAIR   7
Maya Banks

ONE NIGHT...NINE-MONTH SCANDAL   195
Sarah Morgan

Dear Reader,

The Anetakis Tycoons trilogy comes to a close with *The Affair*, Piers Anetakis's story.

Of the three Anetakis brothers, Piers is the most closed off and the most troubled. But he's also the most passionate and emotional.

He's been hurt by past betrayals, but then so has Jewel Henley, the woman Piers meets one night in an intimate, tropical setting. These two are kindred spirits, and they have a lot to offer one another—if they can ever get around their issues of trust.

I'm inviting you along for the exciting conclusion of the Anetakis family's story. Rich, powerful and ruthless, these three men learn that no amount of wealth or privilege can ever fill the places in their hearts only love can reach. Piers and Jewel must navigate many obstacles in their search for happiness. Their love will be tested, and they'll have to offer the one thing not easily given by either: their trust.

Maya Banks

MAYA BANKS

has loved romance novels from a very (very) early age, and almost from the start, she dreamed of writing them, as well. In her teens she filled countless notebooks with overdramatic stories of love and passion. Today her stories are only slightly less dramatic, but no less romantic.

She lives in Texas with her husband and three children and wouldn't contemplate living anywhere other than the South. When she's not writing, she's usually hunting, fishing or playing poker. She loves to hear from her readers, and she can be found on Facebook, or you can follow her on Twitter (@maya_banks). Her website, www.mayabanks.com, is where you can find up-to-date information on all of Maya's current and upcoming releases.

SARAH MORGAN

USA TODAY bestselling author Sarah Morgan writes hot, happy contemporary romance and her trademark humor and sensuality have gained her fans across the globe. Described as "a magician with words" by *RT Book Reviews*, she has been nominated three years in succession for the prestigious RITA® Award from the Romance Writers of America and won the award twice: in 2012 for her book *Doukakis's Apprentice* and in 2013 for *A Night of No Return*. She also won the RT Reviewers' Choice Award in 2012 and has made numerous appearances in their "Top Pick" slot.

Sarah lives near London with her husband and children, and when she isn't reading or writing she loves being outdoors, preferably on vacation so she can forget the house needs tidying. You can visit Sarah online at www.sarahmorgan.com, on Facebook at facebook.com/AuthorSarahMorgan and on Twitter @SarahMorgan_.

MAYA BANKS
THE AFFAIR

Recycling programs for this product may not exist in your area.

ISBN-13: 978-0-373-18078-3

The Affair

Copyright © 2014 by Harlequin Books S.A.

The publisher acknowledges the copyright holders of the individual works as follows:

The Tycoon's Secret Affair
Copyright © 2009 by Maya Banks

One Night...Nine-Month Scandal
First North American Publication 2010
Copyright © 2010 by Sarah Morgan

This edition published by arrangement with Harlequin Books S.A.

For questions and comments about the quality of this book, please contact us at CustomerService@Harlequin.com.

Printed in U.S.A.

www.Harlequin.com

THE AFFAIR

Maya Banks

To Dee, who loved Piers from the start.

Prologue

Jewel Henley shifted on the hospital bed, one hand curled around her cell phone, the other hand pushing aside hot tears. She had to call him. She had no choice.

Having to depend on the man who couldn't get her out of his life fast enough after their one-night stand wasn't a prospect she relished, but for her baby, she'd do anything. Swallow her pride and try to let go of the burning anger.

Her free hand dropped to rest on the burgeoning swell of her belly, and she felt the sturdy reassurance of her daughter's kick.

How would Piers react when she told him he was going to be a father? Would he even care? She shook her head in mute denial. Surely, no matter his feelings for her, he wouldn't turn his back on his child.

There was only one way to find out and that was to

push the send button. His private phone number was already punched in. She may have been fired from her job, but for some reason, she'd held on to the phone numbers she'd been provided upon her hiring.

And still she couldn't bring herself to complete the call. She let the phone drop to her chest and closed her eyes. If only there weren't complications with her pregnancy. Why couldn't she be one of these beautiful, glowing women who were pictures of health?

Her thoughts were interrupted when her door swung open and a nurse bustled in pushing a cart with the computer she used to log her charts.

"How are you feeling today, Miss Henley?"

Jewel nodded and whispered a faint, "Fine."

"Have you made arrangements for your care after your release?"

Jewel swallowed but didn't say anything. The nurse gave her a reproving look.

"You know the doctor won't release you until he's satisfied that you'll have someone to look after you while you're on bed rest."

A sigh escaped Jewel's lips and she held up the phone. "I was just about to make a call."

The nurse nodded approvingly. "Good. As soon as I'm done I'll leave you alone to finish."

A few minutes later the nurse left, and once again Jewel lifted the phone and stared at the LCD screen. Maybe he wouldn't even answer.

Taking a deep, fortifying breath, she punched her thumb over the send button then closed her eyes and put the phone to her ear. There was a brief silence as the call connected, and then it began to ring.

Once. Twice. Then a third time. She was preparing

to chicken out and cut the connection when his brusque voice filled her ear.

"Anetakis."

It came out more of a growl than anything else, and she quickly lost courage. Her breath came stuttering out as more tears welled in her eyes.

"Who is this?" he demanded.

She yanked the phone away and clumsily jabbed at the buttons until the call ended. She couldn't do this. Issuing a silent apology to her unborn baby, she decided that she'd find another way. There had to be something she could do that didn't involve Piers Anetakis.

Before she could dwell too long on such possibilities, the phone pulsed in her hand. She opened it automatically, a second before she realized that he was calling her back.

Only her soft breathing spilled into the receiver.

"I know you're there," Piers barked. "Now who the hell is this and how did you get my number?"

"I'm sorry," she said in a low voice. "I shouldn't have bothered you."

"Wait," he commanded. Then there was a long pause. "Jewel, is that you?"

Oh God. She hadn't counted on him recognizing her voice. How could he? They hadn't spoken in five months. Five months, one week and three days to be exact.

"Y-yes," she finally said.

"Thank God," he muttered. "I've been looking everywhere for you. Just like a damn female to disappear off the face of the earth."

"What?"

"Where are you?"

The questions came simultaneously.

"Me first," he said imperiously. "Where are you? Are you all right?"

She laid there in stunned silence before she gathered her scattered wits. "I'm in the hospital."

"Theos." There was another rapid smattering of Greek that she couldn't have followed even if she understood the language.

"Where?" he bit out. "What hospital? Tell me."

Completely baffled at the turn the conversation had taken, she told him the name of the hospital. Before she could say anything else, he cut in with, "I'll be there as soon as I can."

And then the line went dead.

With shaking hands, she folded the phone shut and set it aside. Then she curled her fingers around the bulge of her abdomen. He was coming? Just like that? He'd been looking for her? None of it made sense.

Then she realized that she'd never told him the most important piece of information. The entire reason she'd called him to begin with. She hadn't told him she was pregnant.

Chapter 1

Five months earlier...

Jewel paused just outside the perimeter of the outdoor bar and stared over the sand-covered floor to the blazing torches lining the walkway down to the beach.

Music played softly, a perfect accompaniment to the clear, star-strung night. In the distance, the waves rolled in harmony with the sultry melody. Soft jazz. Her favorite.

It was pure chance that had directed her to this tiny island paradise. A vacated seat on a plane, a bargain ticket price and only five minutes to decide. And here she was. A new place, a vow to take a few days for herself.

Not being completely impulsive, the first thing she'd done when she'd arrived was to find a new temporary job, and as luck would have it, had learned that the owner of the opulent Anetakis Hotel was going to be in temporary residence here and needed an assistant. Four weeks. A perfect amount of time to spend in paradise before she moved on.

The opportunity had almost been too good to be true. Along with a generous salary, she'd also been given a room at the hotel. It had the makings of a marvelous vacation.

"Are you going out or are you going to spend such a lovely night indoors?"

The vaguely accented male voice brushed across her ears, eliciting a trail of chill bumps down her spine. She turned and was forced to look up for the source of the huskily spoken words.

When she met his eyes, she felt the impact clear to her toes. Her belly clenched, and for a moment it was hard to breathe.

The man wasn't just gorgeous. There were plenty of gorgeous men in the world, and she'd met her share. This one was…powerful. A predator in a sea of sheep. His eyes bore into hers with an intensity that almost frightened her.

There was interest. Clear interest. She wasn't a fool, nor did she indulge in silly games of false modesty.

She stared back, unable to wrest herself from the force of his gaze. Black. His eyes were as black as night. His hair was as dark, and his skin gleamed golden brown in the soft light of the torches. Firelight cast a sheen to his eyes, shiny onyx, glittering and proud.

His jawline was firm, set, a strong tilt that denoted his arrogance, a quality she was attracted to in men.

For a long moment he returned her frank appraisal, and then his lips curved upward into a slight smile.

"A woman of few words I see."

She shook herself and mentally scolded her tongue for knotting up so badly.

"I was deciding on whether to go out or not."

He lifted one imperious brow, a gesture that seemed more challenging than questioning.

"But I can't buy you a drink if you remain inside."

She cocked her head to the side, allowing a tiny smile to relax the tension bubbling inside her. She wasn't a stranger to sexual attraction, but she couldn't remember the last time a man had affected her so strongly right off the bat.

Awareness sizzled between them, almost as if a fuse had been lit the moment he'd spoken. Would she accept the unspoken invitation in his eyes? Oh, she knew he'd asked to buy her a drink, but that wasn't all he wanted. The question was whether she was bold enough to reach out and take the offer.

What could a single night hurt? She was extremely choosy in her partners. She hadn't taken a lover in two years. She just hadn't been interested until this dark-eyed stranger with his sensual smile and mocking arrogance came along. Oh yes, she wanted him. So much so that she vibrated with it.

"Are you here on holiday?" she asked as she peered up at him from underneath her lashes.

Again his lips quirked into a half smile. "In a manner of speaking."

Relief scurried through her belly. No, one night wouldn't hurt. He'd leave and go back to his world.

Eventually she'd move on, and their paths would never cross again.

Tonight…tonight she was lonely, a feeling she didn't often indulge in, even if she spent the majority of her time in isolation.

"I'd like a drink," she said by way of agreement.

Something predatory sparked in his eyes. A glow that was gone almost as soon as it burst to life. His hand came up and cupped her elbow, his fingers splaying possessively over her skin.

She closed her eyes for a brief moment, enjoying the electric sensation that sizzled through her body the moment he touched her.

He led her from the protective awning of the hotel into the night air. Around them the warm glow of torches danced in time with the sweet sounds of jazz. The breeze coming off the water blew through her hair, and she inhaled deeply, enjoying the salt tang.

"Dance with me before we have that drink," he murmured close to her ear.

Without waiting for her consent, he pulled her into his arms, his hips meeting hers as he cupped her body close.

They fit seamlessly, her flush against him, melting and flowing until she wasn't sure where she ended and he began.

His cheek rested against the side of her head as his arms encircled her. Protective. Strong. She reached up, sliding her arms over his shoulders until they wrapped around his neck.

"You're beautiful."

His words flowed like warm honey over jaded ears. It wasn't the most original line, but that was just it.

Coming from him, it didn't sound like a line, but rather an honest assessment, a sincere compliment, one that maybe he'd ordinarily be unwilling to give.

"So are you," she whispered.

He chuckled, and his laughter vibrated over her sensitive skin. "Me beautiful? I'm unsure of whether to be flattered or offended."

She snorted. "I know for a fact I'm not the only woman to have ever called you beautiful."

"Do you now?"

His hands skimmed over her back, finding the flesh bared by the backless scoop of her dress. She sucked in her breath as his fingers burned her flesh.

"You feel it too," he murmured.

She didn't pretend not to know what he meant. The chemistry between them was combustible. Never before had she experienced anything like this, not that she'd tell him that.

Instead she nodded her agreement.

"Are we going to do anything about it?"

She leaned back and tilted her head to meet his eyes. "I'd like to think we are."

"Direct. I like that in a woman."

"I like that in a man."

Amusement softened the intensity of his gaze, but she saw something else in his expression. Desire. He wanted her as badly as she wanted him.

"We could have that drink in my room."

She sucked in her breath. Even though she knew what he wanted, the invitation still hit her squarely in the stomach. Her breasts tightened against his chest, and arousal bloomed deep.

"I'm not…" For the first time, she sounded unsure,

hesitant. Not at all the decisive woman she knew herself to be.

"You're not what?" he prompted.

"Protected," she said, her voice nearly drowning in the sounds around them.

He tucked a finger underneath her chin and forced her to once again meet his seeking gaze. "I'll take care of you."

The firm promise wrapped around her more securely than his arms. For a moment she indulged in the fantasy of what it would be like to have a man such as this take care of her for the rest of her life. Then she shook her head. Such foolish notions shouldn't disrupt the fantasy of this one night.

She rose up on tiptoe, her lips a breath away from his. "What's your room number?"

"I'll take you up myself."

She shook her head, and he frowned.

"I'll meet you there."

His eyes narrowed for a moment as if he wasn't sure whether to believe her or not. Then without warning, he slid a hand around her neck and curled his fingers around her nape. He pulled her to him, pressing his lips to hers.

She went liquid against him, her body sliding bonelessly downward. He hauled her against him with his free arm, anchoring her tight to prevent her fall.

He licked over her lips, pressing, demanding her to open. With a breathless gasp, she surrendered, parting her mouth so his tongue could slide inward.

Hot, moist openmouthed kisses. He stole her breath and returned it. His teeth scraped at her lip then captured it and tugged relentlessly. Unwilling to remain a passive participant, she fired back, sucking at his tongue.

His groan echoed over her ears. Her sigh spilled into his mouth.

He finally pulled away, his breaths coming in ragged heaves. His eyes flashed dangerously, sending a shiver over her flesh.

Then he shoved a keycard into her hand. "Top floor. Suite eleven. Hurry."

With that he turned and stalked back into the hotel, his stride eating up the floor.

She stared after him, her body humming and her mind in a million different pieces. She was completely shattered by what she'd just experienced.

"I must be insane. He'll eat me alive."

A low hum of heady desire buzzed through her veins. She could only hope she was right.

She turned on shaking legs and walked slowly into the hotel. It wasn't that she was being deliberately coy by putting her mystery man off. Mystery man… She didn't even know his name, but she'd agreed to have sex with him.

Then again, it had a certain appeal, this air of mystery. A night of fantasy. No names. No expectations. No entanglements or emotional involvement. No one would get hurt. It was, in fact, perfect.

No, she wasn't being cute. But if she was going to go through with this, it would be on her own terms. Her dark-eyed lover wouldn't have complete control of the situation.

With more calm than she felt, she went up to her room. Once there, she surveyed her reflection in the bathroom mirror. Her hair was slightly mussed and her lips swollen. Passion. She looked as if she'd had an encounter with the very essence of passion.

The sultry temptress staring back at her wasn't a woman she recognized, but she decided she liked this new person. She looked beautiful and confident, and excitement sparked her eyes at the thought of what waited for her in suite eleven.

After a lifetime of loneliness, of being alone, the idea of spending the night in a lover's arms was so appealing that it was all she could do not to hurry out to the elevator.

Instead she forced herself to take steadying breaths. She stared at herself until the wildness faded from her eyes and coolness replaced it. Then she smoothed her long blond hair away from her face.

Satisfied that she had herself under control, she walked out of the bathroom to sit on the bed. She'd wait fifteen to twenty minutes before she headed up. No need to seem too eager.

Chapter 2

Piers prowled his suite, unaccustomed to the edginess that consumed him ever since he'd parted ways with the blond bombshell downstairs. He stopped his restless pacing and poured a drink from the crystal decanter on the bar, but he didn't drink it. Instead he stared at the amber liquid then glanced at his watch for the third time.

Would she come?

He cursed his eagerness. He felt like an errant teenager sneaking out of the house to meet a girlfriend. His reaction to the woman couldn't be explained except in terms of lust and desire.

He wanted her. Had wanted her from the moment he spotted her staring longingly through the open doorway of the hotel. He'd been mesmerized by the picture she portrayed. Long and sleek with slender legs, a narrow waist and high, firm breasts. Her hair fell like silk over her shoulders and down her back and his fingers itched to dive into the tresses and wrap them around his knuckles while he devoured her plump lips.

Even now his groin ached uncomfortably. Never had he reacted so strongly to a woman, and it bothered him even as the idea of taking her to bed fired his senses.

A soft knock at his door thrust him to attention, and he hurried across to open it. She stood there, delightfully shy, her ocean eyes a strange mixture of emerald and sapphire.

"I know you gave me a key," she said in a low voice, "but it seemed rude to just barge in."

He found his voice, though his mouth had gone dry as soon as she spoke. He reached for her hand, and she placed it trustingly in his. "I'm glad you came," he said huskily as he pulled her forward.

Instead of leading her farther inside, he wrapped his arms around her, molding her to the contours of his body. She trembled softly against him, and he could feel her heart fluttering like the beat of hummingbird wings.

Unable to resist the temptation, he lowered his mouth to hers, wanting to taste her again. Just once. But when their lips met, he forgot all about his intention to sample.

She responded hotly, her arms sliding around his body. Her hands burned into his skin, through the material of his shirt as if it wasn't there. His impatience grew. He wanted her naked. Wanted him to be naked so he could feel her skin on his.

Thoughts of taking it slow, of seducing her in measured steps flew out the window as he drank deeply of her sweetness. He wasn't sure who was seducing whom, and at this moment, it didn't matter.

His lips scorched a path down the side of her neck as his fingers tugged impatiently at the fastenings of her dress. Smooth, creamy skin revealed itself, and his mouth was drawn relentlessly to the bare expanse as her dress fell away.

She moaned softly and shivered as his tongue trailed over the curve of her shoulder. He pushed at the dress, and it fell to the floor leaving her in only a dainty scrap of lacy underwear.

All his breath left him as he looked down at the full round globes of her breasts. Her nipples puckered and strained as if begging for his attention. The tips were velvet under his seeking fingers. He toyed with one and then the other before cupping one breast in his palm and lowering his head to press a kiss just above the peach areola.

Her breath caught and held, and she tensed as his tongue lazily traced downward to suck the nipple into his mouth.

Her taste exploded in his mouth. Sweet. Delicate like a flower. So feminine. Perfect. His senses reeled, and he pulled away for a moment to recoup his control. *Theos* but she drove him mad. He reacted to her like a man making love to his first woman.

Already his manhood strained at his pants, and he was dangerously close to flinging her on the bed and stroking into her liquid heat.

Finesse. He must take it slower. He wouldn't allow her such power over him. He would make her as crazy as she made him, and then and only then would he take her.

Jewel grabbed his shoulders as her knees buckled. She needn't have worried. He swept her into his arms and carried her toward the bedroom just beyond the sitting area of the suite.

He laid her on the bed then stood back and began to hastily strip out of his clothing. There was something incredibly sexy about a man standing over her as he undressed. His eyes burned into her, heating her skin even from a distance.

First his shirt fell away revealing smooth, muscled shoulders, a rugged chest and narrow waist with enough of a six-pack to suggest he wasn't an idle businessman. Hair dotted the hollow of his chest, spreading just to his flat nipples. It was thicker at his midline, trailing lower to his navel, tapering to a faint smattering just above the waist of his pants.

She stared hungrily at him as he unfastened his trousers. He didn't waste time or tease unnecessarily. He shoved them down his legs, taking his boxers with him. His erection sprang free from a dark nest of hair. Her eyes widened at the way it strained upward, toward his taut belly. He was hugely aroused.

Her question must have shone on her face. He crawled onto the bed, straddling her hips with his knees. "Was there any doubt that I wanted you, *yineka mou?*"

She smiled up at him. "No."

"Rest assured, I want you very much," he said huskily. He lowered his head until his mouth found hers in a heated rush.

Her entire body arched to meet him, wanting the contact, the warmth and passion he offered. It had been so long since she'd purposely sought out the company of another person, and this man assaulted her senses. He flooded her with a longing that unsettled her.

He pushed her arms over her head until she was helpless beneath him. He didn't just kiss her, he devoured her. There wasn't an inch of her skin that didn't feel the velvet brush of his lips.

Her gasp echoed across the room when he licked and suckled each breast in turn. His tongue left a damp trail down her midline as he licked down to the shallow indention of her navel. There wasn't a single muscle that wasn't quivering in sharp anticipation.

His hands followed, his palms running the length of her body, tracing each curve, each indention, and settled on her hips. He tucked his thumbs underneath the thin string holding her underwear in place, and then he pressed his mouth to her soft mound still covered by transparent lace.

She cried out softly, unnerved by the electric sensation of his mouth over her most intimate place, and yet he hadn't even made contact with her flesh.

His hands caressed their way down her legs, dragging the underwear with it. At her knees, he simply ripped impatiently, rending the material in two. He quickly discarded it and returned impatient fingers to her thighs.

Carefully, he spread her, and she began to shake in earnest.

"Don't be afraid," he murmured. "I'll take care of you. Trust me tonight. You're so beautiful. I want to give you the sweetest pleasure."

"Yes. Please, yes," she begged.

He kissed the inside of her knee. With a brush of his lips, he moved higher, kissing the inside of her thigh, and then finally brushing over the curls guarding her most sensitive regions.

With a gentle finger, he parted her. "Give me your pleasure, *yineka mou.* Only to me." And then his mouth touched her. She bucked upward with a wild cry as his tongue delved deep. It was too much. It had been too long. Never had she reacted so strongly to a man.

"So responsive. So wild. I can't wait to have you."

He rolled away, and she gave a sharp protest until she saw he was only putting on a condom. Then he was back, spreading her thighs, stroking her to make sure she was ready for him.

"Take me. Make me yours," she pleaded.

He closed his eyes, his fingers tight at her hips. He spread her wide and surged into her with one hard thrust.

Her shocked gasp spilled from her lips. Her fingers tightened at his shoulders, and she lay still, simply absorbing the rugged sensation of having him inside her.

His eyes flew open. "Did I hurt you?" he demanded harshly, the strain evident on his face as he held himself in check.

She touched his cheek, trying to soften the lines. His eyes glittered dangerously, and she realized just how close he was to the edge of his control. In that moment, she relished her power, and she wanted to taunt the beast. She wanted to experience the wildness she could see lurking beyond the iron facade.

"No," she said softly. "You didn't hurt me. I want you so much. Take me now. Don't hold back."

To emphasize her request, she dug her nails into his shoulders then lifted her hips in a move that lodged him deeper inside her.

He made one last effort to hold back, but she wouldn't allow it. Wrapping her legs tightly around his waist, she arched into him, reaching for him, pulling him closer. She wanted him. She *needed* him.

He dropped down, surrendering with a growl. He gathered her close, fastening his lips to the vulnerable skin of her neck as his body took over. Harder and faster, his power overwhelmed her. There was a delicious mix of erotic pain and sensual bliss. Heaven. It wasn't something she'd ever experienced before. It was like riding a hurricane.

"Let go," he rasped in her ear. "You first."

She complied without argument, surrendering completely to his will. Her orgasm flashed, terrifying and thrilling all at the same time. She spun wildly out of control, her cries mixing with his.

Then he was moving faster, and harder, driving into her with savage intensity. His lips fused to hers almost in a desperate attempt to stanch his own sounds, but they escaped, harsh and masculine.

Then he stilled inside her, his hips trembling uncontrollably against hers. He smoothed his hands, now gentle, over her face, through her hair and then he gathered her close, murmuring words she didn't understand against her ear.

When his weight grew too heavy, he shifted to the side, pulling her into his arms. He slipped from the warm grasp of her body then rolled away from her for a moment to discard the condom.

She waited with breathless anticipation. Would he want her to leave now or would he want her to spend the night? She was too sated and boneless to even think about getting up, but neither did she want any awkward situations.

He answered her unspoken dilemma by pulling her back into his arms and tucking her head underneath his chin. A few moments later, his soft breathing blew through her hair. He had fallen asleep.

Cautiously so as not to awaken him, she curled her arm around his waist and snuggled deeper into his embrace. Her cheek rested against the hair-roughened skin of his chest, and she inhaled deeply, filling her nostrils with his male scent.

For the space of a stolen moment she felt safe. Accepted. Even cherished. It was silly if she dwelled on it, but tonight she wouldn't. Tonight she just wanted to belong to someone and not to feel so alone in the world.

Even in sleep, he seemed to sense her disquiet. His arms tightened around her, bringing her even closer to his warmth. She smiled and gave in to the sleepy pleasure seeping into her bones.

Piers awoke unsure of the time, a rarity for him. He usually woke every morning before dawn, his mind alert and ready to take on the day's tasks. Today however sleep clouded his brain, and uncharacteristic laziness permeated his muscles. Something soft and feminine stirred his senses, and he woke enough to realize that she was still in his arms.

Instead of rolling away, of distancing himself immediately, he remained there, breathing in her scent. He should get up and shower, make it clear the interlude was over, but he hung on, unwilling to send her away just yet.

She stirred when his hands smoothed over her back,

down to her shapely buttocks and over the curve of her hip. He had to have her again. One more time. Even as warning bells clanged in his mind, he was turning her, sliding over her as he reached to the nightstand for another condom.

As her eyes fluttered sleepily, he slid inside her, slower this time, with more patience and care than he'd taken her the night before. He didn't want to chance hurting her, and if he was honest, he wanted to savor this last encounter.

"Good morning," she murmured in a husky voice that sent a shudder over his body.

He thrust deeper then leaned down to capture her mouth. "Good morning."

She yawned and stretched like a cat, wrapping her arms around his neck to pull him down again when he drew away. Sleek and beautiful, she matched his movements, rocking gently against him.

If last night had been the storm, this was a calm rain afterward. Gentle and extremely satisfying.

He tugged her hair from her face, unable to resist kissing her again and again. He couldn't get enough of her. The thought that he didn't want her to go rose in his mind. Before it could take root, he tamped it back down, determined not to get caught in an emotional trap.

He'd existed for too long without such entanglements, and he'd be damned if he allowed it to happen again.

She enveloped him in her tight grasp, her sweet depths clinging to him as he withdrew and thrust forward. He set an easy pace, one that would prolong their pleasure.

And when he could no longer delay the surge of exquisite pleasure, he pushed them both over the edge, leaving them gasping for breath and shaking in each other's arms.

For a long moment he lay there, still sheathed deeply inside her, his face buried in her sweet-smelling hair.

Then reality encroached. It was morning. Their night together was over, and it was best to end things now before things had a chance to get messy.

He rolled away abruptly, getting up from the bed and reaching for his pants.

"I'm going to take a shower," he said shortly when she did nothing more than watch him from her perch in his bed, her eyes probing him with a wary light.

She nodded, and he disappeared into the bathroom, his relief not as great as his regret. And when he returned a mere ten minutes later, he found her gone from his bed, from his hotel room. From his life.

Yes, she'd understood well the rules of the game. Maybe too well. For a moment he'd allowed himself to wish that maybe, just maybe she'd still be lying there. Warm and sated from his lovemaking. Belonging to him.

Chapter 3

Jewel stood outside the third floor offices of the Anetakis Hotel and smoothed a hand through her hair for the third time. It was a bad nervous habit and one destined to bring down more tendrils from the elegant knot she'd fashioned.

Instead she placed her palms over her skirt and removed nonexistent wrinkles as she waited admittance into Piers Anetakis's office.

She knew she looked cool and professional, a look she strove hard for. The woman who'd let loose with such abandon two nights before no longer existed. In her place was an unreadable face devoid of any emotion.

Still, despite her best efforts, thoughts of her lover drifted erotically through her mind. She'd left while he was in the shower, but she'd hoped to run into him again. A chance meeting. Maybe it would lead to another night even though she'd sworn it would only be one.

It was just as well. He was probably already gone back to wherever it was he lived. She'd move on herself in a few more weeks, armed with enough money to sustain her travels.

At times, she wondered what it would be like to settle in one place, to have all the comforts of home, but such an idea was alien to her. She'd learned long ago that a home wasn't in the cards for her.

She glanced down at her watch. Two minutes past eight. She was to have been summoned at eight. Apparently promptness wasn't one of Mr. Anetakis's strong points.

She clutched her briefcase to her and stared out the window to the waves crashing in the distance. The sea lost some of its romance in the daylight. It was still beautiful and striking, but at night under the flicker of torches and the glow of the moon, it took on a life of its own.

Her mouth twisted ruefully. She was still thinking of her dark-eyed lover. He was hard to forget, and she knew she'd be thinking of him for a long time to come.

Behind her the door opened, and an older woman stuck her head out and smiled at Jewel. "Miss Henley, Mr. Anetakis will see you now."

Jewel pasted a bright smile on her face and marched in behind the woman. Across the room Mr. Anetakis stood with his back to them, a cell phone stuck to his ear. When he heard them come in, he turned and Jewel halted. Her mouth flew open, and her eyes widened in shock.

To his credit, Mr. Anetakis merely raised an eyebrow in recognition, and then he closed his phone and nodded to the other lady.

"You can leave us now, Margery. Miss Henley and I have a lot to discuss."

Jewel swallowed nervously as Margery quietly left the room and shut the door behind her. Her fingers curled around her briefcase, and she held it almost like a shield as Mr. Anetakis stared holes through her. God, how this must look.

"You have to know I had no idea who you were," she said in a shaky voice before he could speak.

"Indeed," he said calmly. "I could see the shock when I turned around. Still, it makes things a bit awkward, wouldn't you say?"

"There's no reason things should be awkward," she said crisply. She moved forward, holding an outstretched hand. "Hello, Mr. Anetakis. I'm Jewel Henley, your new assistant. I trust we'll work well together."

His lips twisted into a sardonic smile. Before he could reply, his phone rang again.

"Excuse me, Miss Henley," he said in a cool voice. Then he picked up his cell phone.

He wasn't speaking English, but it was obvious the phone call wasn't to his liking. He frowned and then outright scowled. He barked a few words into the receiver before muttering something unintelligible and snapping it closed.

"My apologies. There is something I must attend to at once. You can see Margery in her office, and she'll get you…set up."

Jewel nodded as he strode out the door. As soon as

the door shut, all her breath left her in a whoosh that left her sagging. Of all the rotten luck. And to think she'd hoped they'd run into each other again so they could have a repeat performance.

On wobbly knees she went to find Margery and then prayed that she'd get through the next four weeks without losing her composure.

Piers got out of the helicopter and strode toward the car waiting to pick him up. As they drove toward the airport where his private jet awaited, he snapped open his phone and placed the call that he'd been deliberating over since he left his office.

His human resources manager for the island hotel picked up on the second ring.

"What can I do for you, Mr. Anetakis?" he asked once Piers had identified himself.

"Jewel Henley," he bit out.

"Your new assistant?"

"Get rid of her."

"Pardon? Is there a problem?"

"Just get rid of her. I want her gone by the time I return." He took a deep breath. "Transfer her, promote her or pay her for the entirety of her contract, but get rid of her. She can't work under me. I have a strict policy about personal involvement with my employees, and let's just say she and I have history."

He waited for a moment and when he didn't hear anything, he said, "Hello?" He cursed. The connection had been cut. Oh well, he didn't require a response. He just wanted action.

Even if he hadn't already been extremely distrustful of situations that seemed too coincidental, his brother's assistant had sold valuable company plans to their competitor. After that debacle, they'd all assumed very strict requirements for the people working closest to them. They could ill afford another Roslyn.

Still, his chest tightened as the car stopped outside his plane, and he got out to board. He wasn't so much in denial that he could refute that the night had been more than just a casual one-night stand. Which was all the more reason to cut ties now. He wouldn't give up any power, no matter how subtle, to a woman ever again.

Jewel sat in Margery's chair behind her desk filling out a mountain of paperwork while Margery puttered around in the background making phone calls and grumbling at the printer when it didn't spit out the appropriate documents.

She'd spent the morning on pins and needles, waiting for Piers to return so they could at least try and air things out and get it behind them. The old saying about an elephant in the room was appropriate, only Jewel felt like there was an entire herd.

At lunch, she went down to the small café and nibbled on a sandwich while watching the seagulls divebomb tourists who had bread to feed them. If Margery let her on the company computer this afternoon, she'd email Kirk and let him know she'd arrived on the island and would be staying a few weeks.

He was her only friend, but they rarely saw each other. He was forever taking assignments to far-flung places, and she was equally determined to travel her own way. It amused her that they were essentially lost souls who wandered from place to place. Neither had a home, and maybe that was why they understood each other.

An occasional email, sometimes a phone call, and every once in a while they crossed paths on their travels. Those were good times. It was nice to connect to another person even if it was only for a few hours. He was as close to a brother or family member as she'd ever imagined having.

After finishing her sandwich, she tossed the wrapper and walked back to the employee elevator. Would Piers be back? A flutter abounded in her stomach, but she swallowed back her nervousness and forged ahead. It wouldn't do to let him know she was put off by their unintentional relationship. If he could be cool about it then so could she.

When she walked back into Margery's office, Margery looked up, a grim expression on her face. "Mr. Patterson wants to see you immediately."

Jewel's brow crinkled. Maybe it was more personnel stuff to sign. Lord knows she'd had enough paperwork this morning to choke a horse. With a resigned sigh, she turned and left Margery's office and went several doors down to the human resource manager's cubicle.

He looked up when she tapped on the frame of his open door.

"Miss Henley, come in. Have a seat please."

She settled down in front of him and waited expectantly. He cleared his throat and tugged at his collar in an uncomfortable motion. Then he leveled a stare at her.

"When you hired on, it was with the condition that it was a temporary position. You were to be Mr. Anetakis's assistant for the duration of his stay here."

"Yes." They'd been through all of this and she was impatient to get on with it.

"I'm sorry to say that he no longer requires an assistant. He's had a change of plans. As such, your services are no longer required."

She stared, stunned, for a long moment. "Excuse me?"

"Your employment here is terminated effective immediately."

She stood, her legs trembling, her fingers curled into tight fists. "That bastard. What a complete and utter bastard!"

"Security will escort you to your room and wait while you collect your things," he continued as if she hadn't let loose with her tirade.

"You can tell Mr. Anetakis that he is the lowest form of pond scum. Verbatim, Mr. Patterson. Make sure he gets my message. He's a gutless piece of chicken shit, and I hope he chokes on his damn cowardice."

With that she turned and stormed out of his office, slamming the door as hard as she could. The sound reverberated down the hallway, and a few people stuck their heads out of their cubicles as she stalked past.

Unbelievable. He hadn't even had the courage to fire her himself. He let his personnel director handle it while he ran for the hills. What a crock.

Two security guards fell into step beside her when she neared the elevator. It pissed her off that she was being treated like a common criminal.

She rode the elevator with them in stiff silence. They walked behind her to her door and positioned themselves on either side of the frame while she went in. How long would they give her before bursting in?

The thought amused her even as rage crawled over her in waves.

Shedding her uncomfortable heels, she sank onto the bed like a deflated balloon. Damn the man. She had enough money to get off the island, but little else. Certainly no money to plan her next venture. She'd spent what she had to get here and taken the good-paying job to restock her resources. With the money earned in this job, she would have been able to travel, albeit economically, for the next six months without worrying about finances.

Now she faced the only choice available to her if she wanted a roof over her head. Going back home to San Francisco and the apartment that belonged to Kirk was her only option.

It had been an agreement between them. If she ever needed a place to stay, she was to go there. The utilities were taken care of each month and the pantry was stocked with staples.

She didn't even have a way to contact him other than email, and sometimes he went weeks without checking it. She just hoped he hadn't planned one of his rare trips home at the same time she'd be there.

Her fingers dug into her temples, and she closed her eyes. She could look for work here on the island, but she'd already exhausted most of her possibilities when this job had landed in her lap. Nothing else paid nearly as well, and now she had no desire to stay where she might actually run into Piers Anetakis. The worm.

San Francisco was it, she admitted with forlorn acceptance. Hopefully she could land a job, save up some money. Having a rent-free place to stay would be helpful but she hated to take advantage of Kirk's generosity.

"Damn you, Piers Anetakis," she whispered. He'd managed to turn the most beautiful night of her life into something tawdry and hateful.

With a resigned shake of her head, she knew there was little point in feeling sorry for herself. There was nothing to do but pick up and go on and hopefully learn a lesson in the process.

Chapter 4

Five months later...

Piers descended the steps of his private jet and strode across the paved runway to the waiting car. The damp, chilly San Francisco air was a far cry from the warm, tropical air he was used to. He hadn't taken the time to pack appropriate clothing, and the thin silk shirt and light suit coat didn't offer much in the way of protection from the pervading chill.

The driver had already been instructed as to Piers's destination, so he sat back as the car rolled away from the airport toward the hospital where Jewel was being treated.

What had happened to her? It must be serious if she'd broken down and phoned him after he hadn't been able to uncover her whereabouts for five months.

Guilt was a strong motivator, and yet his efforts had come to naught.

No matter. He now knew where she was. He'd see to it that she had the best care and settle an amount on her to compensate her loss of employment, and then maybe he could get her out of his head.

When they finally rolled up to the hospital, Piers wasted no time hurrying in. At the help desk he was given Jewel's room number, and he rode the elevator to the appropriate floor.

At her door, he found it slightly ajar and issued a soft knock. Not hearing any summons, he pushed the door open and quietly walked in.

She was barely more than a rumpled pile of sheets on the bed, her head propped haphazardly on her pillow. Her eyelashes rested on her cheeks, and her soft, even breathing signaled her sleep.

Even in rest, she looked worried, her face drawn, her brow wrinkled. Her fingers were clutched bloodlessly at the sheet gathered at her chest. And yet she was as beautiful as he remembered, and unfortunately for him, he'd been haunted by her beauty for the last five months.

He removed his suit coat and tossed it over the chair beside her bed and then settled himself down to sit and wait for her to wake. The slight movement alerted her, and her eyes flew open.

Shock registered as soon as she saw him. Her eyes widened in what looked to be panic. Her hands moved immediately to her stomach in a protective gesture he'd be blind to miss.

Then he saw what it was she was protecting. There

was an unmistakable swell, a taut mound that shielded a baby!

"You're pregnant!"

Her eyes narrowed. "Well, you needn't sound so accusing. I hardly got that way by myself."

For a moment he was too stunned to realize her implication, and then when it came, it trickled like ice down his spine. Old memories came back in a wave, and hot anger quickly melted away the cold in his veins.

"Are you saying it's mine?" he demanded. Already his mind was moving in a whir. He wouldn't be trapped again by a conniving woman.

"She," Jewel corrected. "At least refer to your daughter as a human being."

Damn her. She knew that by personalizing the vague entity she shielded that he'd be inhuman not to react.

"A daughter?"

Against his will, his voice softened, and he found himself examining her belly closer. He impatiently brushed aside her cupped hands and then snatched his own hand back when her belly rippled and jumped beneath his fingers.

"*Theos!* Is that her?"

Jewel smiled and nodded. "She's active this morning."

Piers shook his head in an attempt to brush away the spell. A daughter. Suddenly he envisioned a tiny little girl, a replica of Jewel but with his dark eyes. Damn her for making him dream again.

His expression hardened, and he once again focused his attention on Jewel. "Is she mine?"

Jewel met his steady gaze and nodded.

He swore softly. "We used protection. *I* used protection."

She shrugged. "She's yours."

"You expect me to accept that? Just like that?"

She struggled to sit up against her pillows, her fingers clenched into tight balls at her sides. "I haven't slept with another man in two years. She's yours."

He wasn't the gullible fool he'd been so many years ago. "Then you won't object to paternity testing."

She closed her eyes wearily and sank back into the covers. Hurt flickered in her eyes when she reopened them, but she shook her head. "No, Piers. I have nothing to hide."

"What is wrong with you? Why are you here in the hospital?" he asked, finally coming around to the matter at hand. He'd been completely blindsided by the discovery that the child she was pregnant with was... could be his.

"I've been ill," she said in a tired voice. "Elevated blood pressure. Fatigue. My doctor said my job had a lot to do with it, and he wants me to quit. He says I *must* quit, that I don't have a choice."

"What the devil have you been doing?" he demanded.

She lifted one shoulder. "Waitressing. It was all I could find on such short notice. I needed the money before I could move somewhere else. Somewhere warmer. Somewhere I could make more money. It's very expensive here in San Francisco."

"Then why did you come here from the island? You could have gone anywhere."

She cast him a bitter glance. "I have an apartment

here. One that is paid for. After I was fired, I had little choice in where to go. I had to have a place to sleep. I intended to save enough money and then go somewhere else."

He flinched as guilt consumed him. Damn, but this was a mess. Not only had he had her fired, but he'd sent a pregnant woman into a bad situation.

"Look, Jewel, about your firing…"

She held up a hand, her expression fierce. "I don't want to discuss it. You're a coward and a bastard of the first order. I wouldn't have *ever* spoken to you again if our daughter didn't need you, if *I* didn't need your help."

"That's just it. I never intended for you to be fired," he said patiently.

She glared at him. "That's hardly comforting given that I *was* fired and that I *was* escorted out of your hotel."

He sighed. Now wasn't the time to try and reason with her. She was growing more upset by the minute. If she chose to believe the worst in him, and it was obvious she did, he was hardly going to change five months' worth of anger and resentment in five minutes.

"So what is it that you need from me?" he asked. "I'll help in any way I can."

She stared at him, suspicion burning brightly in her ocean eyes. Maybe he was wrong to want his daughter to have his eyes. No, she should definitely have Jewel's eyes. Dark-haired like him, but with her mother's sea-green eyes. Or were they blue? He could never tell from one moment to the next.

Then her shoulders sank, and she closed her eyes.

"My physician won't discharge me until he's certain I have someone to care for me."

She said the latter with a measure of distaste, as if it pained her to be dependent on anyone.

"I'll be on bed rest until my surgery."

Piers sat forward. "Surgery? Why do you need surgery? I thought you said you were only ill. Blood pressure." He knew enough about that from his sister-in-law's pregnancy to know that the prescribed treatment for stress or elevated blood pressure was merely rest and to be off one's feet. "You can't have surgery while you're pregnant. What about the baby?"

She stared back at him patiently. "That's just it. When they did a sonogram to check on the baby, they found a large cyst on one of my ovaries. Instead of shrinking, as a lot of cysts do during the course of the pregnancy, this one has gotten larger, and now it's pressing on the uterus. They have no choice but to remove it so that it won't interfere with the pregnancy or possibly even harm the baby."

Piers cursed. "This operation, is it dangerous? Will it harm the baby?"

"The doctor doesn't think so, but it has to be done soon."

He cursed again, though he didn't allow the words past his lips. He didn't want to be ensnared in another situation where he stood to lose everything. Once a fool, but never again. This time things would be done on his terms.

"You're going to marry me," he announced baldly.

Chapter 5

"You're out of your mind," Jewel burst out.

Piers's eyes narrowed. "I'd hardly say my speaking of marriage constitutes an unsound mind."

"Crazy. Certifiable."

He bristled and let out an irritated growl. "I am not crazy."

"You're serious!"

She stared at him with a mixture of stupefaction and horror.

His breath escaped in a long sound of exasperation.

Her mouth fell open. "For the love of God. You think I'd *marry* you?"

"There's no reason to sound so appalled."

"Appalled," she muttered. "That about covers my reaction. Look, Piers. I need your help. Your support. But I don't need marriage. Not to you. Never to you."

"Well if you want my support, you're damn well going to have to marry me for it," he growled.

"Get out," she bit off. She held a trembling hand up to point to the door, but Piers caught it and curled his fingers around hers. He brought it to the edge of the bed and gently stroked the inside of her wrist.

"I shouldn't have said that. You made me angry. If you're pregnant with my child, of course you'll have my support, Jewel. I'll do everything I can to provide for you and our daughter."

Astounded by his abrupt turnaround, she could only stare at him, her tongue flapping to try and come up with something, anything to say. How could he still affect her this way after all he'd done?

"Then you'll say no more about marriage?"

His lips tightened. "I didn't promise that. I have every intention of marrying you as quickly as possible and definitely before this surgery."

"But—"

He held up his hand, and to her utter annoyance, her mouth shut, cutting off her protest.

"You are having a dangerous surgery. You have no family, no one to be with you, to make decisions if the worst should happen."

A cold trickle of dread swept down her spine. How did he know anything about her family? Had he had her investigated? Her stomach rolled as nausea welled. She couldn't bear for anyone to know of her past. As far as she was concerned it didn't exist. She didn't exist.

"There has to be another way," she said faintly. Already the strain of him being here, of standing up against this hard man, was wearing on her.

It must have been obvious, because his expression softened noticeably. "I'm not here to fight with you. We have a lot to work out and not much time. I need to speak with your doctor and have you transferred to a better facility. I'll want a specialist to take over your care. He can give us a second opinion on whether this surgery is the best solution with you pregnant. I'll see to the arrangements for our wedding."

"Stop right there," she said as fury worked its way up her spine until her neck was stiff and locked. "You won't come barging in here, taking over my life and making decisions for me. I'm not some brainless idiot who needs you to rush in and save the day. I've spoken to the doctors. I'm well aware of what needs to be done, and I will make the decision as to what is best for me and my daughter. If that bothers you, then you can take yourself right back to your island and leave me the hell alone."

He held up a placating hand. "Don't upset yourself, Jewel. I'm sorry if I've offended you. Taking over is what I do. You asked for my help, and I'm here to offer it, and yet now you don't seem to want it."

"I want your help without conditions."

For a long moment they stared at each other, neither backing down as the challenge was laid.

"And I'm afraid that I'm unwilling to just sit back and not have a say."

"You're not even convinced this is your child," she threw out.

He nodded. "That's true. I'd be a fool to blindly accept your word. We hardly know each other. How do I know you didn't set the entire thing up? Regardless, I'm willing to help. I have much to make up for. For now I'm willing to go with the assumption that you're carrying my daughter. I want us to marry before you have any further medical treatment."

"But that's just insane," she protested.

He continued on as if she hadn't spoken. "I'll have an agreement drawn up to protect both our interests. If it turns out you've lied and the child is not mine, the marriage will immediately be terminated. I'll provide a settlement for you and your daughter, and we'll go our separate ways."

She didn't miss the way he said "your daughter," the way he purposely distanced himself from the equation. If she lied. She almost shook her head. She would have had to have jumped directly from his bed into another man's for the timing to be such that the baby could be someone else's. What he must think of her. Hardly a basis for marriage.

"And if she is yours?" she asked softly.

"Then we remain married."

She was already shaking her head. "No. I don't want to marry you. You can't want this either."

"I won't argue about this, Jewel. You will marry me and you'll do it immediately. Think about what's best for your daughter. The longer we spend arguing, the longer you and the baby are at risk."

"You really are blackmailing me," she said in disbelief.

"Think what you want," he offered with a casual shrug.

"She is your child," she said fiercely. "You get those damn tests done, but she's yours."

Piers nodded. "I'm willing to concede that she could

be mine. I wouldn't have offered marriage if I didn't think the possibility existed."

"And yet you don't want to wait for those results before you tie us together?"

"How strangely you put it," he said with mild amusement. "Our agreement will allow for any possibility. As I've said, if it turns out you've lied to me, our marriage will end immediately. I'm prepared to be generous in spite of the lie, but it will be on my terms. And if, as you said, that she is my daughter, then the best course is for us to be married and provide a stable home for her."

"With two parents who can barely tolerate one another."

He raised one eyebrow. "I wouldn't go that far. I'd say we got on quite well together that night in my hotel room."

A deep flush worked its way over her cheeks. "Lust is no substitute for love, trust and commitment."

"And who is to say those things won't follow?"

She stared at him in astonishment.

"Give it a chance, Jewel. Who is to say what the future holds for us. For now, it isn't wise to dwell on things that might not even be an issue. We have your surgery to contend with and of course the results of the paternity test."

"Of course. Silly me to consider the cornerstones of marriage when in fact we're considering getting married."

"There is no need to be so sarcastic. Now, if we're finished, I suggest you get some rest. There are many things to be done, and the sooner I arrange everything, the sooner you can be at ease."

"I haven't said I'll marry you," she said evenly.

"No, and I'm waiting for your answer."

Frustration beat at her temples. How infuriating was this man. Arrogant. Convinced of getting his way each and every time. And yet, the jerk was right on all counts. She needed him. Their daughter needed him.

Sadness crept over her, and she lay back, closing her eyes. She felt disgustingly weepy. This was so far removed from the way she'd dreamed things might be one day. In her more sane moments, she'd accepted the fact that she'd probably never marry, never have someone she could absolutely trust. Trust just wasn't in her makeup. And yet, it hadn't stopped her fanciful daydreams of a strong, loving man. Someone who wouldn't abuse her trust. Someone who would love her unconditionally.

"It won't be as bad as that," Piers said gently as he took her hand in his once more.

She opened her eyes to see him staring intently at her.

"All right, Piers. I'll marry you," she said wearily. "But I'll have conditions of my own."

"I'll provide a lawyer to represent your interests. He can look over my part of the agreement and advise you accordingly."

How sterile and cold it all sounded. More like a hostile business takeover than a marriage. A delicate shiver skirted up her spine and prickled her nape. There was no doubt that she was making a mistake. Perhaps the biggest mistake of her life. But for her child, she'd do this. She'd do anything. From the moment she discovered she was pregnant, her child became everything to her. She wouldn't lose her daughter. If she had to marry the devil himself, she'd grit her teeth and bear it.

"How about I choose the lawyer and have him bill you," she offered sweetly.

To her surprise he chuckled. "Don't trust me? I suppose you have no reason to. Of course. Choose your lawyer and have him send me the bill."

Her eyes narrowed. He was positively magnanimous, but then he could afford to be now that he'd won.

"Is there anything you need? Anything you'd like me to bring you?"

She hesitated for a moment. "Food."

"Food? They don't feed you here?"

"Really good food," she said hopefully. "I'm starving."

He smiled, and she felt the jolt all the way to her toes. Damn the man for looking so disgustingly appealing. She didn't want to be attracted to him anymore. Her hand smoothed over her belly in another silent apology. She didn't regret a single thing about their night of passion, but it didn't mean she wanted to dwell on it forever.

"I will see what I can do about getting you some really good food. Now, get some rest. I'll be back after a while."

As if she would rest now that he'd arrived and turned her life upside down.

Then he surprised her by leaning down and brushing his lips across her forehead in a surprisingly tender gesture. She held her breath, enjoying the brief contact. As he drew away, his fingers trailed down her cheek.

"I don't want you to worry about anything. Just rest

and get well and take good care of your…our daughter."

He seemed to struggle with the last as if he was making a concession to her claim, and yet, he looked grim. Maybe he had no wish for children. Tough. He now had a daughter, and he might as well get used to the idea.

He gave her one last look and then turned to walk briskly from the hospital room. When the door shut behind him, Jewel let out her breath in a long whoosh.

Married.

She couldn't imagine being married to such a hard man. She'd had enough hard people in her life. Emotionless, cold individuals with no heart, no love. And now she was consigned to a marriage that would be a replica of her childhood.

Her hands rubbed and massaged her swollen belly. "It will never be like that for you, sweetie. I love you so much already, and there'll never be a day you won't know it. I swear. No matter what happens with your daddy, you'll always have me."

Chapter 6

"I've done a terrible thing," Piers said when his brother, Chrysander, muttered an unintelligible greeting in Greek.

Chrysander sighed, and Piers could hear him sit up in bed and fight the covers for a moment.

"Why is it becoming commonplace for my younger brothers to call me in the middle of the night with those exact words?"

"Theron messed up lately?" Piers asked in amusement.

"Not since he seduced a woman under his protection," Chrysander said dryly.

"Ahh, you mean Bella. Why do I imagine that it was she who did the seducing?"

"You're straying from the topic. What is this terrible thing you've done, and how much is it going to cost?"

"Maybe nothing. Maybe everything," Piers said quietly.

A curse escaped Chrysander's lips, and then Piers heard him say something to Marley in the background.

"Don't worry Marley over this," Piers said. "I'm sorry to have disturbed her sleep."

"It's too late for that," Chrysander growled. "Just give me a moment to go into my office."

Piers waited, drumming his fingers on the desk in his hotel room. Finally Chrysander came back on the line.

"Now tell me what's wrong."

Just like Chrysander to get to the point.

"I had an affair—a brief affair, a one-night stand really."

"So?" Chrysander asked impatiently. "This isn't new for you."

"She was my new assistant."

Chrysander cursed again.

"I didn't know she was my assistant until she showed up for work. I had her fired."

Chrysander groaned. "How much is she suing us for?"

"Let me finish." This time it was Piers who was impatient. "I didn't intend to fire her at all. I asked my human resources manager to transfer her, or promote her or pay her for her entire contracted term, but he only heard the get rid of her part and fired her. She disappeared before I could remedy the situation, and I wasn't able to locate her. Until now."

"Okay, so what's the problem?"

"She's in the hospital. She's ill, she needs surgery… and she's pregnant."

Dead silence greeted his announcement.

"*Theos,*" Chrysander breathed. "Piers, you can't let this happen again. Last time—"

"I know," Piers said irritably. The last thing he needed was a recap of that disaster from his brother. It was bad enough he'd been made a complete fool of, but his brothers had witnessed the entire debacle.

"Are you certain the child is yours?"

"No. I've asked for paternity testing."

"Good."

"There's something else you should know," Piers said. "I'm going to marry her. Soon, as in the next few days."

"What? Have you lost your mind?"

"Funny, that's what she asked me."

"I'm glad one of you has sense then," Chrysander said heatedly. "Why on earth would you marry this woman when you don't even know if the child is yours?"

"It's amazing how the tables have turned," Piers said mildly.

"Don't even start. I heard the same thing from Theron when he was so set on marrying Alannis. Never mind that I was right about what a disaster that would be. You two warning me about Marley was an entirely different situation, and you know it. You don't have a relationship with this woman. You slept with her one night, and now she claims to be pregnant with your child, and you're going to marry her? Just like that?"

"She needs my help. I'm not stupid. I'm having our lawyer draw up an ironclad agreement that provides stipulations for the possibility that the child isn't mine. For now, with her surgery looming, it's best that we marry. This way I can make decisions for her care and that of the child's. If it does turn out to be my daughter, how would I feel if I had sat back and done nothing while I waited for the proof?"

"Daughter?"

"Yes. Apparently Jewel is pregnant with a girl."

Despite his doubts and his heavy suspicions, he couldn't help but smile at the image of a little girl with big eyes and a sweet smile.

"Jewel. What's her last name?"

"Oh no you don't, big brother. There's no need to get all protective and have her background dug up. I can handle this myself. You just concern yourself with your wife and my nephew."

"I don't want you hurt again," Chrysander said quietly.

And there it was. No matter how much he wanted to avoid the past, it was always there, hanging like a dark cloud. Unbidden, the image of another child, a sweet baby boy, dark-haired with a cherubic smile and chubby little legs, came painfully to mind. Eric. Not many days had gone by that Piers hadn't thought of him in some form or fashion, but not until now had such pain accompanied the memories.

"This time, I'm going to make sure that my interests are better protected," Piers said coldly. "I was a fool then."

Chrysander sighed. "You were young, Piers."

"It was no excuse."

"Call me if you need me. Marley and I would like to come to your wedding. It will be better if family is there."

"There's no need."

"There is every need," Chrysander said, interrupting him. "Let me know the details, and we'll fly out."

Piers's hand gripped the phone tighter. It was nice to have such unconditional support. And then he realized the irony. He hadn't exactly offered Jewel his unconditional support. He'd strong-armed her and taken advantage of her situation.

"All right. I'll call when I have the arrangements made."

"Be sure and let Theron know as well. He and Bella will want to be there."

Piers sighed. "Yes, big brother."

Chrysander chuckled. "This is a small thing I ask. It's not as if you've ever listened to me before."

"Give Marley my love."

"I will—and Piers? Be careful. I don't like the sound of this at all."

Piers hung up the phone. He should call Theron, but he couldn't bring himself to face another inquisition. Especially now that Theron had joined the ranks of the deliriously happy. He'd be appalled that Piers was going to marry a woman he barely knew, a woman who might well be lying to him.

Instead he phoned his lawyer and outlined his situation. Then he arranged a security detail for Jewel. He and his brothers took no chances with those close to them after what had happened to Chrysander's wife, Marley. Next he called to see when Jewel's doctor would next be making his rounds. He intended to be there so he'd know exactly what was going on.

Lastly, he called a local restaurant and arranged for a full-course dinner to be prepared for pickup in an hour.

* * *

Jewel was ready to fidget right out of the bed. She'd only gotten up to use the bathroom, and now she'd decided she'd had enough. The doctor was releasing her tomorrow now that someone had shown up to take *care* of her. She had to work to keep the snort of derision from rising in her throat.

She could do without Piers Anetakis's brand of caring.

The thin hospital gown offered little in the way of modesty, and so after showering, she dressed in a pair of loose-fitting sweats and a maternity shirt. She toweled her hair as dry as she could and left it loose so it would finish drying.

She had settled in the small recliner to the side of her bed when the door opened, and Piers strode in carrying two large take-out bags.

She sat forward nervously as his gaze swept over her. Then his eyes narrowed, and he set the bags down on the bed.

"You should not have showered until I was here."

Her mouth fell open in shock. "What?"

"You could have fallen. You should have waited for me to help or at least called for the nurse."

"How do you know I didn't call for one of the nurses?"

He stared inquisitively at her, his eyes mocking. "Did you?"

"It's none of your business," she muttered.

"If you're pregnant with my child, it's every bit of my business."

"Look, Piers, we need to get something straight right now. Me being pregnant with your child does not

give you any rights over me whatsoever. I won't allow
you to waltz in and take over my life."

Even as the sharp protest left her lips, she realized
how stupid she sounded. That's precisely what he had
done so far. Taken over. What else explained the reason for this marriage he proposed?

She bit her lip and looked away, her hand automatically moving to her belly in a soothing motion.

Piers began taking food out of the bags as if she'd
said nothing at all. The smells wafted through her nostrils, and her stomach growled. Heavenly.

She raised an eyebrow. She wouldn't have thought
he'd give much thought to what she could or couldn't
have.

"Thank you, I'm starving."

He prepared a plate and handed it to her along with
utensils. Then he fixed a plate for himself and settled
on the edge of the bed.

"I can get back into the bed so you have a place to
sit," she offered.

He shook his head. "You look comfortable. I'm
fine."

They ate in silence, though she knew he watched
her. She refused to acknowledge his perusal, though,
and concentrated on the delicious food instead.

When she couldn't eat another bite, she sighed and
put down her fork.

"That was wonderful, thank you."

He took the plate and set it on the counter along
the wall. "Would you like to get back into bed now?"

She shook her head. "I've had enough bed to last
a lifetime."

"But shouldn't you be in bed with your feet up?" he persisted.

"I'm doing well. The doctor wants me on moderated bed rest until my surgery. That means I can get up and move around. He just doesn't want me on my feet for long periods of time."

"And this job you had, you were on your feet all the time?" he asked with a frown.

"I was waitressing. It was necessary."

"You should have phoned me the minute you knew you were pregnant," he said fiercely.

Her expression turned murderous. "You had me fired. You told me quite plainly that you wanted nothing further to do with me. Why on earth would I be calling you? I wouldn't have called you now if I hadn't needed you so badly."

"Then I suppose I'll have to be grateful you needed me."

"I don't need you," she amended. "Our daughter does."

"You need me, Jewel. I have a lot to make up for, and I plan to do just that. We can talk about your firing when you aren't in the hospital and you're feeling better."

"About that," she began.

He raised an eyebrow. "Yes?"

"The doctor is releasing me in the morning."

"Yes, I know. I spoke to him before I came back to your room."

Her fingers curled into tight fists, but she kept the frustration from her expression. Or at least she tried.

"I don't need you hovering over me at every moment. You can drop me off at my apartment—"

Before she got any further he shook his head resolutely, his expression implacable.

"I've arranged for the rental of a house until your surgery. I'll take you there of course. I've hired a nurse to see to your needs—"

It was her turn to break in, her head shaking so stiffly that her neck hurt.

"No. Absolutely not. I won't have some nurse hired to babysit me. It's ridiculous. I'm not an invalid. I have to stay off my feet. Fine, I can do that without a nurse."

"Why must you be so difficult?" he asked mildly. "I'm only doing what is best for your health."

"If you want to hire someone, hire a cook," she muttered. "I'm terrible at it."

Amusement curved his hard mouth into a smile. It was amazing what a difference it made in his face. He looked almost boyish. She stared at him in astonishment.

"A cook can be arranged. I, of course, wish to see that my daughter and her mother are well fed. Does this mean you aren't going to fight moving in with me?"

She made a sound of protest, but it quickly died. She'd walked right into that one. With a long suffering sigh, she uttered a simple, "No."

"See, that wasn't so hard, now was it?"

"You can quit the gloating. It's not very attractive on you."

His grin broadened. The amazing thing was, it made him look quite charming. *Dangerous, Jewel. He's dangerous. Don't fall for that charm.*

"I'm going to take you home with me, Jewel," he said patiently. "There's little point in arguing. All the arrangements have been made. Tomorrow I hope to see to the wedding arrangements. Understandably, concerns for your health came before our marriage, but once I have you settled in, I'll see to the necessary plans."

The beginnings of a headache thrummed at her temples. Was this what her life was going to be like? Him calling all the shots and her meekly following along? Not if she could help it. Right now, she was tired, worried and more than a little stressed, and as weak as it made her feel to hand everything over to him, it also felt good to relinquish her problems. Even if it was just for a little while.

"Does your head hurt you?" he asked.

She drew her hand away, unaware until now that she'd been rubbing her forehead. "Stress," she said in a shaky voice. "It's been a long couple of weeks. I'm tired."

What an idiot she was, outlining her weaknesses in stark detail. As if he hadn't already honed in on her disadvantages.

To her surprise, he didn't make any sharp or sarcastic remarks. He took her hands gently in his, and lowered them to her lap. Then he carefully helped her up.

Too stunned to do more than gape at him, she cooperated without complaint. He stepped behind her and sank down onto the seat, pulling her down onto his lap.

She landed with a jolt of awareness that five long months hadn't diminished in the least. There was still potent chemistry between them, much to her dismay.

His warmth wrapped around her, soothing her despite her rioting emotions. She was almost in complete panic when his fingers dug into her hair and began massaging her scalp.

A soft moan of surrender escaped her. Bliss. Sheer, unadulterated bliss. His strong fingers worked to her forehead and then her temples.

Bonelessly she melted further into his chest. He stiffened slightly and then relaxed as he continued his ministrations. For several long minutes, neither spoke, and only the sound of her soft breathing could be heard.

"Better?" he asked softly.

She nodded, unable to form coherent words. She was floating on a cloud of sheer delight.

"You are worrying yourself too much, *yineka mou*. The stress is not good for you or the baby. Everything will be all right. You have my word on it."

The statement was intended to comfort her, and she did appreciate his effort. But for some reason, his vow sounded ominous to her ears. Almost like this was a turning point in her life where nothing would ever be the same. Like she was giving up control, not just for the short term.

Of course things are changing irrevocably, you idiot. You're pregnant and getting married. How much more change could you possibly make?

Still, she tried to draw some comfort in the serious promise in his voice. He didn't trust her. She didn't think he even particularly liked her, but he desired her, that much was obvious. And she desired him. It wasn't enough. Not even close, but it was all they had.

Not exactly a prime start to a marriage.

Chapter 7

Jewel tilted her head so she could see out the window as Piers pulled through the gates of a sprawling estate covered in lush green landscaping and well manicured shrubbery. The house came into view when they topped the hill, and her eyes widened in appreciation. Despite the size of the grounds, the house was what she'd deem modest in comparison.

Still it was gorgeous. Two stories with dormers and ivy clinging to the front. He'd said he rented the place. Who knew such places were for rent?

He parked in front of the garage that was adjacent to the main house. Behind them, the car carrying her newly assigned security detail pulled in. Before she could get out, one of the guards appeared and opened her door. He hovered protectively, shielding her…from what? Only when Piers reached for her hand, did the guard step away.

"I'm not helpless, you know," she said dryly when he tucked her against his side. But she would have been lying if she denied that having his help thrilled her in an inexplicable way. His body was warm and solid against hers. Strong. The idea that she wasn't alone nearly brought her to her knees.

"I know this," he said in his brusque accent. "But you've only just gotten out of the hospital, and you're carrying a child. If at any time you need help, it is certainly now."

She relaxed against him, refusing to spoil their first moments home with senseless, petty arguments.

Home. The word struck her in the chest, and even as she thought it, she shook her head in mute denial. She had no home.

"Is there something wrong?" he asked as they stopped at the door.

Embarrassed over her emotional display, she uttered a low denial.

He opened the door, and they stepped into the expansive foyer. Beyond was an elegant double staircase curving toward the top where a hallway connected the two sides of the house.

"Come into the living room, and I'll see to your things."

She allowed him to lead her to a comfortable leather couch that afforded a view of the patio through triple French doors. It would be a perfect breakfast spot, she thought with longing. The morning sun would shine perfectly on the garden table.

What would it be like to have a home like this? Filled with laughter and children. And then it occurred to her that it was entirely possible that part of that dream would come true.

She looked down at the gentle mound covered by her thin shirt and slowly smoothed her hand over it. The baby kicked, and Jewel smiled.

She wanted to give her daughter all the things she'd never had, the things she longed for. Love, acceptance. A stable home.

Would Piers provide those things? Everything but love. Could Jewel love her baby enough to compensate for a father who didn't want her or her mother?

Damn if she hadn't done what she'd sworn never to do.

Piers traipsed inside the living room, hauling her two suitcases with him.

"I'll take these upstairs, and then I'll be down to make us some lunch. Is there anything you need in the meantime?"

Unnerved by his consideration, she shook her head. "I'm fine."

"Good, then I'll be right back."

She heard him rattle up the stairs, and she returned her perusal moodily to the outside. No longer content to look from afar, she got up and walked to the glass doors. She pressed her hand to the panes as she gazed over the magnificently rendered gardens.

It was extremely beautiful, but it almost looked sterile, as if no one ever touched it, or even breathed on it for that matter. It seemed…artificial. Not a living, breathing entity. Not like the ocean. It was always alive, rolling, sometimes peaceful and serene and at other times angry and forbidding.

A hand slipped over her shoulder, and she jumped.

As she turned, she saw that Piers stood behind her, his expression mild and unthreatening.

"Sorry if I startled you. I called from across the room, but you didn't hear me obviously."

She offered a half smile, suddenly nervous in his presence.

"It's beautiful, isn't it?"

"Yes, it is," she agreed. "I prefer the ocean, though. It's more…untamed."

"You find these gardens tame?"

"Mmm-hmm."

"I suppose I can see your point. Would you like to eat now? I had something dropped by before we arrived. It will only take a few minutes to warm everything up."

She turned sideways to face him. "Could we eat outside? It's a beautiful day."

"If you wish. Why don't you go on outside. I'll bring out the food in a moment."

His footsteps retreated across the wooden floors. When he was gone, she slipped out of the French doors and onto the stone patio.

The coolness caused her to shiver, but it was a beautiful day, one of the few where nothing marred the blue sky, and she didn't want to waste it by returning indoors.

She settled into one of the chairs to wait for Piers. It seemed odd to have this arrogant man waiting on her. He was clearly used to having the tables turned and being served.

The doors opened, and Piers elbowed his way out carrying two trays. He was a man of continuing surprises. He'd shown up at the hospital in time for her release, wearing a pair of faded jeans and a casual polo shirt, a far cry from the expensive designer clothing she knew he usually wore. He looked almost approachable. No less desirable, but definitely less threatening. In a more cynical moment, she wondered if he'd done it on purpose to lull her into a false sense of security.

He set a tray in front of her then placed his own across the table before taking a seat. She picked up her fork but made the mistake of looking over at him before she began to eat. He was staring intently at her, his food untouched.

"We have a lot to talk about, Jewel. After you eat, I plan to have the conversation we should have had a long time ago."

He sounded ominous, and a prickle of unease swept over her. What was left for them to discuss? He'd demanded she marry him, and she'd agreed. He'd demanded she move in with him, and she'd agreed. Quite frankly her acquiescence was starting to irritate the hell out of her.

They ate in silence, though she knew he watched her. The heat of his stare blazed over her skin, but she refused to acknowledge his perusal. He already had enough power over her.

When she'd finished, she put her fork down, and still refusing to look at him, she turned her gaze back to the gardens.

"Ignoring me won't help."

Finally she turned, sure she must look guilty. Now she felt childish for being so obvious, but the man made her nervous.

"We need to clear the air on a few matters. Mainly your firing."

She stiffened and clenched her fingers into small fists. "I'd just as soon not discuss it. No good can come of it, and I *am* supposed to keep my stress level down."

"I never intended to have you fired, Jewel. It was a despicable thing to have happened to you, and I accept full blame."

"Well who the hell else's fault would it be?" she demanded.

"It wasn't what I intended," he said again.

"Whether you intended it or not, it's what happened. Mighty coincidental that I got the sack as soon as you found out who I was, wouldn't you say?"

Piers blew out his breath, and his gaze narrowed. "You aren't going to make this easy, are you?"

She leaned back, this time giving him the full intensity of her stare. "Why should it be easy for you? It wasn't easy for me. I had no money left, no job. I came here because it was the only place I had to stay, and waitressing was the only quick job I could land. Then I started getting sick." She stopped and shook her head. She wasn't going to get into it with him.

"You're right. I'm sorry."

He looked and sounded sincere. Enough so that her next question slipped out before she could think better of it.

"If I wasn't supposed to be fired, how exactly did I end up sacked and escorted out of the hotel?"

Piers winced and dragged a hand through his hair. "As I said, it's completely my fault. I told my human resources manager to reassign you, or promote you or even to pay you for the term of your contract but I'm afraid the first words out of my mouth were to get rid of you. The rest, unfortunately, he didn't hear because the connection was severed. By the time I returned to the hotel and discovered the misunderstanding, you were gone. I had no luck tracing your whereabouts. In fact, I'd given up ever hearing from you again until you called."

She stared at him in disbelief. First, she couldn't believe he'd actually admitted his wrongdoing. Second, she couldn't fathom him looking for her afterward. It sounded suspiciously like he genuinely regretted what had happened.

"I don't get it," she said with genuine confusion. "Why couldn't we have just been adults about it? Why was it so important to you to get rid of me? I realize it wasn't an ideal situation, but it was an honest mistake. Neither of us knew who the other was or God knows I wouldn't have gone to bed with you that night."

"Then I guess it's a good thing you didn't know who I was," he said softly.

She looked down at her belly. "Yes, I don't regret it now at all."

"Did you then?"

He didn't look offended, only genuinely curious. He'd been honest with her so far, so she couldn't be anything other than completely honest with him.

"No. I didn't regret our night together."

He seemed satisfied with her answer. "To answer your question, it wasn't personal. What I mean is that it's not as if it was something you did. I have a strict policy about allowing anyone to work closely with me who has had any sort of a personal relationship with me. It's a necessary rule, unfortunately."

She raised an eyebrow. "You say that as if you were once burned."

"In a manner of speaking. My brother's personal assistant was enamored with him, but she was also selling company secrets and framed my sister-in-law."

"Sounds like a soap opera," Jewel muttered.

He chuckled. "It seemed like one at the time."

"You could have simply told me. You owed me that much given the fact we had spent the night together," she said, pinning him with the force of her gaze. "If you'd been up front with me, none of this would have happened. There would have been no misunderstanding."

"You're right. I'm afraid the shock of finding out who you were made my judgment particularly bad. I'm sorry."

His quietly spoken apology softened some of her anger. If she was honest, she still held resentment for the easy way he'd summarily dismissed her from his life. Not that she'd expected undying love and commitment, but hadn't the night meant something? Even enough to rate a personal dismissal instead of the job being handed off to a stooge?

Still, if this marriage was to be anything short of difficult and laced with animosity, she knew she had to let go of some of that resentment. Be the bigger person and all that jazz. Funny how taking the high road was never particularly fun.

"I accept your apology."

Surprise flickered in his dark eyes. "Do you really, I wonder?"

"I didn't say you were my best friend," she said

dryly. "Merely that I'd accepted your apology. It seems the thing to do in light of our impending nuptials."

Amusement replaced the surprise. "I have a feeling we're going to get along just fine together, *yineka mou.*" His gaze dropped to her stomach. "That is if you're telling me the truth."

For a moment, pain shadowed his eyes, and she wondered what sort of hell occurred in his past that would make him so distrustful. It went beyond mistrust. He didn't *want* to be the father of her child. He wanted her to be a liar and a deceiver. It was as if he knew how to handle those. But a woman telling him the truth? That was the aberration.

She must be insane to walk into this type of situation. There was every way for her to lose and no way to win.

"It does me little good to tell you that you're the father when you're determined not to believe me," she said evenly. "We'll have the paternity tests done and then you'll know."

"Yes. Indeed we'll know," he said softly.

"If you'll excuse me, I need to go dig out my laptop," she said as she rose from her seat. "I need to send an email."

"And I have arrangements to make for our wedding."

She nodded because if she tried to say anything, she'd choke. Not looking back at him, she hurried to the doors and went inside. Piers hadn't told her which bedroom was hers, but she'd find it easily enough.

She hit the stairs, and after going into three rooms on the upper level, she found her bags lying on the bed.

She unpacked her clothing first and put everything away before settling back onto the bed with her laptop. She checked her email, but didn't see anything from Kirk. Not that she expected to. Sometimes they went months with no communication depending on his assignment and whether she was in a place she could email him. Still, she felt like she owed him an explanation, and so she spilled the entire sordid tale in an email that took her half an hour to compose.

When she was done, she was worn out and feeling more than a little foolish. There was no advice Kirk could offer, but she felt better for unloading some of her worries. He'd know better than anyone her fears of marriage and commitment.

Leaving her laptop open, she leaned back on the soft pillows to stare up at the ceiling. Contemplating her future had never been quite so terrifying as it was now.

Piers walked up the stairs toward Jewel's room. She'd been sequestered for two hours now. Surely that was enough time to have completed her personal business.

He stopped at her door and knocked softly, but he heard no answer from within. Concerned, he pushed open the door and stepped inside.

Jewel was curled on her side, her head buried in the down pillows. Sound asleep. She looked exhausted.

Her laptop was precariously close to the edge of the bed, and he hurried over to retrieve it before it fell. When he placed it on the dresser, the screen came back up and he saw that a new email message was highlighted by the cursor. It was from someone named Kirk.

With a frown, he scrolled down the preview screen to read the short message.

Jewel,
I'm on my way home. Don't do anything until I get there. Okay? Just hang tight. I'll be there as soon as I can hop a flight.
Kirk

Piers stiffened. Hell would freeze over before he'd allow this man to interfere in his and Jewel's relationship. She'd agreed to marry him, and marry him she would. He didn't question why it was suddenly so important that the wedding take place, but he'd be damned if he let another man call the shots.

With no hesitation, he clicked on the delete button and then followed it to the trash bin to permanently delete it from her computer. Afterward, he pulled her email back up and then replaced the laptop on her bed, making sure it was far enough from the edge so that it wouldn't topple over.

For a long moment, he stood by her bed and stared down at her sleeping face. Drawn to the pensive expression, even in rest, he touched a few strands of her blond hair, smoothing them from her cheek.

What demons existed in her life? She didn't trust him. Not that he blamed her, but it went beyond anger or a sense of betrayal. She wore shadows like most women wore makeup. Somewhere, some way, someone had hurt her badly. They had that in common.

As much as he'd like to swear never to hurt her and

to protect her from those who would, he knew that if she'd lied to him about the child, that he'd crush her without a second thought.

Chapter 8

Jewel studied the unsmiling face of the man she'd chosen to represent her interests and wondered if any lawyer had a sense of humor or if they were all cold, calculating sharks.

But then she supposed when it came to her future and that of her child, she wanted the biggest, baddest shark in the ocean.

"The agreement is pretty straightforward, Miss Henley. It is in essence a prenuptial agreement which states that Mr. Anetakis's assets remain his in the event of a divorce and that yours remain yours."

Jewel snorted in amusement. What assets? She didn't have a damn thing, and Piers knew it.

"What else?" she asked impatiently. With a man like Piers, nothing could be as simple as it appeared. There were strings, hidden provisions. She just had to find them. "I want a complete explanation, line by line."

"Very well."

He shoved his glasses on and picked up the sheaf of papers as he took his seat again.

"Mr. Anetakis will provide a settlement for you regardless of the paternity of the child you carry. If DNA testing proves the child his, then he will retain custody of the child in the event of a divorce."

Her mouth fell open. "What?" She made a grab for the paper her lawyer held, scanning the document until she found the clause he referred to.

"He's out of his damn mind. There is no way in hell I'll sign anything that gives up custody of my child."

"I can strike the clause, but it's possible he won't agree."

She leaned forward, her breath hissing through her teeth. "I don't give a damn what he agrees to. I won't sign it unless this so-called clause is removed in its entirety."

Furious, she stood and snatched the paper back as the lawyer reached for it. "Never mind. I'll see to it myself."

She stormed out of the lawyer's office into the waiting room where Piers sat. He was sitting on the far side, his laptop open and his cell phone to his ear. When he looked up and saw her, he slowly closed the laptop.

"Is there a problem?"

"You bet there is," she said behind gritted teeth.

She thrust the offending piece of paper at him, pointing to the custody clause.

"If you think I'm signing anything that gives away custody of my child, you're an idiot. Over my dead body will I ever be separated from my child. As far as I'm concerned, you can take this…this prenuptial agreement and stick it where the sun doesn't shine."

He raised one dark eyebrow and stared back at her in silence.

"You don't seriously think that I would give up custody of *my* child, do you? If indeed it turns out I am the father."

She threw up her hands in exasperation. "You just don't miss a chance to take your potshots at me. I'm well aware of the fact that you don't believe this child is yours. Believe me, I get it. Reminding me at every opportunity just serves to further piss me off. And haven't you ever heard of a thing called joint custody? You know, that thing called compromise, where the parents consider what's best for the child and agree to give her equal time with her parents?"

"If the child is mine, I don't intend to see her on a part-time basis, nor do I intend I should have to work around your schedule. I can certainly provide more for her than you can. I'm sure she'd be much better off with me."

She curled her fingers into a tight fist, crumpling the document as rage surged through her veins like acid.

"You sanctimonious bastard. Where do you get off suggesting that my child would be better off with you? Because you have more money? Well big whoop. Money can't buy love, or security. It can't buy smiles or happiness. All the things a child needs most. Quite frankly, the fact that you think she would be so much better off with you tells me you don't have the first clue about children or love. How could you? I doubt you've ever loved anyone in your life."

Her chest heaved, and the paper was now a crumpled, soggy scrap in her hand. She started to hurl it at his feet, but he quickly rose and gripped her wrist, preventing her action. His eyes smoldered with rage, the first sign of real emotion she'd seen in him.

"You assume far too much," he said icily.

She wrenched her hand free and took a step backward. "I won't sign it, Piers. As far as I'm concerned this marriage doesn't need to take place. There is no amount of desperation that would make me sign away my rights to my child."

He studied her for a long moment, his face as immovable as stone. "All right," he finally said. "I'll have my lawyer strike the clause. I'll call him now and he can courier over a new agreement."

"I'd wait," she said stiffly. "I'm not finished with my stipulations yet. I'll let you know when we're done."

She turned and stalked back into the lawyer's office, only to find him standing in the doorway, amusement carved on his face when she'd sworn he couldn't possibly have a sense of humor.

"What are you looking at?" she growled.

He sobered, although his eyes still had a suspicious gleam. "Shall we get on to your additions to the agreement?"

Three hours later, the final contract had been couriered from Piers's lawyer's office, and she and Piers read over and signed it together.

Jewel had insisted on an ironclad agreement that stated they would share custody of their child but that she was the primary custodian. She could tell Piers wasn't entirely happy with the wording, but she'd been resolute in her refusal to sign anything less.

"Clearly you've never learned the art of negotiation," Piers said dryly as they left the lawyer's office.

"Some things aren't negotiable. Some things *shouldn't* be negotiable. My child isn't a bargaining chip. She never will be," she said fiercely.

He held up his hands in mock surrender. "All I ask is that you see my side of the equation. As determined as you are to retain custody of your child, I am equally determined not to let go of mine."

Something in his expression caused her to soften, some of her anger fleeing and leaving her oddly deflated. For a moment, she could swear he seemed afraid and a little vulnerable.

"I do see your point," she said quietly. "But I won't apologize for reacting as I did. It was a sneaky, underhanded thing to do."

"I apologize then. It was not my intention to upset you so. I was simply seeking to keep my child where she belongs."

"Maybe what we should be doing is working to prevent a divorce in the first place," she said tightly. "If we manage to make this marriage a success as you have suggested, then we won't have to worry about custody battles."

He nodded and opened the car door for her. She settled in but he stood there for a long moment, his hand on the door. "You're right. The solution is to make sure it never comes down to a divorce."

He quietly closed her door and strode around to his side. He slid in beside her and started the engine.

"Now that the unpleasantness is out of the way, we should move on to the more enjoyable aspects of planning a wedding."

Thus began an afternoon of shopping that made her head spin. Their first stop was at a jeweler. When they were shown a tray of stunning diamond engagement rings, she made the mistake of asking the price. Piers clearly wasn't happy with her question, but the jeweler answered her with ease. It was all she could do to scrape her jaw off the floor.

She shook her head, putting her hands out as she backed away from the counter. Piers caught her around the waist and pulled her back with tender amusement.

"Don't disappoint me. As a woman it's supposed to be ingrained for you to want to pick the biggest, most expensive ring in the shop."

"Indeed," the shop owner said solemnly.

"It's not good form to ask the price anyway," Piers continued. "Just pick the one you want and pretend there are no price tags."

"Your fiancé is a very wise man," the man behind the counter said. Laughter shone in the merchant's eyes, and Jewel relaxed at their teasing.

Trying not to think about the fact that what one ring cost could feed an entire third world nation, she went about studying each setting. After trying on no less than a dozen, she found the perfect ring.

It was a simple pear-shaped diamond, flawless as far as her untrained eye could tell. On either side was a small cluster of tiny diamonds.

"Your lady has exquisite taste."

"Yes, she does. Is this the one you want, *yineka mou?*" Piers asked.

She nodded, ignoring the sick feeling in her stomach. "I don't want to know how much it cost."

Piers laughed. "If it will make you feel better, I'll match the cost of the ring with a donation to the charity of your choice."

"Now you're making fun of me."

"Not at all. It's nice to know my new wife won't break me inside of a year."

He was trying hard to keep from laughing, and she leveled a glare at him. She marveled at the ease in which he flipped his credit card to the cashier, as if he were paying for a drink instead of a ring that costs thousands upon thousands of dollars.

He slid the ring on her finger and curled her hand until it made a fist. "Leave it on. It's yours now."

She glanced down, unable to keep from admiring it. It *was* a gorgeous ring.

"Now that the ring is out of the way, we should move onto other things like a dress and any other clothing you might need."

"Wow, a man who likes to shop. However have you existed as a single man this long?" she teased.

His expression became shuttered, and she mentally sighed at having once again said the wrong thing at the wrong time.

Determined to salvage the rest of the day despite its rocky start, she tucked her hand into his arm as they left the jeweler.

"I'm starving. Can we eat before we attack the rest of the shopping?"

"Of course. What would you like to eat?"

"I'd love a big, nasty steak," she said wistfully.

He laughed. "Then by all means, let's go kill a cow or two."

Chapter 9

The fact that Jewel hid in her room didn't make her a
coward exactly. It just made her reserved and cautious.
Downstairs, Piers greeted his family who had flown in
for the wedding. She still couldn't understand why. It
wasn't as if this was a festive occasion, the uniting of
kindred souls and all that gunk that surrounded marriage ceremonies.

All she knew about the rest of the Anetakis clan was
that Piers had two older brothers, and both were re-
cently married, and at least one child had been added.
Hers would be the second.

And from all Piers had told her, his brothers were
disgustingly in love.

She closed her eyes in recognition that she was
green with envy, and she dreaded having to meet these
disgustingly happy people.

They'd know it wasn't all hearts and roses between

her and Piers. For that matter, she was sure Piers had told them the entire truth and that they were marrying because of a one-night stand and a faulty condom.

She stared back at her reflection in the mirror and tried to erase the glum look from her face. The dress she'd chosen for the occasion was a simple white sheath with spaghetti straps. The material gathered gently at her breasts, molding to her shape then falling over her belly where it strained and then hung loose down her legs.

She'd debated on whether to put her hair up or leave it down, but Piers had seemed to delight in her hair the night they met and so in a moment of sheer vanity, she brushed it until it shone and let it hang over her shoulders.

And now she procrastinated like the coward she was, knowing everyone was downstairs waiting for her.

Still bereft of the courage needed to walk down those stairs, she walked to her window to look down over the gardens. The sky was overcast and light fog had descended over the grounds. A perfect fit to her melancholy mood.

For how long she stood, she wasn't sure. A warm hand slid over her bare shoulder, but she didn't turn. She knew it was Piers.

Then something cool slithered around her neck, and she did turn her head.

"Be still a moment," he said as he reached under her hair to fasten a necklace at her nape. "My wedding gift to you. There are earrings to match, but I honestly couldn't remember if your ears were pierced or not."

She put a hand to the necklace and then hastened to

the mirror so she could see. A gasp of surprise escaped when she saw the exquisite diamond arrangement.

"Piers, it's too much."

He smiled over her shoulder. "My sisters-in-law inform me that a husband can never do too much for his wife."

She smiled back. "They sound like smart women."

"There, that wasn't so bad was it?"

Her brow crinkled. "What?"

"Smiling."

Her eyes flashed in guilty awareness. He held out the box with the earrings, and she gazed in wonder at the large stones twinkling back at her.

"Are your ears pierced?"

She nodded. "I seldom wear earrings, but they are pierced."

"Then I hope you'll wear these today."

She took them and quickly fastened them in her ears. When her gaze returned to his, she found him watching her intently.

"Speaking of my sisters-in-law, they're anxious to meet you."

"And not your brothers?" she asked.

"They are a bit more reserved in their welcome. They worry for me. I'm afraid it's a family tradition to try and ruin the nuptials of the others," he said dryly.

She didn't know whether to laugh or feel dismay. Finally laughter won out. "Well at least you're honest. For that I'm grateful. It will keep me from making a fool of myself in their presence."

He shrugged. "You have nothing to be reserved about. You are to be my wife and that fact affords you the respect you are due. Theron is the soft touch in the family anyway. You'll have him eating out of your hand in no time."

She couldn't imagine anyone related to Piers being a soft touch.

"Are you ready?" he asked as he slipped his hands over her shoulders. He squeezed reassuringly as if sensing her deep unease. "We have just enough time for you to be introduced to my family before the minister is due to arrive for the ceremony."

Inhaling deeply, she nodded. He took her hand firmly in his and led her out of the bedroom and down the stairs. As they neared the bottom, she heard the murmur of voices in the living room.

Butterflies scuttled around her stomach, and the baby kicked, perhaps in protest of her mother's unease.

When they rounded the corner, Jewel took in the people assembled in the living room with a bit of awe. The two men were obviously Piers's brothers. There was remarkable resemblance. Both were tall and dark-haired, but their eyes were lighter than Piers's, a golden hue while Piers's were nearly black.

The two women standing next to his brothers were as different as night and day. Before she could continue her silent perusal, they looked up and saw her.

The brothers gave her guarded looks while the two women smiled welcomingly. She was grateful for that at least.

"Come, I'll introduce you," Piers murmured.

They closed the distance, stopping a few feet from the two couples.

"Jewel, this is my oldest brother Chrysander and his wife, Marley. Their son, Dimitri, is with his nanny for the day."

Jewel offered a tremulous smile. "I'm happy to meet you."

Marley smiled, her blue eyes twinkling with friendliness. "We're happy to meet you too, Jewel. Welcome to the family. I hope you'll be happy. When are you due?"

Jewel blinked and then returned her smile. "I'm a little over five months along."

"Hello, Jewel," Chrysander said in his deep voice.

She swallowed and nodded her greeting to Piers's oldest brother. Intimidating. How could anyone stand to be around the three of the Anetakis brothers at the same time?

Piers turned to the other couple. "This is my brother Theron and his wife, Bella." Piers's entire expression softened into a fond smile when he touched Bella's arm. She smiled mischievously back at Piers and then looked up at Jewel.

"We're both happy to meet you, Jewel," Bella said. She nudged Theron with her elbow. "Aren't we, Theron?"

"Of course, Bella *mou*," he said in a teasing tone. It was as if all attempt to maintain a serious air went out the window when he looked at his wife. Then he turned his attention to Jewel. "Welcome to our family. I'm not sure whether to offer my congratulations or my condolences on marrying my brother."

Jewel smiled at his attempt at humor, and Piers snorted.

"If you're quite through insulting me, I'll offer everyone a drink to celebrate the occasion. The minister should be here at any moment to perform the ceremony."

The others watched her curiously as Piers left her side to collect a chilled bottle of champagne. He passed glasses to everyone and then popped the cork.

When he came to her, he handed her a glass of mineral water instead. She was touched by his thoughtfulness and smiled her thanks.

Chrysander cleared his throat, and Marley slipped her arm into his. "Our best wishes for a long and... happy marriage," he added after a slight pause.

They raised their glasses in a toast, and for a moment, Jewel wished, oh how she wished that it was all real, and that this was her family and that she and Piers were in love and expecting their first child with all the joy of a happily married couple.

She dreamed of Christmas celebrations, birthdays and get-togethers just for the heck of it and a loud rambunctious family, loyal to a fault.

Tears pricked her eyelids as she bade goodbye to that dream and embraced her reality. She hastily gulped her water in an effort to regain control of her emotions.

Piers stood at her side and bent his head low to her ear. "What is it, *yineka mou?* What has upset you?"

"I'm fine," she said, pasting on a bright smile.

The doorbell rang, and she jumped.

His fingers cupped her elbow, and he rubbed a thumb across her skin in a soothing manner. "It's just the minister here to marry us. I'll go let him in."

She almost asked him not to go, but how silly was she to be worried about being left alone with his relatives? She chanced a glance at the two couples, standing so close, so lovingly together, and her heart ached all over again.

"Between you and Marley, Theron is going to get all the wrong ideas," Bella said to Jewel.

"And how is this?" Theron demanded.

"All these babies and pregnant women," she said mischievously. "I fully expect Theron to start hinting about knocking me up any day now."

Jewel laughed, charmed by Bella's easy humor and how relaxed she was around everyone. Clearly she wasn't worried about her place in this family. No one seemed to mind her outrageous statement in the least.

Marley tried to stifle her laughter while Chrysander just groaned. Theron's eyes took on a sensual light that almost made Jewel feel like a voyeur.

"Oh no, Bella *mou*. We have much practicing to do before we get you pregnant."

"See, Jewel, it's not so hard to train the Anetakis men," she said cheekily. "Marley has whipped Chrysander into admirable shape, while I have turned Theron to my way of thinking. I can't imagine you being any less successful with Piers."

"Theron, keep your woman quiet," Chrysander said mildly. "She's inciting discontent among the female ranks."

Marley elbowed him sharply, but her eyes were alight with amusement and love.

Piers walked back in with an elderly man, their heads turned in conversation. When the minister saw Jewel, he smiled and went forward, his hands outstretched.

"You must be the bride to be. You look lovely, my dear. Are you ready for the ceremony to begin?"

She swallowed and nodded, though her legs were trembling.

The minister introduced himself to the others, and after a few moments of polite conversation, Piers motioned that he was ready to begin.

It was all quite awkward, at least for Jewel. The rest acted as if this was the sort of ceremony they attended every day. Piers and Jewel stood in front of the minister while each couple flanked them.

Her throat tightened as she listened to Piers promise to love, honor and cherish her all the days of his life and until death do they part. And then it struck her square in the face that she wanted him to love her. Why? Did that mean she loved him? No, she didn't. She couldn't. She didn't know how to love any more than she knew how to be loved. But it didn't stop the yearning inside.

When the ceremony concluded, Piers brushed a perfunctory kiss across her lips and then stepped back to receive his brothers' somewhat muted congratulations.

Chrysander insisted on taking them all out to eat afterward, and a limousine took all three couples into the heart of the city to an upscale restaurant that boasted delicious seafood.

She was hungry, but the idea that she was now married effectively put a damper on her appetite. She picked and pushed at her food until finally Piers took notice.

He picked up her hand, and the band he'd placed on her finger just hours before gleamed behind the diamond engagement ring in the low light.

"Are you ready to return home?" he whispered so the others wouldn't hear. "I can send them on at any time."

"They're your family," she protested. "I've no wish to cut short your visit."

He laughed. "You're very thoughtful, *yineka mou,* but I see them often, and if there is ever a time I can send them away, surely my wedding day is one of them? They would understand—having had their wedding nights not too long ago."

She froze as his meaning became clear. Surely he wasn't thinking that…no, he couldn't, could he? He'd been present when her doctor said there was no reason she couldn't indulge in lovemaking, but she'd assumed that Piers had taken it as the doctor thinking they were in a normal relationship. Did this mean he wanted to make love to her? To actually consummate the marriage?

His hand covered hers, idly stroking the tops of her fingers as he turned to the others and told them that he and Jewel were ready to go.

There were hugs, polite kisses and teasing goodbyes. Piers hugged each of his sisters-in-law, and she could tell that he regarded them with great affection. It was quite a change to the way he looked at her with so much distrust in those dark eyes.

And then they were on their way. Piers had left the limousine to the others and called for a car to pick them up. The ride home was quiet, and finally, unable to stand the tension, she turned her head in the darkness of the backseat only to see him staring at her, those dark eyes nearly invisible.

"What is bothering you, *yineka mou?*"

"Are you expecting a wedding night?" she blurted.

White teeth flashed as he smiled. It was a decidedly predatory smile, and it sent shivers down her spine.

"But of course. You're my wife now. A wedding night usually does follow a wedding, does it not?"

"I...I just wasn't sure, I mean this isn't a real marriage, and I didn't think you wanted much to do with me."

"Oh, I intend for it to be very real," he said softly. "Just as I intend for you to spend tonight and every night in my bed."

Chapter 10

All she had to do was say no. It wasn't as if Piers would force her. Jewel stepped from the car, her hand in Piers's as he pulled her to his side. A shiver overtook her when the night chill brushed her skin, and she unconsciously moved closer to his warmth.

The question was, did she want to tell him no? And what purpose would it serve except to make him further distrust her and her motives?

As soon as the thought materialized, she clenched her teeth in anger. If the only reason she could muster to go to bed with him was so that he'd trust her more then she needed a serious reality check, not to mention she needed a few more brain cells.

Admit it, you want him.

And there it was. She did. The one night they'd shared burned brightly in her memory. She was married to him, and she wanted him to love her. She wanted him to trust her, and neither could happen if she maintained the distance between them.

Determined to embrace her marriage without being a martyr, she slipped her fingers tighter through Piers's and hurried alongside him into the house.

"I know today was hard for you, *yineka mou.* I hope it wasn't too taxing for you and the baby."

Had he changed his mind about making love to her? It sounded like he was offering an out. Or was he simply giving her the choice?

"I'm perfectly all right," she said softly as they stepped into the foyer.

He turned, putting his hands gently on her upper arms. "Are you?"

She stared back, knowing what he was really asking. Slowly she nodded, her senses firing in rapid succession.

"Be sure, Jewel. Be very sure."

Again she nodded, and before she could say or do anything else, he pulled her to him and covered her mouth hotly with his.

He swallowed her breath, took every bit of air and left her gasping for more. How was it he made her so weak? She sagged against him, clutching desperately at his shirt.

His tongue invaded her mouth, sliding sensuously over her lips and inside, tasting her and giving her his taste.

"Sweet," he murmured. "So sweet. I want you, *yineka mou.* Say you want me too. Let me take you upstairs. I want to make love to you again."

"Yes. Please, yes." She gasped when he swung her into his arms. "Piers, no, I'm too heavy."

"Do you doubt my strength?" he asked in amusement as he mounted the stairs.

"I'm huge," she said in exasperation.

"You're beautiful."

He carried her through the doorway to the master bedroom and laid her carefully on the bed. With gentle fingers he slipped the thin straps over her shoulders and let them fall. He tugged farther until the dress eased over her sensitive breasts, the material scraping lightly at her nipples.

Farther and farther, it inched over her belly, then to her hips and finally down her legs. When it swirled around her ankles, he pulled it free and dropped it on the floor.

Sharp tingles raced up her legs when he rasped his palms back up to her hips where he tucked his thumbs underneath the lace of her panties. Then he lowered his mouth and pressed a kiss to her taut belly as he slid the underwear down and then free. Her legs parted in exquisite anticipation as his mouth traveled lower and lower still.

Cupping her behind, he gently spread her wider, and his tongue found her in a heated rush. She arched off the bed, twisting wildly as pleasure consumed her.

His mouth found her again and again, gentle and worshipping. It was hard to breathe, hard to think, hard to do anything but feel. Her orgasm built, and every muscle in her body tightened in response. Just when she knew she couldn't bear it any longer, he pulled away, and she whimpered in protest.

"Shhh." He murmured to her again in Greek, raining soft words over her skin as he moved up her body. How had he gotten his clothes off without her noticing?

Flesh against flesh, smooth, comforting, a balm to her reeling senses. His mouth closed around one taut nipple, sucking and tugging. One hand cupped her rounded middle, his fingers splayed possessively over their child. It was the first movement he'd made to actually acknowledge her presence, and she wondered if he even knew what he was doing.

"Open your legs for me, *yineka mou.* Welcome me inside."

She could barely make herself respond. She shook and quivered as he settled between her thighs, his shaft nudging impatiently.

And then he was inside her in one smooth thrust.

She cried out and gripped his shoulders, her nails digging deep.

"That's it. Hold on to me. I've got you."

Their lips fused, their tongues tangling wildly as their bodies met and retreated. Pressure built until she simply couldn't bear it any longer. Her release exploded with the force of a hurricane.

He followed, surging into her, over and over, his husky groan filling her ears as he poured himself into her.

She closed her eyes, allowing sweet fuzzy bliss to encompass her, and when she gained awareness, it was to Piers's arms wrapped tightly around her, her body tucked into his side.

His lips moved through her hair as his hand went to cup her backside in a possessive gesture. She melted bonelessly into him and sighed in contentment. The wispy hairs on his chest tickled her nose and whispered across her lips, but she didn't move. She felt safe. More than that, she felt loved.

* * *

Jewel awoke the next morning to Piers sitting on the side of the bed holding a tray with breakfast and a single long-stemmed rose. He had only a pair of silk pajama bottoms on, and her gaze was drawn to his muscled chest, a chest she'd slept on for most of the night.

"Good morning," he said. "Are you hungry?"

"Starved," she admitted as she sat up in bed.

Then she realized she was still nude, and she yanked at the sheet, a hot flush surging up her neck and to her cheeks.

Piers caught her hand, stopping the sheet from its upward climb. "Don't be shy with me. I've seen and tasted every inch of your sweet body."

She slowly uncurled her fingers and relaxed her tense shoulders. He leaned in and kissed her long and slow, his lips exploring hers. This fantasy he spun allured her, drew her in and surrounded her in its firm grip.

A night of making love, breakfast in bed, tender kisses and gentle words.

If only it were all real.

Was he playing with her? Toying with her emotions? How could he act with such caring when he thought she was a liar and a manipulator?

"I'd give a lot of pennies for your thoughts right now."

She blinked and looked up to see him staring intently at her. No, he didn't really want to know what she was thinking. It would put the frown he so often wore right back on his face, and right now, she enjoyed the odd tenderness in the dark depths of his gaze.

"I'm thinking this is a nice way to wake up," she said with a smile.

He rubbed his thumb over her bottom lip and then trailed his fingers over her cheek, pushing back the wayward strands of her hair.

"Eat your breakfast. Your appointment is in two hours."

An appointment she'd forgotten in the aftermath of her wedding. She was scheduled for a sonogram as part of her pre-op workup. Afterward, she'd have more blood drawn and talk to the scheduling clerk about when she would be admitted to the hospital.

He placed the tray over her legs then handed her the utensils. "I'm going to go shower and shave. I have a few calls to make, and then I'll drive you to your appointment."

She glanced at his lean jaw, shadowed by the night's growth. Unable to resist, she lifted fingers to touch the hard edge of his chin and brushed the tips over the rough surface. His eyes closed as he leaned into her palm.

"Thank you."

He pulled away. "You're welcome. I'll leave you to eat now."

She watched as he walked away, his long stride eating up the floor. Despite the fact she had a delicious meal in front of her, her thoughts were of Piers in the shower, water sluicing over his muscled body. If she were daring, she'd go join him, but she had to admit, she had reservations about approaching him. So far, she'd allowed him to make the moves. It gave her an opportunity to study him and to figure out more about this man who'd upended her life.

Again she looked down at the sparkling diamond on her third finger. The weight was odd. She hadn't grown used to it yet, but she was fascinated by the sight and also by the meaning. In many ways it was a stamp of possession. She belonged to someone.

Realizing she'd spent too much time daydreaming, she hurriedly ate. After showering and dressing, she ventured downstairs where she found Piers in his study on the phone.

When he looked up and saw her standing at the door, he held up one finger to signal he'd be just a minute and then turned back to the phone.

Not wanting to intrude, she retreated back to the living room to wait. He wasn't long. He was tucking his phone into his pocket when he strode into the living room.

"I've arranged for a chef for the time we're here. He'll arrive this afternoon in time to prepare tonight's dinner."

"You didn't really need to do that. I was only teasing."

"On the contrary. It was an excellent idea. You certainly don't need to be on your feet cooking, and if it was left to me, I'm afraid you'd grow tired of my limited culinary repertoire."

"You're shamelessly spoiling me," she protested, though it sounded weak even to her.

He half-smiled, something flickering in his eyes. It was that same look he always seemed to wear around her. "That's the idea." He looked down at his watch. "Are you ready? We ought to leave now in case traffic is bad."

She nodded and rose from her perch on the couch.

When they arrived for her appointment, Piers surprised her by staying at her side every step of the way. She'd imagined that he might sit in the waiting room, but he went back and listened with concentration to everything the nurse and the doctor had to say.

When it came time for her sonogram, Piers was like a child in a candy store. He studied each image, and one time he almost touched the screen.

"Is that her?" he asked as he pointed to one tiny fist.

The sonogram tech smiled. "She's sucking her thumb. Here's her chin," he said, tracing a small curve on the screen. "Here's her fist. She's got her thumb in her mouth."

Tears simmered in Jewel's eyes as she stared in awe at her child. "She's beautiful."

Piers turned to her, his voice husky and oddly emotional. "Yes, she is, *yineka mou.* Very beautiful like her mother."

"What about the cyst?" Jewel asked anxiously. "Has it gotten smaller?"

"Unfortunately no. I'll have to compare the measurements to the last we recorded, but I think it's grown a little larger."

Jewel's face fell, and she closed her eyes. Somehow she'd hoped for a small miracle. That maybe the cyst would shrink so she wouldn't have to undergo surgery. She didn't want to risk anything that would harm her baby.

Piers found her hand and squeezed reassuringly. "We'll speak with the doctor and all will be well."

She clung to him, basking in his confidence. She needed it desperately because hers was flagging.

The sonogram tech rolled the portable machine out

of her room, and she and Piers waited in anxious silence. He seemed far too calm, but then what did she expect? He didn't want this child. Didn't even believe it was his.

But he's here.

That meant something, didn't it?

The silence was disturbed when the doctor came back in, his expression pensive as he studied her chart.

"Miss Henley, it's good to see you again."

Piers cleared his throat. "It's Mrs. Anetakis now. I'm her husband, Piers." He thrust out his hand to shake the doctor's, and Jewel blinked as she watched Piers take control of the situation.

He and the doctor spoke of her condition and upcoming surgery as if she weren't in the room. At first she listened in befuddlement, and then anger stirred. This was her health, her child.

"I will decide when the surgery is to be scheduled," she said fiercely.

Piers touched her once on the knee. "Of course, *yineka mou.* I am merely trying to understand all that is at stake here."

She flushed, sure she sounded petty and difficult, but she could literally feel the threads of her life slipping away, becoming permanently tangled in his.

"It should be done soon, Mrs. Anetakis," the doctor said. "I've consulted with a colleague of mine who will be assisting. It's a delicate surgery to be sure, but we feel confident of its success."

"And my baby?" she whispered.

He offered a soothing smile. "Your child will be fine."

"All right."

As they prepared to leave, the nurse gave Jewel instructions for when to report to the hospital. The entire thing scared her to death. Before she'd been able to put it out of her mind, but now it was there, staring her in the face.

"Come," Piers said quietly. He guided her toward his car and settled her inside.

For the first several miles, they drove in complete silence. Jewel stared out at the passing scenery, her mind occupied with the coming surgery.

"Tell me something. If you could live anywhere, anywhere at all, where would it be?"

Startled by the unexpected question, she turned to look at him. "The beach, I suppose." She smiled suddenly. "I've always dreamed of one of those big houses that overlooks the beach from a cliff." Her eyes closed as she imagined the sound of the waves crashing on the rocks. "A patio to watch the sun set in the evenings. What about you?"

His eyes never left the road, but she could feel him tense slightly.

"I've never given it much thought."

"Where did you live before? I mean before all this?"

A sardonic smile quirked his lip. "I don't have a permanent residence. I travel often and when I'm not away on business, I choose one of my hotels and I stay there."

"Your life sounds a lot like mine."

He cocked his head to the side and glanced at her for a moment. "How so?"

She shrugged. "No home."

He frowned as though he'd never had such a thought. And then his lips twisted ruefully. "I suppose you're right. Indeed I have many residences but no home. Perhaps you can solve that for me, *yineka mou*."

They pulled into the long drive to the house, but it wasn't until they came to a stop in the circle drive that Jewel saw the car parked in front of them. Was Piers expecting more company?

Then her gaze traveled to the front entrance and to the man sitting on the steps by the door.

"Kirk!"

As soon as the car stopped, she flew out and ran toward her friend.

Kirk rose when he saw her, a deep scowl on his face. But he caught her as she ran into his arms and hugged her fiercely.

"What the devil is going on, Jewel?" he demanded.

"I think that should be what I'm asking," Piers said coolly.

Jewel turned to see Piers staring at them, his eyes steely.

"Piers, this is a good friend of mine, Kirk. Kirk, this is Piers…my husband."

Kirk swore. "Damn it, Jewel, I told you to wait until I got here."

She swung back around to Kirk. "What are you talking about?"

"I emailed you after you emailed me telling me your situation and that you were marrying this guy." He made an angry sweeping motion toward Piers.

"But I didn't get any email. I swear. I had no idea if you'd even get mine."

Piers stepped to Jewel's side and wrapped an arm around her. He held her so tightly that she couldn't move.

"And did you rush all this way to offer us your congratulations?" Piers asked smoothly. "I'm sorry to say you missed the ceremony."

Kirk frowned even harder. "I'd like to talk to Jewel alone. I'm not leaving here until she convinces me that this is what she wants."

"Anything you have to say in front of my *wife,* can be said in front of me."

"Piers, stop," she said sharply. "Kirk is a very dear friend, and I owe him an explanation." She pried herself away from Piers and laid her hand on Kirk's arm. "Have you eaten anything?"

Kirk shook his head. "I hopped a flight and came straight here."

"Come in then. We can go out on the patio to eat, and we can talk."

She could have broken a stone on Piers's face. Without a word, he turned and stalked away, disappearing into the house.

"Nice guy," Kirk muttered.

Jewel sighed. "Come on in. I'll get us something to eat."

Chapter 11

Piers stood in the living room, sipping his drink and staring broodingly to the terrace where Jewel sat entertaining her guest.

Just who was this Kirk to her? Was he the father of her child? Had he left her high and dry and now had a change of heart? For all he knew, the two of them could be taking him on the ride of his life.

His eyes narrowed when he saw Jewel smile and then laugh at something Kirk had said. Then they both stood and Kirk drew her into his arms, hugging her tightly.

Piers's fingers curled into tight fists at his side. Then, before they returned inside, he walked away, determined not to give her the satisfaction of rising to her bait.

He was halfway across the room when he realized

what he was doing. Running. That made him more furious than the thought of her making a fool of him. No woman was going to force him into retreat.

He turned to face them when the French doors opened. His gaze swept coldly over Kirk and then Jewel. She answered him with a frown, her eyes reproachful.

"Everything cleared up?" he asked mildly.

"Not really," Kirk said in a tight voice. "I've offered my assistance to Jewel so that her only alternative isn't marriage to you."

"How kind, only it's too late. She's my wife."

"Divorces are easy enough to get."

"I suppose they are, providing I was willing. I'm not."

"Stop it, both of you," Jewel demanded. "Kirk, please. I appreciate your help more than you know, but Piers is right. It's too late. We're married, and I want to make the best of it."

Kirk's expression softened as he looked at Jewel. "If you need anything at all, get in touch with me. It might take me a few days to get to you, but I'll be there, okay?"

Jewel smiled and hugged him tightly. "Thank you, Kirk. I appreciate everything you've done and for letting me stay in the apartment."

So it was Kirk's apartment and not Jewel's. She obviously hadn't been exaggerating when she said she had no money and no place to stay.

Guilt crowded into his mind again at the idea of her alone and in desperate need of help.

Kirk kissed her forehead and then pulled away. "If you're sure there isn't anything I can do, I'm going to head back to the airport and see if I can hop a flight today. If I'm lucky, I can be back on location in a day and a half."

"I'm just sorry you made the trip for nothing. If I'd gotten your email, I would have told you not to bother coming."

Piers fought to maintain a neutral expression. Deleting the email had backfired on him. If she was telling the truth.

She walked Kirk to the door, and they both disappeared outside. A few minutes later, Piers heard the car drive away and then Jewel came back inside, her expression stormy.

"What the hell was all that about?" she demanded.

He raised an eyebrow at the force of her anger. She was bristling from head to toe and her eyes shot ocean-colored daggers at him.

"Funny, I should be asking you that question."

"What are you talking about? Kirk is a good friend of mine. The only friend I have. If you have a problem with that, you can take a hike."

"So fiercely loyal," he murmured. "I wonder, though, if that loyalty extends to me?"

"Cut the crap, Piers. If you want a fight, let's fight, but I don't have time for little psychological games."

"Is that what we're doing? Fighting? It's a little soon for our first marital spat, wouldn't you say?"

"Go to hell."

With that, she turned and stomped up the stairs. A few seconds later, the door to her bedroom slammed with enough force to shake the house.

So she had a temper. He'd purposely baited her for no other reason than his anger over his apparent jealousy. The woman had him tied in knots, and he didn't like that one little bit.

If this Kirk was so hot to trot to come to Jewel's aid, where had he been when she really needed him? If he was the father of her child, had he deserted them both and was now only back because he had competition? Or was this an elaborate hoax for them both to con him out of a fortune? He must have played right into Jewel's hands when he offered her a generous settlement if the child turned out not to be his and they divorced. It was probably her plan all along.

But then the entire scheme hinged on him granting her a divorce. He smiled coldly. He couldn't wait to inform her that there would *be* no divorce.

Dinner was quiet and strained. Jewel was still furious over the way Piers had acted toward Kirk, and Piers's face was cast in stone. He ate as though nothing had occurred between them at all, and that made her even angrier. How were they supposed to have an argument when he didn't cooperate?

Dessert was served, and as much as she wanted to enjoy the decadent chocolate tart, it tasted like sawdust.

"I've been thinking," Piers said. He spoke coldly, with no warmth or inflection in his voice.

She didn't answer and continued to concentrate on dissecting her dessert.

"I no longer feel that divorce is an option."

Shocked, she dropped her fork, and winced at the loud clatter. "What? You believe that the baby is yours now? Before we get the results?"

He raised an eyebrow in a manner meant to make

her feel inferior and at a disadvantage. It was mocking, almost as if he were laughing at her.

"I'm not a fool, Jewel. You'd do well to remember that."

"Then why this nonsense about a divorce? The child is yours, but you've never been inclined to believe that. Why on earth would you suggest there be no divorce until you're sure?"

"Maybe I'm just letting you know that your plan won't work. I won't grant a divorce, regardless of whether the child is mine."

He seemed to be studying her, waiting for a reaction. What kind of reaction? What was he thinking now?

And then it hit her like a ton of bricks. Her mouth fell open in disgust.

"You think this is a scheme to extort money from you. You think that Kirk is the father, and that I'm some whore sleeping with both of you."

She hadn't imagined that anyone had the power to hurt her anymore. Long ago, she'd developed impenetrable armor against the kind of pain other humans inflicted. Despite it all, hurt overwhelmed her. She felt betrayed even though she never imagined she had his loyalty.

With shaking legs, she clumsily got out of her chair, shoving it backward with more force than was necessary. She was determined not to break down in front of him. Before she escaped the room, she turned one last time to him.

"Who did this to you, Piers? Who made you into a bastard who won't trust anyone, and how long will it take you to figure out that I'm not her?"

She hurried away, no longer able to stand his brooding gaze.

Instead of retreating upstairs, she let herself out the French doors and ventured into the gardens. A chill chased away the flush of anger, and she gathered her arms close to her as she walked down a spiraling pathway deeper into the heart of the greenery.

Old-fashioned streetlamps lit most of the paths. Finally she found a round, stone table with a circular bench. It was the perfect place to sit and enjoy the night air.

What had she done? She rubbed her stomach absently, thinking about her daughter and the future. A future that didn't seem quite as bright as it had before. Piers was being vengeful over a perceived wrong she hadn't dealt him, and so he'd decided, as if she had no choice or say in the matter, that there wouldn't be a divorce.

Oh, she knew according to his stipulations that there would never be a divorce because she knew the child was his. Only he seemed convinced otherwise.

What kind of life had she consigned herself and her child to? Would Piers's attitude soften toward their daughter when he learned the truth? And what about Jewel? Would she forever be relegated to just being the woman who gave birth to his daughter or would he soften toward her as well?

"You shouldn't be out here alone."

She whirled around, her anger surging back when she saw Piers standing there, hands shoved insolently into his pockets.

"I'm hardly alone, am I? No doubt there are countless security men surrounding me."

He nodded as he walked closer. "Yes, but you shouldn't take such a risk just because I have a security detail."

"Tell me, Piers, will your security detail protect me from you?" she asked mockingly.

"Interesting choice of words. I feel as though I'm the one in need of protecting."

She turned away, her shoulders shaking. "I want out, Piers. Immediately."

She heard his swift intake of breath and his hiss of anger.

"I've just told you I won't grant you a divorce."

"At this point, I couldn't care less. It isn't as if I ever intend to marry again. I just want to be away from you. Keep your damn settlement. I don't want anything from you. Just my freedom. I'll leave immediately."

She lurched forward, taking the spiraling pathway that would lead her back to the house, but Piers was beside her in an instant, his hand tight around her arm.

"You can't go anywhere at this hour, Jewel. Be sensible."

"Sensible?" She laughed. "Now you tell me to be sensible. I should have been sensible the moment you walked back into my life and took it over."

"Stay until morning. You won't have to concern yourself with me asserting my husbandly rights."

"And you'll let me go?" she asked incredulously.

"If you still want to, then yes."

She studied him in the dark, and shook her head at the emotionless set to his face. Did he feel anything ever? Did he have a soul or had he given it away long ago?

"All right then. I'll leave first thing in the morning. Now if you'll excuse me, I'd like to go to bed."

Piers watched her go, his chest tight with something that felt remarkably like panic. Of all the reactions he might have expected, this wasn't one of them. When confronted with her deception, he'd expected tears, recriminations, even pleas to help her anyway. He hadn't expected her to tell him to go to hell and leave. Where was the profit in that?

Now he was stuck with thinking of a way to persuade her to stay. Until he figured out this puzzle, he needed her where he could find her at all times. For the first time, a surge of excitement tingled his nape. Could it be that she was really pregnant with his child? That this time, he had rights where the child was concerned?

If so, there was no way he would let Jewel walk out of his life.

Chapter 12

Unable to sleep, Jewel spent her time packing her clothing. She hadn't even unpacked everything yet, so the task didn't take her long. The rest of her time was spent sitting on the bed, her hands braced on the mattress as she silently stewed.

Why had she married Piers? It was a stupid decision, and yes, she'd been desperate, but not so desperate that she had called Kirk. No, she'd called *Piers* and then allowed him to take over and demand she marry him.

Face it. You're a hopeless dreamer.

All of the things she supposedly no longer believed in had guided her every step for the last five months. Was it any wonder she'd royally screwed up?

At two in the morning, she was lying in bed, in the dark, staring toward the window at the full moon spilling through the panes. She'd just closed her eyes and considered that she might finally fall asleep when sharp pain lanced through her side, stealing her breath with its intensity.

She drew her knees up in automatic defense, and another tearing pain ripped through her abdomen. She couldn't breathe, couldn't think, couldn't even process what she needed to do.

When the agony let up, she rolled toward the edge of the bed. Fear was as strong as the pain now. Fear for her child. Was she losing her baby?

Tears blurred her vision as she groped for a handhold. Her feet dangled above the floor when pain assaulted her again. She fell the rest of the way, landing with a thump on her side. She lay there, gasping for air, tears rolling down her cheeks as wave upon wave of pain shredded her insides.

Piers, she had to get to Piers.

She pushed her palm down on the surface of the floor, trying to lever herself up. The pain was unrelenting now. Nausea rolled through her stomach, swelling in her throat until she gagged.

She clamped her mouth shut and took deep breaths through her nose.

"Piers!"

It sounded weak, and her door was closed.

"Piers!" she said louder, and collapsed again when pain slashed through her side again.

Oh God, he wasn't coming. He probably couldn't hear her, and she couldn't get up.

Tears slipped faster down her cheeks, and she moaned helplessly as the tearing sensation overwhelmed her.

Then she heard the door fly open. The light flipped on, and footsteps thumped across the floor.

"Jewel! What's wrong? Is it the baby?"

Piers knelt beside her, his hands flying across her body and her stomach. He started to turn her, and she cried out in pain.

"Tell me what's wrong, *yineka mou*. Tell me how to help you," he said desperately.

"Hurt," she gasped out. "I hurt so much."

"Where?"

"My side, my stomach. Low—around my pelvis. God, I don't know. It hurts everywhere."

"Shhh, I'll take care of you," he said soothingly. "It'll be all right. I promise."

He gathered her in his arms and lifted her up.

"Will you be all right if I lay you on the bed for a moment? I need to get dressed, and then I'll drive you to the hospital."

She nodded against his chest, unable to form even a simple word.

He strode into his bedroom and settled her on the same bed they'd made love in the night before. His scent surrounded her, and oddly, offered her comfort.

It seemed to take him forever to dress, but finally he was back, pulling her to him. He hurried down the stairs and outside into the chilly night.

"I'm going to put you in the backseat so you can lie down," he murmured. "I'll have you at the hospital quickly. Try to hold on, *yineka mou*."

She curled into a ball as soon as he put her down and clenched her fingers into tight fists to combat the urge to scream.

Not the baby. Please don't let it be the baby.

She barely registered the car stopping or Piers picking her up again. There were voices around her, a prick in her arm, the cold sheets of a bed, bright lights and then a strange man peering down into her eyes.

"Mrs. Anetakis, can you hear me?"

She nodded and tried to speak. Piers squeezed her hand—how long had he been there holding it?

"The cyst on your ovary has caused your tube to torque. I've called in your obstetrician. He wants us to prep you for surgery."

A low whimper erupted from her throat. Piers moved closer to her, smoothing his free hand through her hair in a comforting gesture.

"It will be all right, *yineka mou.* The doctor has assured me that you will receive the best care. Our baby will be just fine."

Our baby, she thought drowsily. Had he said our baby or was she imagining it? She couldn't quite get her thoughts together. The pain had diminished and she felt like she was floating on a light cloud.

"What did you do to me?" she asked.

She heard a light chuckle from the nurse at her head.

"Just something to make you more comfortable. We'll be wheeling you in to surgery in just a moment."

"Piers?"

"I'm here, *yineka mou.*" Again his hand stroked her hair, and she turned into his palm, her eyes fighting to stay open.

"You said our baby. You believe she's yours?"

There was a hesitation, and she blinked harder to keep him in focus. There were worry lines crowding his forehead. Was he concerned for the baby?

"Yes, she is mine," he said huskily. "She's our

daughter, and you'll take good care of her during the surgery, I'm sure. Rest now and don't try to speak. Let the medicine take the pain away."

She gripped his hand tightly, afraid that if she let go, he'd leave. The bed going into motion startled her, and she pulled his hand closer.

"Don't go."

"I'm not going anywhere," he said soothingly.

His lips brushed across her forehead, and she relaxed, closing her eyes and allowing the pain to leave her.

The voices dimmed around her. Then Piers kissed her again and told her softly that he would be waiting for her. Why? Where was he going? She wanted to ask but couldn't muster the energy to do anything more than lie there.

The bed rolled again and suddenly she was in a frigid room. She was lifted and transferred to a much harder surface, and it was cold. A cheerful voice sounded in her ear and asked her to count backward from ten.

She opened her mouth to comply but nothing came out. She even managed to open her eyes, but by the time she mentally made it to eight, everything went black.

Piers paced the confines of the surgery waiting room like a caged lion, edgy and impatient. He checked his watch again only to find that three minutes had passed since the last time he'd checked it. Damn it, how long would it take? Why weren't they telling him anything?

"Piers, how is she?"

Piers looked up to see Theron striding into the waiting room, his hair rumpled as if he'd rolled out of bed and onto the plane. But then he had. Piers felt guilty for dragging his brother out of bed in the middle of the night, but he was grateful to have him here.

Piers briefly embraced his brother and the two sat down.

"I don't know yet. They took her in a few hours ago, but I haven't heard anything since."

"What happened? Is the baby all right?"

"The cyst on her ovary caused a tubal torsion. She was in unspeakable pain so they took her to surgery to remove the cyst and probably the tube as well. She was scheduled for surgery in a week's time anyway so this just moved up the timeline."

"And the baby?"

"There are…risks, but they've assured me they'll do everything they can to prevent anything from happening to the baby."

"How long has she been in surgery?"

"Four hours," Piers said bleakly. "What could be taking so long?"

"You'll hear something soon," Theron said comfortingly. "Have you called Chrysander?"

Piers shook his head. "There was no need. It would take him too long to get off the island and come here. By the time he did, it would all be over with."

"Still, you should call him. He'd want to know, he and Marley both."

"I'll call them when I know how she is."

The two brothers sat in the waiting room. After a while Theron left and returned with coffee for the both of them. Piers sipped the lukewarm brew, not really tasting it.

"You're different, you know."

Piers looked up in surprise. "What are you talking about?"

"You seem more settled…more content even. I noticed it in your eyes when we were here for the wedding."

"As opposed to what?" he asked mockingly.

"As opposed to the way you've existed ever since Joanna screwed you over and left with Eric."

Piers flinched. No one ever mentioned Eric to his face. He was sure his family probably said a lot behind his back, but never when he was around. The pain was still too fresh.

"Don't ruin your chance at happiness, Piers. This is your chance to have it all."

"Or lose it all again. Maybe I already have."

"What do you mean?"

Piers took another gulp of the coffee and put the cup aside.

"She was going to leave me in the morning. Her bags were already packed when I found her on the floor in terrible pain."

"Want to talk about it?" Theron asked carefully. "I've been accused of being dense once or twice by a certain woman in my life."

"You seem so sure it's me who is the problem," Piers said dryly.

"You're a man, and men are always in the wrong. Haven't you learned anything yet?"

The corner of Piers's mouth lifted in a smile. Then he sobered. "I was an ass."

"Yes, well, it won't be the last time. It seems an inherent part of our genetic makeup."

"A male friend of hers showed up yesterday to come to her rescue. I didn't take it very well."

"No one can blame you for that. It's part of being territorial."

Piers snorted. "Next you'll be telling me that we're all cavemen stomping around and marking our territory like dogs."

"Quite an image you've conjured there, little brother. I imagine that's precisely what we do, just not in the literal sense."

Theron glanced sideways at Piers.

"So she was going to leave you because you didn't appreciate her male friend showing up?"

"I might have accused him of fathering her child and the two of them of running a scam to extort money from me."

Theron winced. "Damn, when you decide to pull off the gloves, you go for the full monty."

"As I said, I was an ass. I was angry. I told her that I wouldn't grant her a divorce, and she told me to take my settlement and go to hell."

"Doesn't sound much like a woman after your money, does it?"

He'd thought the same thing himself.

"I want to trust her, Theron."

"And that frightens you."

And there it was in a nutshell. Funny how his brother cut so quickly to the heart of the matter. Yes, he wanted to trust her, but he was afraid, and it infuriated him.

"I don't want to ever allow a woman that much power over me again."

Theron sighed and put his hand on Piers's shoulder. "I understand, really I do. But you can't shut yourself away from the world for the rest of your life just because you got hurt once."

"Hurt?" Piers made a derisive sound. "I wish it was only hurt. She took from me what I loved most in the world. Somehow that goes beyond simple hurt."

"Still, as cliché as it sounds, life goes on. I want you to be happy, Piers. Chrysander and I worry about you. You can't go on traveling from one hotel to another your entire life. At some point you need to settle down and start a family. Jewel has given you that opportunity. Perhaps you should make the most of it. Give her a chance."

"Mr. Anetakis."

Both men yanked their heads up as a nurse appeared in the waiting room.

"Mrs. Anetakis is out of surgery. You can visit her in recovery for a moment if you like."

Piers shot up and hurried over to the nurse. "Is she all right? The baby?"

The nurse smiled. "Mother and baby are fine. The surgery went well. The doctor will stop in to talk to you in recovery before she's taken to a room. She's going to be very groggy, but you can talk to her for a moment if you like."

"I'll wait here," Theron said. "You go ahead."

"Thank you," Piers said sincerely. Then he turned to follow the nurse to see Jewel.

Chapter 13

Her pain was different. It wasn't as agonizingly sharp as before. Instead it had settled to a dull ache, not as deep as it had been, but on the surface. Jewel tried to shift and gasped when it felt as though her belly had been ripped in two.

"Careful, *yineka mou.* You mustn't try to move. Tell me what it is you need, and I will help you."

Piers. She opened her eyes, squinting as the light speared her eyeballs. She quickly shut them again and cautiously opened them a slit as she tried to bring him into focus.

And then she remembered.

"The baby," she whispered. She reached her hands out in panic, feeling for her belly then gasping as more pain crashed through her system.

Piers took her hands and pulled them gently away from her belly.

"The baby is fine, as are you. See?" He carefully levered one of her hands to the swell of her belly but wouldn't allow her to exert any pressure.

She looked down at the unfamiliar feel of bulky bandages, but the swell was still evident. Tears flooded her eyes as her insides caved in relief.

"I was so afraid. I can't lose her, Piers. She's everything to me."

He cupped her cheek and rubbed his thumb over the damp trail underneath her eye. "Your surgery was a success. The doctor says the baby is doing well. They've been monitoring you for contractions." He gestured toward a machine at the side of her bed. "See? You can see and hear her heartbeat."

She turned her head and tuned into the soft *whop whop whop* sound that echoed in the still room.

"It's really her?"

Piers smiled. "Yes, our daughter is making her presence known."

She caught her breath as suddenly she remembered the scene just before they'd taken her to surgery. At first she thought surely she'd imagined it, but no, here again he was staking his claim. Why had he changed his mind?

"Thank you for getting me here so quickly," she said in a low voice. "I was so afraid I wouldn't be able to get to you."

He sobered as he gazed intently at her, his dark eyes seeming to absorb her. "You wouldn't have suffered for as long as you did if I had been there with you. From now on, you'll sleep in my room in my bed so if anything like this happens again, I'll know immedi-

ately. I don't like to think what could have happened
if I hadn't heard you call out."

She processed his statement, blinking the cloudi-
ness from her mind. Everything was so fuzzy, and he
confused her more than ever. It was as if their argument had never happened, as though he hadn't accused
her of trying to pawn off another man's child on him.

"There will be plenty of time to talk later," he
chided gently. "You're worn out and in pain. You need
rest. I'll be here when you wake up. You can ask the
questions I see burning in your eyes then."

She shook her head and winced when the movement caused a ripple of pain through her belly. "No, I
have to know now. You said—implied—some terrible
things, Piers. I won't stay with a man who thinks so
little of me, not even for my daughter. Kirk is willing
to help me get back on my feet. I should have called
him in the first place."

"But you didn't," he said mildly. "You called me,
as you should have. I think it best if we leave Kirk out
of the equation."

She started to protest but he held a finger over her
lips.

"Shhh, don't upset yourself. I owe you an apology,
yineka mou. I'm sure it won't be the last I ever have to
offer you. I would appreciate your patience with me.
I'm not an easy man. I realize this. I should not have
implied what I did. From this day forward, we go on
as a family. You're having my child. We owe it to her
to be a solid parental unit, not one where I continu-
ally upset you and cause you such stress. If you'll give
me another chance, I'll prove to you that our marriage
will work."

She stared at him in absolute stupefaction. His sincerity was etched on his face. His eyes burned with it. There was no arrogance to his voice, just simple regret.

Something inside her chest, perilously close to her heart, unfurled and loosened. Forgotten for a brief moment was the pain that throbbed in her abdomen and the fuzziness caused by the pain medication. Warmth, blessed and sweet, hummed through her veins. Hope. It had been so long since she'd felt such a thing that she hadn't identified it at first. For the first time, she had hope.

He drew her hand to his mouth and pressed a soft kiss inside her palm. "Do you forgive me? Will you give me another chance to make things right?"

"Yes, of course," she whispered, her voice so shaky that her words came out in barely a croak.

"And you'll stay? There'll be no more talk of leaving?"

She shook her head, too choked to say anything more.

"You won't regret it, *yineka mou*," he said gravely. "We can make this work. We can do this."

She smiled and then grimaced as pain radiated from the center of her body. Piers leaned forward, directing her attention to the small device lying beside her on the bed. He picked it up and pressed it into her palm.

"This is for pain. You press the button here, and it injects a small amount of medication into your IV. You can press it every ten minutes if you have the need."

He depressed the button himself, and a split second later, she felt the slight burn as it entered her vein. The relief was almost instantaneous.

"Thank you."

"I will take care of you and our baby," he said solemnly. "I don't want you to worry about a thing except to get better."

She smiled up at him, her eyelids fluttering sleepily.

"Tired," she said in a half murmur.

"Then sleep. I'll be right here."

She turned toward his voice, and when he started to move his hand from hers, she curled her fingers around his, keeping them laced. He relaxed and tightened his grip on her hand.

"When am I getting outta here?" she mumbled as she fought the veil of sleep.

He chuckled lightly. "There's no hurry. You'll leave when the doctor feels it's safe for you to do so. In the meantime enjoy everyone fussing over you."

"Just you," she muttered just before she surrendered to the dark.

"Are you sure everything is prepared?" Piers said into his mobile phone as he entered Jewel's room.

Jewel looked up and smiled and Piers held up one finger to signal he would be finished shortly.

"Good. Very good. I owe you one, and I have no doubt that you'll collect."

He snapped his phone shut and hastened to Jewel's side. He bent down and brushed his lips across hers in greeting.

"How are my girls today?"

"Your daughter is very active, which is a blessing and a curse."

Piers gave her a sympathetic look. "Do her movements aggravate your incision?"

She grimaced. "I think she's playing target practice. She's has uncanny accuracy for kicking that precise spot."

"I'm sorry. I know it must be painful for you."

"The alternative doesn't bear thinking about, so I'm grateful for her movements."

"Has the doctor been by to see you yet?"

"He came by while you were out. He said if all goes well today and I have no further contractions, that I can be released tomorrow. I'm to be on strict bed rest for a week and then I can get up and around as long as I don't overdo it."

"And I will see to it that you obey his instructions to the letter."

She was careful not to laugh, but she grinned in amusement. "Why do I get the feeling you're going to enjoy my convalescence?"

He gave her an innocent look. "Why would you think such a thing?"

"Because you're a man used to bossing people around and having them obey you implicitly," she said darkly.

"You say this as if it was a bad thing."

This time she did chuckle and promptly groaned when her belly protested. Piers gave her a disapproving frown, and she rolled her eyes.

The past several days had been good considering she was stuck in a hospital bed. After the first day, the nurse had come in to help her get up, and Jewel had spent fifteen minutes trying to argue that there was no need for her to get up when every movement nearly split her in two. It was the threat of a catheter that finally gave her the motivation to endure sitting up and standing.

Piers had been wonderful. The brooding man who'd so insolently told her there would be no divorce had seemingly disappeared, and was replaced by someone who saw to her every need. She had to admit that he was trying very hard to put their past disagreements behind them.

A light knock sounded at the door, and to her surprise, Piers's brothers and their wives crowded into her room. She must have looked as mortified as she felt because Piers squeezed her hand.

"Don't worry, *yineka mou.* You look beautiful. They won't stay long enough to tire you. I'll see to it."

He was lying through his teeth, but she loved him for it.

The thought hit her between the eyes and was more painful than the stapled incision in her belly. Love? Dear God, she'd fallen in love with him.

She tried to smile, but what she wanted to do was crawl into a deep, dark hole. How could she have allowed herself to fall in love with him—with any man? Apparently she hadn't had enough hurt in her life. No, she obviously wanted to pile on more pain and disappointment.

It was all well and fine to want to be loved, but to offer her love on a silver platter? She was just asking for rejection.

"Jewel? Have we come at a bad time?" Marley asked quietly.

Jewel blinked and saw that the two couples were standing at the foot of her bed, studying her intently.

"No. No, of course not. I'm sorry. I'm still a bit muddled. It's probably all the pain medication they've funneled through me."

Beside her Piers frowned, and she just hoped he'd remain quiet about the fact she hadn't had pain medication in three days. The doctor hadn't wanted her to be on any narcotic for an extended period of time. It was too risky for the baby.

She smiled brightly at Bella and Marley and opted to keep her gaze away from Chrysander and Theron. They intimidated the hell out of her, and she wasn't in the habit of giving up that kind of advantage to anyone.

"How are you feeling?" Bella asked as she moved forward.

She perched on the side of Jewel's bed and flipped her long dark hair over her shoulder.

"Has Piers been bullying you? Marley and I can take him outside and rough him up for you."

Jewel smiled and swallowed to keep from laughing.

"Don't make her laugh," Piers growled. "It hurts her too much. Besides, I have you and Marley wrapped around my finger, remember?"

Chrysander let out a loud guffaw. "Don't let him fool you, Jewel. All either woman has to do is look at this idiot brother of mine, and he gives them whatever they want, much to mine and Theron's dismay."

"As if you both don't spoil them shamelessly," Piers said dryly.

"That may be true, but a woman can never have too many men at her disposal," Marley said cheekily.

"There is only one man at your disposal, *agape mou*," Chrysander growled. "And you would do well to remember that."

Jewel watched the interaction between the three brothers and Bella and Marley, and for the first time, she didn't feel like an outsider. The horrible feeling of intense longing didn't hit her like it did the first time she'd met them. This time she felt more of an equal, as if she belonged in this intimate circle of family members.

"You must be feeling better," Bella said from her perch on the bed. "You're smiling so beautifully. You look quite radiant for someone who has just undergone surgery."

"It's the pregnancy," Theron said slyly. "A woman never looks more beautiful than when she is pregnant."

"Nice try," Bella said dryly. "Your flattery will get you nowhere. And if you start lusting after pregnant women, I'll make it so you'll never be able to father children."

Jewel couldn't help but laugh when Theron all but paled. She put her hand over her belly and groaned, but even amidst the pain, it felt so good to laugh. She felt lighter than she had in a long time.

"Are you all right?" Piers asked quietly.

She waved him off. "I'm fine. Truly." Then she turned to Bella. "Why do I get the feeling this is an ongoing battle between you and Theron?"

Bella grinned. "If Theron had his way, I'd have already popped out a veritable brood of children, but I'm too young, and we have so much to do together before I think of having babies. I'll eventually give in and fill his nursery, but until then I live to torment him."

Jewel studied Theron's face as Bella spoke. His eyes shone with love for his wife, and she knew that he didn't exert any real pressure. It was obviously a long-standing joke between them.

"Besides, Marley has taken it upon herself to pro-

vide enough Anetakis children for both of us," Bella
added with a smirk.

Piers eyebrows shot up. "Marley?"

Marley blushed while Chrysander smiled smugly
and wrapped his arm around her waist. It was a possessive gesture not lost on Jewel.

"You're pregnant again?" Piers demanded.

"In seven months she'll give me the daughter I
want," Chrysander said arrogantly.

"And if it's another son?" Marley challenged.

Chrysander looked down at her, passion blazing
in his eyes. "Then we'll simply try again until we get
it right."

Marley and Bella both laughed, and Jewel joined
them, holding her belly all the while.

What a marvelous family. A family that she was
now a part of. It was simply too much to take in.

"We should probably go now," Chrysander said as
he studied Jewel. "You look as though you're in pain,
and we don't want to tire you out. We simply wanted
to come by to check in on you and to let you know that
if there is anything you need, anything at all, just let
us know. You're family now."

She stared back at him, tears in her eyes. "Please,
don't go. You're not bothering me a bit. I've so enjoyed
having you all."

"Tell me," Bella said, leaning forward to capture
Jewel's attention. "Are they letting you have real food
yet? I'm simply dying for some pizza. Theron thinks
it's barbaric, and so I'm shamelessly using you as an
excuse to get some really greasy, cheesy pizza."

"You call that real food?" Theron asked in mock
horror.

"Oh, I'd love pizza," Jewel said with real longing. "Double pepperoni and extra cheese. Oh, and light sauce if no one objects."

"Tell you what," Bella said. "We'll order one our way and let the rest fend for themselves. What you suggested sounds positively divine."

Jewel looked hopefully at Piers who sighed in resignation.

"What man can possibly say no to a woman when she looks at him that way?"

Both Theron and Chrysander laughed.

Chrysander clapped Piers on the back. "Now you're learning, little brother. Now you're learning."

Chapter 14

"I have a surprise in mind," Piers said as he wheeled her out of the hospital's front entrance. "It will take a while to execute, so what I want you to do is relax and try to rest as much as possible."

A flutter of excitement bubbled in her stomach. She felt like a kid at Christmas. For someone who'd never gotten accustomed to any sort of surprise, she was fast finding she liked them very much. Or at least the anticipation of having one.

Piers's security detail stood outside the limousine awaiting their arrival. One opened the back door, and Piers scooped Jewel up from the wheelchair and carefully placed her in the seat, taking extra care not to jostle her. Then he walked around to the other side while all but one of his security team slipped into a car parked behind the limousine. The last man got into the front with the driver.

"Where are we going?" she asked curiously when they went the opposite direction of the house she and Piers had been staying in.

"The airport."

She raised her eyebrows. "Where are we going?"

Familiar excitement lit her veins. She loved to travel for the excitement of going to a new place, meeting new people and experiencing different cultures. Only this time she wasn't going alone, and that thrilled her more than she would have thought possible.

He smiled and reached over to take her hand. "If I told you, it would spoil the surprise."

"But my clothes, my things. I haven't packed."

"All taken care of," he said smoothly. "This is why I hire a staff."

"Did you pack my chef?" she asked mournfully. "He made the most delicious food."

Piers chuckled. "I assure you, you won't go hungry."

A while later they pulled up next to a small jet parked on a private airstrip. Piers waited while his security got out and boarded the plane. Then he walked around to her side and picked her up.

"I'll take her if you like, Mr. Anetakis," Yves offered. He was the only one who Jewel knew by name. The rest were a mystery to her, but then Yves seemed more of a personal bodyguard for Piers while the rest operated on the perimeter.

Piers shook his head. "Thank you, Yves, but I'll take Mrs. Anetakis to the plane."

Each step he took was in careful consideration of her comfort. When he reached the steps to the plane, he ducked down and walked inside.

Never before had she seen the inside of a private

jet, and if she'd been expecting a smaller version of a regular airliner, she was mistaken. There were seats in the front covered in soft, supple leather that looked incredibly luxurious and comfortable. Beyond them was a sitting area with a recliner and a couch along with a coffee table, television and a mini bar.

Piers followed the direction of her gaze. "After we take off, I'll show you the rest. There's a bedroom in the back of the plane that you can lie down in. There's also a small kitchenette, so if you want anything, you've only to let the flight attendant know."

Her eyes widened. "Flight attendant? You have one for the plane?"

"Of course. She travels with the pilot. They're a husband and wife team. It's an arrangement that suits them well. Now, would you like a window or an aisle seat?"

"Window," she said.

He carefully settled her in place and then took the seat next to her. Before fastening his seat belt, he reached over and gingerly buckled hers into place, leaving it loose around her belly.

The flight attendant walked up with a smile and greeted Piers. Then she turned her smile on Jewel. "I'm very happy to meet you, Mrs. Anetakis. If there is anything I can get you during the flight, don't hesitate to ask. We'll be cleared for takeoff shortly. Would you like something to drink while you wait?"

Jewel shook her head. "No thank you. I'm fine for now."

Minutes later, they taxied down the runway and took off. Jewel leaned her head on Piers's shoulder and snuggled into his warmth. As curious as she was to see the rest of the plane, getting up and moving hurt too much. She was perfectly content to remain here for the duration of the flight.

"You're still not going to tell me where we are?" Jewel asked several hours later as their car wound its way along a curving highway.

Piers smiled. "Patience, *yineka mou.* I think you'll find it's well worth the wait."

She sighed and relaxed in her seat. Wherever they were, it was beautiful and unspoiled. She'd lay odds it was in the Caribbean or some similar tropical place. Were they going to one of his hotels?

They stopped at a security gate where Piers punched in a code. Huge iron gates swung slowly open, and they continued up the drive.

Lush greenery abounded. It was like driving into a private paradise. Flowers, plants, fountains and even a mini waterfall cascaded over rocks in the distance.

And then she saw the house. Her mouth fell open at the sight of the stunning cottage, well if you could call something so huge a cottage. But despite its size, it had the look of a cozy, stone cottage. It looked positively homey.

"Is this where we're staying for the time being?" she asked when the car pulled to a stop beside another large fountain with flowers floating serenely in the pool surrounding it.

"This is your house, *yineka mou.* It now belongs to us."

She was struck positively speechless.

"But the best is yet to come," he said.

She watched him walk around the front of the car and wondered how on earth it could get any better?

He helped her from the car and motioned his security men who were standing several feet away. They quickly disappeared while Piers put a strong arm around her waist and urged her toward a walkway leading around the house.

And then she heard it. The distant sounds of waves crashing. She inhaled deeply, catching the salty air in her nostrils.

"Oh, Piers," she breathed.

They topped a small rise between a section of gardens and the wooden deck jutting from the house over a sharp cliff. She looked out and all she could see was a great expanse of ocean. Brilliant blue, so stunning it almost hurt her eyes to look at. It sparkled like a million sapphires.

The walkway continued, smooth in places and at other areas it became a series of steps leading down to the beach. The house was situated on the cliff in a secluded cove between two outcroppings. It afforded them a small stretch of sandy beach, completely private.

It was the most magnificent view she could have imagined. And it was theirs.

"I don't know what to say," she whispered. "This is my dream, Piers. I can't believe this is ours."

"It's yours, *yineka mou.* My wedding gift to you. I have it on good authority it comes equipped with a full staff, including a certain chef you've grown extraordinarily fond of."

She threw her arms around him, ignoring the painful jolt to her incision. "Thank you. It's so wonderful, Piers. I don't know how I'll ever be able to thank you."

"By taking good care of yourself and my daughter,"

he said seriously. "I don't want you taking the pathway down to the beach unless I'm with you."

"I promise," she said joyfully. Right now she'd promise him the moon.

"Come inside. Dinner has been held for us. We'll eat on the terrace and watch the sun go down."

She went eagerly, anxious to see the inside of the house. He gave her a quick tour of the downstairs before they walked onto the deck in the back. Their places had been set, and she eased into her chair to wait for the food.

"It's so gorgeous," she said in awe. She was completely and utterly overwhelmed by the knowledge that she lived here now, that this place was hers. It was all simply too good to be true.

"I'm glad you like it. I was afraid I wouldn't have everything in place before you were released from the hospital."

"You didn't already own it?"

"I had my representatives looking for just the perfect place the day you told me where you'd like to live more than anywhere else. When they found this place, I knew it was perfect. The sale isn't quite final, but I convinced the owner to allow us to take possession of it until all the paperwork can be finished."

She was unable to keep the wide smile from forming on her face. "That's the most wonderful thing anyone has ever done for me."

He put his hand over hers, his palm warm and soothing. "Tell me, *yineka mou*. Has anyone ever done a wonderful thing for you? I get the impression yours has not been an easy life."

She stiffened and tried to withdraw her hand, but

he wouldn't allow it. His grip tightened around her fingers, but his touch stayed soothing the entire time.

"What is it you won't tell me?" he asked quietly. "Surely there should be no secrets between a man and his wife."

She turned away to stare at the ocean, the breeze blowing across her cheeks and drying the invisible tears she shed.

"It's nothing so dramatic," she said matter-of-factly. "My parents died when I was very young. I barely remember them, and even now I wonder if the people I remember aren't just one of the many foster families I was shuttled through."

"You had no relatives to take care of you?"

She shook her head. "None that would, anyway."

A young woman came out then carrying a tray of food, and Jewel sighed in relief. She didn't miss Piers's frown, which told her the conversation wasn't closed, just delayed.

Still, nothing good would come of her rehashing the past.

They ate in companionable silence. Jewel enjoyed the sounds and smells of the ocean and found herself more relaxed than she'd been in longer than she could remember.

As the sun dipped lower on the horizon, the sky faded to soft hues of pink and purple with threads of gold spreading from the disappearing sun. The ocean shimmered in the distance, reflecting the brilliance of the sunset.

She hadn't realized she'd long since stopped eating, so entranced by the view was she. Only when the maid returned to collect the dinner plates, did Jewel break from her reverie.

"You look tired, *yineka mou*," Piers said gently. "I think I should take you upstairs so you can get ready for bed."

She yawned and then chuckled at how easily she'd given herself away. "Bed sounds really good right now. Does the bedroom have windows we can open? I'd love to be able to hear the ocean."

"I think you'll find the view from our bedroom magnificent, and we can certainly open the windows if that is your wish."

He helped her to her feet and they returned inside. They took the stairs slowly, and she bit her lip when the upward movement put awkward pressure around the area of her incision. Her entire belly felt bruised and tender.

When they entered the master bedroom, she let out a sound of pure delight. The entire back wall that faced the ocean was glassed in from floor to ceiling. She left Piers's side to peer over the water, her palms pressed to the cool glass.

Her throat suspiciously tight, she turned to face Piers. "This has been the most wonderful day. Thank you so much."

"I'm glad you approve," he said huskily.

She returned her attention to the view, watching as the last bits of the orange glow from the sun disappeared into the sea.

"What about your work? Your hotels?"

He came to stand beside her, studying the ocean with her.

"Most of my work can be handled from here. I have

a phone, my computer and a fax machine. There will be times I need to travel. Up to now, I've always done the bulk of the traveling, but I find myself unwilling to continue on that track. Either my brothers will have to help shoulder the load or we'll hire someone to do most of the traveling."

"You won't miss it?" she asked lightly.

"A few months ago I would have said yes, very much, but now I find myself more reluctant to be away from my wife and our child."

Warmth spread through her chest. How like a family they sounded. She wasn't entirely certain what had caused him to change his tune, but she had no desire to question it. She only hoped it lasted.

Chapter 15

For the next several days, Jewel rested and recovered under the watchful eye of Piers and the staff he'd hired. It seemed odd at first to have other people in the house, but they blended so seamlessly into the background that Jewel quickly became accustomed to their presence.

Piers even had a physician come to the house to check her incision and remove the staples so she wouldn't have to make the trip into town.

In short, she was spoiled and pampered endlessly, and she was fast becoming bored out of her mind. She was positively dying to explore her surroundings. A trip down to the beach was foremost on her wish list, but she also wanted to go beyond the grounds of their estate and see the rest of the island.

According to Piers, the island was small and not yet discovered by the many tourists that flocked to the

Caribbean. Fishing was the main source of industry for the locals. There were plans to build an elaborate resort, an exclusive playground for the wealthy where no expense would be spared and guests would be lavished with personal attention.

The goal was to keep the island as private and as unspoiled as possible while still providing an influx of capital for the locals.

Jewel broached the subject of a trip down to the beach over breakfast, the day after the doctor had removed her staples and pronounced her fit.

Piers frowned for a moment. "I'm not sure you should be descending the stairs this soon after your surgery, *yineka mou.*"

"But I'll have you to hang on to," she cajoled. "Please, Piers. I'm about to go stir-crazy. I've watched from a distance for so long, I'm beginning to feel like I'm viewing postcards."

He smiled. "I find I can deny you nothing. All right. After breakfast we'll go down to the beach. I'll have the cook prepare a picnic lunch."

She bounced on her seat like an excited child. "Thank you. I can't wait to see it!"

"Be sure and wear some comfortable shoes. I don't want you slipping on the steps."

She smiled at his solicitousness. How perfect things were right now. Gone was the feeling that at any moment her world could come crashing down around her. If only…if only he'd open up to her.

For days she'd argued with herself, vacillated from having the courage to ask and having it disappear. The other problem was that if she managed to get him to talk to her about his past then she'd be forced to speak of her own.

Soon, she promised herself. But not this morning. Nothing was going to ruin their outing to the beach.

Picnic basket in one hand, his other firmly wrapped around hers, Piers made his way down the steps carved into the face of the cliff. With each downward movement, the sounds of the ocean got louder and Jewel became more excited.

When their feet finally hit the sand, Jewel stopped and looked up at the impressive rocky cliffs looming over and around them, isolating their stretch of beach from the rest of the world.

"It's like we're in our own little world," she said in awe.

Piers smiled. "No one can see you except by boat, and I have it on good authority the locals don't fish this end of the island."

"Conjures up all sorts of naughty possibilities, doesn't it?"

His eyes glittered in response. "You can be sure once you are well that I'll be all too willing to indulge in some of those possibilities."

She laughed and kicked off her shoes, digging her toes into the warm sand. Unable to resist the lure of the foaming waves, she hurried toward the water's edge, anxious to feel the water swirling around her ankles.

The cascading water met her and rushed over her feet. She threw out her arms to embrace the breeze and smiled in absolute delight as her hair billowed behind her. Closing her eyes, she inhaled deep and wished she could stop time, right here in this perfect moment.

"You look like a sea nymph," Piers said. "More beautiful than a woman should be allowed to look."

She turned to see him standing beside her, his pants rolled up to his knees, his feet bare.

"Is it safe to swim here?"

He nodded.

"We'll have to do it sometime."

"You look happy, *yineka mou*. Have I made you so?"

The vulnerability that flashed in his dark eyes made her catch her breath. This strong, arrogant man was as human as the next person. Not questioning the wisdom of doing so, she flung herself into his arms, wrapping hers around his neck.

"You're so good to me, Piers. You do make me so very happy."

Tentatively, he returned her embrace and as she pulled her head away to look at him, their eyes met. Their lips were but an inch apart, and she licked hers nervously, in anticipation of what she knew was about to happen.

Instead of waiting on him, she pulled him close, fitting her mouth to his. He seemed willing to let her dictate the pace, and she explored his mouth thoroughly, learning every nuance, his taste, feeling the warmth of his tongue.

His fingers were a soft whisper against her neck. They delved farther into her hair, holding her closer as she deepened the kiss. The salt from the ocean danced on their tongues, mixing with the heady sweetness of their passion.

Finally she pulled away, gazing up at him through half-lidded eyes. "And do I make you happy?" she asked huskily.

He ran his thumb over her cheekbone, stroking to the corner of her mouth. "You make me very happy."

She smiled brilliantly at him then grabbed his hand and tugged him farther down the beach. "Come on! Let's explore."

Indulgently, he allowed her to pull him along. They covered every inch of the beach from cliff to cliff. By the time they returned to where the picnic basket lay, she was starving.

"Help me with the blanket," she said as she unfurled the brightly colored quilt. Laughing, she fought with the billowing material as it refused to cooperate.

"Here, let me."

Piers wrestled the blanket to the sand and piled their shoes at each corner to hold it down.

"Now hurry and sit before it flies away again," he said.

She gingerly eased down and dragged the basket into the middle of the quilt. Piers sat beside her and they began divvying up the food.

The sun shone bright above them, and the sand glistened like tiny jewels, scattered to the water's edge. She sighed and turned her face up into the warmth.

"You look very content, *yineka mou*. Like a cat sunning herself."

"Haven't you ever wished that a single moment could last forever?"

He became pensive as though he were giving her question serious consideration. "No, I can't say I have, but if I were given to such flights of fancy, then today would be one such time."

She smiled. "It is perfect, isn't it?"

"Yes. It is."

They finished eating, and Jewel lay back on the blanket, enjoying the sounds and smells of the ocean. The warmth of the sun's rays lulled her to sleep, and before she knew it, she was being shaken awake.

"It's time to return to the house, *yineka mou.* The sun will be setting soon."

She yawned and blinked lazily as his face came into view. She smiled up at him and held up her hand so he could help her.

Together they collected the remnants of their lunch, and Piers packed them and the blanket into the basket. He reached for her hand when they arrived at the bottom of the steps, and she slipped her fingers into his.

Tonight. Tonight she'd broach the subject of his past, and for the first time, she wouldn't avoid hers. She wanted to know his secrets, the source of the pain she saw lurking in the depths of those shuttered eyes.

Would he share those secrets or would he block her out? And should she press him on something that clearly he had no wish to discuss?

True to his word, after the night Piers had found Jewel on the floor of her bedroom writhing in pain, she'd slept each night in his bed. In deference to her incision, he spooned against her back, and she enjoyed the warmth and security his muscled body offered.

Most nights she wondered if they'd resume their lovemaking after the tenderness left her abdomen. Tonight, however, she lay there, cuddled against his chest, gathering her courage to broach the subject of his past.

"Piers?"

"Mmm-hmm."

Carefully she started to turn over to face him.

"Will you tell me who hurt you so badly?"

He went still, and she wished the lamp was on so she could gauge his reaction.

"Who made you so distrustful of women?" she continued on. "And why is it that you don't want this to be your child."

He put a finger on her lips. "That's where you're wrong, *yineka mou.* I want her to be mine very much."

Jewel cocked her head to the side. "But you seem so convinced that she isn't."

He turned on his back to stare up at the ceiling. She tentatively cuddled into the crook of his arm and laid her head on his shoulder. When he didn't resist, she relaxed, allowing her fingers to trail through the hairs on his chest.

"Ten years ago I met and fell in love with a woman. Joanna. I was young and stupid and convinced I had the world by the tail."

"Don't we all at that age," she said with a slight smile.

He chuckled. "I suppose you're right. Anyway, she became pregnant, and so we married right away."

Jewel winced at the similarities but remained quiet as he continued.

"She gave birth to a boy. We named him Eric. I adored him. I was as happy as a man can be. I had a beautiful wife who seemed devoted to me. I had a son. What more could I ask for?"

Jewel's mouth turned down unhappily. She could only imagine what he'd say next.

"And then one day I came home to find her packing. Eric was two years old. I remember him crying the entire time I tried to reason with Joanna. I couldn't understand why she was leaving. There hadn't seemed to be any problems. I had no warning.

"Finally, when I told her that she could leave but there was no way in hell I'd let my son go, she told me that he wasn't my child."

Jewel sucked in her breath. "And you believed her?"

A derisive sound escaped his lips. "No, I didn't believe her. But to make a long story short, her lover who she was involved with when she and I met had devised the perfect plan to milk me for all they could. Several months and a paternity test later, it was proved that Eric wasn't my son. Joanna took him and a great deal of my money, and I haven't seen either since."

"Oh, Piers, I'm so sorry," she whispered. "How horrible of her to allow you to fall in love with a child you thought was yours and then to yank him so cruelly away. How could she do that to either of you?"

Piers trailed his fingers up and down her bare arm.

"I have nightmares sometimes. I hear Eric calling to me, asking why I won't help him, why I left *him*. All I can remember is the day they left, and how Eric screamed and cried, how he stretched his arms out trying to get to me, and all I could do was watch her walk away with my son. It's a sight I'll never get out of my mind."

"You miss him."

"He was my entire world for those two years," he said simply. "I realize now that I didn't love Joanna. I was infatuated with her, but I did love Eric."

Jewel rose up and cupped his cheek in her palm as she lowered her mouth to his. Then she drew his hand down to her swollen belly where their daughter bumped and turned between them.

"She's yours, Piers. Yours and mine."

"I know, *yineka mou.* I know."

Chapter 16

"Piers looks more at ease than I've ever seen him," Marley said to Jewel as the two stood on the patio overlooking the ocean.

Jewel turned to the other woman and smiled. "Really? I hope I can take credit for it."

Bella laughed as she took another sip of her wine. "Of course the credit is yours. I'd swear the man is in love."

Jewel bit her lip and turned away. She wanted Piers to love her, but he'd never said the words. She wasn't sure he was capable of offering his love to another woman after what had happened with Joanna.

"Your house is beautiful, Jewel," Marley said. "I just wish it wasn't so far away from Greece."

"Or New York," Bella said dryly. "You think Piers planned it this way?"

Jewel grinned. "But we have jets at our disposal, don't we?"

"Hmm, you're right," Marley said thoughtfully. "The world shrinks quite a bit when airplanes are involved. No reason we couldn't all meet in New York for some shopping. Theron is a soft touch, and he'd no doubt accommodate us."

Bella glared over at Marley. "Just because he isn't an ape swinging from tree to tree and beating his chest while muttering stuff like 'you my woman' doesn't mean he's a softy."

"She's very protective and possessive when it comes to Theron," Marley said with a roll of her eyes. "All I meant was that of the three brothers, Theron would be the most accommodating when it comes to us wanting to get together. Chrysander and Piers would spend a month planning the security team."

Bella nodded. "You're right about that."

Jewel looked at the two women in question. "Piers mentioned what had happened to Marley when I asked him why the need for all the security people. Has nothing been resolved yet?"

Marley sighed unhappily. "As a matter of fact, we think the men who kidnapped me have been arrested. Chrysander got the call yesterday but we didn't want to ruin our time here. When we leave, we're flying back to New York with Bella and Theron so that I can identify the suspects."

Bella threaded her arm around Marley's waist and squeezed. "I'm so sorry, Marley. What rotten timing for you when you've been so ill with the new baby."

Marley smoothed a hand over her still flat stomach.

"Chrysander is worried it will be too much, and he's still feeling so guilty. He hates that I have to do this."

Jewel touched her hand in a comforting gesture. "Still, what a relief to know that they've been apprehended. I can only imagine the fear you've been living in."

"And the inconvenience it's caused you and Bella," Marley added. "I know that Theron and Piers have taken extra precautions because of the potential threat to anyone close to them. Maybe we can all relax a little now."

Bella held up her glass in a toast. "To freedom and relaxation."

Jewel held up her glass of water as did Marley and the women clinked the crystal.

"I'm so glad you're all here," Jewel said.

Bella looped her arm through Jewel's. "We're grateful you've made Piers so happy. He's been so...hard."

Marley nodded. "It took him a long time to accept me. Of course now he'd do just about anything if I needed him, but it wasn't like that in the beginning."

Jewel sobered. "Marley, do you think you could pull Chrysander to the side for me? There is something I'd like to discuss with him, something I'd prefer Piers not to know right now."

Marley lifted a brow. "Okay, I can do that, but you should know that Bella and I are insatiably nosy, and you'll have to fill us in first."

Jewel laughed and squeezed Marley's hand with her free one. "I'll tell you after Chrysander. That way you two don't try to talk me out of it."

"Uh-oh," Bella said with a groan. "I don't like the sound of that."

"I'm too curious to try and dissuade her," Marley said. "If you'll stay out here, Jewel, Bella and I will make sure Piers is occupied while you talk to Chrysander."

"Thank you."

The two women disappeared indoors leaving Jewel to gaze out over the sea. She was so absorbed by the view, that she didn't hear Chrysander when he came out.

"Marley tells me you'd like to speak with me."

Startled, she made a quick turn, and swallowed as she stared back at Piers's older brother. He raised a brow in surprise.

"Do I frighten you, Jewel?"

"Oh no, of course not…okay, yes, you do," she admitted.

"It is certainly not my intention," he said formally. "Now tell me, what can I do for you?"

She twisted her fingers nervously in front of her. This was probably a stupid idea, and Chrysander would probably tell her she was out of her mind. He might even be angry that she intended to pry into Piers's past.

"Piers told me about Joanna…and Eric."

Chrysander's eyes grew cold.

"I know how hurt he was by what happened."

Chrysander sighed and moved closer to Jewel. "He was devastated, Jewel. Hurt is a very tame word for what he went through. He loved Eric, considered him a son for two years. Can you imagine thinking a child is yours for that long? And then having him snatched away?"

She swallowed and lowered her gaze. "No, I can't imagine. It would devastate me too."

"Perhaps you can understand now that he's told you about them."

She looked up again, braving Chrysander's stare. "That's just it. I want your help."

Chrysander's brows came together in confusion. "My help? With what?"

"Finding Eric."

"No. Absolutely not. I won't allow Piers to go through that all over again."

Jewel put her hand over Chrysander's when he turned to go back inside.

"Please. Hear me out. Part of the problem was that Piers never got to say goodbye. He never got any closure. His wound is still raw and bleeding. He's still grieving for that two-year-old he lost. His only memory of Eric is of the day she left with him, how Eric screamed and cried for him. Maybe if he could see him now it would help to ease some of that pain. I can only imagine that he's wondered over the years if Eric is happy, if he's well, if he's needed anything. If he saw that Eric wasn't hurting, maybe it would go a long way to healing the awful pain Piers feels."

"You would do this?" Chrysander asked. "You would willingly bring a child back into his life that he loved? Risk contact with a woman he once loved just to make him happy again?"

"Yes," she said huskily. "I would do anything to ease his hurt."

Chrysander studied her for a long moment. "You love my brother very much."

She closed her eyes and turned away. "Yes," she whispered. "I do."

"All right, Jewel. I will help you."

She grabbed his hand. "Thank you."

"I just hope when this is all over that my brother is still speaking to me," he said wryly.

She shook her head vigorously. "I'll tell him you had nothing to do with it. I'll take sole responsibility."

"My brother is a lucky man, I think."

"I just hope he thinks so," she said wistfully.

"Give him time. I have no doubt he'll figure it out." Chrysander leaned forward and kissed her forehead. "I'll do some digging and let you know what I come up with."

Bella slipped out through the glass doors. "I'm afraid we've held him off for as long as possible. I hope you're done, because Theron and Piers are convinced we're plotting some evil."

Chrysander chuckled. "Bella, I have no doubt that where you're concerned, it's absolutely true. I haven't forgotten that you dragged my wife into a tattoo parlor not so many months ago."

Jewel burst out laughing. "A tattoo parlor? You have to tell me about this, Bella. Did Chrysander have a heart attack?"

"He might have bellowed a bit loudly just before he dragged us out," Bella said with an innocent grin.

Jewel wrapped an arm around Bella in a show of loyalty.

"Just what we needed around here. Another woman to cause trouble," Chrysander said with a mock groan.

The door opened, and this time Marley came out with Theron and Piers on her heels. Both men wore expressions of suspicion as they surveyed Chrysander laughing with Bella and Jewel.

"Whatever he's said, don't believe a word," Theron said as he dragged Bella back against his side.

"Why do I gain the impression that my family is plotting against me?" Piers murmured as he went to stand at Jewel's side.

She wrapped her arms around him, hugging him close. Then she leaned up to brush her lips across his jaw. "You're being paranoid. Chrysander was just divulging all your family secrets."

Both Theron and Piers donned expressions of horror. Chrysander held up his hands. "Don't worry. I've told them nothing you'll be sorry for later."

"You mean there is dirt they'd be sorry for?" Bella asked. "Do tell. Theron always acts as if I'm the troublemaker in the family."

Jewel relaxed against Piers and enjoyed the laughing and teasing that went on between the others. She already liked Bella and Marley so much, and she was beginning to lose her uneasiness around Theron and Chrysander. To their credit, both men had seemingly accepted her presence in Piers's life.

Piers's hand went to her belly as it often did, rubbing lightly over the swell. She wasn't even sure he realized what he was doing, but it made her heart ache with love for him.

She was beginning to realize that for all his coldness and aloofness that he was a man of great passion. When he loved, he did so with everything he had. How fortunate both her and her child would be to have his love and devotion. She would never have to worry about being alone or of being accepted again.

"Are you ready for dinner, *yineka mou?*" he murmured close to her ear. "I have it on good authority that the chef has prepared all your favorites tonight."

"Hmmm, I think I could get used to being so spoiled," she said with a sigh.

"You're easily satisfied," he teased.

"I just want you," she said seriously.

Fire blazed in his eyes, and his grip tightened around her midsection.

"Don't tempt me so or I'll forget we have guests and take you upstairs to bed."

"And this would be bad why? Your brothers all have wives. Surely they'd understand."

He laughed and kissed her on the nose. "You're bad for my control, *yineka mou.* Come, let's go eat. I'll carry you up to bed later."

Chapter 17

"Mrs. Anetakis, there is a call for you."

Jewel looked up to see the maid holding the cordless phone out to her. She took it and smiled her thanks at the younger woman. After she'd retreated, Jewel put the phone to her ear.

"Hello?"

"Jewel, this is Chrysander. I have some information for you about Eric. I'm glad you asked me to look into this. The news is not good."

Jewel frowned and got up from her seat at the breakfast table on the terrace. She ducked back inside so she could better hear over the distant roar of the ocean.

"What's wrong?"

"I found him. He's in foster care. He was made a ward of the state of Florida two years ago. He's been through six homes in that time."

"Oh no. No, no, no," she whispered. Her fingers curled tightly around the phone as she battled tears. This would destroy Piers.

"Jewel, are you all right?"

She swallowed the knot in her throat. Memories that she'd spent her life suppressing boiled to the surface.

"I'm okay," she said shakily. "Thank you for doing this, Chrysander. I'd appreciate it if you could email me all the information you have. I want to thoroughly investigate this before I tell Piers."

"I understand. I'll send it over as soon as we get off the phone. And, Jewel, if you need any further help from me, let me know."

"Thanks, Chrysander. How is Marley doing?"

Chrysander sighed. "It's been difficult for her. She's already ill with the pregnancy, and the stress of having to identify the kidnappers and give more statements is getting to her."

"I'm sorry," she offered softly. "Will you be much longer in New York? Will she have to remain there for the trial?"

"Not if I can help it," he said fiercely. "The District Attorney has offered a plea bargain. If they accept it, then they'll forgo a trial, and Marley will be finished with this nightmare."

"Give her my love, please."

"I will. Let me know if there is anything else I can do."

"I will, Chrysander."

She hung up the phone and then went to find her laptop. A few minutes later, she received Chrysander's email. She frowned as she read through the details. A few phone calls would have to be made, but she couldn't wait to tell Piers what she'd discovered. There was no need for Eric to be in foster care when he had a family all too willing to take him in.

Piers sank into his chair behind his desk and looked ruefully at the piles of mail in front of him. Never before had he been so lax when it came to work matters. He had Jewel to thank for his inattention lately.

His emails were in the hundreds, his voice mail had reached capacity, and he hadn't opened mail in several days. His brothers would give him hell, but they'd also be happy to know that work wasn't his life any longer.

With a sigh, he powered up his computer so he could sift through the backlog of emails. Then he reached for his phone and turned on the speaker so he could weed through voice mails. Most were routine reports from various construction projects. A few minor emergencies from panicked hotel managers, and one offer to buy the new hotel in Rio de Janeiro. That one made him smile. There weren't many corporations that could afford one of the Anetakis's hotels. They spared no expense.

As soon as the voice mails were squared away, he dialed Chrysander's number. He wanted to check in on Marley and find out the results of their trip to New York to identify her kidnappers.

When he received no answer, he called Theron instead. They spent several minutes talking about business. Theron brought him up to speed on Chrysander and Marley and then conversation drifted back to business.

As he chatted, he idly sorted through the envelopes piled on his desk. When he got to one addressed to him from the laboratory that had performed the paternity test, he froze.

"I'll speak to you later, Theron. Give Bella my love."

He hung up and stared at the envelope in front of him. A smile eased his face as he fingered the seal. Here would be the proof of his paternity. In black and white, irrefutable proof that he was a father.

Last time it had gone the other way, and he'd lost everything that mattered most to him. This time… this time it would be perfect. He had a daughter on the way. His child.

Mine.

The surge of possessiveness that rocketed through his body took him by surprise.

He tossed the envelope aside. There was no need to open it. He knew what it would say. His trust in Jewel also surprised him, but he realized he did indeed have faith in her. He trusted her not to betray him.

After sorting through a few more envelopes he glanced back over at the letter. He should open it and revel in the feeling. Then he could go find Jewel and make mad, passionate love to her.

The idea made him tighten with need.

He felt like celebrating. Maybe he'd take Jewel on a trip to Paris. She loved to travel, and her doctor had pronounced her fully recovered from her surgery. To be on the safe side, he could schedule a check-up and a sonogram. Then they could take the private jet. They could make love in Paris and then maybe go on to Venice. Take the honeymoon they hadn't been able to take when they'd gotten married.

He picked up the envelope again, smiling as he

turned it over. He only hesitated a moment before tearing it open and unfolding the letter within.

He scanned the contents, the perfunctory remarks thanking him for his business, and finally he got to the bottom where the results were posted.

And he froze.

He read it again, sure that he'd missed something. But no, there it was in black and white.

He wasn't the father.

Icy rage flooded his veins, burning, billowing until he thought he would explode. Again. It had happened again, only this time it was different. So very different.

What had she hoped to accomplish? Would she, like Joanna, wait for him to form an attachment to the child before leaving? Use the child as a bargaining tool?

Was Kirk the father or was he yet another man she dangled from her fingertips like a windup toy?

Older and wiser? He wanted to puke at his stupidity. In his arrogance, he'd imagined that he'd never be deceived as he'd been in the past, but what had he done to prevent it?

He looked down at the offending document again. His hands were shaking too much to keep it still. Damn her. Damn her to hell.

She'd wormed her way into his life, into his family's lives. His sisters-in-law loved her, and his brothers had accepted her. Because of him. Because he'd brought her into their unsuspecting midst.

Never had he felt so sick. He wished he'd never opened the damn thing.

What a fool he'd been. What a fool he'd always be. All this time wasted on building a relationship that was based on lies and treachery. He'd bought the house of her dreams, done everything in his power to make her happy.

And worse, he'd bought into the fantasy as well. He'd begun to believe that they could be a family. That he'd been gifted another chance at a wife and child. That he'd finally been given hope.

He stared bleakly at the paper in his hand. The worst part was he had to have played right into her hands by offering her a settlement regardless of her child's paternity. She won either way. And him? He'd lost everything.

Jewel clutched the printouts to her chest and hurried to Piers's office. She knew it would hurt him to find out Eric's fate and that Joanna had abandoned him two years ago, but the most important thing was getting Eric out of his current situation.

Nausea rose in her throat at the thought of the young boy in so many foster homes. Had he harbored the same hopes she had when she was a little girl, only to be disappointed over and over?

She didn't knock but burst through the door, breathless from her pace. She stopped abruptly when she saw Piers sitting at his desk, a document crumpled in his hand, his expression so horrible that she nearly forgot why she'd come.

"Piers?"

He turned his cold gaze to her, and she shivered as a chill washed up her spine.

She took a step forward. "Is everything all right?"

He rose slowly with calculated precision. "Tell me, Jewel. How did you think you would get away with it?

Or did you just want to prolong the truth until you had me completely wrapped around your finger?"

Her heart sank. How had he found out about Eric? Why was he so angry?

"I was on my way to tell you now. I thought you'd want to know."

He laughed but the sound was anything but joyous. It skittered abrasively over her skin, and she shrank away from his obvious anger. Rage. That was the word for it. He vibrated with it.

"Oh yes, Jewel. I wanted to know. Preferably when this whole charade began. Did you enjoy hearing me spill my guts about Joanna and the deception she perpetrated? Did it give you satisfaction to know that yours was even more sound?"

She shook her head in confusion. What was he talking about?

"I don't understand. Why are you so angry? And at me? I didn't do this, Piers."

He gaped incredulously at her. "You didn't lie to me? You didn't try to foist another man's child off on me? You amaze me, Jewel. How you manage to sound the victim. The only victim here is me and the poor child you're pregnant with."

Hurt crashed over her, making her fold inward in a familiar defense mechanism she'd perfected over the years.

"You hate me," she whispered.

"Are you suggesting that I could love someone like you?" he sneered.

He thrust the paper forward. "Here is the truth, Jewel. The truth you never saw fit to give me. The truth I deserved."

She took the paper with a shaking hand, tears obscuring her vision. It took her three times to make sense of the words and when she realized what it said, she went surprisingly numb.

"This is wrong," she said in a low voice.

Piers snorted. "You'd still keep up the pretense? It's over, Jewel. These tests don't lie. It states with absolute certainty that there is no chance I could be the father of your child."

She stared up at him, tears trickling down her cheeks. He was cold. So cold. Hard. And unforgiving.

"You've waited for me to fall," she choked out. "You've been waiting for this since the day I called you. It's the only outcome that was acceptable to you. You weren't going to be satisfied until you proved I was no better than Joanna."

"You have quite a flair for dramatics."

She scrubbed angrily at her tears, furious that she'd allowed him to make her cry. "The results are wrong, Piers. This is your child. *She* is your child."

Something flickered in his eyes at her vehemence, but then he blinked, and it was gone, replaced with ice.

There would be no convincing him. He'd already tried and convicted her. She had some pride. She wouldn't beg. She wouldn't humiliate herself. She'd never allow him to know how shattered she was by his rejection. Or how much she loved him.

She lifted her chin and forced herself to stare evenly at him, steeling herself until she could no longer feel the shards of pain that pelted her.

"Someday you'll regret this," she said quietly. "One day you'll wake up and realize that you threw away something precious. I hope, for your sake, you don't take too long and that one day you can find the happiness you're so determined to deny yourself and others around you."

She turned stiffly, her heart breaking under the weight of her pain. She gripped the papers she'd intended to show Piers and held them close to her chest as she walked away. He made no effort to stop her, and she knew he wouldn't. He'd stay here, holed up in his refuge until she'd gone.

Methodically she took the stairs to the master bedroom. She got out a suitcase and began putting her clothing inside.

"Mrs. Anetakis, is there something you need?"

Jewel turned to see the maid standing in the doorway wearing a perplexed look.

"Could you arrange for a car to take me into town?" Jewel asked. "I'll be ready in fifteen minutes."

"Of course."

Jewel turned back to her packing, willing herself not to break down into more tears. She would survive this. She had survived worse.

When she had packed everything she thought she'd need, she smoothed out the papers that had all the information about Eric. No matter that she and Piers were no longer together, she couldn't allow that child to remain in the system, unwanted and tossed from family to family.

She closed her eyes and sighed. This would be so much easier with the money and power of the Anetakis name. Slowly she opened her eyes again and frowned. She may not have the money but she did have the name. Yes, Piers had provided a settlement for her in the case of a divorce, but who knows how long it would take to lay hands on it. She needed money now. Eric couldn't wait.

She went to her dresser and pulled out the diamond necklace and earrings Piers had given her on her wedding day. With one fingertip, she stroked the brilliant stones, remembering the way he'd fastened the necklace at her nape.

Between her engagement ring and the necklace and earrings, she should be able to raise enough cash to rent a place in Miami. But she'd need enough money to remain solvent until she would collect her settlement from Piers.

"Mrs. Anetakis, the car is ready for you."

Jewel closed her suitcase and smiled her thanks. She looked one more time around the room she'd shared with Piers and then walked down the stairs behind the maid.

When she was settled into the car, she directed the driver to take her to the airstrip. She didn't have time to call for Piers's jet, though she didn't have any qualms about using it. She had no desire to be stuck here in this place for any longer than necessary. She'd take the first flight off the island, and go to New York to see Bella and Marley and pray that they'd help her save Eric.

Chapter 18

"Jewel, what on earth are you doing here?" Bella asked as she all but dragged Jewel inside the doorway. "Does Piers know you're here? Did he come with you?"

Jewel swallowed the knot in her throat. Damn if she was going to get all weepy again.

Marley appeared behind Bella, her face soft with sympathy.

"What happened?" Marley asked.

Despite her resolve, Jewel burst into tears. Bella and Marley flanked her, each wrapping an arm around her as they guided her into Bella's living room.

"Are Chrysander and Theron here?" she managed to ask around her sobs.

"No, and they won't be back for a while," Bella said soothingly. "Now sit down before you fall over. You look dead on your feet."

Jewel perched on the edge of the couch while the other women took a seat on either side of her.

"What has that idiot brother-in-law of mine done?" Marley asked grimly.

Jewel tried to smile through her tears at Marley's show of loyalty. "I'm afraid he'd say it was what I'd done to him."

Bella snorted. "With that man, I'd hardly believe that. Besides, it's easy to see that you're crazy in love with him."

Jewel buried her face in her hands. "That's just it. He believes the absolute worst of me."

Marley put a hand on her shoulder and squeezed. "Tell us what happened."

With little reluctance, Jewel spilled the entire sorry tale from start to finish, including the part about Joanna and Eric and the paternity results.

"What an idiot," Bella said scornfully. "Did he even call the laboratory to double-check the results? Did he question them at all? Clearly there was some mix-up at the lab."

Jewel gave her a watery smile. "Thank you for believing in me. But the thing is, he got what he was waiting for. He's been waiting since the start for me to fall off the pedestal, so to speak. He hasn't been able to believe in a woman since Joanna."

"So what are you going to do?" Marley asked. "You're in love with him."

"But he doesn't love me. Moreover, he doesn't want to love me. I can't live with someone who distrusts me as much as he distrusts me."

"What about Eric?" Bella questioned. "Surely you won't leave him in his current situation."

"No," Jewel said fiercely. "And that's why I've come. I need your help."

Marley put her hand on Jewel's. "Anything."

"I pawned the jewelry that Piers gave me. It's enough to rent a small place in Miami so I can set up a permanent residence. But I'll need enough money socked away that the state will see me as a stable, financially able parent for Eric. I won't get a settlement from Piers until the divorce, and I have no idea how long that will take."

Bella grinned. "The lovely thing about having my own money, is that I don't need to rely on the Anetakis billions. No offense, Marley."

"None taken," Marley said dryly.

"I have some cash on hand that I can give you, and I'll wire you more funds so that you can rent something a little better than a 'small place' in Miami. If small is good, then bigger is better, right?"

Jewel squeezed both women's hands. "Thank you so much. I was so worried that you'd hate me, that you'd believe that I'd deceived Piers."

Marley sighed. "I have a feeling that Piers is going to wake up one day and realize he's made the worst mistake of his life. I almost wish I was there to see it."

"Don't feel so bad, Jewel," Bella said soothingly. "I'm afraid all of the Anetakis men are rather dense when it comes to love."

"So true," Marley agreed.

"You'll keep us posted on how things go with Eric? I'd love to meet him," Bella said.

"Of course I will."

"Do you have travel arrangements for your trip to Miami?" Marley asked.

Jewel shook her head. "Not yet. I've barely had time to breathe. I came straight here from the island."

Bella stood, her expression one of take charge. "First things first. We're going to go have a nice girly lunch followed by an afternoon of complete pampering at the spa. God knows you pregnant women need it. Then we're going to arrange for a private jet to fly Jewel to Miami, and I'll have a driver waiting there to pick her up and take her wherever she needs to go. Piers may be a dumb ass, but you're still family."

Jewel burst into tears again, and Bella groaned.

"Is it any wonder I have no desire to procreate? Pregnancy turns women into hormonal messes."

Marley dabbed quickly at her eyes, and Jewel burst out laughing. Marley joined her, giggling through her tears and finally Bella joined them as well.

"Okay, enough sniffling. Let's get out of here before the men return. I'll leave them a note telling them I've taken Marley off for an afternoon of debauchery. They won't be the least bit surprised," Bella said with a grin.

"Promise me you'll both visit me in Miami," Jewel said fiercely. "I'll miss you both terribly. I've always wanted a family—sisters—and I couldn't ask for better sisters than you two."

"Oh, I'll visit," Marley promised. "I'll blame it all on Bella. It's my standard excuse and keeps me out of trouble with Chrysander. Theron loves her so much that he's frighteningly indulgent with her."

"You're both very lucky," Jewel said wistfully.

Marley gave her a stricken look. "I'm so sorry, Jewel. That was incredibly thoughtless of me."

"Blame it on the pregnancy," Bella said. "Surely

having a parasite inside you sucking all your brain cells has to negatively impact you sooner or later."

Marley and Jewel both cracked up.

"You're so delightfully irreverent," Jewel teased. "It's no wonder Theron loves you so."

"Come on, let's go, let's go. My man radar tells me the menfolk will be home soon. The more distance we put between here and where we're going, the less likely they'll be able to track us down."

They linked arms and headed out the door only to be stopped by Reynolds, Theron's head of security.

Bella sighed and cast a baleful look in the man's direction. "Can we count on you for a little discretion or will you break your neck reporting to Theron?"

Reynolds cleared his throat. "That will depend on where you think you're going."

Marley pressed forward. "What we have here, sir, is a damsel in distress. A very pregnant damsel in distress. She is in sore need of a day at the spa. You know, where we do all those frightening girly things that scare the devil out of men."

Reynolds swallowed and paled slightly. "Well as long as it's that and not a more inappropriate place."

Bella glared at him as she walked by him to the car. "You're never going to let me live down that strip club, are you?"

"Strip club?" Jewel asked. "This I've got to hear."

"And I'll tell you all about it once we're wrapped in mud from head to toe," Bella said as they got into the car.

Bella leaned forward as Reynolds got into the front seat. "There's one more thing, Reynolds. This is top secret stuff. You didn't see Jewel, don't know who she is, never saw her in your life, *capiche?*"

Reynolds nodded solemnly. "Who?"

Bella smiled in satisfaction and leaned back in the seat once more.

"He's really an okay guy when he doesn't have a corncob wedged up his arse."

"I heard that," Reynolds commented.

Bella grinned and winked at the other two women.

"Okay, girls, a day at the spa it is. Then we'll get Jewel to the airport and on her way to Miami."

Piers stared broodingly into the surf, hands shoved into the pockets of his trousers—pants that he hadn't changed out of in three days. He looked and felt like he'd been on a monthlong bender. He hadn't showered or shaved. The staff avoided him like the plague, and when he did come into contact with them, they all glared at him with disapproving eyes. As if he'd been the one to drive her away.

And he had, in a way. He hadn't made it easy for her to stay. No, he hadn't asked her to leave in so many words, but what woman would stay with a man who'd been so cruel, so derisive?

He closed his eyes and inhaled the sea air that Jewel so loved. She loved the ocean like he loved her. Passionately.

Love was supposed to be without barriers or conditions. He'd never offered that to Jewel. He hadn't even offered his unconditional support. No, he'd demanded and she'd given. He'd taken and she'd offered.

What a bastard he was.

How was she supposed to have ever been able to tell

him the truth when he made it impossible for her to do so? He'd all but told her that he'd toss her out without thought if he found out she'd lied.

And the truth was he didn't care.

He'd realized it the moment he'd found her gone. He didn't care if the baby was his biological child or not. Jewel was married to him, which meant both belonged to him. He would be the baby's father because it was what Jewel wanted. It was what *he* wanted.

He hadn't loved Eric any less even knowing that he wasn't his biological child. He already loved his daughter, and nothing would change that. He'd ruined his chance at having a family. A wife and a daughter. All because he'd been so sure Jewel was another Joanna.

Jewel was right. He'd been waiting for her to fail, for her to give him the ammunition he needed to destroy her because it beat him being destroyed a second time. She was right about another thing, and it hadn't taken him long to realize it. He'd destroyed something very precious.

"I love you, *yineka mou,*" he whispered. "I don't deserve your love, but I can give you mine. I can try to make up for the many wrongs I have done to you. Please forgive me."

Just saying the words he'd vowed never to give another woman freed something buried deep in his soul. He breathed deeply, as past hurts fell away, carried on the wind further out to sea. He'd allowed himself to be ruled by bitterness and anger for too long. It was time to let go and embrace his future with Jewel.

He turned and strode back to the stone steps leading up to the house. He began barking orders as soon as he stepped inside. At first he was met by cold re-

sistance, until the staff figured out what it was he was
doing. Then there was a flurry of activity as everyone
stumbled over themselves to provide him what information they could.

"I called a car for her to drive her into town," one
of the maids offered.

When the driver was summoned, he said he'd driven
her to the small airport and carried her single bag inside.

Frustrated, Piers took the car to the airport to question the ticket agent, but not even the Anetakis name
was able to yield him any results. No one would tell
him what, if any, flight Jewel took—or to where.

Kirk.

The name shot back through his memory. Of course.
She had often gone back to Kirk's apartment when she
needed a place to stay. Surely that's where she would
go. She seemed to trust this fellow, and there was genuine affection and concern between them.

He looked down in disgust. He couldn't go anywhere looking as he did right now. He'd likely be arrested for vagrancy.

On his way back to the house, he phoned his pilot
and instructed him to be fueled and ready to depart
within the hour.

He was going to find Jewel and bring her and their
child back where they belonged. Home.

Chapter 19

Piers stood outside the San Francisco apartment and knocked. A few moments later, the door opened, but it wasn't Jewel who stared back at him. It was Kirk.

"Is Jewel here?" Piers asked stiffly.

Kirk's eyes narrowed. "Why would she be here? Why isn't she with you?"

Piers closed his eyes. "I had hoped she'd come here. Do you have any idea where else she might go?" It galled him to ask for this man's help, but to find Jewel, he'd do anything.

"You better come in and tell me what the hell is going on," Kirk said.

Piers followed him inside and the two sat down in the living room.

"Spill it," Kirk said.

"I said some terrible things to her," Piers admitted.

"I wasn't thinking straight. I was angry and I lashed out."

"About?"

Knowing he needed this man's help, Piers poured out the entire story from start to finish. Maybe if he seemed remorseful enough, Kirk wouldn't think he was a total bastard and give him any information he had on Jewel.

"You are a first-class jerk, aren't you? Jewel wouldn't lie about something like that. Did she ever tell you about her childhood? I'm guessing not or you wouldn't have shoveled that horse manure at her."

"What are you talking about?"

Kirk made a sound of disgust. "From the time her parents died when she was barely older than a toddler, she was shuttled from one foster family to another. The first few were merely temporaries as the state tried to place her in a more permanent environment. The first was a real gem of a family. The oldest son tried to abuse her. She told her caseworker, who thankfully believed her. So she was placed in another home, this time with another foster child, a girl about her age. What Jewel didn't know was that the family never had any intention of taking both girls. They took two so they could choose. And it wasn't Jewel they chose. So she lost a family she'd grown to trust and a sister she loved."

"*Theos,*" Piers said through tight lips.

"Things started looking up when a couple who couldn't have children decided they wanted to adopt Jewel. She went to live with them. The adoption was nearly final when the mother discovered she was pregnant. After years of infertility, she'd stopped trying and now she was suddenly pregnant. They couldn't afford more than one child, and you can imagine which one they chose. Once again, Jewel was rejected."

Piers closed his eyes. Just as he'd rejected her and her baby.

"After that, she didn't believe in happy endings any longer. You might say she grew up fast. She went through the motions of the system until she was old enough to be out on her own. Since then she's moved around constantly, never settling in one place, never forging ties with people. Never having a home. She simply doesn't believe she deserves one."

Kirk stared hard at Piers. "You've taken the one thing from her guaranteed to hurt her the most. *If* you find her, don't expect her to welcome you back with open arms."

Piers stared back at the other man, his stomach churning. "If she contacts you will you let me know immediately? She's pregnant and alone. I need to find her so I can make this right."

Kirk studied him for a long moment before finally nodding. Piers handed him his card.

"Call me day or night. It doesn't matter."

Kirk nodded and Piers rose to leave.

"Where will you go now?" Kirk asked when he saw Piers to the door.

"To New York to see my brothers. Something I should have done already," Piers said grimly.

Piers knocked on his brother's door and waited with dread for it to open. He didn't like facing his brothers with his mistakes, and he liked asking for their help even less, but if it would get Jewel back, he'd do anything.

"Piers? What the devil are you doing here? Why didn't you call to let us know you were coming? And where's Jewel?"

Piers looked up, wincing at the barrage of questions coming from Theron.

"Can I come in?"

Theron stepped to the side. "Of course. We were just about to sit down for dinner. I have to say, you look awful."

"Thanks," Piers said dryly.

They walked into the formal dining room, and Chrysander, Marley and Bella all looked up. Only Chrysander seemed surprised. The two women were more subdued.

Chrysander's sharp gaze found him. "What's happened?" he asked bluntly.

"Jewel left me," he said bleakly.

Theron and Chrysander both began talking at once while the women merely exchanged glances and remained silent.

"That doesn't make sense," Chrysander said. "Not after she spent all that time—"

Marley cut him off with a sharp elbow to his gut. Then she frowned at him and shook her head. Chrysander gave her a curious look but remained silent.

Bella stood, her hands on her hips. "Why did she leave you, Piers?"

Her voice was deceptively soft. It reminded Piers of the reason men feared women so much to begin with.

"Bella, perhaps Piers would prefer not to tell us such private things," Theron suggested.

Marley raised an eyebrow. "He's here, isn't he? He obviously wants our help. We deserve to know if he deserves it or not."

Piers winced. "If you want to know the truth, no, I don't deserve your help, but I'm asking for it anyway."

"Why?" Bella demanded.

Piers looked at both women. "Because I love her, and I made a terrible mistake."

"So you called the stupid lab and they figured out it was all a mistake then?" Marley said furiously.

Chrysander and Theron turned to Marley and Bella. Marley flushed and cast an apologetic look at Bella, who merely shrugged.

"I haven't called the lab. I don't care about the bloody results. I love her and our child. I don't give a rat's ass who the biological father is. She's my daughter, and I don't plan to give her or Jewel up."

"Why do I get the impression that we're the only two without the faintest clue what the devil is going on?" Theron said to Chrysander.

"No, but I bet our lovely wives could fill us in," Chrysander said as he rounded on Bella and Marley.

Both women crossed their arms over their chests and pressed their lips together.

Frustration beat at Piers's temples. He walked past his brothers to stand in front of Marley and Bella.

"Please, if you know where she is, tell me. I have to make this right with her. I love her."

Marley sighed and glanced over at Bella.

"I might have helped her get a place in Miami," Bella hedged.

Chrysander's eyebrows went up. "But isn't that where…"

Marley shot him another furious glance.

"Where in Miami?" Piers said, ignoring the exchange between Marley and Chrysander.

"If you go down there and upset her again, I'll personally sic every member of Theron's security team on you," Bella threatened.

"Just tell me, Bella. Please. I need to see her again. I need to make sure she and the baby are all right."

"When I spoke to her yesterday, they were just fine," Marley said casually.

"It would appear that you and Bella have been very busy women," Chrysander said darkly.

Marley sniffed. "If things were left to you men, the world would be a disaster."

"I think we've been insulted," Theron said dryly.

Bella thrust the piece of paper she'd been writing on toward Piers. "Here's her address. She trusted me, Piers. Don't screw this up."

Piers hugged her quickly and kissed her on the cheek. "Thank you. I'll bring her back for a visit as soon as I can."

Jewel smoothed her hand over Eric's hair as he slept and smiled at how peaceful and innocent he looked. Tucking his blanket around him, she turned to tiptoe from his bedroom.

Once in the kitchen, she prepared a cup of decaf tea and sipped the soothing, warm brew.

Her arrival in Miami couldn't have come at a better time. Eric had been taken from his previous home and was awaiting placement along with several hundred other children. It had taken several days to complete the paperwork, have the home study and background checks, but Eric was finally hers.

At first he'd been silent and restrained. No doubt he thought his placement with her was as temporary as all his other ones. She didn't try to persuade him any differently. It would take time to win his trust.

The important thing was that he had a home now. Thanks to Bella's generosity, they both had a home.

After checking on Eric one last time, she went into the living room and settled into her favorite chair. Nights were difficult, when all was silent. She missed Piers and the easy companionship they'd developed.

She had nearly dozed off in her chair when the doorbell rang. She got up quickly so it wouldn't disturb Eric and went to look out the peephole. No one knew her here, and she was wary of anyone knocking on her door. Surely Social Services wouldn't pay a surprise visit at this time of night.

What she saw shocked her to the core.

Piers. Outside her door, looking worried and a little haggard.

With fumbling fingers, she unlocked the deadbolt and opened the door a crack.

"Jewel, thank God," he said. "Please, can I come in?"

Her grip tightened on the door as she stared through the crack. Anger, pain—so much pain—surged through her veins. What could he possibly have to say to her that hadn't already been said?

She steeled herself, opened the door just enough that she could see him and he could see her.

"I won't ask how you found me. It isn't important."

He started to interrupt, holding up one hand in a plea, but she shook her head.

"No, you've said enough. I let you say all those things, and I took it, but I don't have to now. This is my home. You have no rights here. I want you to leave."

Something that looked suspiciously like panic spasmed in his eyes.

"Jewel, I know I don't deserve even a moment of your time. I said and did unforgivable things. I wouldn't blame you if you never spoke to me again. But *please,* I'm begging you. Let me in. Let me explain. Let me make things right between us."

The sheer desperation in his voice unsettled her. She wavered on the brink of indecision, her anger warring with the desire to relent and let him through the door. He stared at her with tortured eyes and slowly, she stepped back and opened the door wider.

He was inside in an instant. He gathered her in his arms and buried his face in her hair.

"I'm sorry. I'm so sorry, *yineka mou.*"

He kissed her temple, then her cheek and then clumsily found her lips. He kissed her with such emotion that it staggered her.

"Please forgive me," he whispered. "I love you. I want you and our baby to come home."

She pulled away, holding onto his arms for support. "You believe she's yours?" She couldn't keep the bitterness or suspicion from her voice.

"I don't care who the biological father is. She's mine. Just as you are mine. We're a family. I'll be a good father, I swear it. I love her already, and I want us to be a family, Jewel. Please say you'll give me another chance. I'll never give you any reason to leave me again."

He gathered her hands in his, holding them so tightly that she was sure her fingers were bloodless.

"I love you, Jewel. I was wrong. So wrong. I don't deserve another chance, but I'm asking—no *begging*—for one because there's nothing I want more than for you and our daughter to come home."

She stood there, mouth wide open, trying to process everything he flung at her. He loved her. He still didn't think he was the father. He didn't *care* if he wasn't the father. He wanted her and the baby back.

Her throat swelled, and her nose stung as tears gathered in her eyes. How difficult must this have been for him, to come all this way, thinking that the baby wasn't his, but wanting them anyway, accepting them anyway.

She should be angry, but the results had confirmed his worst fears, and yet it didn't matter.

He'd humbled himself in front of her, made himself as vulnerable as a man could make himself. She had only to look at the sincerity burning like twin flames in his eyes to know that he spoke the truth.

He loved her.

"You love me?"

She needed to hear it again. Wanted it so desperately.

"I love you so much, *yineka mou.*"

She shook her head. "What does that mean, anyway?"

"What does what mean?"

"Yineka mou."

He smiled. "It means my woman."

"But you called me that the first night we made love."

He nodded. "You were mine even then. I think I fell in love with you that very night."

Tears welled in her eyes, and she swallowed back the sob that clawed its way up her throat.

"Oh, Piers. I love you so much."

She threw herself back into his arms, holding onto him as tightly as she could. He held her just as firmly, his hands stroking her hair. Then his palm slid down to cup her belly.

He trembled against her, his big body shaking with emotion. When he spoke, there was a betraying crack that told her how close he was to breaking.

"How is our child?"

She closed her eyes as tears slipped from the corners. Then she reached down to hold on to his wrist as she stepped away.

"She's yours, Piers. I swear it to you. I haven't slept with another man. Only you. Please tell me you believe me. I know what the tests said, but they were *wrong*."

He stared back at her, hope lighting his eyes. He swallowed and then swallowed again. "I believe you, *yineka mou*."

She closed her eyes and hugged him again, burying her face in his strong chest.

"I'm sorry for hurting you, Jewel. I won't do so again, you have my word."

"There is something I must tell you," she said quietly.

He stiffened against her and slowly drew away, his eyes flashing vulnerability.

"You should sit down."

"Just tell me. There is nothing we can't work out."

She smiled. "I hope you won't be angry at what I've done."

"We can fix it. Whatever it is. Together, *yineka mou.*"

She took his hands in hers as they sat on the couch. "I came to Miami to find Eric."

He went completely still. "Why?"

"I thought you needed closure. I thought if you could see him happy and well adjusted that you could carry that memory instead of the one where he screamed and cried as his mother took him away."

"And did you find him?"

There was anticipation in his voice that told her how eager he was to know of Eric's well-being.

"Yes, I found him," she said softly.

Her grip tightened around his hands.

"Joanna abandoned him two years ago."

"What?"

Anger exploded from him in a volatile wave. He bolted from the couch, his hands clenched into fists at his sides.

"Why didn't she bring him to me? She knew I loved him. She knew I'd take him in."

Jewel shook her head sadly. "I don't know, Piers. He was taken into foster care and has been there for the last two years."

"This must be rectified. I won't allow him to remain in foster care. Not like you were, *yineka mou.* I won't allow your pain to be his."

She stood beside him, touching his arm. "How did you know about me?"

Piers looked at her with such pain in his eyes. "Kirk

told me when I went to San Francisco looking for you. *Theos,* Jewel. I am so shamed by the way I treated you."

"Piers, Eric is here," she said gently.

His mouth dropped open in shock. "Here?"

She nodded. "He's asleep in his bedroom. You see, I couldn't allow him to remain in foster care either. I knew how much he meant to you, and I know how painful my childhood was. I searched for Eric before we split up. It was why I came to your office that day. I was going to tell you that I'd found him and that he was in foster care. I thought we could both fly to Miami to get him."

He closed his eyes and let out a groan. "Instead, I drove you away, and you came here yourself to take care of him."

"He's here, and he very much needs a mother and a father."

"You would do this? You would take in a child that is not your own?" he asked.

"Isn't that what you plan to do? What you planned to do when you thought our daughter was not your own?"

He gathered her close in his arms, his body trembling against hers. "I love you, *yineka mou.* So much. Never leave me again. Not even if I deserve it."

She laughed lightly. "I won't. Next time, I'll stay and fight, which is what I should have done this time. You won't get rid of me so easily again."

"Good," he said gruffly. "Now let's go see our son."

Epilogue

"She's the most beautiful girl in the world," Piers said proudly as he held up six-week-old Mary Catherine for his brothers to admire.

"You can only say that because Marley is having another boy," Chrysander pointed out.

"Listen to them," Bella said in disgust. "Why is it that babies turn men's minds to mush?"

"I thought that was good sex," Marley said mischievously.

"Well, that too," Jewel said with a laugh.

Eric stood with the Anetakis men, looking absurdly proud of his little sister. Jewel's heart never failed to swell when she saw the love between father and son.

Eric's adoption had become final just two weeks before Mary Catherine had been born. A week later, Piers had received a frantic phone call from the laboratory that had performed the paternity test. They had, indeed, made a mistake and mixed up his results with someone else's. Piers had been horrified all over again over the fact that he'd blasted Jewel, but she reminded him that he'd taken her word on faith long before he knew the results were in fact in error. That was enough for her.

Bella had been quick to point out that all they'd needed to do was wait for Mary Catherine to be born because no one in their right mind would ever deny that she was an Anetakis through and through.

She was dark haired and dark eyed, and blessed with the olive complexion of her father. She was for all practical purposes a miniature Piers.

Jewel looked around at her family, all gathered at her home on the cliff overlooking the sea. There was so much happiness here. It was hard to believe at times that it was all hers. That she had a family. That she belonged. She and Piers had both been drifters for so long, but somehow they'd found their way to one another and had at long last found what mattered the most. A home.

"I'd like to propose a toast," Chrysander said as he raised his glass. "To the Anetakis wives. I've no doubt they'll keep us on our toes well into our old age, and I plan to enjoy every minute of it."

"Here, here," Theron said as he raised his own.

Piers turned to smile at Jewel, and she rose to stand by his side as they both looked down at the bundle in his arms. She put out her arm, and Eric snuggled against her side.

"I'd also like to propose a toast," Jewel said. "To

Bella. May she give Theron a house full of girls all as beautiful and as sassy as she is."

"Bite your tongue," Bella said, but her eyes twinkled merrily.

Theron put his arm around his wife. "God help me if that is true. One Bella is all this world needs."

"I'd like to propose a toast to love and friendship," Marley said. She pulled Jewel and Bella away from their husbands and linked her arms around them both.

Jewel and Bella squeezed back.

"To love and friendship," they both echoed.

* * * * *

Dear Reader,

I love marriage-reunited stories. I enjoy exploring the intensity of emotion and conflict that comes from a past relationship, which is why I wrote *One Night…Nine-Month Scandal*— except that in this case the marriage didn't happen. Four years ago Greek tycoon Alekos Zagorakis left schoolteacher Kelly at the altar. Now he wants her back in his life, but Kelly has other ideas…until one passionate encounter with her rich, powerful ex leaves her pregnant. Suddenly her simple life is complicated. Alekos is a man who knows what he wants and he wants her, but this proud man has to earn the right to be back in her life.

Writing for the Harlequin Presents line allows me to feed my addiction to strong, sexy alpha heroes and I'm thrilled to be in this volume with Maya Banks, who writes such brilliant alpha men. If you enjoy this story, I hope you'll try one of my longer single title books for Harlequin HQN. The O'Neil Brothers series is available now! For more information and extracts check out my website at www.sarahmorgan.com!

Thank you for reading.

Sarah

xx

ONE NIGHT...
NINE-MONTH SCANDAL

Sarah Morgan

Chapter 1

'I don't care if he's on a conference call, this is urgent!'

The voice outside his office belonged to his lawyer and Alekos paused in mid-sentence as the door burst open.

Dmitri stood there, papers in his hand, his face a strange shade of scarlet.

'I'll call you back,' Alekos drawled and hit the button to disconnect himself from his team in New York and London. 'Given that I've never seen you run anywhere in the ten years you've worked for me, I assume you're the bearer of bad tidings. A tanker has sunk?'

'Quickly.' The normally calm, steady Dmitri sprinted across the spacious office, banged into the desk and spilled the papers over the floor. 'Switch on your computer.'

'I'm already online.' Intrigued, Alekos shifted his gaze to his computer screen. 'What am I supposed to be looking at?'

'Go to eBay,' Dmitri said in a strangled voice. 'Right now. We have three minutes left to bid.'

Alekos didn't waste time pointing out that placing bids with an online auction-house didn't usually form part of his working day. Instead he accessed the site with a few taps of his fingers.

'Diamond,' Dmitri croaked. 'Type in "large, white diamond".'

A premonition forming in his mind, Alekos stabbed the keys. No; she couldn't have. *She wouldn't have.*

As the page sprang onto his screen, he swore softly in Greek while Dmitri sank uninvited onto the nearest chair. 'Am I right? Is it the Zagorakis diamond? Being sold on eBay?'

Alekos stared at the stone and felt emotion punch deep in his gut. Just seeing that ring made him think of *her*, and thinking of her set off a chain reaction in his body that shocked him with its intensity. He struggled to shake off the instantaneous assault on his senses triggered by those rebel thoughts. Even after four years of absence she could still do this to him, he thought grimly. 'It's the diamond. You're sure she is the seller?'

'It would appear so. If the stone had come on the market before now we would have been notified. I have a team checking it out right now, but the bids have already reached a million dollars. Why eBay?' Bending down, Dmitri gathered together the papers he'd dropped. 'Why not Christie's or Sotheby's, or one of the big, reputable auction-houses? It's a very strange decision.'

'Not strange.' His eyes fixed on the screen, Alekos laughed. 'It's entirely in character. She'd never go to Christie's or Sotheby's.' Her down-to-earth approach had been one of the things he'd found so refreshing about her. She'd been unpretentious—an attribute that was a rare commodity in the false, glittering world he inhabited.

'Well, whichever.' Dmitri tugged at his tie as if he were being strangled. 'If bids have reached a million dollars then there's a high probability that someone else knows this is the Zagorakis diamond. We have to stop her! Why is she doing this now? Why not four years ago? She had plenty of reason to hate you then.'

Alekos leaned back in his chair, considering that question. When he spoke, his voice was soft. 'She saw the pictures.'

'Of you and Marianna at the charity ball? You think she heard the rumours that the relationship is serious?'

Alekos stared at the ring taunting him from the screen. 'Yes.'

The ring said it all. Its presence on the screen said *this is what I think of what we shared.* It was the equivalent of flinging the diamond into the river, only far, far more effective. She was selling it to the highest bidder in the most public way possible and her message was clear: this ring means nothing to me.

Our relationship meant nothing.

She was in a wild fury.

His own anger slashed like the blade of a knife and he stood up suddenly, taking this latest gesture as confirmation that he'd made the right choice with Marianna. Marianna Konstantin would never do anything as vulgar as sell a ring on eBay. Marianna was far too discreet and well-bred to give away a gift. Her behaviour was always impeccable; she was quiet and restrained, miserly with her emotions and, most importantly, she didn't want to get married.

Alekos stared at the ring on the screen, guessing at the depth of emotion hidden behind the sale. Nothing restrained there. The woman selling his ring gave her emotions freely.

Remembering just how freely, his mouth tightened. It would be good, he thought, to cut that final link. This was the time.

Watching the clock count down on his computer screen, Alekos made an instantaneous decision. 'Bid for it, Dmitri.'

His lawyer floundered. 'Bid? How? You need an account, and there is no time to set one up.'

'We need someone just out of college.' Swift and decisive, Alekos pressed a button on his phone. 'Send Eleni in. Now.'

Seconds later, the youngest PA on his team appeared nervously in the doorway. 'You wanted to speak to me, Mr Zagorakis?'

'Do you have an eBay account?'

Clearly stunned by the unexpected question, the girl gulped. 'Yes, sir.'

'I need you to bid for something. And don't call me sir.' His eyes on the screen, Alekos watched as the clock ticked down: two minutes. He had two minutes in which to retrieve something that should never have left his possession. 'Log in, or whatever it is you do to put in a bid.'

'Yes, sir. Of course.' Crumbling with nerves, the girl hurried to his desk and entered her username and password. She was shaking so badly that she entered her password incorrectly and Alekos clamped his mouth shut, sensing that if he showed impatience he'd just make her more nervous.

'Take your time,' he said smoothly, sending a warning glance towards Dmitri who looked as if he were about to have a stroke.

Finally entering her password correctly, the girl gave him a terrified smile. 'What bid do you want me to place?'

Alekos looked at the screen and made a judgement. 'Two-million US dollars.'

The girl gave an audible gasp. *'How much?'*

'Two million.' Alekos watched the clock counting down: sixty seconds. He had sixty seconds to retrieve an heirloom that he never should have given away. Sixty seconds to close the door on a relationship that never should have happened. 'Do it now.'

'But the limit on my credit card is only f-five hundred pounds,' the girl stammered, 'I can't afford it.'

'But I can. And I'm the one paying for it.' Glancing at the girl's ashen features, Alekos frowned. 'Do *not* pass out. If you faint now, I won't be able to bid for this ring. Dmitri is head of my legal team—he will witness my verbal agreement. We now have thirty seconds, and this is very important to me. Please.'

'Of course, I—sorry.' Her hands shaking, Eleni tapped the amount into the box, hesitated briefly and then pressed enter. 'I—I'm—I mean *you're*—currently the highest bidder,' she said faintly and Alekos lifted an eyebrow.

'Is it done?'

'Providing no one puts in a last-minute bid.'

Alekos, who wasn't taking any chances, promptly put his hands over hers and entered four-million dollars.

Five seconds later, the ring was his and he was pouring the shaking girl a glass of water.

'I'm impressed. Under pressure you responded well and you did what needed to be done. I won't forget it. And now,' he kept his voice casual, 'I need to know exactly where to send the money. Does the seller give you a name and address?'

Ignoring Dmitri's startled glance, Alekos reached for a pen and paper.

He needed to decide whether to do this in person or hand it over to lawyers.

Lawyers, his common sense told him. *For all the reasons you haven't tracked her whereabouts over the past four years.*

'You can email any questions you have,' Eleni said weakly, her eyes on the diamond on the screen. 'It's a beautiful ring. Lucky woman, ending up with that on her finger. Wow. That's so romantic.' She looked at him wide-eyed and Alekos didn't have the heart to disillusion her.

Had he ever been romantic? If being romantic was to indulge in an impulsive, whirlwind romance then, yes, he'd been romantic. Once. Or maybe 'blinded by lust' would be a more accurate assessment. Fortunately he'd come to his senses in time. With a cynical smile at his own expense, Alekos reflected on the fact that a business approach to relationships, such as the one he had with Marianna, was vastly preferable. He'd had no particular wish to understand her, and she'd showed no interest in trying to understand him.

That was so much better than a girl who tried to climb into your thoughts and then seduced with raw, out-of-control sex that wiped a man's brain.

Feeling the tension ripple across his shoulders, Alekos stared out of the window as Dmitri hastily ushered the girl out of the room, promising to deal with all the financial aspects of the transaction.

Closing the door firmly, the lawyer turned to face Alekos. 'I'll arrange for the funds to be transferred and the ring collected.'

'No.' Driven by an impulse he decided was better not examined, Alekos reached for his jacket. 'I don't want that ring in the hands of a third party. I'll collect it myself.'

'In person? Alekos, you haven't seen the girl for four years. You decided it was best not to get in touch. Are you sure this is a good idea?'

'I only ever have good ideas.' Closure, Alekos thought grimly, striding towards the door. Hand over the money, take the ring and move on.

'Breathe, breathe, breathe. Put your head between your legs—that's it. You're *not* going to faint. OK— that's good. Now, try telling me again—slowly.'

Lifting her head, Kelly mouthed the words. No sound came out. She wondered whether it was possible to go mute with shock. It felt as though her entire body had shut down.

Her friend glared at her in exasperation. 'Kel, I'm giving you thirty seconds to produce sound from your mouth and then I'm throwing a bucket of water over you.'

Kelly dragged in air and tried again. 'Sold—'

Vivien nodded encouragingly. 'You've sold something—right. What have you sold?'

'Sold.' Kelly swallowed. 'Ring.'

'OK, *finally* we're making progress here—I'm getting that you've sold a ring. Which ring?' Viv's eyes suddenly widened. 'Holy crap, not *the* ring?'

Kelly nodded, feeling as though all the air had been sucked out of the room. 'Sold ring—eBay.' She felt dizzy and light-headed, and she knew she would have been lying on the floor in a dead faint by now if she hadn't already been sitting down.

'All right, well, that's good.' Her expression cautious, Vivien's smile faltered. 'I can understand why that seems like such a big thing. You've been wearing that ring around your neck for four years—which is probably four years too long given that the rat who gave it to you didn't turn up for the wedding—but you've finally seen the light and sold it, and I think that's great. Nothing to worry about. No reason to hyperventilate. Do you need to breathe into a paper bag or something?' She looked at Kelly dubiously. 'You're the same colour as a whiteboard, and I'm rubbish at first aid. I closed my eyes in all the classes because I couldn't stand the revolting pictures. Am I supposed to slap you? Or do I stick your legs in the air to help blood flow? Give me some clues here. I know the whole thing traumatised you, but it's been four years, for crying out loud!'

Kelly gulped and clutched her friend's hand. 'Sold.'

'Yes, yes, I know! *You sold the ring!* Just get over it! Now you can get on with your life—go out and shag some stranger to celebrate. It's time you realised that Mr Greek God isn't the only man in the world.'

'For four-million dollars.'

'Or we could just open a bottle of—*what? How much?*' Vivien's voice turned to a squeak and she plopped onto the floor, her mouth open. 'For a moment there I thought you actually said four-million dollars.'

'I did. Four-million dollars.' Saying the words aloud doubled the shaking. 'Vivien, I don't feel very well.'

'I don't feel very well either.' Vivien gave a whimper and flapped her hand in front of her face. 'We can't both faint. We might bang our heads or something, and our decomposed bodies would be discovered weeks from now, and no one would even find us because your place is always such a mess. I bet you haven't even made a will. I mean, all I own is a load of unwashed laundry and a few bills, but *you* have four-million dollars. Four-million dollars. God, I've never had a rich friend before. Now I'm the one who needs to breathe.' She grabbed a paper bag, emptied out two apples and slammed it over her mouth and nose, breathing in and out noisily.

Kelly stared down at her hands, wondering if they'd stop shaking if she sat on them. They'd been shaking since she'd switched on her computer and seen the final bid. 'I—I need to pull myself together. I can't just sit here shaking. I have work to do. I have thirty English books to mark before tomorrow.'

Vivien pulled the bag away from her face and sucked in air. 'Don't be ridiculous. You never have to teach small children again. You can be a lady of leisure. You can walk in there tomorrow, resign and go for a spa day. Or a spa decade!'

'I wouldn't do that.' Shocked, Kelly stared at her friend, the full implications of the money sinking home. 'I love teaching. I'm the only one not looking forward to the summer holidays. I *love* the kids. I'll miss the kids. They're the nearest I'm ever going to get to a family of my own.'

'For crying out loud, Kel, you're twenty-three, not ninety. And, anyway, you're rich now. You'll be a toy girl, or a sugar mummy or something. Men will be queuing up to impregnate you.'

Kelly recoiled. 'You don't have a romantic bone in your body, do you?'

'I'm a realist. And I know you love kids. Weird, really; I just want to bash their heads together most of the time. Maybe you should just give me the money and *I'll* resign. Four-million dollars! How come you didn't know it was worth that much?'

'I didn't ask,' Kelly mumbled. 'The ring was special because he gave it to me, not because of its value. It didn't occur to me it was that valuable. I wasn't really interested.'

'You need to learn to be practical as well as romantic. He might have been a bastard, but at least he wasn't a cheapskate.' Vivien sank her teeth into one of the apples that she'd tipped out of the paper bag, talking as she ate. 'When you told me he was Greek, I assumed he was a waiter or something.'

Kelly flushed. She hated talking about it because it reminded her of how stupid she'd been. How *naïve*. 'He wasn't a waiter.' She covered her face with her hands. 'I can't even bear to think about it. How could I ever have thought it could have worked? He is super-cool, super-intelligent and super-rich. I'm not super-anything.'

'Yes you are,' Vivien said loyally. 'You're—you're, um, super-messy, super-scatterbrained and—'

'Shut up! I don't need to hear any more reasons why it didn't work.' Kelly wondered how anything could possibly still hurt this much after four years. 'It would be nice if I could think of just one reason why it might have worked.'

Vivien took a large bite of apple and chewed thoughtfully. 'You have super-big breasts?'

Kelly covered her chest with her arms. 'Thanks,' she muttered, not knowing whether to laugh or cry.

'You're welcome. So how did Mr Super Rich make his money?'

'Shipping. He owns a shipping company—a big one. Lots of ships.'

'Don't tell me—super-big ones? Why did you never tell me this before?' Munching away, Vivien shook her head in disbelief. 'This guy was a multi-millionaire, wasn't he?'

Kelly rubbed her foot on the threadbare carpet of her tiny flat. 'I read somewhere he was a billionaire.'

'Oh, right—well, who's counting? What's a few-hundred million between friends? So—don't take this the wrong way—how did *you* meet him? I've been alive the same number of years as you and I've never met a single millionaire, let alone a billionaire. Some tips would be welcome.'

'It was during my gap year. I trespassed on his private beach. I didn't know it was private; I'd left my guide book somewhere and I was in a bit of a dream, looking at the view, not reading the signs.' Misery oozed through her veins. 'Can we talk about something else? It isn't my favourite subject.'

'Sure. We can talk about what you're going to do with four-million dollars.'

'I don't know.' Kelly gave a helpless shrug. 'Pay for a psychiatrist to treat me for shock?'

'Who bought the thing?'

Kelly looked at her blankly, worried that her brain appeared to have stalled. 'Someone rich?'

Viven looked at her with exasperation. 'And when do you hand it over?'

'Some girl emailed me to say it would be collected in person tomorrow. I gave them the address of the school in case they turn out to be dodgy.' She pressed her hand to the ring that she wore on a chain under her shirt and Vivien sighed.

'You never take it off. You even sleep in the thing.'

'That's because I have a problem with my personal organisation,' Kelly said in a small voice. 'I'm afraid I might lose it.'

'If you're trying to hide behind the "I'm untidy" act, forget it. I know you're untidy, but you wear the ring because you're still stuck on him, and you've been stuck on him for four years. What made you suddenly decide to sell the ring, Kel? What happened? You've been acting awfully weird all week.'

Kelly swallowed hard and fiddled with the ring through her shirt. 'I saw pictures of him with another woman,' she said thickly. 'Blonde, stick-thin—you know the type. The sort that makes you want to stop eating, until you realise that even if you stopped eating you still wouldn't look like that.' She sniffed. 'I suddenly realised that keeping the ring was stopping me from moving on with my life. It's crazy. *I'm* crazy.'

'No, not any more. Finally you're sane.' Vivien

sprang to her feet and flung her hair out of her eyes in a dramatic gesture. 'You know what this means, don't you?'

'I need to pull myself together and forget about him?'

'It means no more cheap pasta with sauce from a jar. Tonight we're eating takeaway pizza with extra toppings, and you're paying. Yay!' Vivien reached for the phone. 'Bring on the high life.'

Alekos Zagorakis stepped out of his black Ferrari and stared at the old Victorian building.

Hampton Park First School.

Of course she would have chosen to work with children. What else?

It had been the day he'd read in the press that she was planning on four children that he'd walked out on her.

With a grim smile that was entirely at his own expense, he scanned the building, automatically noticing the things that needed doing. The fence was torn in several places and plastic covered one section of the roof, presumably to prevent a leak. But the surroundings weren't responsible for the ripple of tension that spread across his shoulders.

A bell rang, and less than a minute later a stream of children poured through the swing doors and into the playground, jostling and elbowing each other. A young woman followed the children out of the door, answering questions, refereeing arguments and gently admonishing when things grew out of hand. She was dressed in a simple black skirt, flat shoes and a nondescript shirt. Alekos didn't give her a second glance. He was too busy looking for Kelly.

He studied the ancient building, deciding that his information must be wrong. Why would Kelly bury herself in a place like this?

He was about to return to his car when he heard a familiar laugh. His eyes followed the sound, and suddenly he found himself taking a closer look at the young teacher in the black skirt and sensible heels.

She bore no resemblance to the carefree teenager he'd met on the beach in Corfu, and he was about to dismiss her again when she tilted her head.

Alekos stared at her hair, fiercely repressed by a clip at the back of her head. If that clip was released and her hair fell forward… He frowned, mentally stripping off the drab garments so that he could see the woman concealed beneath.

Then she smiled, and he sucked in a sharp breath because it was impossible not to recognise that smile. It was wide, warm and generous, freely bestowed and genuine. Dragging his eyes from her mouth, Alekos took a second look at the sensible skirt. He could see now that she had the same long, long legs. Legs designed to make a man lose the thread of his conversation and his focus. *Legs that had once been wrapped around his waist.*

Shouts of excitement snapped him out of his perusal of her wardrobe. A group of boys had noticed the car, and instantly he regretted not having parked it round the corner out of sight. As they sprinted across the playground to the flimsy fence that separated the school from the outside world, Alekos stared at them as another man might stare at a dangerous animal.

Three little heads stared at him and then the car.
'Wow—cool car.'
'Is it a Porsche? My dad says the best car is a Porsche.'
'When I grow up, I'm going to have one like this.'
Alekos had no idea what to say to them so he stood
still, frozen by his own inadequacy as they rattled the
fence, small fingers curling between the wire as they
stared and admired.

He saw her head turn as she checked anxiously
on her charges. Of course, she would notice instantly
when one of her flock had wandered from safety. She
was that sort of person. A people person. She was
messy, scatty, noisy and caring. And she wouldn't have
greeted a group of children with silence.

She saw the car first and Alekos watched as the colour fled her face, the sudden pallor of her skin accen-
tuating the unusual sapphire-blue of her eyes.

Obviously she didn't know any other men who
drove a Ferrari, he thought grimly. The fact that she
was shocked to see him increased his anger.

What had she expected, that he'd sit by and watch
the ring—*the ring he'd put on her finger*—sold to the
highest bidder?

Across that stretch of nondescript tarmac, that
school playground that was no one's idea of a romantic venue for a reunion, wide blue eyes met fierce black.

The sun came out from beyond a cloud, sending a
spotlight of bright gold onto her shining head. It reminded him of the way she'd looked that afternoon on
his beach in Corfu. She'd been wearing a minuscule,
turquoise bikini and a pretty, unselfconscious smile.

With no desire to climb aboard that train of thought,
Alekos dragged his mind back to the present.

'Boys!' Her voice was melting chocolate with hints of cinnamon—smooth with a hint of spice. 'Don't climb the fence! You know it's dangerous.'

Alekos felt the thud of raw emotion in his gut. Four years ago she would have hurled herself across the playground with the enthusiasm of a puppy and thrown herself into his arms.

The fact that she was now looking at him as if he'd escaped from a tiger reserve added an extra boost to his rocketing tension-levels.

Alekos looked at the boy nearest to him, the need for information unlocking his tongue. 'Is she your teacher?'

'Yes, she's our teacher.' Despite the warning, the boy jammed the toe of his shoe in the wire fence and tried to climb up. 'She doesn't look strict, but if you do something wrong—pow!' He slammed his fist into his palm and Alekos felt a stab of shock.

'She hits you?'

'Are you kidding?' The boy collapsed with laughter at the thought. 'She won't even squash a spider. She catches them in a glass and lifts them out of the classroom. She never even shouts.'

'You said "pow".'

'Miss Jenkins has a way of squashing you with a look. Pow!' The boy shrugged. 'She makes you feel bad if you've done something wrong. Like you've let her down. But she'd never hurt anyone. She's non-violent.'

Non-violent. Miss Jenkins.

Alekos inhaled sharply; so, she wasn't married. She didn't yet have the four children she wanted.

Only now that the question was answered did he

acknowledge that the possibility had been playing on his mind.

She crossed the playground towards him as if she were being dragged by an invisible rope. It was obvious that, given the chance, she would have run in the opposite direction. 'Freddie, Kyle, Colin.' She addressed the three boys in a firm tone that left no doubt about her abilities to manage a group of high-spirited children, 'Come away from the fence.'

There was a clamour of conversation and he noticed that she answered their questions, instead of hushing them impatiently as so many adults did. And the children clearly adored her.

'Have you seen the car, Miss Jenkins? It's so cool. I've only ever seen one in a picture.'

'It's just a car. Four wheels and an engine. Colin, I'm not telling you again.' Turning her head, she looked at Alekos, her smile completely false. 'How can I help you?'

She'd always been hopeless at hiding her feelings, and he read her as easily now as he had four years ago.

She was horrified to see him, and Alekos felt his temper burn like a jet engine.

'Feeling guilty, *agape mou*?'

'Guilty?'

'You don't seem pleased to see me,' he said silkily. 'I wonder why.'

Two bright spots of colour appeared on her cheeks and her eyes were suddenly suspiciously bright. 'I have nothing to say to you.'

He should have greeted that ingenuous remark with the appropriate degree of contempt, but the ring had somehow faded in his mind, and now he was thinking something else entirely. Something hot, dangerous and primitive that only ever came into his head when he was with her.

Their eyes locked and he knew she was thinking the same thing. The moment held them both captive, and then she looked away, her cheeks as fiercely pink as they had been white a few moments earlier. She was treating him as if she didn't know why he was here. As if they hadn't once been intimately acquainted. *As if there wasn't a single part of her body that he didn't know.*

A tiny voice piped up. 'Is he your boyfriend, miss?'

'Freddie Harrison, that is an extremely personal question!' Flustered, she urged the children away from the fence with a movement of her hand. 'This is Alekos Zagorakis, and he is *not* my boyfriend. He is just someone I knew a long time ago.'

'A friend, miss?'

'Um, yes, a *friend.*' The word was dragged from her and the children looked suddenly excited.

'Miss Jenkins has a boyfriend, Miss Jenkins has a boyfriend...' the chant increased the tension in her eyes.

'Friend is not the same as boyfriend, Freddie.'

'Of course it's not the same thing.' One of the boys snorted. 'If it's a boyfriend, you have sex, stupid.'

'Miss, he said the sex word *and* he called me stupid. You said no one was to call anyone stupid!'

She dealt with the quarrel skilfully and dispatched the children to play before turning back to Alekos. Glancing quickly over her shoulder to check that she couldn't be overheard, she stepped closer to the fence. 'I cannot *believe* you had the nerve to come here after four years.' Every part of her was shaking, her hands, her knees, her voice. 'How could you be so horribly, hideously insensitive? If it weren't for the fact the children are watching, I'd punch you—which is probably why you came here instead of somewhere private. You're scared I'd hurt you. What are you *doing* here?'

'You know why I'm here. And you've never punched anyone in your life, Kelly.' It was one of the things that had drawn him to her. Her gentleness had been an antidote to the ruthless, cut-throat business-world he inhabited.

'There's always a first time, and this might well be it.' She lifted her hand to her chest and pressed it there, as if she were checking that her heart was still beating. 'Just get it over with, will you? Say what you have to say and go.'

Distracted by the press of her breasts against her plain white shirt, Alekos frowned. It was virtually buttoned to the throat; it was perfectly decent. There was nothing, absolutely nothing, about what she was wearing that could explain the volcanic response of his libido.

Infuriated with both himself and her, his tone was sharper than usual. 'Don't play games with me, because we both know who will win. I'll eat you for breakfast.' It was the wrong analogy. The moment the words left his mouth, he had an uncomfortably clear memory of her lying naked on his bed, the remains of breakfast scattered over the sheets as he took his pleasure in an entirely different way.

The hot colour in her cheeks told him that she was remembering exactly the same incident.

'You don't eat breakfast,' she said hoarsely. 'You

just drink that vile, thick Greek coffee. And I don't want to play anything with you. You don't play by the same rules as anyone else. You—you're a *snake*!'

Struggling with his physical reaction to her, Alekos stared down into her wide eyes and realised in a blinding flash that she genuinely didn't know he was the one who had bought the ring.

With a cynical laugh at his own expense, he dragged his hand through his hair and swore softly to himself in Greek.

That was what happened, he reminded himself grimly, when he forgot that Kelly didn't think like other people. His skill at thinking ahead, at second guessing people, was one of the reasons for his phenomenal business success, but with Kelly it was a skill that had failed him. She didn't think the way other women thought. She'd surprised him, over and over again. And she was surprising him now. Seeing the sheen of tears in her eyes, he sucked in a breath, realising with a blinding flash of intuition that she hadn't sold the ring to send him a message. She'd sold the ring because he'd hurt her.

In that single moment, Alekos knew that he'd made a grave error of judgement. He should not have come here in person. It wasn't easy on him, and it wasn't fair on her. 'You have four-million dollars of my money in your bank account,' he said calmly, resolving to get this finished as quickly as possible for both their sakes. He watched as shock turned her eyes a darker shade of blue. 'I've come for my ring.'

Chapter 2

Kelly stood in the classroom, gulping in air.

Alekos had bought the ring?

No, no, *no*! That wasn't possible. Was it? Thumping her fist to her forehead, she tried to think straight, wondering why it hadn't occurred to her that it could be him.

Because billionaires didn't trawl eBay, that was why. If she'd thought for a moment that he would find out about it, she would never have sold it.

As the full consequences of her actions hit her, Kelly gave a low moan.

Instead of purging him from her life, she'd brought him back into it.

When she'd seen him standing at the fence, she'd almost passed out. For one crazy moment she'd thought he was there to tell her he'd changed his mind. That he'd made a mistake. *That he was sorry.*

Sorry.

Kelly covered her hand with her mouth and stifled a hysterical laugh. When had Alekos ever said sorry? Had he even mentioned the tiny fact that he hadn't turned up at the wedding? No. There hadn't been a hint of apology in his indecently handsome face.

'Are you all right, miss?' A small voice cut through her panic. 'You look sort of weird and you ran in here like someone was after you.'

'After me?' Kelly licked dry lips. 'No.'

'You look like you're hiding.'

'I'm not hiding.' Her voice was high-pitched and she stared at her class without seeing them. Why, oh why, had she run away? Now it was going to look as though she really cared, and she didn't want him thinking that. She wanted him to think that she was doing fine and that breaking up with him had done nothing but improve her life. That selling her ring had been part of de-cluttering, or something.

Kelly tried to breathe steadily. She'd spent four years dreaming about seeing him again. She'd lain in bed at night imagining bumping into him——a feat which had really challenged the imagination, given that he moved in a different stratosphere. But never, not once, had she actually thought it might happen. Certainly not here, without warning.

'Is there a fire, Miss Jenkins?' A pair of worried eyes stared at her—little Jessie Prince who always worried about everything, from spelling tests to terrorists. 'You were running. You always tell us we're not supposed to run unless there's a fire, Miss Jenkins.'

'That's right.' Fire, and men you never wanted to see again. 'And I wasn't running, I was, er, walking very quickly. Power walking. It's good for fitness.' Was he still outside the school? *What if he waited for her?* 'Open your English books. Turn to page twelve and we'll carry on where we left off. We're writing our own poem about the summer holidays.' Maybe she should have just handed him the ring, but that would have meant revealing the fact she was wearing it round her neck, and there was no way she was giving him the satisfaction of knowing what it meant to her. The only thing she had left was her pride.

There was a rustle of paper, a hum of low chatter and then a loud commotion at the back of the class.

'Ow! He punched me, miss!'

Kelly lifted her hand to her forehead and breathed deeply. *Not now.* Discipline problems were the last thing she needed. Her head throbbed and she felt sick. She desperately needed space to think, but if there was one thing teaching didn't give you it was space. 'Tom, come to the front of the class, please.' She waited patiently while he dragged his feet towards her sulkily, and then crouched down in front of the little boy. 'You don't just go around punching people. It's wrong. I want you to say sorry.'

'But I'm *not* sorry.' He glared at her mutinously, his scarlet cheeks clashing with his vivid hair. 'He called me a carrot-head, Miss Jenkins.'

Finding it almost impossible to focus, Kelly took a deep breath. 'That wasn't nice, and he's going to apologise too. But that doesn't change the fact you punched him. You should never punch anyone.'

Not even arrogant Greek men who left you on your wedding day.

'S'not my fault I've got a temper. It's cos of my red hair.'

'It's not your hair that punched Harry.' *How had she been supposed to know he was the one who had bought the ring?*

A child behind her piped up. 'My dad says if someone is mean to you, you should just thump them and then they'll never be mean to you again.'

Kelly sighed. 'Alternatively we could all just try and think more about each other's feelings.' Raising her voice slightly, she addressed the whole class. 'We need to understand that not everyone is the same. We need to show tolerance: that's going to be our word for the day.' She stood and walked to the front of the class, feeling twenty-six pairs of eyes boring into her back. 'T-o-l-e-r-a-n-c-e. Who can tell me what it means?'

Twenty-six hands shot up.

'Miss, miss, I know—pick me, pick me.'

Kelly hid a smile. It didn't matter how stressed she was, they always made her smile. 'Jason?'

'Miss, that man is at the door.'

Twenty-six little necks craned to get a better view of their visitor.

Kelly glanced up just as Alekos yanked open the door and strode into the room.

Mute with horror, she just stared at him, registering with numb despair the sudden increase in her pulse rate. *Was this how her mother had felt about her father?* Had she felt this same rush of excitement even though she knew the relationship was hopeless?

Alekos changed the atmosphere in a room, Kelly thought dizzily. His presence commanded attention.

There was a discordant scraping of chairs and desks

as the children all stood up and Kelly felt a lump in her throat as she saw them looking at her for approval. When she'd first taken over the class, they'd been a disjointed rabble. Now they were a team.

'Well done, class,' she said huskily. 'Lovely manners. Everyone gets two stars in their book.' It comforted her, having them there. It gave her strength to turn and face Alekos as he strode towards her. 'This isn't a good time. I'm teaching.'

'It's a perfectly good time for me.' His eyes clashed with hers; Kelly felt her face turn scarlet and her legs tremble violently as she remembered the passion they'd shared.

She held onto her composure for the benefit of the twenty-six pairs of watching eyes. 'We have a visitor—what didn't he do?'

'He didn't knock, Miss Jenkins.'

'That's right.' Kelly conjured a bright smile, like a magician pulling a rabbit from a hat. 'He didn't knock. He forgot his manners and he broke the rules. So he and I are just going to pop outside so that I can give him a little lesson on the behaviour we expect in our classroom, and you're going to finish writing your poem.'

She turned to leave the room but Alekos closed his hand around her wrist, dragging her against his side as he faced the goggle-eyed children.

'Let me teach you all a really important life lesson, children.' His Greek accent was more pronounced than usual, his eyes dark, as he surveyed the class with the same concentration and focus that he undoubtedly brought to his own boardroom. 'When something is important to you, you go for it. You don't let someone walk away from you, and you don't stand outside a door waiting for permission to enter. You just do it.'

This unusually radical approach was greeted with stunned, fascinated silence. Then several little arms shot into the air.

Alekos blinked. 'Yes, you?' Rising to the challenge, he pointed to a boy in the front row.

'But what if there are *rules*?'

'If they're not sensible, then you break them,' Alekos said immediately and Kelly gasped.

'No! You do not break them. Rules are there to—'

'Be questioned,' Alekos said with arrogant assurance, his deep male voice holding the children transfixed. '*Always* you must question and ask yourself "why?" Sometimes rules must be broken for progress to be made. Sometimes people will tell you that you can't do something. Are you going to listen?'

Twenty-six heads moved from side to side doubtfully and Kelly tugged at her wrist, trying to disengage herself so that she could take control.

A choked laugh bubbled up in her throat. Who was she kidding? She was never going to be able to gain control in the classroom again.

Alekos didn't release her. 'Take now, for example. I need to talk to Miss Jenkins, and she doesn't want to listen. What am I going to do? Am I going to walk away?'

A hand shot up. 'It depends how important it is to speak to her.'

'It is very important.' Alekos emphasised each word carefully as he addressed the captivated class. 'But it's also important to make the other person feel they are having a say in what happens, so I am willing to concede a point. I will let her choose where we have the conversation. Kelly?' He turned to face her, his eyes glittering dark. 'Here or outside?'

'Outside.' Kelly spoke through clenched teeth and Alekos smiled and turned back to the children.

'This is an example of a successful negotiation: it should be a win-win situation. We both have something we want. And now I am going to take Miss Jenkins outside and you are going to—to write one-hundred words on why rules should *always* be questioned.'

'No, they're not!' Kelly made a choked sound in her throat. 'They're going to write their poem.'

'Fine.' His eyes lingered on her mouth for a moment before sliding back to the enraptured class. 'You can write a poem—about the benefit of breaking rules. It was very nice to meet you all. Work hard and you will succeed in life. Remember—it's not where you come from that matters, it's where you're going.' His hand still locked around Kelly's wrist, he strode back out of the classroom giving her no choice but to follow him.

Outside the classroom, she leaned against the wall, shaking. 'I can't *believe* you just did that.'

'You're welcome,' he drawled. 'My going rate for motivational speaking on the international circuit is half a million dollars, but in this case I'm willing to waive my fee for the benefit of the next generation.'

Kelly's mouth opened and shut. 'I wasn't thanking you!'

'Well, you should be. Tomorrow's entrepreneurs won't emerge from a group of rule-enslaved robots.' Studying her face, he gave a sardonic smile. 'Something tells me I'm not going to be given two stars in my book.'

Almost exploding with frustration, Kelly curled her hands into fists. 'Don't you know *anything* about children?'

The smile disappeared along with the mockery. Without it his face was cold, hard and handsome. 'No.' His voice was taut and his expression suddenly guarded. 'Nothing. I spoke to them as adults, not children.'

'But they're not adults, Alekos. Do you know how much trouble we have with discipline?' She was desperately aware of his fingers on her wrist and the sexy look in his eyes as he looked down at her. 'When I took over that class they couldn't even sit still on a chair for five minutes.'

'Sitting still is an overrated pastime. Even in board meetings I often walk around. It helps me think. You should be encouraging them to question, not trying to churn out obedient clones all doing as they're told. *Why* did you sell my ring?'

Kelly studiously ignored his question. 'Without rules, society would fall apart.'

'And without people bold enough to break rules, society would never progress,' he purred. 'And I'm not here to—' Before he finished his sentence, hysterical shrieks came from along the corridor and there was the sound of feet running.

'Miss Jenkins, there's a flood! There's water everywhere!'

Alekos gave a driven sigh. 'Where do you go for peace and quiet in this place?'

'I can't have peace and quiet—this is a school.'

A group of children ran towards them, Vivien close behind them.

'Oh, Kelly.' She looked hugely stressed and there were huge wet patches on her skirt. 'There's a flood in the girls' changing rooms. Water everywhere. It's pouring out of somewhere. Can this lot go in your room while I go to the office? We're going to have to find a plumber, or a—' she gave a helpless shrug '—I don't know who to ring. Any ideas? The whole school is going to be under water soon; maybe I should phone for a submarine. We need someone who knows about pipes and water.'

'I know about pipes and water.' Clearly exasperated, Alekos inhaled deeply. 'Where is this flood? Show me. The sooner it is solved, the sooner I can have you to myself.'

Suddenly noticing him, Vivien's eyes widened and she looked slightly stunned.

Accustomed to that reaction from women seeing Alekos for the first time, Kelly bowed to the inevitable. 'This is Alekos. Alekos, my friend and colleague, Vivien Mason.'

'Alekos?' Vivien's eyes slid questioningly to Kelly, who gave a helpless shrug.

'He's the one who bought the ring.'

'Ring?' Vivien adopted a vacant expression which might have been convincing if it hadn't been so exaggerated. 'Oh, that old thing you keep in the back of your underwear drawer? I remember it—vaguely.'

Kelly's face turned as red as a traffic light and she was horribly aware of Alekos's interested stare.

'Anyway, about this flood.' Vivien glanced over her shoulder. 'I'll call a plumber, shall I?'

Alekos was looking at the water trickling into the corridor. 'Unless he has super powers, your school will be under water before he arrives. Get me a tool box—something—whatever you have in this school,' he ordered. 'And turn off the water at the mains.' With that, he strode along the corridor, leaving Kelly gaping after him.

'Alekos, you can't.' Her eyes slid over his shockingly expensive suit and handmade shoes, and he turned his head and gave a mocking smile, reading her mind in a single glance.

'Don't judge a book by its cover—isn't that what you English say? I flew straight from meetings in Athens. Just because I'm wearing a suit, doesn't mean I can't weld a pipe. Get me something to work with, Kelly.'

'He can look that good *and* weld a pipe? Colour me bright green with envy,' Vivien murmured faintly and Kelly gave her a shove.

'Go and turn the water off.'

By the time the water was turned off and they'd located a rusty metal box of tools hidden in the caretaker's cupboard, Alekos had discovered the fault.

'The joint in this pipe has corroded.' He'd removed his jacket and his shirt was soaked, sticking to his lean, muscled torso like another skin. 'What's in that box?'

'I have no idea.' Distracted by the sheer power of his body, Kelly struggled to open the box, staggering under the weight and Alekos frowned down at the assortment of tools.

'Give me that one—no, the one underneath it; that's it.' He proceeded to remove the offending pipe and examine it closely. 'Here is your problem.' He ran his finger over a section of ancient pipe. 'I doubt it's been replaced since the school was built. Doesn't anyone maintain this place?'

Vivien was gazing at his shoulders. 'I don't think our caretaker possesses your skills. And we're a bit short of money.'

'It doesn't need much money, just regular maintenance. Kelly, my phone is in my back pocket—get it out.'

'But—'

'I have my hands rather full at the moment,' he gritted. 'Not to mention being soaking wet. If you could not choose this moment to argue, that would be appreciated.'

Kelly stepped through the water and slipped her hand into his pocket, feeling the hard muscle of his body burn through the wet fabric. Quickly, she closed her fingers around his phone and dragged it out, aware that he was as tense as she was. Four years ago she hadn't been able to keep her hands off his body—and he hadn't been able to keep his hands off hers.

It was something she'd been trying to forget ever since.

Judging from the sizzling glance he sent in her direction, he felt the same way.

Kelly gulped. 'What do you want me to do?'

'Speed dial.' He gave her instructions and she did as he said, then held the phone to his ear so that he could speak. Listening to the flow of Greek, she wished she'd spent less time focusing on his body when they were together and more time honing her language skills. At the very least she should have learned how to say 'get out of my life'.

'Do you know what he's saying?' Vivien hissed and Kelly shook her head just as Alekos ended the call.

'I will have a team here in less than ten minutes.'

'A team?'

'I can fix this pipe for you, but I don't have the equipment. We need a new section of pipe, the same diameter; my security team can locate what we need and have it here. It will do them good to have something useful to do instead of hovering on street corners.' He wiped his damp forehead on his shoulder and then glanced around him in incredulity, taking in the peeling paint. 'If this place were a ship, it would have sunk by now.'

'It makes the *Titanic* look seaworthy,' Vivien agreed fervently and Kelly rolled her eyes.

Being this close to Alekos, and in these circumstances, was the worst possible torture; she didn't need to witness hero-worship from her closest friend. 'Can we just get on with this? Alekos, I'm sure there's somewhere you need to be. Now that you've identified the problem, we can sort it out, so you are free to go.'

'Go? Are you mad?' Vivien's voice was an astonished squeak. 'We're never going to be able to find anyone to fix this at such short notice. He knows what he's doing, why would you want him to go?'

'Because Kelly is feeling uncomfortable being this close to me.' A sardonic smile on his face, Alekos fixed his gaze on her. 'Isn't that right, *agape mou*?'

His use of that particular endearment sent the tension rocketing through her. It reminded her too clearly of intimate moments she was working hard to forget. 'I've changed my mind about selling the ring. I want it to go to a good home, and you're definitely not a good home. And, just because you can roll up your sleeves and fix a leaking pipe, don't think I'm impressed.'

'*I'm* impressed,' Vivien said dreamily. '*Really* impressed. I thought you ran a shipping company. But you can—wow. I mean, *wow.*'

Alekos looked amused. 'I do run a shipping company.'

'But not from behind a desk, obviously.'

'Unfortunately, it usually is from behind a desk. But I have a degree in naval architecture and marine engineering which occasionally comes in useful.' He looked up as a woman walked into the room followed by five men carrying stacks of equipment.

'These men say that—oh.' The school secretary blinked in horror and Kelly formed her lips into something approaching a smile.

'It's all under control, Janet.'

And it was. With Alekos giving orders, the men worked as an efficient team, but what really surprised her was that he did the actual work himself. His team gave him what he asked for and, while he fixed the pipe they set about cleaning up the water and setting up drying machines.

By the time Alekos had finished, a new section of pipe had replaced the old piece that had rusted away and the cloakroom was drying.

Kelly was just trying to slink away when he closed his hand around her wrist like a vice. 'No. No more running.' Hauling her against him, Alekos swung her into his arms; Kelly made a choked sound and clutched at his shoulders for support.

'Alekos! What are you doing? Put me down.'

Half-alarmed, half-laughing in envy, Vivien put a

hand on his arm. 'Whatever you do, don't drop her! Gosh, if you're that desperate you can use my classroom, if you like, it's empty.'

'Put me down!' Kelly snapped, twisting in his arms. 'I want to keep the respect of these children and I won't be able to do that if you're carrying me through the school like—'

'Like a man?' Ignoring her, Alekos said something in Greek to his team and strode out of the door. 'You've put on some weight since you were nineteen.'

'Good.' Kelly banked down the hurt caused by that comment. 'I hope you put your back out.'

'It was a compliment—the extra weight appears to be distributed in all the right places, although I can't be sure without a closer inspection.'

'How can you say things like that when you're involved with another woman? You're disgusting.'

'You're jealous.'

'I'm not jealous. As far as I'm concerned, your sickeningly skinny blonde can have you.' Kelly wriggled, but wriggling just made him hold her more firmly so she lay still, trying not to breathe in his familiar male scent—*trying not to look at the dark shadow of his jaw and the impossibly long lashes.* 'Put me down right now, Alekos.'

His answer was to kiss her, and as she slipped downwards through a hazy mist of thick, swirling desire Kelly heard Vivien's envious voice coming from somewhere in the distance.

'Given the choice of him or four-million dollars, I'd choose him every time. Way to go, Kel.'

Chapter 3

The sleek black Ferrari roared along the narrow roads; Kelly was glad he'd dropped her into the seat because her legs had turned to jelly. 'I can't believe you kissed me in front of everyone. I will *never* be able to look at any of them again.'

'I thought we dealt with your inhibitions four years ago.'

'I was not inhibited! You were just always doing really embarrassing stuff that—'

'You'd never done before. I know.' He shifted gears in a smooth movement. 'I pushed it too fast, but I'd never been with anyone as inexperienced as you.' He was supremely cool and her face burned hot as a furnace.

'Well, I'm sorry!'

'Don't be. I'm Greek; teaching you was the most erotic experience of my life.'

Kelly squirmed. 'And then there was the whole thing with the lights.'

'Lights?'

'You always wanted them on!'

'I wanted to see you.'

Kelly slunk lower in her seat, remembering all the ways she'd tried to hide. 'Haven't you ever heard of global warming? We're supposed to be turning lights off. Anyway, never mind that. I'm not inhibited, but that doesn't mean I've turned into an exhibitionist. And, actually, I just don't *want* to kiss you. The thought of kissing you revolts me.'

Without taking his eyes off the road, he smiled. 'Right.'

It was the smile that flipped her over the edge—that and the fact that her pulse rate still hadn't returned to normal. 'How dare you just barge in here after four years and not even offer so much as an explanation? You're not even sorry, are you? You don't have a con-science. I could never hurt *anyone* the way you hurt me, but you just don't care.'

For a moment she thought he wasn't going to an-swer. His hands whitened on the wheel and his mouth compressed. 'I do have a conscience,' he said harshly. 'That's why I didn't marry you. It would have been wrong.'

'*What?* What sort of twisted logic is that? Oh, never mind.' Kelly closed her eyes, completely humiliated. She'd kissed him back—hungrily, desperately, fool-ishly. 'Why *did* you kiss me, anyway?'

He shifted gears again, his hand strong and steady. 'Because you wouldn't stop talking.'

Kelly's ego shrivelled still further; it was not because she was irresistible or because he just couldn't help himself. He'd kissed her as a method of shutting her up. 'Slow down. I get car sick.' Not for anything would she admit that the kiss had made her dizzy. Alekos knew everything there was to know about kissing a woman, which was just her bad luck, she thought gloomily. Staring out of the window as trees flashed past, she wondered what he'd meant by that comment. Why had his conscience stopped him from marrying her—because it wouldn't have been fair to deprive all those other women of great sex?

She swallowed down a hysterical laugh.

It was almost worth tearing the ring from round her neck just to make this whole thing end. What did she have left to lose? Only her pride. And Alekos wasn't stupid. He probably knew exactly how she felt about him.

She wished now she hadn't given him the address of her cottage, but she'd been so embarrassed by the exhibition he'd created at the school that she'd just wanted to escape.

Her heart pounding, her mouth dry, Kelly tried to think clearly, but it was impossible to think, jammed into this enclosed space with him. The length of his powerful thigh was too close to hers, and every time she risked looking at him the memories came flooding back: his firm, sensual mouth brushing hers, proving to her that she'd never properly been kissed before; his strong, clever hands teaching her what her body could do, stripping away her inhibitions, everything so shockingly intense and exquisitely perfect that she'd felt like the luckiest woman on the planet.

But their relationship had been more than just incredible sex.

It had been laughter and an astonishing chemistry. It had been *fun*.

It had been the most stimulating relationship she'd ever had, before or since.

And the most painful.

There had been moments when she'd thought that losing him would be the end of her—standing there, waiting for a man who didn't turn up. Trying to pretend it didn't matter.

Transported straight back to her childhood, Kelly closed her eyes and reminded herself that it was different. The trouble was that rejection felt pretty much the same, no matter who was responsible.

'Take the next left,' she said huskily. 'I live in the pink cottage with the rusty gate. You can park outside. I'll get you the ring and you can go.'

This was a good test of how she was doing, she told herself. If the only way she could handle her feelings for Alekos was by not seeing him, then what had the past four years been about? Why invest so much time on rebuilding a life so carefully if it could be that vulnerable?

She'd got over him, hadn't she? She'd moved on. Apart from the occasionally disturbing dream involving a virile Greek man and incredible sex, she no longer ached and yearned. Yes, she wore the ring around her neck, but that was going to change. Once she handed it over she was going to do something radical, like joining a project to build a school in Africa or something. And she was going to kiss loads of men until she found someone else who knew how to do it properly. He couldn't be the only person.

Noticing the neighbour's curtains twitching, Kelly groaned. She was giving everyone enough to gossip about for at least two lifetimes. 'Don't you *dare* kiss me here. Mrs Hill is ninety-six and she watches from the window. You'll give her a heart attack.'

Climbing out of the car, she glanced dubiously at Alekos, wondering how he always managed to look completely at home in his surroundings. Boardroom or beach, city or tiny village, he was confident in himself, and it showed. He stood outside her house, the early-evening sunlight glinting off his dark hair, his face so extraordinarily handsome that it took her breath away. Four years had simply added to his raw sex appeal, adding breadth to his shoulders and a hardness to his features that had been missing before.

'This is where you live?'

Kelly bristled. 'We're not all millionaires,' she muttered. 'And it's very bad-mannered of you to look down your nose.'

'I'm *not* looking down my nose.' He shot her an impatient look. 'Stop being so sensitive and stop imagining what I'm thinking because, believe me, you don't have a clue. I'm just surprised, that's all. It's really quiet here, and you are a very sociable person. I imagined you living in London and going to parties every night.'

Not wanting to flatter his ego by revealing what a mess she'd been after he'd left, Kelly fumbled in her bag for her keys. 'I am out every night. You'd be surprised.'

He glanced around him, one eyebrow lifted. 'You're

right. I'd be very surprised. Are you trying to tell me this place comes alive at midnight?'

Kelly thought of the badgers, foxes and hedgehogs that invaded her garden. 'It's really lively. There's a sort of underground nightlife.' It came to something, she thought gloomily, when badgers had a more interesting sex life than you did. But that was partly her fault, wasn't it? After the press had torn her apart, she'd hidden away. 'Wait there; I'll bring you the ring.'

'I'll come in with you. I'd hate to give your neighbour a heart attack, and we're attracting too much attention out here.'

Her eyes slid from his powerful shoulders to his hard jaw and she looked away quickly, her stomach churning. The thought of him in her little cottage made her heart-rate double. 'I don't want you in my home, Alekos.'

His answer to that was to remove the keys from her hand and stride towards her front door.

Enraged, Kelly sprinted after him. 'Don't you *dare* go into my house without invitation!'

'There's a simple solution to that: invite me.'

'I will not. I only invite nice people into my home, and you——' she stabbed his chest with her finger '——are definitely not a nice person.'

'Why did you sell my ring?'

'Why did you leave me on our wedding day?'

He inhaled sharply. 'I've told you.'

'You were doing me a favour—yes, I heard you. You have a warped sense of what constitutes generous behaviour.'

For once he seemed to be struggling to find the right words. 'It was difficult for me.'

'Tell me about it. On second thoughts, don't bother. I don't even want to know.' Kelly decided that she couldn't bear to hear him list all the reasons she was wrong for him. *Couldn't bear to hear him compare her to the skinny, sophisticated blonde she'd seen in the magazine.* 'Come in, if you must. I'll get the ring and then you can go.'

He stood still, immovable. 'I know I hurt you—'

'Gosh, you're quick, I'll give you that.' Kelly snatched the keys back from him and opened her door. She wished he'd just give up and go away, but Alekos didn't give up, did he? It was that unstoppable tenacity that had made him into the rich, powerful man he was. He didn't see obstacles; he had a goal and he pursued it, ploughing down everything in his path if necessary. Yet he was praised as a truly innovative businessman with inspirational leadership-skills. And as for his skills as a lover...

Refusing to think about that, Kelly pushed open her front door, wincing slightly as the door jammed on a pile of magazines. 'Sorry.' She shoved at the door. 'I've been trying to throw them away.'

'Trying?'

Kelly stiffened defensively. 'I find it hard, throwing things away. I'm always scared I'll get rid of something I might want.' Stooping, she gathered the magazines, looked hesitantly at the recycling box and then put them back down on the floor. 'And some of these magazines have some really interesting articles I might want to read again some day.'

Alekos was looking at her intently, as if she were a fascinating creature from another planet. 'You always did drop everything where you stood.' The faint amusement in his eyes was the final straw.

'Yes, well, none of us are perfect, and at least I don't deliberately try and hurt people,' Kelly snapped—then gasped in horror as he smacked his forehead hard on the doorframe. 'Oh—mind out! Poor you—are you OK? Are you hurt? I'll get you some ice.' Sympathy bubbled over until she remembered she wasn't supposed to feel sympathy for this man. 'These cottages are old. You need to bend your head coming through there.'

Rubbing his fingers over his bronzed forehead, he grimaced. 'You need to warn people *before* they knock themselves unconscious.'

'It's not a problem for anyone under six foot.'

'I'm six-three.'

She didn't need reminding. He towered over her, all broad shoulders and pumping testosterone.

Unsettled, Kelly took a step backwards. 'Yes, well, you should have been looking where you were going.'

'I was looking at *you*.' His irritable tone implied he was less than pleased about that fact, but for some reason his reluctant confession really cheered her up.

The fact that she could still make this man miss his step gave her a ridiculous sense of feminine satisfaction. Maybe she wasn't thin and blonde, but he still noticed her whether he wanted to or not.

But satisfaction was short lived as she realised his wide shoulders virtually filled the hallway. Sexual awareness and a cloying, dangerous heat spread through her cosy cottage. Trapping a man like Alekos in this confined space was like putting a tiger in a small cage: fine if you were on the other side of the wire.

Frightened by how quickly her composure was deserting her, Kelly dumped her keys on a pile of unopened letters, wondering why being with him instantly made her think of sex. Their relationship hadn't just been about sex, so why was she suddenly thinking about nothing but it?

Probably because her sex life had been so unfulfilling since they had parted, she thought wistfully. Suddenly she wished she hadn't been so choosy over the last few years. If she'd had an active sex life, maybe she wouldn't be feeling this way.

Maybe that nagging ache wouldn't be present.

The truth was she'd poured her energies into her teaching, ignoring that other side of herself, pretending that it didn't exist.

But it did exist.

It was as if just seeing him had flicked a switch inside her, reminded her what she was missing.

Too aware of his physical presence in her tiny hallway, Kelly walked through to the kitchen.

Alekos followed, this time bending his head to avoid the threat of the low beam. 'This house is a death trap.'

'For some, maybe. Perhaps it senses who is welcome and who isn't. It presents no threat to me whatsoever.'

But he did. Oh yes, *he* did. Just by being within a metre of her, he presented a threat.

It had always been like this between them. That searing awareness, an almost primal reaction that neither of them had ever felt before. The connection had created a fierce maelstrom of emotion from which neither of them had escaped unscathed. It had been scary, she admitted, to realise that such passion existed. Even now it was there, simmering between them like the precursor to a deadly storm. It didn't matter what had happened; she was learning to her cost that sexual attraction was no respecter of logic. 'Wait here. I'll get the ring.'

He glanced around the tiny room. 'Are you going to offer me coffee?'

'Why?'

His smile was barely discernible. 'Because it would be hospitable?'

'And hospitality is so important to you Greeks, isn't it? You'll leave a girl standing alone on her wedding day, but if you turn up uninvited in her home four years later you expect a cup of coffee and a slice of baklava.'

'I've never seen you angry before.'

'Stick around.' Kelly filled the kettle violently, squirting water down her front. 'On second thoughts, don't stick around.'

'Greek coffee, please.'

'I hate Greek coffee. You can have tea.'

He eyed the pot she'd abandoned on the work surface that morning. 'If you hate Greek coffee, why are you drinking it?'

Kelly stared at the offending pot, feeling her face redden. She could hardly tell him that she'd started drinking it because it had reminded her of the happy times they'd spent in Corfu, and that now she actually liked it. 'I—I—'

'It pleases me that you haven't turned your back on everything Greek.'

Making a point, Kelly turned her back on him; maybe it was childish but she didn't care. Pulling open a cupboard, she winced as a packet of rice fell on her head. Replacing it, she reached up and gingerly pulled out a jar of instant. 'This is what I usually drink,' she lied, removing the top with a twist of her wrist. She hadn't opened the jar for at least six months and the granules were stuck together. Gritting her teeth, she chipped at them with a spoon and then tipped them into a mug.

Observing this performance from beneath lustrous dark lashes, Alekos removed his jacket and slung it over the back of a kitchen chair. 'You always were a terrible liar.'

His arms were strong and muscled, and made her think about all the times she'd lain against his hard body, marvelling that this man was with her.

'Whereas you were a master of deceit. You could make love to a woman as if she was the only thing in your world, and then walk away the day of our wedding without so much as a goodbye.'

'Why did you sell the ring?'

Her mind was so firmly locked in the past that it took her a moment to shift to the present. They were having two different conversations, and she could feel the heat boiling under the surface of his bronzed skin. The same passion that had characterised their relationship now had a different focus. He simmered like a volcano waiting to erupt, his attention focused on her in a way that made her heart pound.

He was so physical, she thought weakly. The most physical man she'd ever met.

'Because I no longer have any use for it. It's just a reminder of a very bad decision. I'll get you that ring and then you can leave, preferably smacking your head on the way out.'

Her hands shaking, Kelly made his coffee and pushed it towards him, feeling a pang of guilt as the liquid sloshed over the sides. It went against her nature to be so inhospitable to a guest, but he wasn't a guest, was he? He was an intruder. And it was her nature that worried her. She knew herself too well to lower her guard. She didn't *dare* lower her guard, even for a moment. She was too aware of him for that—too aware of her reaction to him. It appalled her to realise that she could still find him shockingly attractive after what he'd done to her. She should not be noticing those thick, dark eyelashes or the dark stubble on his hard jaw. And she definitely should not be noticing the way his expensive shirt emphasised the width and power of his shoulders. Instead she should remember how it had felt when all that leashed power had been focused on the destruction of their relationship.

Alekos paced the length of her kitchen, which for him took no more than three strides. Clearly it wasn't enough to relieve his simmering tension because he turned impatiently, dragging his hand through his hair in a gesture of frustration that was pure Mediterranean male. Or maybe not, Kelly thought wearily: the gesture was pure Alekos.

'That ring was a gift, and yet you were prepared to sell it to a stranger.' The words erupted from his throat and she stared at him in genuine amazement.

'Why would I keep it?' The ring weighed heavily against her chest. 'Do you think it holds some emotional meaning for me?'

'I gave it to you.'

'Payment for sex.' She wasn't going to let herself think it had been driven by anything else. 'That was all you ever wanted from me, wasn't it? All you think about is sex. Every minute of the day. That was all we ever shared.' Her reference to their passionate physical relationship made his eyes darken, and Kelly licked her lips, wishing she hadn't taken the conversation in that direction.

Mistake, she thought with a flash of panic. Big mistake.

'Not every minute. Every six seconds, is the opinion of experts.' Prowling restlessly around her kitchen, he looked brooding, virile and disturbingly male. 'Men think about sex every six seconds. Which leaves us five to think about other things.'

'Which for you is making money.'

'Are you short of money? Is that why you sold it?' Eyes stormy and menacing, he crossed the kitchen again, closing in on her.

She wasn't afraid of him, she told herself, gripping the work surface with her hands; she definitely wasn't. But there was something about his raw, elemental brand of masculinity that stirred her in a way that came close to terrifying. Being near him gave her a feeling she'd had with no other man and she didn't know if it was good or bad.

Bad, she thought, sucking air into her lungs. *Definitely bad.*

He was right in front of her now, legs spread apart, unapologetically male, his aura of rough sexuality sending the temperature in the room soaring to dangerous levels.

Her body aching with a need she'd suppressed for

far too long, Kelly shoved at his chest with the flat of her hand. 'You're invading my personal space, Alekos. Get away from me.'

'I've spent the last five seconds thinking about coffee,' he said silkily, 'which means I've now moved onto sex.'

She was stupid, stupid to have mentioned sex to this man.

She didn't want to think about sex while she was in the same room as him. It was the one topic they should have avoided. The most dangerous.

But it was already too late.

The heat was spreading through her pelvis, slow and insidious, stealing through her like smoke from a fire. And the fire was raging, curling inside her, ready to burn up everything in its path.

Fighting that reaction, Kelly pushed past him, but he caught her arm and hauled her against him. Their bodies collided with an almost fatal inevitability, and in that single, highly charged instant he read her body. As sure as if he'd stripped her naked, he knew what she was feeling. He'd always known, even before she'd known herself.

That intimate knowledge hovered between them, as acute as it was unwelcome.

Without warning, his mouth came down on hers, hard and demanding. She was dragged back four years, sucked back into a time when passion had ruled thought, when the world had been a perfect place, and when the only thing that had mattered was being with this man.

For a moment she melted. She couldn't breathe or think.

Swamped, Kelly struggled to free herself and dragged her mouth from his. 'No!'

She heard him draw a ragged breath, his eyes blazing into hers as he tried to focus. 'You're right.' His usually accentless English was thickened and pronounced. 'It is crazy.'

'I don't—' Her mouth was burning. Her body was on fire.

'Neither do I.'

If either of them had stepped back, they might have stood a chance.

Instead their mouths collided again with almost brutal force. The raw chemistry that exploded between them was so intense that for a moment she couldn't help herself.

She'd missed this.

She'd missed *him*.

Missed the feel of his mouth. The touch of his hands. Kelly kissed him back hungrily, her mouth every bit as greedy as his, her tongue every bit as bold. But there was anger in her kiss too, and as she felt his response to her she thought, *just look at what you're missing: just look at what you gave up.*

He muttered something in Greek, so shaken that she felt a vicious rush of satisfaction.

Yes, she thought, *it was good and you threw it away. You threw* this *away.*

Purring in her throat, she licked at the corner of his mouth, the caress dangerously provocative. She had no idea what was pushing her—desire? Pride? Revenge? All she knew was that she wanted to be with him again. Just this once.

Without breaking the kiss, Alekos powered her back

against the work surface, jabbed his fingers into her hair and gripped her head. Her fingers were locked in the front of his shirt, dragging him closer. They kissed as if it were their last moment on the planet, as if the future of civilisation depended on their desire for each other, *as if they had never parted.*

Kelly was so turned on she ignored the thought that this was really, really stupid.

His touch was as skilled as she remembered—his kisses as bone-meltingly perfect.

Yes, she was angry with him—blisteringly angry—but that just seemed to intensify the emotions that flared between them. Anger was just another fuel to stoke a fire that was already white-hot. She didn't want to feel like this, but sex had never been the problem between them, had it? Maybe that was why she'd given it up, she thought as she dug her fingers into the hard muscle of his shoulders. She'd known it could never be like this with anyone else. Celibacy had been preferable to disappointment.

'*Theé mou*, we should not be doing this.' He growled the words against her throat and she gasped and slid her leg around his, unwilling to let him go.

'You're right. We shouldn't.'

'You're angry.'

'Boiling mad.'

'I'm *furious* that you sold the ring.'

'I'm furious you're giving it to another woman.'

'I'm not!' He jerked her head back, his gaze black and intense, his voice thickened by the swirly, sultry atmosphere. 'I'm *not* giving it to another woman.'

'I hate her. I hate *you*.'

He breathed in deeply. 'I probably deserve that.'

'You definitely deserve it.' But her hands were on his belt and she heard the breath hiss through his teeth as her fingers brushed against the hard, rigid length of him.

'If we do this, you will hate me even more than you do already.'

'Trust me, that isn't possible.'

His hand slid up her thigh, hooking her leg higher. 'In that case, there is no incentive to stop.' He groaned as his fingers touched bare legs. 'You're wearing stockings?'

'I always wear stockings for work.' *Does she wear stockings, Alekos? Does she do this to you? Does she make you feel this way?*

'Stockings under that prim black skirt.' The prim black skirt hit the floor. 'The whole teacher-outfit thing really turns me on.' He dragged the clip out of her hair, silencing her gasp of pain with his mouth. 'Sorry. Sorry. I didn't meant to hurt you.'

'You always hurt me.' Her hair was all around them and she could feel his hands buried into the soft mass, his fingers biting into her scalp. 'In the scheme of things, a little more pain doesn't count.'

'I know I was a complete bastard.'

'Yes, you were—still are. And now could you please just—?' Rocking her hips against him, she sank her teeth into his lip and Alekos took her mouth hungrily, his hands now locked against her bottom.

'No other woman has ever made me feel the way you make me feel.'

The words sent a thrill of satisfaction through her. 'But I'm sure you've kept looking.'

He buried his face in her neck. 'You were never this wild four years ago.'

She was never this desperate. Kelly's eyes closed. 'Don't talk.'

His answer was to weld his mouth to hers again and kiss her until she couldn't breathe or stand upright. Her hands closed over his shoulders, but what began as a need for support, ended in a caress as her fingers slid over hard, male muscle.

'Kelly...'

'Shut up.' She didn't want to talk about what they were doing. She wasn't sure she even wanted to think about it. Her teeth gritted, she ripped his shirt so that she could get to his chest, hair tickling her fingers as she slid her hands over the hard muscle of his chest. His tie still hung between them but she ignored it, too absorbed by his body to bother undressing him.

To have sex with Alekos was to understand why her body had been invented.

His eyelids were lowered, his eyes half-shut as he watched her. It was a look of such raw, sexual challenge that she shivered.

Later, she thought, I'm going to really regret this.

But right now she didn't care.

He was probably lying about the ring. He was probably going to give it away, but she was going to make sure that he didn't forget *her*, Kelly thought as she trailed her mouth over his jaw, feeling the roughness of stubble graze her lips. Other women had sex with men they didn't know. She'd never done that; for her, sex had begun and ended with this man.

She was achy, needy, and when he backed her to the table and lifted her she just gave a groan of assent, closing her fingers around the glorious velvet length of him.

'Alekos…'

'I need to taste you, I need to…' Muttering something in Greek, he ripped at her shirt, tore at her bra and fastened his mouth over her breast.

Kelly's head fell back, the heat of his mouth like a brand. She squirmed as hot, liquid pleasure pumped through her veins and he lifted his head and devoured her mouth again, both of them crazily out of control.

'Now!' She yanked at his tie, pulling him towards her, and he flattened her to the table and pushed her thighs up. Dragging aside her panties, he entered her in a single, driving thrust that had her crying out his name. It had been so long that it took her a moment to adjust to the size of him. He was hard, full and pulsing hot, and Kelly held herself rigid, afraid to breathe or move. And then his mouth claimed hers again and from then on it was wild, each rhythmic thrust driving away all thoughts of how much she hated him—the fact that this was going to turn out to be a bad decision. He wrapped her thighs around his hips and she dug her nails into his back as she matched his demands with her own.

It was so shockingly good that when his phone buzzed there was no question of him answering it; neither of them were capable of focusing on anything but each other. He had one hand locked in her hair, the other under her bottom, anchoring her in a position designed to give them both maximum pleasure. He thrust hard, fast, his movements so unerringly skilful that she felt her body erupt with sensation. After four years it was never going to last long, and when she felt the first ripples take hold of her she moaned his name. Exquisite pleasure bordered on pain; his fingers tightened in her hair and his mouth locked on hers as he drove them both higher.

They were kissing when the explosion took them. Wave after wave engulfed them, crashing down on them, leaving no room for breath or recovery as they were caught in the web of sensation they'd spun for themselves. They kissed through her choked gasps and through his tortured groan, through the contractions that racked both of them and left them shaken.

His chest was slick against hers, his fingers still digging hard into her bottom as he dragged in air.

Kelly lay stunned, deliciously aware of the weight of him, the *feel* of him. If she'd been young and naive, she might have thought that such incredible sex could only happen when there was love, but she wasn't a naive teenager any more.

Slowly recovering her powers of thought, she realised with a flash of horror that the ring was round her neck. Panicking, Kelly pushed him away and fastened the few remaining buttons on her shirt with hands that shook.

Had he noticed?

No; both of them had been too carried away to notice anything but each other. Even if the ring had bashed him in the face, she doubted he would have seen it.

And now she had to get him out of here before she made a fool of herself. 'I'll get you the ring,' she croaked, walking to the door without looking over her shoulder. Her legs were shaking and her body was on fire but she knew she didn't dare think about what they'd just shared. Not yet. Not now. Later—when she was on her own.

Up in her bedroom, she unfastened the gold chain she wore around her neck and slid the ring into her palm. It glinted and winked at her and she felt a lump build in her throat. It had been next to her skin for four years. It had witnessed her pain and her slow, faltering recovery. Giving it back should feel cathartic—that was the theory.

The practice was something quite different.

Hearing a sound from the hall, Kelly quickly wiped her eyes on the back of her hand and walked back down the stairs.

The front door was wide open.

'Alekos?' Puzzled, she glanced from the open door to the kitchen and then heard the unmistakable, throaty growl of an impossibly powerful engine.

Sprinting to the door, the ring still in her hand, she watched in disbelief as the Ferrari roared away.

Chapter 4

'OK, breathe, breathe…I always seem to be saying that to you; how come you have so much drama in your life? I'm having an exciting day if my card doesn't work in the cash machine.' Juggling a half-eaten tub of chocolate ice cream and a box of tissues, Vivien sat on the sofa next to Kelly. 'How can you be pregnant? You haven't had sex for four years. Even elephants don't take that long.'

Kelly tried to fight her way through the panic. 'I had sex three weeks ago.'

Ice cream and spoon fell to the carpet. 'You had sex *three weeks* ago? But you don't—I mean, who with? You never go out. You're not the one-night-stand type—and three weeks ago was when Alekos…' Vivien's smile faltered and Kelly wrapped her arms around herself, feeling her face heat.

'Yes.' Just admitting it made her want to shrink. *What had she been thinking?*

'*Alekos?*'

'Can you stop saying his name? I seem to remember you being happy enough when he was kissing me.'

'That was a kiss! Last time I checked, a kiss couldn't make you pregnant! Alekos? This is the guy you hate, the guy who ruined your life.' Vivien grabbed a handful of tissues and tried to mop up the worst of the ice cream. 'What an unbelievable mess.'

'I know that.'

'I meant my carpet, not your life—although your life isn't looking too great, either.' Covered in chocolate ice cream, Vivien licked her fingers. 'So is that why he walked out without taking the ring?'

'I don't know. I suppose so, but he didn't talk to me, so I don't know. He just vanished. As usual.' Increasingly agitated, Kelly sprang up and walked around Vivien's tiny living-room.

'Kel.' Vivien's voice was firm. 'It's not that I don't love you or that I don't care deeply about your trauma, but would you mind *awfully* not treading on the bit with the ice cream? You'll walk it all around the flat, and my landlord is going to shred me if the place is covered in chocolate footprints.'

'Sorry.' Kelly stood still, rubbing her hands over her arms, trying to warm herself up. She felt sick; was that pregnancy or panic? 'Sorry. I'll help you clean it up.'

'Forget it. I'll squirt something on it in the morning.' Covering the stain with a cloth, Vivien flung herself in the chair and picked up the tub again. 'So, you don't speak to the guy for four years and then suddenly you have passionate sex. I'm seeing a whole different side to you. I honestly never thought of you as—'

'Sex mad? Sex starved? Maybe this is what happens when you keep men at a distance for too many years. Oh God, what was I thinking, Vivi? He dumps me—' her voice rose '—and what do I do? I reward him by having sex with him. What is the matter with me? Am I sick?'

Vivien eyed her warily. 'I hope not because my carpet has taken enough punishment. How many years?'

'What?'

'You said this is what happens when you keep men at a distance for too many years. How long actually is it since you last had sex?'

Distracted, Kelly racked her brains. 'I think it was about four years ago. Just after—it was part of my Alekos rehabilitation-programme.'

'I gather it didn't work.'

Kelly took slow, deep breaths, trying to calm herself so that she could think clearly. 'Have you ever had a relationship where you just can't help yourself? You *know* it isn't good for you, you know there is going to be agony at the end of it, but something between you is so powerful it just draws you together.'

'No. But my sister-in-law is an alcoholic and that description sounds uncannily close to how she feels about a bottle of vodka.'

'I don't find that analogy comforting. If she went without vodka for four years, would she still feel like that?'

'Oh yes. She says the feeling never goes away. It's just a question of not putting yourself near the vodka.'

'The vodka took me home and barged into my house.'

Vivien blinked. 'This conversation is getting too complicated for me. But vodka sounds like a good idea. I have some somewhere, for emergencies.'

'I'm pregnant,' Kelly said in a high voice. 'I can't drink.'

'But I can. I'll drink for both of us while you decide what you're going to do.' Moments later, Vivien emerged from the tiny kitchen carrying a bottle, her face white. 'Forget that. You don't need to decide what to do, it's been taken out of your hands. There's an enormous limousine outside my flat and I don't know anyone who owns one.'

'What?'

'It's Alekos; it has to be.'

'No!' Panicking, Kelly sprang to her feet. 'It can't be him. Why would he be here? He can't know I'm pregnant.'

'Well, he *was* present at the time of conception,' Vivien said helpfully. 'And he obviously has a planet-sized brain, so there is a possibility that he's considered that as a potential outcome.'

Her breath coming in rapid pants, Kelly pressed her hand to her chest. 'No. *No.*'

'On the other hand, men are a bit thick sometimes, so it's always possible that he's just come for the ring.' Vivien patted her shoulder soothingly. 'In which case, he's going to be leaving with something that's going to cost him a whole load more by the time you've added up nappies, clothes, an iPod and all the stuff kids seem to need now. Then there's university fees, and—'

'Shut *up*, Viv! You can't let him in. Don't let him

in. I haven't decided what to do.' Kelly was panicking badly. 'I need time.'

'Don't be ridiculous! Time isn't going to change anything but your age.' Vivien sprang towards the door. 'But I promise not to say, "hello, Daddy". Or "did you bring the nappies?"'

Kelly sank back onto the sofa with her head in her hands. Was she going to tell him? Of course she was going to tell him. She couldn't deny her child the right to know his father, could she? That wasn't her decision to make.

Maybe they could be one of those couples who seemed to get on perfectly well but just didn't live together. But that would mean shuffling her child backwards and forwards like a lost parcel, and she didn't want to do that.

Kelly groaned and pressed her hand to her forehead. How had this complete and utter nightmare happened to her? If only she hadn't sold the ring, he wouldn't have come looking for her, they wouldn't have had sex and she wouldn't be pregnant.

Just thinking of the word made her shake.

She needed time to think. She wasn't ready to do this now.

The door to Vivien's flat banged. 'You can relax, it isn't him. It's one of his slaves.' Vivien came in dragging a small suitcase and thrust an envelope at her. 'Here we are. You can tip me if you like; round it up to the nearest million.'

'What's that? And where did you get that suitcase?' Kelly slit the letter open and immediately recognised Alekos's bold, dark scrawl. Reading the letter, she gulped.

'Now what?' Vivien snatched the letter from her: *My private jet is waiting for you at the airport. Jannis will drive you. I will see you in Corfu.* 'Kel, any minute now I'm going to poke you in the eye with something sharp. Four-million-dollar diamond rings, Ferraris, limousines, private jets—give me one reason why I shouldn't die of envy?'

Kelly's teeth were chattering. 'The guy left me on my wedding day.'

'True. But honestly, Kelly, private jet,' Vivien said weakly. 'I mean, I bet you get loads of leg room. And the person in front won't recline his seat into your face. No plastic food. How quickly could I get breast implants? I could go instead of you.'

'You can go instead of me if you like because I'm not going.' Kelly stared at the suitcase. 'What's that?'

'Jannis said it was for you.'

'Jannis? You're on first-name terms? You got friendly rather quickly.' Kelly dropped onto her knees and opened the suitcase.

'Oh my goodness—clothes wrapped in tissue paper.' Vivien's voice was faint as she peered over Kelly's shoulder. 'He's bought you a *wardrobe*?'

'Probably because he doesn't want me to show him up arriving dressed in my completely embarrassing black skirt,' Kelly said stiffly, ripping apart tissue paper and pulling out a dress. 'Oh! It's—'

'*Gorgeous.* Is that silk?'

Kelly fingered the beautiful fabric wistfully and then she stuffed it back in the suitcase. 'No idea. Send it back to Jannis.'

'*What?* Kelly, he's inviting you to Corfu. You have to go.'

'He wants me to bring his ring, that's why! I'm his personal delivery-service and this is my payment.'

Vivien was still poking through the contents. 'It's a pretty good payment; these shoes are Christian Louboutin—do you know how much they cost?'

Kelly eyed the height of the heel in disbelief. 'No, but I know the surgery to fix my broken ankle would be a lot. Not to mention all the things I'll probably smash to pieces as I fall trying to walk in those. Vivien, I'm *not* going.'

Vivien folded her arms, a stubborn look on her face. 'If this is about that woman he was seeing, he's not with her any more. I've already told you that. It was all over the papers that they'd split up. Now I know why. He shagged you and realised that you're the only one.'

'If that's supposed to sound romantic, you need to try harder.' But there was no denying that, ever since she'd heard the news that Alekos had parted from that Marianna woman, her mood had lifted. It had been like walking in the darkness and suddenly discovering that you had a torch in your pocket.

'You're pregnant. You're having this man's baby. He has a right to know.'

Kelly's palms were suddenly damp with sweat. 'I *will* tell him.'

'And this is the perfect time. Look at it this way: you tell him about the baby, then you can have a holiday in Greece with the four-million dollars.'

Kelly swallowed, her eyes on the suitcase. 'I think I'd find it hard going back to Corfu.' Everything had happened there. She'd fallen in love. *She'd had her heart broken.*

'Life's hard,' Vivien said in a brisk, practical tone.

'But it's a heck of a lot easier if you have four-million dollars, and at least you're going to face the world wearing Christian Louboutin.'

'I don't think they'll fit over a plaster cast.'

'You hold his arm while you wear them. That's why you have a man.'

'I don't have a man.'

Vivien sighed. 'Yes, you do. You're just not sure if you want him. But look at it this way, Kel—the school holidays start tomorrow and your alternative is being sad and lonely here. Better to be rich and angry in Greece. Go. Put on the dress and the heels and walk right over him.'

Mistake, mistake, mistake...

Kelly sat rigid in the back of the chauffeur-driven car, staring straight ahead as they drove through the middle of bustling Corfu town, up across the mountains that rose in the centre of the island and down through twisty, narrow roads that led through endless olive groves. Each turn in the road revealed another tantalising glimpse of sparkling, turquoise sea and buttercup-yellow sand but Kelly was too stressed to enjoy the scenic temptations of Greece.

On her first trip to this island she'd fallen in love with the place, loving the smells, the sounds and the bright colours that were Greece. Then she'd fallen in love with the man.

Kelly felt nerves explode in her stomach.

If she'd arrived here under different circumstances, she would have been excited and thrilled. Instead she could hardly breathe. Anxiety choked her and all she could feel was panic at the thought of seeing Alekos again.

They hadn't seen each other since that day in her kitchen.

She didn't even know why she'd come. Not really.

Licking dry lips, she stared out of the window. Why had he asked her to bring the ring in person? What was going on in his head? What was he thinking?

Her brain was careering forward like a wild ride at a theme park. One minute hope popped up and she felt a flash of optimism, and then she was confronted by the ugly memory of what he'd done and hope plummeted to earth like a meteorite, leaving her drained and pessimistic.

She couldn't forget that one comment he'd made about him doing her a favour by not marrying her. It had played over and over again in her head during the weeks since he'd walked out of her house, leaving the door wide open.

What exactly had he meant by that?

Was he implying that she'd been too young or something? Kelly gnawed her lip as she stared out of the window. Nineteen *was* pretty young to get married. Perhaps he'd been worried she hadn't seen enough of the world or that she hadn't known her own mind.

The only thing she knew for sure was that she had no idea what was going on in *his* mind, and she needed to know. She needed to know what future there was for her and her baby.

Resting her hand low on her abdomen, Kelly made herself a promise.

Whatever happened, however this turned out, there was one thing she was sure about: she was *not* going to do what her mother had done. She wasn't going to cling onto a relationship that was never going to work.

This wasn't just about her any more. It was about her child.

And she knew how it felt to be the child of parents who absolutely shouldn't have been together.

As the car drove through a pair of elaborate wrought-iron gates, Kelly felt her stomach drop with anticipation. Even the novelty of having a private jet to herself hadn't been able to damp down her apprehension at the approaching meeting. Whatever Alekos was expecting, it probably wasn't the news that she was pregnant.

A stomach-churning cocktail of excitement and dread formed inside her.

Maybe he'd be pleased, she thought optimistically, hunting around for evidence to support that theory.

Alekos was Greek, wasn't he? Everyone knew that Greeks had big families. Everyone knew the Greeks loved children. Unlike their counterparts in England, who had a tendency to treat the arrival of children with the same enthusiasm as vermin, Greek restaurant-owners were delighted when a young family arrived on the premises. They smiled indulgently if children ran around and danced to the music. Family was the Greek way of life.

And that was her dream, wasn't it? The whole 'big family' thing.

That was what she'd always wanted.

Despite her efforts to keep her mind in check, Kelly's thoughts drifted off on a tangent as she imagined what Christmas would be like with lots of small versions of Alekos dragging out prettily wrapped parcels from under the enormous tree. It would be noisy, chaotic, a bit like a day in her classroom, which was one of the reasons she loved teaching. She loved the noisy, busy atmosphere that was created when lots of children were together.

Maybe Alekos felt the same way.

Kelly gave a tiny frown. It was true that Alekos had talked to her class as if he'd been in a board meeting, but he probably just needed practice, didn't he? He needed to understand that he couldn't apply the principles of corporate management to child rearing. He was basically Greek, so that whole 'family' thing should be welded into his DNA.

Maybe, just maybe, they could make this work.

At the very least, they had to try.

How could she ever look her child in the eye and say that she hadn't even tried?

The limousine pulled up in a large courtyard dominated by a fountain, and Kelly gulped. The first time she'd seen Alekos's Corfu home, she'd been shocked into awed silence by the sheer size and elegance of the villa. As someone who had grown up in a small house, she'd found the space and luxury of his Mediterranean hideaway incredibly intimidating.

She still did.

Reminding herself not to scatter her possessions around his immaculate villa, Kelly stepped hesitantly out of the car.

'Mr Zagorakis has instructed me to tell you that he is finishing a conference call and will meet you on the terrace in five minutes.' Jannis urged her inside the villa and Kelly gazed around at the familiar interior, no less daunted now than she'd been four years earlier.

The floors of the villa were polished marble and Kelly picked her way nervously, relieved she hadn't worn the Christian Louboutin shoes. *Death by stilettos,* she thought uneasily, wishing Alekos had installed a handrail. Maybe the Greek aristocracy were given lessons in skating in heels when they were children.

Cautiously eyeing the priceless antiques, she kept her hands pressed to her sides, terrified that she was going to bang into something and send it smashing into a zillion pieces on the mirror floors. Nothing was out of place. Everything looked as though it was where it was supposed to be: no magazines, no half-read books, no unopened letters or junk mail covered in pictures of pizza, no half-drunk mugs of tea.

Feeling as though she was in a museum, Kelly looked round nervously, relieved when Jannis led her through a curved archway that led onto the terrace. No matter how many times she saw the view, it still made her gasp.

The beautiful gardens fell away beneath her, hot-pink oleander and bougainvillea tumbling down the gentle slope to the curve of perfect beach that nestled below the villa.

Kelly blinked in the sudden brightness of the mid-day sun, watching as a yacht drifted silently across the sparkling sea. She felt slightly disconnected, unable to believe that yesterday she'd woken up in her bed in Little Molting and now she was back on the island of Corfu with the sun shining in her eyes.

A lump settled in her throat.

She'd left her dreams here, on a sandy beach, with the sound of the sea in the air.

'Was your journey comfortable?' His voice was

deep, dark and husky, and Kelly froze, desperately conscious that this was the first time she'd seen him since that day in her kitchen. A sizzle of sexual awareness shot through her body and her tongue stuck to the roof of her mouth as she turned.

The air was electric. If either one of them had touched the other, that would have been it. The dangerous glitter of his eyes said it all, and Kelly felt her body grow heavy with longing.

Suddenly she wished there were other people in the villa. She needed someone else to dilute the concentration of sexual tension that threatened to drown both of them.

She didn't *want* to drown. She wanted to think with her head, not react with her body.

Trying to apply caution, Kelly reminded herself that this was nothing like the last time. She'd grown up, hadn't she?

Her own particular fairy tale had most definitely *not* had a happy ending.

'The journey was fine. I've never been on a private jet before. It was, well, private.' She winced as she listened to herself. *Oh for goodness' sake, Kelly, say something more intelligent than that.* But her tongue had apparently wrapped itself into an elaborate knot and her heart was racing at a very unnerving pace. 'It felt a bit weird, if I'm honest.'

Bold dark brows rose in question. 'Weird?'

Kelly shrugged awkwardly. 'It was a bit lonely. And your hostess woman wasn't very chatty.'

A smile touched the corner of his mouth, that same shockingly sensual mouth that knew how to drive a woman from wild to crazy. 'She is not paid to chat. She's paid to make sure you have whatever you need.'

'I needed a chat.'

Alekos breathed deeply. 'I will make sure someone speaks to her about being more, er, *chatty*.'

'No, don't do that; I don't want to get her into trouble or anything, I'm just saying it wasn't as much fun as I thought it would be. There's not a lot of point travelling in a private jet if there isn't anyone to laugh about it with, is there?'

A look of incredulity crossed his handsome features and it was clear he'd never given the matter consideration before. 'The point,' he drawled, 'is that you have the space and privacy to do whatever you want to do.'

'But no one to do it with.' Realising that she probably sounded really ungrateful, Kelly tried to retrieve the situation. 'But it was great not having to queue through customs, and brilliant to be able to lie flat on the sofa.'

'You lay *flat*?'

'So I didn't crease my dress.' Kelly smoothed the fabric, wondering why something so simple as a dress could make you feel good. 'It's linen, and I didn't want to arrive looking as though I'd jumped out the laundry basket. The clothes are great, by the way; thanks. How did you know I had nothing to wear?'

'I didn't. It was a guess.'

Kelly gave an awkward laugh. 'Good guess. My wardrobe is full of stuff that doesn't fit me any more, but I refuse to throw it away because one day I'm going to be a size zero.'

His gaze slid down her body and lingered on her breasts. 'I sincerely hope not.'

That look was all it took. Her breasts tingled and her nipples pressed against the fabric of her dress, defying all her attempts to control her reaction. Not wanting to look down at herself and risk drawing attention to what was happening, Kelly fumbled with the clasp of her purse and pulled out the ring. 'Here. This is yours. This must be the most expensive delivery-service ever, but here you go.' She held out the enormous diamond, frowning when he made no move to take it. 'Well? Go on—it's yours.'

'I gave it to you.'

'Not exactly. I mean, you *did*, but it was supposed to come with a wedding. And, anyway, you bought it back from me,' Kelly reminded him. 'For four-million dollars. And, if you're waiting for me to say I'd rather have the ring than the money, forget it. I've already given away a big chunk of it to pay for the new playground. I can't give you the money back, so you have to take the ring. A better person than me probably wouldn't have taken the ring *or* the money, but I've discovered I'm not a better person. Exposure to wealth has obviously warped me.'

Alekos studied her, a curious look in his intense dark eyes, a smile flickering around his sensual mouth. 'You suddenly find yourself with four-million dollars and you spend the money on a new playground? I think you might need some lessons on the true motivation of the gold-digger, *agape mou*.'

Even though she hated to admit it, the endearment made her heart flutter. Or maybe it was his voice— deep, sexy and chocolate-smooth. This whole thing would be easier, Kelly thought desperately, if she wasn't so drawn to him. It was difficult to push some-thing away when you wanted it more than anything.

The tips of her fingers tingled with the desire to touch, and she linked her hands behind her back to be on the safe side. 'I didn't spend *all* the money, ob-viously. What use is a gold-plated playground? But I found this brilliant climbing-frame—massive—and it comes with this bit that's like a tree house...' Nervous and unsettled, she faltered. *Don't bore him, Kelly.* 'Never mind. Take it from me, it's a good one. And we're having this special surface put down over the summer holidays so that if the kids fall they shouldn't break anything...' Her voice tailed off and she shrugged self-consciously. 'Don't say anything to them. I pretended I was an anonymous benefactor.'

'They don't know the money came from you?'

'No.' A grin spread across her face as she remem-bered the staff meeting. 'They were all guessing. It feels good giving money away to good causes, doesn't it? It makes you go all warm and fuzzy inside. I guess you get that feeling all the time when you give stuff away.'

'I don't give anything away personally. Charitable donations are managed by the Zagorakis Foundation.'

Kelly digested that information with astonishment. 'You mean you have a whole company that gives away your money?'

'That's right. It was set up for that purpose. We do-nate a proportion of income, and they analyse all the applications and make a decision—with my input.'

'But you don't actually get to meet the people you help?'

'Sometimes. Not usually.'

'But don't you feel warm and fuzzy when you know you've helped someone?'

Alekos studied her through heavy-lidded dark eyes. 'I can't honestly say that "warm and fuzzy" features large in my emotional repertoire.'

'Oh. Well, it should, because you've obviously helped loads of people so you *should* feel good about that.' It was confusing, thinking about that side of him. Or maybe it was just the man himself who was confusing. Experience was telling her to be wary, but instinct was telling her to throw herself into his arms. It was probably because he was standing so close. He smelt fantastic, Kelly thought weakly, thrusting the ring towards him again.

'Are you going to take this? It sort of freaks me out, holding it, knowing how much it is worth. It's a good job I didn't know it was that valuable when I owned it. I never would have left the house.'

'Put it on your finger.'

Kelly's eyes flew to his and for a moment everything around her ceased to exist. Had he said...? Did he mean...? Even before her brain had answered the question, her heart performed a happy dance all on its own. He couldn't possibly mean that, could he? He couldn't be proposing...

'W-what did you say?'

'I want you to wear it.' His hands sure and decisive, Alekos took the ring from her and slid it onto the third finger of her right hand.

Her right hand.

Kelly felt the hard slug of disappointment deep in her gut and suddenly she was cross with herself. What was the matter with her? Even if he *had* proposed, she would have said no, wouldn't she? After what happened last time, she wasn't just going to walk back into his arms, no questions asked. No way.

'It looks good there,' Alekos said huskily, and Kelly bit back the impulse to tell him that it had looked even better on her left hand.

The diamond winked and flashed in the bright sunlight, dazzling her as much now as it had four years before. Reminding herself that a diamond didn't make a marriage, she yanked it off her finger before her brain could start getting the same silly ideas as her body. 'I've told you, I've already spent the money. I don't want the ring. I don't understand what's going on. I don't know why I'm here.' Which probably said more about her than him, she thought gloomily: he'd summoned her and she'd come running.

'I wanted to talk to you. There are things that need to be said.'

Kelly thought about the child growing inside her and decided that had to be the understatement of the century. 'Yes.' She squeezed her hand around the ring, feeling the stone cutting into her palm. 'I have a couple of things to say to you, too. Well, one thing in particular—nothing that…' Suddenly she felt horribly nervous about his reaction. What was the best way to tell him—straight out? Lead up to it with a conversation about families and kids? 'It's something pretty important, but it can wait. You go first.' She needed more time to build up her courage. She needed someone like Vivien bolstering her up from the sidelines.

She needed to stop thinking about her own childhood.

'Put the ring back on your finger, at least for now.

I'll pour you a drink—you look hot.' Alekos strolled over to a small table which had been laid by the beautiful pool. 'Lemonade?'

Still rehearsing various ways to spill her own piece of news, Kelly was distracted. 'Oh, yes please. That would be lovely.' Wondering what on earth he wanted to say to her, Kelly slid the ring back on the finger of her right hand as a temporary measure. They could argue about it later. 'So, I read in the papers that you broke up with your girlfriend. I'm sorry about that.'

'No, you're not.' A smile touched his mouth as he poured lemonade into two chilled glasses, ice clinking against the sides.

'All right, I'm trying to *feel* sorry, because I don't want to be a bad person. And I do feel sorry for her, in a way. I feel sorry for any woman who has been dumped by you. I know how it feels. Sort of like missing your step at the top of the stairs and finding yourself crashing to the bottom.'

He winced as he handed her a glass. 'That bad?'

'It feels as though you've broken something vital. Will your cook person be offended if I pick the bits out of this?'

'The bits?'

'The bits of lemon.' Kelly stuck a straw into the glass and chased the tiny pieces of lemon zest around. 'I'm not good with bitty things.'

Alekos inhaled deeply. 'I'll convey your preferences to my team.'

'*Team?* Gosh, how many people does it take to peel a couple of lemons?' She sipped her drink and sighed. 'Actually, it's delicious. Even with the bits. All right, this is all very nice—the whole private jet, pretty clothes and lemon-from-the-tree scene—but don't think I've forgiven you, Alekos. I still think you're a complete b—' her tongue tangled over the word '—bleep.'

'You think I'm a "bleep"? *What* is a "bleep"?'

'It's a substitute for a bad word that I absolutely don't want to say out loud.' Kelly snagged a few more bits of lemon with her straw. 'On television they stick a bleep sound in instead of the swear word. I'm doing the same thing.'

'Which swear word?'

'You have more intelligence than that, Alekos. Work it out for yourself.'

'You don't know one?'

'Of course I do.' Kelly sipped her drink slowly. 'But I'm always very careful with my language. I don't want to slip up in front of the children. I try never to swear, even when severely provoked.'

'I seem to recall that you called me a bastard.'

'Actually, you said that about yourself. I just agreed. It felt good, actually.' Kelly pressed the glass to her arms to cool her overheated skin. 'So why did you make me deliver the ring in person? Why not use a courier or send one of your staff? They can't all be peeling lemons.'

'I didn't want the ring. I wanted you.'

Kelly's heart tumbled and she put her glass down because her hands were suddenly shaking so much that they'd lost their ability to grip. 'You didn't want me four years ago.'

'Yes, I did.'

She looked up at him, reminding herself not to fall

for anything he said. 'You have a funny way of show-ing it.'

'You are the first woman I have ever proposed to.'

'But not the last.'

'I did *not* propose to Marianna.'

'But you were going to.'

'I don't want to hear her name mentioned again. She has no relevance to our relationship. Tell me why you have black circles under your eyes.'

That's right, change the subject, Kelly thought moodily. He obviously didn't want to talk about Marianna. And maybe she didn't, either. 'I have black cir-cles under my eyes because of you. Fighting you is exhausting.'

'Then don't fight me.'

Kelly wondered how her heart could still miss a beat even when her brain was issuing warning signals. Yes, he was gorgeous; there was no denying that he was gor-geous. Everything about him was designed to attract the opposite sex, from the leashed power in his broad shoulders to the haze of black hair revealed by his open-necked shirt. Desire pumped through her veins, her physical response contradicting her emotions.

Natural selection, she thought to herself, scrambling around for an excuse for the way she felt. It helped a little to pretend that she was genetically programmed to be attracted to the strongest, the fittest and the most powerful male of the species. And Alekos Zagorakis was all those things.

But just because she could feel herself sinking didn't mean she was prepared to go down without a fight.

Make a fool of herself as she had first time around? Throw herself at a man who didn't want her? No. Absolutely no. Not even knowing that she was carrying his child.

'If you expect me to just surrender to you then you'll be disappointed. I'll never be submissive.'

'I don't need submissive. I do want honest.'

'That's rich, coming from you. When did you ever tell me what you were truly feeling?'

A muscle flickered in his lean cheek, the merest hint of tension in a personality big on control. 'I don't find it easy to open up, that's true. I'm not like you. You spill out what you're feeling, when you're feeling it.'

'It's how I deal with things.'

'And I deal with things by myself. That's what I've always done. I have never felt the need to confide.'

Kelly picked up her drink again and sipped, brooding on the differences in their personalities. 'So I might as well go home, then.'

'No. There *are* things I need to tell you. Things I should have told you four years ago.'

Judging from his tone, they were going to be things she didn't want to hear. Kelly wondered uneasily if she should just tell him she was pregnant before he said something that would make her want to thump him. Being non-violent was becoming a real challenge around Alekos. 'Am I going to hate you for what you say?'

'I thought you already hated me.'

'I do. In which case, you might as well just get on with it and say whatever it is you want to say.' Ridiculously apprehensive, Kelly shrugged, trying to look cool and casual—as if whatever he said was going to make no difference to her. But it was obviously going to be something important, wasn't it? Whatever it was had stopped him from turning up on his wedding day, which was pretty major from anyone's point of view. And then there was the screaming tension she could feel pulsing from his powerful frame.

'Just say it, Alekos. I'm not great with all this suspense and tension stuff. I *hate* it on those TV shows where they say "and the winner is…", and then they wait ages and ages before they give you the answer, and you're thinking, "for goodness' sake, just get on with it".' Realising that he was looking at her as if she were demented, she gave a tiny shrug. 'What? What's wrong?'

Alekos shook his head slowly. 'You *never* say what I expect you to say.'

Kelly thumped her glass down on the table. 'I just want you to get to the point before the suspense kills me! I embarrassed you? I talked too much? I was messy?' She wrinkled her nose, trying to think which of her other sins might have been sufficient to send him running for the hills. 'I eat too much?'

'I love your body, I find your need to drop your belongings as you walk surprisingly endearing, I have always been fascinated by your ability to say exactly what is on your mind with no filter, and you have *never* embarrassed me.'

The angle of the sun had shifted and it reflected off his glossy dark hair. Somewhere close by an orange fell onto the ground with a dull thud, but Kelly didn't notice. She was too busy trying to hold back the sudden rush of hope that bounded free inside her, like a puppy suddenly let off a lead. 'I never embarrassed you? Not even once?'

'Not even once.' His hot, brooding gaze dropped

to her mouth. 'But I seem to remember that I embarrassed you most of the time.'

Kelly turned scarlet. 'Only when we did it in broad daylight. Why do they call it that—why *broad* daylight? Why not narrow daylight?' Chattering nervously, she broke off as he ran his hand over his face and shook his head in exasperation.

'I'm trying to tell you something, and it isn't easy.'

'Well, please just get on with it! It's honestly not good for you to have this much stress. It furs up your arteries.' Her palms were sweating and her stomach was churning. It was like waiting for an exam result, she thought anxiously, her mind still jumping ahead. Perhaps it *was* the age thing that had caused him to walk away. Maybe he had been worried that she was too young to know her own mind. Or maybe he'd thought their relationship was too much of a whirlwind. If it had been the age thing, that was now fixed, wasn't it? She was older. The kids in her class thought she was positively ancient. She was probably less inhibited. Thinking of their steamy encounter on her kitchen table didn't do anything to alleviate the heat in her cheeks. *She was definitely less inhibited.*

All she had to do was assure him that she'd matured, that she knew her own mind. He'd apologise. She'd be hurt, but forgiving. Her mind sprinted ahead again, weaving happy endings from the threads of disaster.

Alekos breathed in deeply. 'The morning of the wedding I read an interview you'd given to a celebrity magazine. You'd spilled your guts about what you wanted. It was all there on the page.'

Still enjoying a fantasy about their future, Kelly tried to remember exactly what she'd said in that particular interview. 'The press were all over me. Apparently the fact that you'd never shown any interest in marrying anyone before suddenly made me interesting.'

He was going to be really pleased about the baby, she thought dreamily.

They'd live happily ever after. She'd ask him to buy a house in Little Molting; she could still teach her class in September, and once the baby was born they'd come back to Corfu and raise the child here, among the olive groves.

She smiled at Alekos, but he didn't smile back.

Instead his features were hard, like an exquisitely carved Greek statue. 'You said that all you'd ever wanted was a family. You said you wanted four children.'

'That's right.' Kelly wondered whether this would be a good moment to tell him that they already had one on the way. 'At least four.'

Muttering something in Greek, Alekos lifted his hand to the back of his neck, visibly struggling with what he had to say next. 'When I saw that article I realised that we had plunged into this relationship with no real thought to the future. It was all about the present. We hadn't discussed what either of us really wanted. I didn't know what you wanted until I read it in that magazine.' His voice was raw. 'It was only when I saw your interview that I realised we didn't want the same thing.'

'Oh?' Still bathing in her own little bubble-bath of happiness, Kelly gave an understanding smile. 'Honestly, I just wish you'd said something right away. I sort of forgot you were Greek. You always have big families, don't you? Four kids probably seems like nothing to you. We can have more. I'm not worried. I teach thirty back home! How many did you have in mind?'

Alekos closed his eyes briefly and pressed his fingers to the bridge of his nose. 'Kelly...'

'It doesn't worry me. I love kids. And I don't even expect you to do the nappies, as long as you help with all the other stuff.'

'Kelly.' He closed his hands over her shoulders, gripping tightly as he forced her to listen to him. 'I don't want a big family.' He waited a moment, apparently allowing time for those momentous words to penetrate her thin veneer of happiness. 'I don't want a family at all.'

Somehow, Kelly managed to make her mouth move. 'But—'

'I'm trying to tell you that I don't want children. I never did.'

Chapter 5

'*Theé mou*, do something!' His tone dark and dangerous, Alekos glared at the local doctor. The guy had to be almost seventy and appeared to have two speeds—slow and stop. Fingering the phone in his pocket, Alekos wondered how long it would take to fly a top physician in from Athens. 'She banged her head really hard!'

'Was she knocked unconscious?'

Vibrating with impatience, Alekos thought back to the hideous moment when Kelly's head had made contact with the glossy tiles. 'No, because she called me a bleep several times.'

'A *bleep*?'

'Never mind. But she wasn't knocked out. I carried her up to the bedroom and she's been lying here unconscious ever since.'

Glancing at him thoughtfully, the doctor touched the bruise on Kelly's forehead. 'Why did she fall?'

Alekos felt the tension trickle down his spine. This had to be the most uncomfortable conversation he'd had in his life. 'She slipped on the tiles when she was running.'

'And why was she running?'

Two hot spots of colour touched his cheeks and guilt squeezed tight. 'Something had upset her.' Alekos ground his teeth, wondering why he was explaining himself to a doctor so ancient he had undoubtedly known Hippocrates personally. '*I* upset her.'

Apparently unsurprised by that confession, the doctor reached into his bag and removed some pills. 'Nothing much changes there, then. I was called to see Kelly on the day of her wedding: the wedding that never happened.'

So, although he was slow, there was clearly nothing wrong with his memory. Alekos gritted his teeth. Everything that happened today appeared to be designed to make him feel bad. 'Kelly needed a doctor?'

'She was very shocked. And the press were savaging her.'

Feeling as though he'd been slugged in the stomach by a blunt instrument, Alekos drew his eyebrows together, shaken by that graphic description. 'She should have ignored them.'

'How? You're six-foot-three and intimidating,' the doctor said calmly. 'I don't think Kelly has ever been rude to anyone in her life. Even when she was struggling with what had happened, she was still polite to me. Leaving her to the mercy of the press was like throwing raw meat to sharks.'

Wincing at the analogy, Alekos felt as though he was being slowly boiled in oil. 'I may not have handled it as well as I could have done.'

'You didn't handle it at all. But that doesn't really surprise me. What surprised me was the fact that you'd asked her to marry you in the first place.' The doctor closed his case with a hand wrinkled with age and exposure to the sun. 'I remember you coming here to stay with your grandmother as a child. I remember one summer in particular, when you were six years old. You didn't speak for a month. You had suffered a terrible trauma.'

Feeling as though someone had tipped ice down his shirt, Alekos stepped back. 'Thank you for coming so promptly,' he said coldly and the doctor gave him a thoughtful look.

'Sometimes,' he said quietly, 'when a situation has affected someone greatly, it helps to examine the facts dispassionately and handle your fears in a rational manner.'

'Are you suggesting I'm irrational?'

'I think you were the unfortunate casualty of your parents' dysfunctional relationship.'

His emotions boiling, Alekos strode towards the bedroom door and yanked it open. 'Thank you for your advice,' he said smoothly, controlling himself with effort. 'However, what I really need to know is how long you expect Kelly to remain unconscious.'

'She isn't unconscious.' The doctor's tone was calm as he picked up his bag and walked towards the door. 'She's lying with her eyes shut. I suspect she just doesn't want to speak to you. Frankly, I don't blame her.'

* * *

'Open your eyes, Kelly.'

Ignoring his commanding tone, Kelly kept her eyes tightly shut.

She was going to lie here in this safe, dark place until she'd worked out what to do.

He didn't want children. It was just like her dad all over again, only worse.

How could she have been so completely and utterly stupid? How could she not have known?

'Just because you're not looking at me, doesn't mean I'm not here.' His voice rang with exasperation and something else: remorse? 'Look at me. We need to talk.'

What was there to talk about?

He didn't want kids and she was pregnant. As far as she could see, the conversation was over before it had even begun.

What was she going to do?

She was going to have to raise their child completely on her own.

Overwhelmed by the situation, Kelly screwed her eyes up tightly, wishing that she could magic herself back to her tiny cottage in Little Molting and lock the door on the world.

Through the haze of her panic she heard him say something in Greek. The next minute he'd rolled her onto her back and lowered his mouth to hers. Rigid with shock, Kelly lay there for a moment, and then the tip of his tongue traced the seam of her lips, his kiss so gentle that she gave a despairing whimper.

Sensation shot through her and she opened her eyes. 'Get off me, you miserable—' She thumped her fists against the solid muscle of his shoulders. 'I *hate* you, and I hate your horribly shiny floors. I hurt on the outside *and* the inside.'

Alekos grabbed her fists in his hands and pressed them back against the pillows. 'I thought you were non-violent.'

'That was before I met you.'

His answer to that was to lower his head again and deliver a slow, lingering kiss to the corner of her mouth. 'I'm sorry you fell. I'm sorry you hurt yourself.'

Kelly tried to turn her head away but his hand held her still. 'You hurt me far more than your floor. *Stop* doing that—stop kissing me. How dare you kiss me when this whole situation is so horribly complicated and impossible and—get *off* me!'

She tried to wriggle away from him but he shifted over her and used his weight to press her into the bed.

'For both our sakes, lie still,' he gritted. Kelly glared up at him but his hard, intense gaze filled her vision.

'You're not playing fair.' She needed to get away from him. She needed space to think about what was best for the baby.

'I play to win.'

'Well, I'm not in the game any more. I give up. I surrender.' Kelly twisted under him but he put one hand on her hip and held her still.

'*Stop* moving,' he breathed. 'Kelly, I know what I said upset you, but you wanted me to be honest. You said you wanted to know what I was thinking.'

'Well, how was I to know you were thinking such awful things?' She strained against him but that movement brought her into direct contact with his body so she stilled. 'You're Greek! You're supposed to want hundreds of children.'

His expression was suddenly guarded. 'I don't.'

'I gathered that.' Kelly gave a groan and squeezed her eyes shut. This scenario was so far removed from what she'd expected that she had no idea how to deal with it. She needed time to work things out. No matter what happened, this must *not* turn into one of those occasions where she just blurted out what was on her mind. No; this time she was going to think it through, come up with a strategic plan and implement it carefully. She'd tell him when the time was right—when she was properly prepared.

Once she'd made a decision, she'd share it with him, and not before.

Alekos traced gentle fingers over the bruise on her forehead. 'You ought to take the tablets the doctor left.'

Wincing with the pain, Kelly opened her eyes. 'I can't take them.'

'Why not?'

'Because I can't take tablets. Don't ask me why.'

'They will stop your head hurting.' Alekos sounded puzzled and a touch exasperated. 'You just swallow them. What's so hard about that?'

'I just don't want to take them.'

'Why?'

'I said, don't ask me why!'

'Just take them, Kelly.'

'*No*, because I don't want to take anything that might hurt the baby!' The words burst from her mouth like a dam breaking behind a force of water and she felt an immediate rush of anger directed towards herself and him. 'I didn't want to say that. I wasn't ready to tell you yet! I *told* you not to ask me why, but you pushed and pushed, didn't you? I'm going on an assertiveness course.'

Alekos looked as though he'd been shot through the head at close range. 'Baby?'

'I'm pregnant, OK? I'm expecting your baby,' Kelly shrieked. 'That's the baby you don't want, by the way. So I think you'll agree that we're in a bit of a fix.'

White-faced and shaking, Alekos slid into the driver's seat of the Ferrari, started the engine and pressed his foot to the floor.

Baby?

The word echoed through his brain along with all the associated feelings. A child depending on him. A child whose entire happiness was going to be his responsibility. *A child crying on his own.*

A thin film of sweat covered his brow; he swore fluently in Greek and pushed the car to its limits, taking the hairpin bends like a racing driver.

Only when a horn blared did he finally come to his senses.

Treading on the breaks, he stopped the car at the top of the hill, staring down across the olive groves towards the villa.

Kelly was down there somewhere, probably packing her bags.

Crying her heart out.

With a rough imprecation, Alekos looked away, trying to apply logic to a situation that required none.

A baby. All his life he'd avoided this exact situation. And now.

Why had he been so careless?

But he knew the answer to that. One look at Kelly had driven rational thought from his head. Every time he went near her, he behaved in a way that was totally at odds with his ruthlessly structured life.

Yet it wouldn't have been possible to find a less suitable woman if he'd tried.

She wanted four children.

Alekos broke out into a sweat. *Just get your head round one*, he told himself. *That would be a start.*

One baby. One baby depending on him. One baby whose entire future happiness was in his hands.

Alekos lifted his fist to his forehead, his knuckles white. Until this moment he'd never known what it was like to be truly afraid. But right now, right at this moment, he knew fear.

Fear that he'd let the child down.

Fear that he'd let Kelly down.

If he got this wrong, if he blew this, a child would suffer. And he knew only too well how that felt.

'*Theé mou*, what are you doing on your feet? You should be lying down, resting.' His hoarse voice came from the doorway and Kelly quickly scrubbed away her tears, feeling a rush of pure relief that he was still in one piece.

He hadn't gone and done something stupid like driving off a cliff. He was still alive; she didn't have his death on her conscience. Now she could be angry without worrying.

She pulled her nose out of the suitcase she was packing and turned.

Alekos was standing in the doorway to the bedroom, looking like someone who had just dragged himself from the wreckage of a car accident.

Alarmed, she scanned him for signs of injury. Maybe he *had* driven his car off a cliff.

She was the one who had bumped her head, but he was obviously in a far worse state. The moment she'd delivered the news that she was pregnant, he'd sprang from the bed like a competitor in an Olympic sprint, and he'd been out of the starting gates before anyone had said 'go'.

But now he was back. And in a complete state, if his appearance was anything to go by.

His usually sleek hair was ruffled and his shirt was crumpled, but the resulting effect was one of such potent masculinity that the frantic crashing of her heart threatened to fracture her ribs.

If anything, Alekos was even more spectacularly attractive when he was feeling vulnerable than when he was strong and in control.

Kelly fought back an impulse to comfort him, reminding herself that this situation was already more than complicated.

This whole thing would have been easier if he hadn't come back.

She hated the way he made her feel. This was a man who had walked out on their wedding day. A man who had just told her he didn't want children.

So why did she just want to hug him?

'I wasn't expecting you back so soon. Normally it takes you four years to reappear after one of your avoidance sessions.' Not trusting herself not to cry again, Kelly turned her back on him and stuffed the final items of clothing into her suitcase. It didn't seem to matter what he said or what he did, he was still the most gorgeous man she'd ever seen, and just being in the same room as him was enough to send her pulse into overdrive. 'Jannis said you'd taken the Ferrari.' She snapped her mouth shut, remembering too late that she'd been determined not to let him know she'd been worried enough to check on him. Recalling the desperation in her tone when she'd asked Jannis if there were any steep cliffs close by, she blushed. 'What are you doing back here?'

'I live here.' He sounded impossibly Greek. He kicked the door shut with his foot and strode across the bedroom towards her. 'About the baby...'

'*My* baby, not *the* baby.' Her heart tumbled and Kelly tried to ram a shoe into her case. 'Why won't this stuff fit?'

'Because you haven't packed neatly.'

'Life is too short to fold stuff neatly!' Incredibly stressed, Kelly took her frustration out on the suitcase by ramming it shut. 'Life is too short for a lot of things, and being with you is one of them. I wish I'd never sold your stupid ring, I wish I'd never come to Corfu in my gap year and I wish I'd never walked across your stupid floor!''

Alekos looked at her in confusion. 'That was all in the wrong order.'

'I don't care if it was all the wrong order. Having your baby after we've split up is the wrong order, too! Everything in my life seems to happen in the wrong order. Most people think *then* act.' Planting her bottom on the lid, she managed to snap the case shut. 'I act then think, and if that's not the wrong order I don't know what is.' Numb with misery, horrified with herself for losing it, Kelly flopped onto the edge of the bed, aware that Alekos was watching her with the same degree of caution he might show an unexploded bomb.

'You are *very* upset, and I can understand that, but you are forgetting that when I said those things to you I did *not* know you were pregnant.'

'What difference does that make?'

'I was not trying to hurt you.'

'That makes it worse. That shows you truly meant what you said, which puts us in a bit of a fix.' Kelly stood up and hauled the little case off the bed, closing her eyes as a sudden attack of dizziness assailed her. 'Get out of here, Alekos, before I kill you and hide your body under an olive tree.'

'You should not be lifting heavy weights.'

'Fine—I'll *drag* your body there. I won't lift it.'

'I meant the suitcase.' He breathed, and she pushed her hair out of her eyes, feeling foolish.

'Oh; right. I knew that. Obviously. But the suitcase is on wheels. I can push it all the way to Little Molting if I have to.' Grabbing the suitcase, she vowed never, ever to get involved with any man again—especially not a fiercely bright Greek man whose superior intellect made her feel the size of a grain of sand. Why hadn't it occurred to her that he didn't want children? Why hadn't she spotted that?

And what was she supposed to do now?

She was having a child he didn't want. She should have nothing more to do with him. His declaration should have killed her feelings stone dead.

But it hadn't.

She was still crazy about him. She loved him as much now as she had four years ago.

Wishing that love could be switched on and off as easily as her iPod, Kelly wondered what he was going to have to do to her before she fell out of love with him.

Had she no self-respect?

Was this how her mother had felt when she'd realised that she was having the baby of a man who had no interest in being a father?

Alekos said something in Greek and jabbed his fingers through his hair. 'I blame myself for not even thinking that you might be *pregnant*.' His voice was hoarse as he struggled with the word. 'But it didn't occur to me. We didn't—I mean, we *did*, but it was just the once. That time on your kitchen table.'

Kelly flinched. 'Romantic, wasn't it?' Her sarcasm was met by taut silence and then he cleared his throat.

'I made you pregnant on that one occasion?'

'So it would seem. Let's hope our child never asks how, or where, he was conceived.'

He dragged his hand over the back of his neck. 'I assumed you were using contraception.'

'Well, I wasn't. Pass me those shoes, please.'

'Shoes?' Distracted, Alekos followed the direction of her finger and retrieved a pair of abandoned fuchsia-pink stilettos from under the bed. 'You shouldn't wear those with your problem with walking.'

'I don't have a problem with walking.' Kelly opened the case gingerly and fed the shoes in one by one, trying not to let any of the contents escape. 'I have a problem with your floor.'

'Why weren't you using contraception?' Dark lashes lowered over his eyes as he focused on the part of the conversation that interested him.

'Because I didn't need it. It seems I'm genetically

programmed to give myself only to the lower forms of life. If there's a decent, honest, family-loving man around, I go blind. Now you can go and beat your chest and do all the other things you cave-dweller, alpha males do.' Kelly was about to reach for her case again when a strong, brown hand covered hers. She stared at his hand and swallowed. 'Don't touch me. What do you think you're doing?'

'I'm doing the things we cave-dweller, alpha males do,' he drawled. 'Like lifting heavy weights. If you want it lifted, I'll lift it.'

'It's a suitcase, not a piece of fallen masonry. I can manage.'

'I don't want you to do anything which will harm the baby.'

'*My* baby. *My* baby, Alekos! Stop calling it *the* baby. What if it can hear you?' The tension exploded inside her, punctured by fears she'd been afraid to express even to herself. 'What if it *knows* you don't want it?'

There was a long silence during which he watched her with an intensity that made her heart race.

'Don't ever say that,' he said thickly. 'All right, I'm the first to admit that this wasn't what I wanted—I wouldn't have chosen this to happen—but it's happened and it's my responsibility. I'm not walking away from that.'

'Forget it. I don't want to drag you along behind the pram like some sort of prisoner of war. I'd rather do this by myself.'

'*Theé mou*, I'm being honest, Kelly! That is what you wanted, isn't it? If I said to you, yes, I'm thrilled about this baby, would you believe me?'

Choking back tears, Kelly bit her lip. 'No.'

'Exactly. I am telling you how I'm truly feeling. This has been a shock.' The disordered mess of his usually smooth hair was an indication of how much of a shock. 'But I will sort myself out. There is no way I would ever leave the baby without a father.'

'*My* baby!' Kelly yelled, putting her hands over her stomach protectively. 'If you call it *the* baby again, I'll punch you.'

Alekos drew in an unsteady breath. 'How about *our* baby?' he said hoarsely, and something unfamiliar glittered in his eyes as he stared down at her flat stomach. 'How does *our* baby sound to you?'

'It sounds like a particularly tasteless joke.' Not even allowing herself to go there, Kelly reached for the phone. 'How do I buy a ticket on a plane? I need basic Greek.'

Alekos's response to that was to gently prise the phone out of her fingers. 'You have a basic Greek,' he said dryly. 'Me. And I have no idea how to buy a ticket on a plane. I've never bought one. And neither will you. You're going to stay here until we work this out. And *stop* talking about leaving. If the baby can hear you, then he will be feeling really unsettled by now.'

'What is there to work out? I'm pregnant and you don't want children, no matter how much you kid yourself you'll do the right thing. Why don't you want children, anyway?' Exhausted by the dilemma in which she found herself, Kelly shot him an exasperated look. 'Is your ego really that fragile? What sort of selfish, self-absorbed, playboy billionaire are you that you can't even bring yourself to be out of the limelight long enough to have a child?'

Alekos looked at her, his face surprisingly pale, his

magnificent bone structure highlighted by the sudden tension that gripped him. 'The sort who knows exactly how it feels to come second to a selfish, self-absorbed father,' he said flatly. 'The sort who vowed never, ever to mess up a child's life. The sort who lived through hell.'

Breathe, breathe, Kelly said to herself, wishing Vivien were here waving a paper bag at her.

Still stunned by Alekos's confession, she was now completely torn, her plan to get on a plane and fly home blown to the wind by his totally unexpected revelation about his own childhood.

Yet staying didn't make sense, did it?

If ever a relationship was doomed, it was theirs.

But the memory of his strained features was stuck in her head. And those words: *the sort who vowed never, ever to mess up a child's life.*

Torn, she sat for a minute, telling herself that all that mattered was the baby. She had to put the baby first. And yet...

'Oh, for crying out loud.' Kelly removed her shoes and walked barefoot across the tiled floor, where she'd slipped, and out on to the terrace. He'd said that if she wanted to talk he'd be outside.

Fine, they could talk—for five minutes. She'd just check he was all right and then she'd leave.

Her feet made no sound on the terrace and Kelly stood for a moment, puzzled, because there was no sign of him.

Then she heard a splash from the pool.

Glancing in that direction, she watched as Alekos powered his way across the pool, water streaming off his muscular shoulders as he swam, clearly trying to work off his frustration as he cut through the water with explosive force.

His body pulsated with strength and power, and Kelly gave a little shiver, remembering how it felt when all that power and passion was focused on her. Refusing to join him in the pool, she gritted her teeth and sat down on the edge of a sun lounger to wait.

The view was stunning, stretching across the gardens and down to the perfect blue sea. Normally the peace and tranquillity of her surroundings would have calmed her, but she was incapable of feeling calm in the current situation, with Alekos still within her line of vision.

Having swum endless punishing lengths, Alekos sprang from the pool, swept water from his face with his hand and prowled over to her.

Kelly slid back on the seat. 'That's close enough. I—I just came to check you're OK.'

'Why wouldn't I be OK?'

'Because you—you talked about stuff you don't usually talk about.' Out of her depth, she looked at him warily. 'I just wanted to make sure you're all right.'

He gave a wry smile and reached for a towel. 'Typical Kelly,' he said softly. 'You hate me, but you think I might be upset so you have to check I'm all right.'

'I just don't want your death on my conscience.' Finding it impossible to concentrate with all that gleaming male muscle on display, Kelly averted her eyes. 'So, let me just check I've understood this correctly: you're basically saying that you don't want children because you're afraid you'll hurt them, is that right?'

'Yes.'

Kelly chewed her lip, waiting for a full confession to spill out. When he was silent, she prompted him. 'Your dad was selfish? He hurt you?'

'Yes.'

Kelly stared at him in exasperation. 'Can't you say more than "yes"? "Yes" doesn't tell me anything about your feelings. Oh, forget it,' she mumbled. 'You don't want to talk about it, I get that. Whatever it is, you've blocked it out. I heard what you said to the doctor, although I didn't realise at the time what it meant. You'd rather just plough on, pretending it didn't happen, because that's what works for you. The trouble is, that doesn't work for me. I played guessing games last time and I guessed all wrong. I assumed you'd just decided you didn't want me—that I was too inexperienced or something.'

'I loved the fact you were inexperienced.' He knotted the towel around his hips and Kelly swallowed, trying to focus on a different part of him.

'Right. Which just goes to show I'm rubbish at reading your mind. And you won't tell me what's on your mind, so we might as well give up.'

'We are not giving up. But you're right—it is a subject I find hard to talk about.' He poured himself a glass of water from the jug that had been left on the table. 'What is it you want to know?'

'Well, all of it! I want to understand.'

Alekos stared into the glass in his hand. 'My parents had a disastrous marriage. My mother had an affair, my father left her, I was made to choose who I wanted to live with.' He lifted the glass to his lips and drank while Kelly stared at him, absorbing that information slowly, slotting the pieces together in her brain.

'Y-you were made to choose between the two of them?' Shaken, she rubbed her hand over her forehead. 'But—how old were you?'

'I was six. They stood me in a room and asked me who I wanted to live with. I knew that whichever decision I made, it would be the wrong one for them.' His tone grim, Alekos thumped the glass down on the table. 'I chose to live with my mother. I was worried about what she might do if I went to live with my father. She was the more vulnerable of the two of them. She told me that if she lost me she'd die. No six-year-old boy wants his mother to die.'

Six? They'd forced a six-year-old to choose who he wanted to live with? Kelly was appalled. 'That's completely shocking. What about your dad? Didn't he understand what a hideous position you were in?'

His mouth twisted. 'A son is a Greek man's most precious possession. To him, I made the wrong choice. He never forgave me.'

'But—'

'I ceased to exist. I never saw him again.' Alekos looked at her and for once there was no mockery in his eyes, no hint of humour. Just a hard, steely determination. 'I never, ever want any action of mine to hurt a child. And it happens. All too easily. So now you understand why I overreacted to the revelation that you want at least four children. It came as a shock.'

Kelly licked her lips. 'I wish you'd told me.'

'We weren't doing that much talking, were we? Most of our communication was physical.' He gave a cynical laugh. 'To call our relationship a whirlwind would be like calling Mount Everest a molehill.'

'I did plenty of talking,' Kelly muttered, feeling a sudden stab of guilt. She'd never asked him that much about himself, had she? She'd never pushed him to talk about his family or his hopes. She'd been thinking about her dreams, not his. 'It didn't occur to me you were thinking that way. You just seemed so confident about everything. You seemed to know exactly what you wanted.'

'I did know what I wanted. Or, at least, I thought I did.' Alekos pulled her to her feet and drew her towards him. 'Things change. Life throws things at you that you weren't expecting.'

Without her shoes, she barely reached his shoulder. For a brief, indulgent moment Kelly leaned her forehead against smooth, bronzed skin, breathing in the tantalising scent of him. 'Yes, life does throw the unexpected. This doesn't feel like the fairy tale.'

He gave a cynical laugh. 'Some of those fairy tales were pretty nasty, *agape mou*. How about the wicked witch and the fairy godmother?'

'The fairy godmother was good. You mean the wicked stepmother.'

'Her too. I told you I'd make a terrible father; I don't even know the right stories,' Alekos lifted her chin with strong fingers. 'How is your poor head?'

'Aching. Like the rest of me. I feel as though I've been trampled by a herd of cows. I'm never wearing shoes in your house again.' But the thing that ached most was her heart—for him. For the small child who had been forced to make an impossible choice by parents too selfishly absorbed by their own problems to put him first. And for herself, who now had to make an equally impossible choice.

Leave and live without him, or stay and risk that he'd walk away again?

She had no idea what to do, which decision to make.

Alekos drew his thumb slowly over her lower lip. 'You're never wearing shoes again? How about clothes?' His voice was husky. 'Perhaps you'd better not wear those, either.'

'Don't. I can't think when you do that.' Kelly tried to pull away but he held her firmly, his hand warm against her back. 'I'm completely and utterly confused now. I always thought you were a totally together, sorted-out person.'

'I am in my business life,' Alekos drawled, sliding his hand into her hair and trailing his mouth along her jaw. 'It's just in my personal life I manage to mess up in spectacular fashion.' This surprisingly honest admission disabled her pathetic attempt to resist him.

She felt impossibly torn.

'We can't get back together for the sake of a baby you never wanted.'

He cupped her face in his hands and brought his mouth down on hers.

'I brought you here *before* I knew you were pregnant.'

'If you were that keen on mending fences, why didn't you come back to England?'

'Because in England it rains even in July, and here in Corfu I can guarantee that you will be walking round in a bikini.' His eyes gleamed dark with the promise of seduction. 'Or less. I'm that shallow.'

'It can't be all about the sex, Alekos!' Her hand slid

to the hard muscle of his shoulders and she pushed him away. 'Having sex is the easy part. It's the relationship bit that's the hard bit.'

'I know that.'

'You don't want a baby. I don't see a solution.' But she wanted one badly. *So badly.*

'We'll find one together.' He took her mouth then, plundering the depths with skilled strokes of his tongue, stirring up emotions she'd struggled to keep under control. His hard body pressed against hers and the flat of his hand kept them welded together while his mouth created a storm of passion.

Kelly melted into him.

He was the only man who'd ever been able to do this to her. The only man who could make her act against her better judgement.

He groaned something in Greek against her mouth, then switched to English. 'For weeks I have wanted to do this—since that time in your kitchen I have thought of nothing else. You have been driving me wild, *erota mou.*'

Kelly lifted her hands, speared his hair with her fingers and let herself go. The taste of him was so dangerously good that she gave a low moan. The sun beat down on their heads and the birds flew playfully across the surface of the pool, but neither of them noticed, so intent were they on each other.

It was the sound of a door slamming close by that caused them to break apart.

Kelly gasped. 'Y-you're just confusing me.'

'There's nothing confusing about it.' Alekos had his hand behind her head and he drew her mouth to his again. 'You want this as much as I do.' The air was humid, thick with sexual tension, and like a drowning person being swept downstream Kelly struggled to keep her head above the water.

'Four years ago you really hurt me.'

'I know.'

'You didn't even explain.' She was looking at his mouth so close to hers, at the sensual curve of his lips and the dark shadow of his jaw. 'You were really horrid.'

'I know that too; I was a real bleep.' His voice was husky and his black lashes shielded eyes that smouldered with the promise of sex. 'I can make it up to you. I can make this work. We can find a way.'

'I don't see how. Don't you *dare* kiss me again, Alekos—don't you dare—not until I tell you it's OK.' Kelly tried to pull away but he was stronger than her and he wasn't afraid to use that strength when it suited him.

His kiss was a devastating reminder of what they shared: power play. 'You are going to forgive me, *agape mou*,' he murmured, taking her lower lip gently between his teeth. 'You are angry, I know, but that is good because it shows you still care.'

'It shows that I have more sense than to let you back into my life again.' But the words lacked conviction, not just because that brief kiss had left her weak and shaking, but also because of the baby. She didn't want to just walk away, did she? It wasn't that simple. But if she stayed there was a strong chance that he'd hurt her again, and this time he'd be hurting their baby too. 'I can't do this, Alekos. I can't put myself through that again. I can't risk it.'

He cupped her face in his hands. 'You want me, you know you do.'

'No, actually, I don't know that at all.' She struggled against her feelings. 'It's just a physical thing.'

'If you don't want me, and it's just a physical thing, why have you been wearing my ring around your neck for four years?'

Kelly's eyes flew wide. 'Who told you that?'

'I saw it after we made love in your kitchen,' he said huskily, brushing his mouth over hers. 'I didn't know you'd been wearing it for four years. That was a guess that you just confirmed. But you have to admit that it says something.'

'It says that you're devious.'

'It says that what we shared has never gone away.' He leaned his forehead against hers. 'Stay, Kelly. Stay, *agape mou*.'

'No, because I can't think straight when I'm near you, and I need to decide what to do without being influenced,' Kelly moaned, turning her head away. 'I'm pregnant, Alekos, and you don't want children. So, tell me how this can ever work! Or are you suddenly going to pretend you've discovered this is what you've always wanted?'

He breathed out slowly. 'No, I'm not pretending that. But it's happened. That changes things. I admit that hearing about the baby is a shock, but we will work it out.'

'How?'

'I don't know.' He was brutally honest. 'I need some time to get used to the idea. But, in the meantime, you leaving won't help the situation.'

'If I stay, we'll just end up in bed, and that won't

help the situation either.' Ripped apart with indecision, Kelly stared at him. 'Last time it was all about the sex. You said that yourself. If I stay, then it has to be different.'

'Different in what way?'

'It has to be about the whole relationship.' She pulled away from him and stared at her suitcase. She didn't know what to do. And the only person she could talk it through with was the same person who made it an impossible decision. If his desire not to have children was so deep rooted that he'd left her on her wedding day, that wasn't going to change, was it?

On the other hand, it was impossible not to admire the fact that he was still standing here. That took courage, didn't it? That showed he was serious about trying to make it work.

Unless it really was all about the sex.

There was only one way to challenge that possibility.

'We'll sleep in separate bedrooms,' she blurted out impulsively and his eyes flared dark with shock.

'Fine,' he said tightly. 'Separate bedrooms. If that's what you want.'

Astounded that he'd agreed so readily, Kelly didn't know whether to be impressed or disappointed. *Was it what she wanted?* She wasn't sure, but now that she'd suggested it she had to follow through. '*And* you have to tell me what you're thinking. All the time. I want to know, because I'm obviously not good at reading your mind and it's exhausting trying to guess.'

His gaze slid over her. 'You're hot, and you should get out of your clothes. I want you naked.'

Feeling as though she was boiling inside, Kelly

glared at him in exasperation. 'I'm trying to have a proper conversation! Do you think you could possibly think about something other than sex for a moment?'

'You told me to tell you what I'm thinking,' he said silkily. 'That's what I was thinking.'

Kelly's face burned. 'In that case, I want you to censor your thoughts. I don't want to hear the ones that involve sex.'

'Censor my thoughts.' Alekos arched an eyebrow and his eyes gleamed with sardonic humour. 'So you want me to tell you everything I'm thinking, as long as it's what you *want* me to be thinking. This is complicated, isn't it?'

'You built a billion-dollar business from nothing but a rowing boat,' Kelly said stiffly. 'I'm sure you can rise to the challenge if you really want to. And now I'm going to unpack my case.'

'The staff will do that.'

'I'd rather do it myself.' She needed an excuse to have a few minutes without him looking at her. She needed to think, and she couldn't do that when he was standing this close.

A faint smile touched his mouth. 'Why not just tip the contents of the case over the floor and have done with it?'

'You may think I'm messy, but I happen to think you're far too uptight and controlling.' Flying into defence mode, Kelly lifted her chin. 'There's something suspicious about someone who needs everything in their life to be neatly ordered. Spontaneity can be a healthy thing. You might want to remember that.'

And *she* needed to try and remember why on earth

she'd thought it would be a good idea to suggest separate bedrooms.

Kelly stalked back inside the villa, wishing she had more control over her mouth.

She'd just consigned herself to endless sleepless nights. If he was going to talk about sex all the time, the days weren't looking too restful either.

Chapter 6

'So, where exactly are we going tonight?' Kelly lay on a sun lounger next to the pool, sipping lemonade with no bits, trying not to think about sex.

Why was it, she wondered gloomily, that when you knew you couldn't have something you just thought about it all the time?

And why was it that Alekos, who usually crashed straight through any decision he didn't like, had accepted this one without argument?

Not that she could accuse him of not being attentive. Over the past few weeks, he had apparently expressed every thought in his head, some of them so hot that she'd been relieved they were on their own in the villa. He'd also presented her with flowers, jewellery, a book he thought she'd enjoy and a new iPod to replace the one she'd accidentally dropped in the pool—but he hadn't touched her. Not once.

And not once had he challenged her request for separate bedrooms.

'We're flying to Athens.' Apparently oblivious to the fact that she was reaching boiling point, he scrolled through the messages on his BlackBerry, occasionally typing in a response. His cool, relaxed demeanour was in direct contrast to her own increasing stress levels.

Kelly was agonisingly aware of him.

It didn't help that he'd chosen to sit on the edge of her sun lounger, as close to her as possible without touching. Sneaking a look at him, she felt a sharp dart of desire pierce her body. Her eyes slid to his muscular legs and her belly clenched.

Was he doing it on purpose, sitting this close?

She pulled her knees up, worried that her thighs would look fat pressed against the sun lounger.

The fact that he was spending so much time with her, surprised her. Over the past couple of weeks he'd only left her side a couple of times, to attend meetings in Athens that couldn't be conducted on the phone. Apart from that, they'd been together at the villa, and the fact that he'd made that compromise for her had Kelly even more confused.

It was a big sacrifice for a guy like Alekos who was completely driven in his work and constantly in demand. The fact that he was making such huge adjustments in his schedule for her was incredibly flattering. In fact it would have been all too easy to fall back into their old relationship with no thought. Every minute of the day, she had to remind herself to be wary.

Living together was becoming all too intense, she thought to herself, watching him lean forward, transfixed by the ripple of muscle and display of strength.

It was all too intense. It was a good thing they were going out.

'Is this a date or something?' Horribly conscious of him, Kelly wished she hadn't risked the bikini. It drew his gaze, and his smouldering, sizzling attention was sending her hormones screaming into the danger zone.

His gaze lingered on hers and then his sensual mouth curved into a smile. 'More of a business dinner than a date. I want you with me tonight.'

The words made Kelly's insides soften to pulp. He wanted her with him. He was including her in his life. He was sharing things with her.

Their relationship was progressing. Obviously it *had* been a good idea to suggest separate bedrooms. She shifted slightly on the sun lounger, wishing that denying herself didn't feel quite so difficult. The chemistry between them was electric. Even without touching him she could feel the tension in his muscles. She was experiencing the same tension. By imposing bedroom limits all she'd done was increase the sexual temperature around them to dangerous levels.

'This meeting—' she curled her legs up so that there was less chance of brushing against him '—tell me what I'm supposed to say. I don't want to say or do the wrong thing.'

'I am not expecting you to close a deal,' Alekos said dryly. 'Just to be yourself.'

'What do I have to wear? Will it be smart?'

'Very. I have already arranged a selection of clothes to be taken to our Athens home so that you can choose something you like.'

Our Athens home.

The words made the breath catch in her throat and

Kelly allowed a little flame of hope to bloom inside her. Would he be talking about 'our' home if he was planning to walk out on her again? No. He was talking as if they were a couple. A partnership.

The fact that she'd never heard him talk like that before raised her spirits, and she sat patiently while he took phone call after phone call, some in English, some in Greek.

Determined not to be impressed by the influence he wielded, Kelly pondered the evening ahead. 'So, how long are we spending in Athens?'

'Just one night. My pilot is picking us up in an hour.'

'An *hour*?' Losing her pretence at cool, Kelly sat upright in a flash of panic. 'I have one *hour* to get ready to go and meet a load of people I'm supposed to impress? That's all?'

'I'm the only person you have to impress,' he said smoothly. 'And I assumed you would get ready when we arrive in Athens. I have arranged for some people to help you.'

'What sort of people?' Torn between relief and outrage, Kelly frowned at him. 'A plastic surgeon?'

'*Not* a plastic surgeon. I don't think you're in need of one of those.' There was laughter in his eyes. 'A stylist and a hairdresser.'

'Stylist? I'm not in need of a plastic surgeon but I *am* in need of a stylist?' Her confidence punctured, Kelly pushed her hair behind her ear. 'Are you saying you don't like my style?'

He sighed. 'I love your style. But most women consider that sort of thing a treat.' His smile faded and his eyes narrowed warily. 'Did I get it wrong? Because I can cancel.'

'No,' Kelly said hurriedly. 'Don't cancel. It might be quite—' she shrugged '—fun, I suppose. Maybe they'll give me one of those seaweed-wrap things that makes you lose a stone in five minutes.'

'If they do that, then they'll never work for me again. Why are women always so incredibly conscious about their weight?'

'Because men are incredibly shallow,' Kelly said with dignity, swinging her legs off the sun lounger.

'Where are you going?'

She picked up her sunglasses and her book. 'I'm going to get ready.'

'You can get ready when we arrive at Athens.'

'I'm getting ready to get ready. I can't face a stylist looking like this.'

Clearly out of his depth, Alekos dug his hand into his hair. 'I will *never* understand women.'

'Stick at it. You're a bright man; you'll get there eventually.'

His house was in the smartest district of Athens, tucked away from the other mansions and hidden at the end of a long, winding drive.

Approaching from the air, Kelly felt slightly faint.

It was huge. Beneath her she could see the architecturally beautiful villa with its wide terrace facing over the city of Athens. An ancient vine offered shade, and water cascaded over a series of stones and into an incredible swimming pool. It was a smooth curve, an oasis of clear, turquoise water framed by tumbling bougainvillea and hot-pink oleander.

Kelly thought of her tiny rented cottage in Little

Molting. When she stood in her kitchen, she could almost touch all four walls. This was another world.

Feeling overwhelmed and more than a little intimidated, she clutched her seat as the helicopter settled on a circular pad a little distance from the villa.

Four powerfully built men immediately came into view.

Kelly lifted her eyebrows. 'Who are they?'

'Part of my security team.'

'Is there something you're not telling me?'

'In Athens I am more careful,' Alekos said shortly, unclipping her seat belt and urging her towards the door. 'Wealth makes you a kidnap target. I want to be able to get on with my work without looking over my shoulder.'

Kelly was affronted on his behalf. She knew his ever-expanding business had created literally thousands of jobs, many of which went to Greeks. She knew him to be fiercely patriotic, supporting local charities and numerous good causes. It was one of the things she'd loved about him when they'd first met.

Following him along the path and into the villa, it was impossible not to stare because it was, without doubt, the most impressive home she'd ever seen. When they'd been together before, they'd spent all their time at his villa in Corfu, so she'd never seen his main residence.

Acres of costly marble and glass gave a sleek, contemporary feel to the place. Beautiful artwork added splashes of colour to the white walls; the furnishings were simple and elegant but the overall feel was one of incredible wealth and privilege. All of it a million miles from her own incredibly ordinary background.

'We don't have much time.' Without breaking stride, Alekos led her up a wide staircase and pushed open a door. 'The staff are all waiting to help you. I will leave you to get ready.'

'But—' Kelly had a million questions she wanted to ask, but he was already striding away from her, his mobile in his hand as he fielded yet another phone call.

Humbled and frustrated by the constant demands on his attention, she stood there feeling like an intruder.

'Miss Jenkins?' A woman hurried across the room towards her, her black hair caught up in an elegant knot at the base of her neck. 'I'm Helen. If we could make a start?'

Relieved to have a purpose, Kelly followed her into a suite of rooms and stared in disbelief at the racks of clothes in front of her. It was as if an exclusive store had been opened up for her use alone. In the short time she'd spent with Alekos four years ago, she'd never seen this side of his life. They'd spent time walking barefoot on the beach; they'd shared dinner on the terrace of his villa wearing the same clothes they'd worn to visit a local market.

Now his life was laid out in front of her.

Two other women were hovering but it was obvious that it was Helen who was in charge. 'If we could start by choosing the dress, Miss Jenkins, then we can decide on hair and make-up.' Her eyes narrowed, she studied Kelly and then walked briskly to the rails. 'I think I have something that would be perfect.'

Kelly, who had been worrying about exactly what constituted 'perfect' for a business dinner, stared as the woman whisked a dress off the rail. 'Hot pink?'

'You will look spectacular. Colours of the Mediter-

ranean.' Helen slipped the dress off the hanger. 'Your
eyes are the colour of the sea, your hair the colour of
washed sand and this dress—' she shrugged '—is the
colour of oleander. Do you like it?'

Kelly stared at the mouth-watering silk confection
on the hanger. 'I'm trying to look grown-up and sophisticated—I thought maybe something safe. Something black?'

The woman gave her a pitying smile. 'Black is for
funerals. I was told that tonight is a celebration. Why
don't you slide into the bath that Nina has prepared for
you and then we'll try this for a change. If you don't
like it, we'll find something else.'

A celebration?

Kelly's heart fluttered. As she slid into scented
water in the largest bath-tub she'd ever seen, she wondered exactly what they were going to be celebrating.

It must be something big if Alekos was going to
all this trouble.

And he'd wanted her here, which meant it couldn't
be business-related or he would have done that on his
own.

It must be about *them*, she thought to herself with
a shiver of excitement. Over the past few weeks they
hadn't really discussed the future; they'd been concentrating more on the present and their relationship.
Which was good, she told herself. That was the right
way to do it.

And if a small part of her was slightly disappointed
that Alekos hadn't mentioned the baby, then another
part of her understood. This was a big thing for him,
wasn't it? And he was nothing like her; he didn't deal

with problems publicly. He worked them out quietly for himself.

She needed to be patient and give him time.

The fact that he'd brought her here proved that he saw them as a couple. She was part of his life now.

Reflecting on the likely nature of the forthcoming 'celebration', Kelly trailed her fingers through the frothy, scented bubbles. Obviously they were going to be celebrating something that hadn't happened yet.

Her heart gave a spring and she felt a flutter of excitement.

Was he going to propose?

She racked her brains to think of other reasons to celebrate, but nothing came to mind. Exams, new jobs: it couldn't be any of those things.

Lying in the warm water, Kelly tried to work out whether she'd say yes straight away or make him wait.

But why make him wait? What would be the point of that? She loved him—she'd never stopped loving him—and now she was having his child. It was a pointless waste of time pretending that she didn't want to be with him.

Her excitement levels rose to almost agonising proportions, and Kelly could barely sit still as one of the girls washed and conditioned her hair.

'I dare not do too much to it or I will be in trouble with the boss.' Helen trimmed it and then blow dried it into soft waves. 'He is right that you have beautiful hair.'

'Alekos said that?'

'"I need her to stun the crowd, Helen",' Helen parroted as she repeated her instructions from Alekos. '"But don't touch her hair. She has beautiful hair. And, whatever you do, don't cut it short or you will never work for me again".'

Taking the fact that she had to stun a crowd to be yet more evidence that he was introducing her to the world as someone important in his life, Kelly beamed. 'You work for him a lot?'

Helen smiled and reached for the make-up she'd already spread across the table. 'He used to fly me to Corfu to blow dry his grandmother's hair. She always loved to look her best, but she found it harder and harder to travel because of her health, so Alekos took me to her. He adored her.'

'Oh.' Surprised by that revelation, Kelly realised that Alekos had rarely mentioned his grandmother. 'I never knew her. She died before I met him. He told me that the Corfu villa was once hers.'

The doctor's words flew into her head.

I remember you coming here to stay with your grandmother as a child. I remember one summer in particular, when you were six years old. You didn't speak for a month. You had suffered a terrible trauma.

Corfu had been his sanctuary, she realised as she allowed Helen to apply her make-up. But he didn't talk about it, did he? She wondered whether that was something Alekos would ever open up and discuss.

'You look stunning,' Helen enthused, standing back to admire the finished effect. 'Now, the dress.' She snapped her fingers and Nina passed it across. Slipping it deftly over Kelly's head, Helen straightened it and stood back, eyes narrowed. 'And now the shoes.'

Nina appeared again with something in her hand and Kelly pulled a face. 'I'll never be able to walk in those. I have a bit of a problem with shoes and shiny floors.'

'That's why God invented man. Alekos will hold your arm.' Helen placed them on the floor in front of her. 'They are perfect.'

As Kelly slid her feet into the shoes, Helen frowned at her. 'We just need to decide on jewellery—the neck is too bare.'

'Are you ready?' Alekos strode into the room with his phone to his ear, spectacularly handsome in a white dinner-jacket, an impatient frown touching his bronzed forehead as he clearly tried to conduct a conversation and finish dressing.

A black bow-tie hung round his neck ready to be tied and cufflinks gleamed at his wrists.

When he saw her, his conversation dried up and Kelly felt her heart beat faster.

She didn't need to look in the mirror to know that Helen had done her job well. Looking into his eyes was enough.

Impossibly excited about the celebration, and feeling incredible, Kelly turned and walked over to the mirror, treating him to a view of her bare back. The dress dipped low and she took his sudden indrawn breath to be a compliment. She needed that compliment because one glance in the mirror had told her that she looked nothing like herself. Normally she chose to wear black because it was safe. There was nothing safe about hot pink. It was bold and brave, but at the same time light-hearted and fun.

What bothered her most was that the dress was undeniably sexy.

And she wasn't sure it was a good idea to dress like this in front of Alekos.

They were supposed to be taking the whole sex element out of their relationship, weren't they?

On the other hand, if they were going to be celebrating what she thought they would be celebrating, then what better way to make their relationship complete?

'You look beautiful.' His voice husky, he dismissed the staff with a barely discernible movement of his head. 'I have something for you.'

Kelly's heart accelerated.

Staring up at him dreamily, she waited, wondering why he'd bought her another ring when she already had a beautiful one on her hand—the wrong hand, admittedly, but that could be easily rectified.

Alekos drew in a deep breath. 'But first there is something I want to say to you.'

Kelly smiled up at him mistily. 'There's something I want to say to you too.' *I love you. I've never stopped loving you.*

'I want to end this farce of sleeping in separate beds,' he breathed. 'It's driving me crazy. I can't concentrate on my work, I'm not getting any sleep.'

'Oh.' Slightly surprised by his approach, Kelly readjusted her expectations. It probably wasn't altogether surprising that he'd approached it from that angle, she reasoned. He was a healthy male with a powerful sex-drive. 'I feel the same way. It's driving me crazy, too.'

'I want a real relationship with you, and that includes sex.'

A real relationship.

'That's what I want too,' she whispered, her heart

pounding as Alekos slid his hand behind her neck and pulled her mouth to his.

'I can't help myself.' He groaned the words against her lips. 'I have to just—'

'Oh yes.' The erotic slide of his tongue unleashed emotions that she thought she had well under control. After weeks of abstinence, Kelly went up in flames. She forgot that they were supposed to be going out. She even forgot that she was waiting for him to propose. Her body felt hot and tight, and everything inside her was focused on the moment.

Desperate for him, she gave a moan of encouragement as she felt his rough palms slide up her bare thighs. Her hand went to the button of his trousers and she felt the hard ridge of his arousal straining against her fingers.

His mouth was hot and demanding on hers, and Alekos bunched the silk dress as he shifted it out of the way impatiently. Kelly's arms locked around his neck and he lifted her where she stood, his dark eyes burning into hers as he gripped her hips.

'Kelly...'

'Yes, now,' she groaned. There was a brief pause and then he lowered her to the ground, his breathing a harsh rasp.

'Wait—we shouldn't.'

On fire and just desperate, Kelly clutched at the front of his dress shirt. 'Why?' She was breathless. 'I thought—'

'No.' His voice vibrating with tension, Alekos closed his hands over her arms and put her away from him. 'Not here. Not like this. That isn't what I meant.'

'No?'

'Later.' Smoothing her dress over her trembling body, Alekos took her face in his hands and kissed her. 'I don't want a few crazy minutes with you,' he said huskily. 'I want more than that.'

She wanted more than that too.

She wanted for ever, and when Alekos put his hand inside his jacket Kelly felt her heart stop.

'Alekos?'

'I have something for you.' His tone husky, Alekos withdrew a long, midnight-blue velvet box from his pocket. Kelly stared at it blankly, her brain refusing to compute the information that her eyes were transmitting. A long box: that was the wrong shape, wasn't it?

'What's that?' Her mind tried to explain away the anomaly. Maybe they'd run out of small boxes in the jewellers, or maybe he'd thought it would be more fun to disguise the gift as something different.

She was on the verge of telling him that he honestly hadn't needed to buy her another ring when he flipped open the box and watched her face in anticipation.

Kelly stared down at the glittering necklace, unable to pretend any longer.

'It's a necklace.'

Not a ring. A necklace.

'It will look perfect with your dress.' Alekos slid his fingers under the diamonds. 'I wanted to give you a present.'

He was giving her a present, Kelly thought wildly, not a future.

A necklace.

Not a ring.

Not a proposal.

Staring at the diamonds dangling from his fingers,

Kelly felt the same way she'd felt when fallen flat on her face on the tiled floor. She was winded. Breathless. Slightly removed from reality.

Shocked and feeling quite ridiculously foolish, she didn't have a clue what to say, but she knew she had to say something because he was staring at her expectantly.

'I—' Nothing came out of her mouth. 'I don't know what to say.'

'You looked stunned.'

'Yes.' Her voice was flat; monotone. 'I am.'

'Diamonds do have that effect on people.'

Kelly forced herself to say something. 'It's very pretty. Thank you.' Her voice was stilted and polite, like a child thanking someone for a gift because a strict parent was looking at her expectantly.

Aware that Alekos was watching her with astonishment, Kelly realised that her response was probably less than appropriate, given the value of the gift, but she couldn't help it.

Somehow over the past few hours she'd managed to convince herself that he was going to propose—that the celebration that Helen had mentioned, was going to be their engagement.

Hot, embarrassing tears scalded her eyes. 'Thanks—it's lovely.'

'Then why are you crying?'

'I'm just—' She cleared her throat and tried to pull herself together. 'Well, a bit stunned. I wasn't expecting this.' Complete idiot that she was, she'd been expecting something different.

'I thought it could mark this new stage in our relationship.'

'The sex stage, you mean?'

'This necklace isn't about sex, Kelly.' Eyes narrowed, he watched her cautiously. 'Is that what you think?'

'No. No, I don't think that. I— Just ignore me. I'm pregnant, and pregnant women are often *emotional*.' She emphasised the word slightly, watching for signs of discomfort on his part, but he seemed perfectly calm. In fact, his only emotion was concern for her.

'Would you like to lie down? I wanted you to be there with me tonight, but if you're not well...'

He wanted her by his side, she reminded herself.

All right, so he hadn't proposed, but their relationship was going in the right direction. She was being horribly unrealistic thinking that their relationship would be fixed in a few weeks. It was going to take much more than that, wasn't it?

She had to be patient.

Trying to calm herself down, Kelly pulled away from him and walked across to the mirror on legs so shaky it was as if she'd forgotten how to walk. He hadn't proposed, but things had changed between them. She could sense it.

For a start he'd called this house 'our' home, not 'my' home. And he had agreed to her suggestion that they leave sex out of the relationship, which showed that he was at least trying to accommodate her wishes. He saw her as his partner, not just a sex object. And, most importantly, when she'd said the word 'pregnant' he hadn't made a dash for his Ferrari.

That had to be a good sign.

Chapter 7

Simmering with frustration across the table, Alekos watched with mixed feelings as Kelly charmed the group of high-powered businessmen. Bringing her with him had been a strategic move on his part to soften what would otherwise have been a difficult meeting. On the one hand he was relieved that the business side of things was going well, on the other he was raw with jealousy as he watched one of the younger men make her laugh.

It had been a long time since he'd seen Kelly so relaxed and happy.

She looked as though a light had been switched on inside her, as if she'd thrown off a weight of worry.

They were seated on the terrace of one of the best restaurants in Athens, shielded from other diners by a terrace of vines.

It was a perfect, blissful setting.

Alekos had never felt so on edge.

Not only was his temper reaching boiling point as he watched the young man flirt openly with Kelly, but his body still throbbed with sexual arousal because that one, torrid encounter in his villa had been nowhere near enough to satiate an appetite that had been building for far too long.

As Kelly leaned forward to reach for her water, the hot-pink dress gaped slightly and he saw a faint hint of shadow at the place where her breasts dipped. Sure that the other man was enjoying that view far more than the sights of Athens, Alekos tightened his fingers around his glass. He sat ultra-still, holding onto control by a thread.

Apparently oblivious to the danger he was facing, his business rival carried on his conversation. 'When Alekos said he was bringing a woman, we were not expecting someone like *you*.'

Listening to Kelly's delighted response to that outrageous flattery, Alekos tapped a slow and deadly rhythm on the table, his thoughts as black as thunder.

Was she doing it on purpose?

Was she trying to stoke his anger and jealousy?

'What do you think, Alekos?' It was Takis who spoke, the elder of the group of bankers. 'Will the expansion have a negative effect on profits?'

'I think,' Alekos purred as he watched the young man reach out to touch Kelly's golden hair, 'that if Theo does not take his hands off my woman within the next two seconds I will look elsewhere for finance.'

The man froze and his hand dropped to his lap.

Alekos smiled. 'Good decision.' He switched to Greek, knowing that Kelly wouldn't be able to follow the conversation. 'Touch her again and you will find yourself working at the supermarket checkout.'

Kelly was staring at him as if he'd gone mad.

Maybe he had, Alekos thought savagely, noticing that his knuckles on the glass were white. Never before had he lost control during what was, essentially, a business meeting. For once in his life he hadn't cared about the end, only the means; if the means meant allowing some guy barely out of his cradle to paw Kelly, he wasn't interested.

Takis broke the sudden stillness around the table. He laughed and lifted his glass. 'Never underestimate what a Greek man will do when defending his woman, heh? We will drink to young love.' There was a faint ping as he tapped his glass against Alekos's. 'This relationship is serious, no?'

Alekos saw Kelly blush.

'It is time you settled down, that's good.' Takis gave a fatalistic shrug, as if it were a fate that befell every man eventually. 'You will need strong sons to take over that shipping business of yours. Kelly is not Greek, but—' he smiled forgivingly '—never mind. She is beautiful, and I can tell that she will give you strong sons.'

Alekos felt the familiar rush of blind panic. Sons: more than one. *Lots of children, all depending on him for their happiness and well-being.*

He reached for his wine glass and drank.

'The sooner you start, the better.' Takis didn't seem to notice the sudden crackle of tension and the stillness of Kelly's shoulders. 'The job of a Greek wife is to have Greek babies.'

Wondering whether Takis was tightening the screw

on purpose, Alekos winced as he anticipated Kelly's outrage at that blatantly sexist comment. Intent on heading off bloodshed, he decided to intervene before she exploded. Their relationship, he thought, was too delicately balanced to weather too great a storm. 'This discussion is a little premature,' he said smoothly, but if he'd expected gratitude from Kelly he was disappointed.

She looked him in the eyes, her face as white as the napkin she placed carefully on the table in front of her.

'You think the discussion is premature? I think overdue would be a better word, don't you?'

Detecting something in her tone, Alekos lowered his glass slowly, aware of the sudden interest from everyone in the restaurant.

Her eyes suspiciously bright, Kelly stood up, her chair scraping on the floor. 'Excuse me,' she muttered stiffly. 'I need to use the bathroom.'

Exchanging looks of embarrassment and fascination, the men rose to their feet in a gesture of old-fashioned courtesy, and Alekos took one look at the ultra-shiny floor of the restaurant and decided that he'd better follow her.

He sprang upright, threw a final, fulminating look of warning towards the young businessman who was now several shades paler than he'd been at the beginning of the evening and followed Kelly.

The thin spike of her heel echoed on the marble, each angry tap a furious indicator of her mood. A few paces behind her, Alekos was treated to a close-up view of her incredible legs and wondered whether they could get away with leaving before dessert.

'You'd better take my arm before you slip,' he

drawled as he lengthened his stride to catch up with her. 'And maybe you'd better not talk so much next time. I know Takis is old-fashioned when it comes to his views on women, but you almost blew that.'

'*I* blew it? You denied our baby!' She whirled to face him, her eyes furious and hurt. 'You're never going to change, are you? I'm just kidding myself. This past few weeks I thought you were coming round to the whole idea, but the truth is that you'd just buried it. You're just doing what you do best—pretending it isn't happening!'

'That is not true.'

'It *is* true.' She virtually spat the words at him. 'When Takis said you should be thinking of babies, you said it was a little premature. Well, how much time do you need, Alekos?'

'I have no intention of discussing my private life with Takis Andropolous.'

'Oh, stop kidding yourself, Alekos! You don't want this baby. You never did. The only reason you're sticking with me is because you want sex. And don't you *dare* tell me that I was the one who almost blew the meeting—*you* were the one who sat there, all jealous and possessive, glaring at me across the table when I'm trying to chat to that guy *you* made me sit next to! You were the one who started a tirade of Greek, knowing I wouldn't be able to understand a word anyone was saying, and you were the one who left me sitting there drowning in all this testosterone and chest thumping while you lot were all glaring at each other!'

Alekos watched in appalled fascination as she drew breath. 'Kelly—'

'I haven't finished! I could have forgiven you for all

that because you've obviously got some weird views on women that come with being Greek, but I will *never* forgive you for denying the existence of my baby.'

Swearing under his breath, Alekos shot a fulminating look at the riveted diners. 'I did *not* deny the existence of our baby.'

'You did! And don't you *dare* call it *our* baby. You haven't once mentioned it over the past few weeks. You buy me flowers, jewellery, anything you think might soften me up so that I'll have sex with you, but do you think of the baby? No. Do you mention the baby? No. And *don't* use bad language in front of our child. I may not speak Greek, but I can tell from your tone of voice that you were saying something that no one under the age of eighteen should hear.'

In the interests of self-preservation Alekos decided that this probably wasn't a good time to point out that the baby wasn't even born yet. 'I wasn't softening you up so that I could have sex with you. If that was all I was interested in, then I would have just kissed you.'

'And that would have reduced me to rubble, is that what you're saying? Because you think you're such a sex god?' Her rage bubbled higher. 'You're arrogant, egotistical—'

'Kelly, you need to calm down.'

'Do *not* tell me to calm down!' She was literally shivering with emotion, her eyes bright and feverish in a face that was ghostly pale. 'This relationship ends now. This is not what I want for my child, and it isn't what I want for myself. I'm going home, and don't bother following me.' Her hands shaking, she tugged the ring off her finger and stuffed it into his hand. 'That's it. It's over. I want to go back to Corfu tonight because I can't bear to spend a single night under the same roof as you. Babies can sense things, you know. I'll fly back to England in the morning.' Barefoot, her head held high, she stalked towards the entrance of the restaurant without bothering to look over her shoulder.

Sodden with misery, Kelly lay alone in the middle of the huge bed in the villa in Corfu, drifting in that hazy place between sleep and wakefulness. Somewhere in the background there was a clacking sound which she assumed to be the ceiling fan. She pulled the pillow over her head, feeling too low and exhausted to summon the energy to do anything about it.

By the time Alekos's pilot had flown her back to the island and the car had taken her back to the villa, it had been the middle of the night—not that it had made a difference, because she hadn't slept anyway.

Her eyes were sore with crying and there were too many thoughts bouncing around her head for her to have any hope of sleep.

The distinctive tread of male footsteps in her bedroom made her freeze with horror. Peeping from under the pillow, Kelly gave a horrified squeak.

Alekos stood there wearing the same dinner-jacket he'd worn the night before, only now the collar of his shirt was undone and the bow-tie was looped around his neck. His arms were loaded with packages and he stopped dead, apparently transfixed by the sight of her on the bed.

Still groggy, Kelly rubbed her eyes and tried to concentrate, but already her heart was racing, as it always did when he walked into a room. 'What are you doing here? And why are you still wearing your dinner-jacket? You look as though you've been up all night.'

'I have been up all night.' His dark eyes glittered with raw sexual appraisal and she remembered, belatedly, that she was naked.

'Stop staring at me.' Her face scarlet, she made a grab for the silk bedcover, but she was lying on it and the process of extracting it turned into a writhing wrestling-match between her and the sheets that brought a sheen of sweat to Alekos's brow.

'Enough!' Depositing the parcels on the nearest chair, he strode across the room, yanked the bedcover free and threw it over her. '*Theé mou*, do you do this on purpose?'

'Do what on purpose?'

'Torment me.' He stepped back with his hands in the air as if touching her had scalded him; Kelly, awash with hormones and hideously overtired, exploded with emotion.

'Don't blame me! You're not even supposed to be here. I wanted to be on my own.' Too late, she realised that the clacking sound hadn't been the fan—it had been his helicopter landing.

'Tough.' Alekos shrugged off his jacket and threw it across the bottom of the bed. 'Our deal was that I was supposed to tell you what I'm thinking, so I came here to tell you what I'm thinking.'

'That was before, and—'

'Are you going to let me speak or do you want me to silence you in my favourite way?' His silky tone made her stiffen defensively and Kelly held the cover to her chin like a shield.

'I don't want you to touch me. Just say what you

need to say and then go. I've booked myself on a flight at eleven o'clock.'

His eyes fixed on hers, Alekos drew in a deep breath. 'Last night at the restaurant you accused me of denying the existence of the baby. But that wasn't what I was doing.'

Kelly didn't give an inch. 'Well, it sounded like it from where I was sitting, and if you've come here to make excuses then you've wasted your time.'

'Kelly, you know I am a private man,' he said in a raw tone. 'I don't find it easy spilling my thoughts to everyone, that isn't what I do. I am fully aware that our relationship is at an extremely delicate point—do you really think I was going to risk destabilising that by announcing your pregnancy to a bunch of strangers? Is that really what you wanted me to do?'

Too upset to consider a different point of view, Kelly sat stiff in the bed. 'You've been denying this baby ever since the moment I told you I was pregnant. I know you didn't want this. I know this is probably the worst thing in the world that could have happened to you, and pretending that isn't the case is just kidding yourself, Alekos. You're just hoping that the whole electric, sex-chemistry thing will somehow get us through this whole tangled mess.'

'That is *not* what I'm thinking. And it's true that finding out that you're pregnant has been difficult for me—I'm not denying that.' His voice was thickened, his accent more pronounced than usual. 'And I probably haven't coped with it as well as I should have done, but I *have* been trying. I readily agreed to your request that we sleep in separate rooms because part of me agreed with your reasoning.'

'Oh.'

'Yes, *oh*.' Visibly tense, he removed his cufflinks and rolled up the sleeves of his shirt. 'I admit that the sex between us does cloud judgement. I know I hurt you four years ago, but I am determined not to do it again, which is the other reason I agreed. I am trying to do as you asked and respect the boundaries you set for our relationship.'

'It's very unfair of you to suddenly start being so reasonable just because you know I'm angry,' Kelly muttered. 'And don't think for a moment that it changes anything. Even if you're behaving like a reasonable person on the surface, I know you're still trying to pretend this whole baby thing isn't happening.'

He threw her a shimmering glance. 'I thought that the idea was that we focus on the relationship. You told me you didn't want to be with me just because of the baby—that it had to be right for us. I agreed. So I've been focusing on *us*. I bought gifts for you because I wanted to spoil *you*, but you interpret that as me ignoring the baby. If I'd bought gifts for the baby, you would have said that I was only trying to fix things because you were pregnant.'

Kelly swallowed and scraped her hair behind one ear. 'Maybe,' she said in a small voice. 'Possibly. Perhaps. Are you saying I'm unreasonable?'

'No.' He breathed out unsteadily. 'But I'm trying to point out that I can't win. Whatever I do can be misinterpreted if that's what you're determined to do. You don't trust me, and I don't blame you for that. In the circumstances it would be odd if you did. I know I have to earn your trust. I'm trying to do that.'

'You're turning this all around to make me feel bad.

And none of that explains why you behaved like a cave-man last night over dinner. You virtually thumped that guy! I know he was incredibly boring, but that's no excuse. I don't like violence.'

'And I don't like men trying to poach my woman.'

'You're very possessive.'

'I'm Greek.' Alekos gave a dangerous smile. 'And, yes, I'm possessive. That is one accusation I am not denying. Nor am I apologising. The day I smile on you flirting with another man is the day you know our relationship is dead. I will fight for our relationship, *agape mou*, even if that means offending your non-violent principles.'

Reluctantly fascinated by that unapologetically male, territorial display, Kelly found that her heart was pounding. 'I wasn't flirting with another man. I wasn't even enjoying his company,' she squeaked, a strange weakness spreading through her limbs as she eyed his pumped-up muscles and darkened jaw. 'If you want the honest truth, he was the most boring, creepy person I've ever sat next to.'

His eyes glittered dark and deadly. 'You were laughing and smiling. I've never seen you so happy.'

'You told me it was an important business meeting. I presumed you wanted me to be polite! And I was happy because, up until the point where you completely lost your mind, I really thought we were doing OK. You were being really nice to me; you called it *our* home, not *my* home, and I thought that meant we were making real progress, and—'

'Our home?' Alekos interrupted her, a curious look in his eyes, and Kelly gave a little shrug.

'That's what you called it: "our home". It made me feel all warm and fuzzy.'

'Warm and fuzzy? This is the same feeling you got from giving away a lump of money to a good cause, no?' Looking slightly dazed, Alekos jabbed his fingers into his hair and Kelly chewed one of her fingernails, wondering whether it was even possible for two people so different ever to understand each other.

'You made us sound like a pair,' she mumbled, trying to explain. 'A couple. We were an *us*. I honestly thought things were going really well, that's why I was happy. And when I'm happy I smile.'

His attention caught by that frank declaration, Alekos studied her intently. 'I presumed you were happy because of him.'

'I was happy because of *you*.' Kelly twisted the bedcover in her fingers. 'But don't get big-headed, because believe me it didn't last very long. You were completely vile during that dinner. And actually I feel pretty unappreciated, I can tell you, given that I worked so hard to be nice to him for your sake.'

'For my sake?'

'You told me it was an important meeting. I worked very hard to be nice to them and not let you down. And I was doing really well until you said that thing about the baby.' Remembering how she'd stalked out of the restaurant and left him to handle them on his own, Kelly covered her face with her hands, mortified. 'Now I feel bad. Which is horrible, because actually ninety percent of this was actually your fault.'

'I completely agree.'

Taken by surprise, Kelly peeped through her fingers. 'You agree?'

'Yes, I was monumentally insensitive. Until you pointed it out, it hadn't occurred to me how easy it would have been for you to misinterpret my reluctance to discuss the baby with strangers—but now I see that, yes, of course you were going to feel that way after I'd told you that I didn't want children.' Alekos yanked the bow-tie away from his neck and dropped it on top of the jacket. 'I have been up all night, trying to find ways of convincing you that I do want you and the baby.'

Distracted by the cluster of dark curls at the base of his throat, Kelly gulped. 'Up all night? Gosh, poor you, you must be so tired. Perhaps you'd better have a nap or something.'

'Sleep is not at the top of my list of priorities at the moment. Sorting this out is more important.' Alekos paced over to the chair where he'd deposited the parcels. 'I *do* think about the baby. Just to prove it to you, I thought it was time to deliver these: I've been buying them over the past few weeks, but I was afraid that if I gave them to you you'd take it the wrong way.' Filling his arms with the brightly wrapped boxes, he gave a rueful smile. 'It seems that by not giving them you took it the wrong way, so there doesn't seem any point in waiting.'

'What are they?' Kelly stared at the precarious tower of gifts in fascination. 'If that's jewellery, then you're going to need a bigger girlfriend.'

'It's not jewellery. None of this is for you. I bought gifts for the baby.'

Kelly blinked in amazement at the mountain of carefully wrapped presents. He'd bought gifts? For the baby? 'I—I'm not even two months' pregnant. We don't know what sex it is...'

'I did the wrong thing?' Alekos was as tense as a bow. 'I can take them back.'

'No. Don't do that.' He'd bought presents for the baby. Just when she'd thought he'd blocked it out of his mind, he'd been buying stuff.

'All right, now I feel really, *really* horrible,' Kelly confessed in a thick voice, and he gave a wry smile.

'I wasn't trying to make you feel horrible,' he said gruffly. 'I was trying to please you. That isn't proving as easy as I thought it would.'

'Thanks. That makes me feel even more horrible. What did you buy?'

'Open them and look.' Alekos gently spilled the parcels onto the bed and Kelly stared at the assortment of packages in disbelief.

'There are loads of them. I'm having one baby, not sextuplets.'

'I went shopping a couple of times when I flew to Athens.' Looking distinctly uncomfortable, he undid another button on his shirt. 'It's possible I may have got a little carried away.'

Touched that he'd thought about the baby during his hideously busy working day, and feeling more and more guilty that she'd misjudged him so badly, Kelly lifted the first parcel, which was large and extremely squashy. Ripping off the paper, she pulled out a huge brown bear sporting a red ribbon. 'Oh. It's *gorgeous*.'

'I thought if I bought one with a blue ribbon you'd be angry with me for assuming the baby was going to be a boy, and if I'd bought a pink ribbon and the baby was a boy then we would have had to change the ribbon…' His voice tailed off as he watched her face. 'So I thought red was best. Is it OK?'

Kelly, who had never before considered the purchase of a child's toy to involve a complex decision-making process—certainly not for a man who made decisions involving tens of millions of dollars every day—was stunned by the agonies he'd clearly endured in making his choice. 'It's really lovely. Perfect.' Noticing that the label said 'not suitable for children under eighteen months', she tucked it under the red ribbon so that he wouldn't see it, and made a mental note to position the bear in a strategic point in the nursery where the baby could see but not touch. 'I know the baby will love it.'

She opened the next parcel and found another bear, identical to the first. Bemused, but extra-careful not to hurt his feelings, she smiled brightly. 'Another one. That's—great. Fantastic.' *What was he thinking? A bear for every day of the week?*

'You're thinking I've gone mad.'

'I'm not thinking that,' Kelly lied, and Alekos gently removed the bear from her grasp and stared down at it, a strange look in his eyes.

'My bear was the one constant in my life when I was little,' he said huskily. 'No matter how up and down my life, my bear was always there. I slept with him every night. And then one day I lost it. I took it to my grandmother's, left it in the back of a taxi and never saw it again. I was devastated.' He lifted his head and gave her a mocking smile. 'Tell that to the press and you'll ruin my reputation for good.'

Hot tears scalded her eyes as she thought of the little boy losing his beloved bear. 'I—I'd never tell that to anyone,' she stammered, a lump in her throat. 'But couldn't you have got it back? Couldn't they have just phoned the taxi firm?'

'No one thought it was important enough.' Alekos handed the bear back to her carefully. 'I wanted our baby to have two identical bears, just in case. A spare is always useful. Maybe you can put one in a drawer or something. Then, if we have a crisis, we can sneak the other one into its place and avoid all that heartbreak.'

'OK, we'll do that.' The tears spilled down her cheeks, and Alekos looked at her in horror.

'Why are you crying? What have I done? Too many bears—not enough bears?'

'It isn't the bear,' she sobbed. 'I love the bears. Both of them. It's the fact that you had to go to sleep without it. I keep thinking about you, just six years old having to choose between your mum and dad, and it's just vile and hideous; it's no wonder you're a bit screwed up about things.' Tears smeared her face and Alekos muttered something in Greek.

'You're crying over something that happened to me twenty-eight years ago?'

'Yes.' Kelly scrubbed her hand over her cheeks and tried to pull herself together. 'I think being pregnant might be making me a little bit emotional.'

'Very possibly,' Alekos said faintly, handing her a tissue. 'Just a little bit. I was worried I'd made a mistake with the bears.'

'The bears are beautiful.' She blew her nose hard. 'Both of them. And having a spare is a completely brilliant idea. I feel really bad now that I accused you of denying the baby when you'd already bought all that stuff. I want to make it up to you. I'm sorry I'm crying; I'm just so tired and I feel bad.'

'You have nothing to feel bad about,' he said softly, removing her tears with his thumb. 'I know I'm not good at this. And it's not surprising you're tired after last night. I upset you badly. I know I'm doing it all wrong, but I am trying, *agape mou.*'

'I know. What else have you bought?' It was an agonisingly tender moment and Kelly opened the other parcels one by one, touched by the variety of things he'd purchased. There were more toys, clothes in neutral colours and books in both Greek and English.

'I thought he ought to learn both languages.' Alekos watched her face as she unwrapped parcel after parcel. 'I want him to know that he is Greek.'

'*She.*' Kelly emphasised the word carefully as she stacked the books that undoubtedly wouldn't be read until the child was at least four. She grabbed another tissue and blew her nose hard, not even wanting to think about how she must look. '*She* will also be half-English.'

'It is going to be a boy, I know it.'

'Even you can't dictate the sex of the child.' But Kelly was incredibly touched by the gifts. Most of them were completely inappropriate for a newborn, but it was the thought. 'They're all lovely, Alekos.'

'Good. So, now I have proved to you that I'm thinking of the baby, and you have explained to me that you weren't flirting, so everyone is happy.' Dragging his eyes away from her bare shoulders, Alekos sprang from the bed and strolled towards the bathroom. 'And now I'm going to take a long, cold shower because, while I agree with the theory of separate bedrooms, I am finding the reality rather hard to sustain. I'll meet you on the terrace for breakfast once I have given myself frostbite.'

Chapter 8

Kelly stood with her hand on the door to the bathroom, listening to the sound of water running.

Raising her eyes to the ceiling, she gave herself a lecture. *What was wrong with her?* Whether they had sex or not wasn't going to have an adverse effect on how this relationship progressed. In fact, she was fast coming to the conclusion that the opposite was true: abstaining made it hard to think about anything *but* sex. It was like giving up chocolate: the moment you knew you couldn't have it, it became impossible to think of anything else.

Kelly opened the door before she could change her mind.

Alekos stood under the shower with his eyes closed, the stream of water running off his broad shoulders onto his washboard-flat abdomen and down his hard thighs.

Kelly gulped and quickly lifted her eyes, but that didn't help much because then she just found herself looking at the perfect symmetry of his handsome face and the sensual lines of his mouth.

Dropping her robe on the floor, she moved silently across the bathroom, walked under the stream of water and slid her arms around his waist.

'I wondered how long you were going to stand there just looking,' he drawled, and Kelly glanced up at him.

'You had your eyes shut. How did you know I was standing there?'

'I can sense you.' His eyes opened and he gave a slow, dangerous smile. 'That, and I heard the door open. Unless my housekeeper has suddenly developed a desire to see me naked, it had to be you.'

Kelly was fairly sure that every one of his female household-staff harboured a desire to see him naked, but she tried to block out that fact.

She gasped as water trickled over her shoulder. 'You weren't kidding about the cold shower. This water is *freezing.*'

'You can take that as a compliment.'

Shivering, her teeth chattering and her flesh covered in goose bumps, Kelly giggled. 'Is it really that bad?'

His answer was to guide her hand to the bold swell of his erection. 'Bear in mind that this is with the aid of *really* cold water.'

Kelly closed her hand over him and heard the breath hiss through his teeth. 'I'd say the cold water isn't working. Maybe we need to try something else.' Turning off the flow of water with her hand, she dropped to her knees and took him in her mouth.

She didn't need to understand Greek to pick up the

shock in his tone, shock that quickly turned to a groan of pleasure as her mouth caressed the whole thick, velvet length of him. He was hot and hard, and she heard the harsh rasp of his breathing as she used her lips and tongue, driving him wild.

'Kelly...' His voice raw, he lifted her to her feet and looked down at her, his eyes narrow slits of burning desire. 'You never did that before.'

'That was before—this is now.' The heat of his erection brushed against her belly and as his hungry mouth caught hers in a hot, sexy kiss a shudder ran through her.

She wanted to tell him how she was feeling, but the words wouldn't string themselves together into a coherent sentence.

Alekos pressed her back against the wall of the shower and Kelly gasped as his hand slid between her thighs. She was trying to work out how to breathe and say his name at the same time when his fingers slipped skilfully inside her. As he touched in all the right places, sensation pooled in her pelvis and her eyes drifted shut.

She was on fire, every single part of her was on fire, and she tried to tell Alekos that he needed to turn the cold water on again, but his mouth was devouring hers and she couldn't catch her breath to speak.

She wanted to tell him that she felt incredible— that he was incredible—but before she could speak, he scooped her up in his arms and carried her through to the bedroom.

'I'm still wet,' Kelly mumbled dizzily and he gave a slow, dangerous smile.

'I know you are, *agape mou*.' Gently pushing her legs apart, he slid down her body, proving his point.

Aware of the hot scorch of the late-morning sun shining directly through the open doors, Kelly squirmed in embarrassment, but he ignored her attempts to close her legs, clamping her wrists together with one hand and using the other to do exactly as he wanted.

With each caress, each skilful, intimate stroke of his tongue, he brought her closer and closer to orgasm. As Kelly wriggled and squirmed in an attempt to relieve the burning sensation in her pelvis, Alekos pinned her hips with his hands, subjecting her to something close to sensual torture.

His tongue was slick and clever, his fingers skilled and knowing, and Kelly felt heat spread through her like a flash fire. Her climax hit with the shattering force, the pleasure pushing her higher and higher as she cried out his name and dug her nails into the smooth muscle of his shoulders. Her pleasure went on and on and he experienced every moment of it with her, his fingers buried deep inside her, his mouth tasting her pleasure.

While she was still shaking in the aftermath, Alekos slid up her body, pushed her thighs still wider and entered her with a smooth, purposeful thrust that joined them completely. Kelly cried out his name as white-hot lightning shot through her, searing her body with sensations so overwhelming that she couldn't breathe.

He made a rough sound deep in his throat and then his mouth came down on hers, the erotic demands of his kiss sending the excitement spinning higher and higher. Cupping her bottom in his hand, Alekos lifted her and thrust deep, the slow, sensual movement of his hips creating almost unbearable pressure as he filled her.

Kelly locked her arms around his neck, and when he lifted his head and looked into her eyes the connection between them deepened to something so incredibly personal that she felt something unravel inside her.

Alekos slid his hand over her thigh, encouraging her to curl her leg across his back. Kelly did as he urged, feeling the sensations intensify as he drove deep, each skilled thrust propelling them both towards climax. The heat was unbearable; her nerve endings were sizzling and when the explosion finally came it took both of them down together. The power of it shocked her and she dug her nails into his shoulders again, her heart pounding, her body slick against his as he drove into her for a final time.

Breathless, stunned, she lay there listening to his harsh breathing, feeling the tension in his slick shoulders. And then he gathered her against him and hugged her tightly. 'Tell me I wasn't too rough.'

Feeling too weak to speak, all Kelly could manage was a brief shake of her head, and Alekos frowned as he pushed her tangled hair away from her face with a gentle hand.

'I was too rough?'

'You were perfect,' she croaked and he gave a slow, satisfied smile as he rolled onto his back, holding her against him.

'I was trying to be extra-gentle,' he murmured, kissing the top of her head. 'But you're so much smaller than me.'

Pressed against the hard muscle of his shoulder, Kelly was well aware of that fact. 'You're—it was—'

'Incredible.' His grip on her tightened. '*You* were incredible. Especially given the amount of light in the room.'

Kelly's face burned at the memory of his intimate exploration. 'You didn't exactly give me a choice.'

'After your performance in the shower, *erota mou*, it is a waste of time pretending to me that you are a shrinking virgin.' A sardonic gleam in his eye, Alekos ran his tongue over the seam of his mouth suggestively, and Kelly wondered how it was that she could still feel completely desperate for him.

'Maybe you do need a bit more practice.' She slid her hand slowly down his body, entranced by the differences between them. Her thigh was pale against the bronzed, hair-roughened length of his, soft against hard and strong, feminine against masculine.

'Keep doing that and we won't be getting up today.' Alekos gave a slow smile and closed his hands over her hips, shifting her so that she straddled him.

Feeling him pressed hard against her, Kelly gave a soft gasp. 'What are you doing?'

'I happen to like the view from here,' he said huskily, his jaw clenching as Kelly took the initiative and slowly slid herself onto his erection.

From this angle she was able to watch his face and she felt a flash of satisfaction as his eyes darkened. Slowly rotating her hips, she took him deeper, and this time she was the one who shackled his hands, pinning them above his head as she rode him.

It gave her a sense of power, holding him there,

even though she knew he could free himself in a minute and take control.

Leaning forward, she licked at his mouth, smiling against his lips as she felt his strong fingers biting into her hips.

'*Theé mou*, you feel incredible,' he groaned, meeting each swirl of her hips with his own rhythmic thrusts. Kelly's hair fell forward, forming a curtain as they kissed, their bodies moving together as everything grew sharper and hotter.

She felt him tense beneath her, felt his grip on her hips tighten, and then his final thrust hurled them both forwards into an explosion of sensation. The intensity of her orgasm shattered her and she pressed her mouth to the sleek skin of his shoulder, sobbing his name as they tumbled over the edge together.

'Why four children?' His mobile in his hand, Alekos leaned across and adjusted the angle of Kelly's hat, making sure that her skin was protected from the burning heat of the sun.

'It just seems like a nice number. I was an only child. I always thought childhood was probably easier if there were more of you. A sister would have been great, someone to laugh, cry and paint your toenails with. How about you?'

'I've never felt much of a need for someone to paint my toenails with.'

Kelly grinned and emptied another blob of sunscreen onto her leg. 'I'm quite relieved about that, actually.'

'Do you want me to rub that in for you?'

'No.' Blushing, she smoothed the cream over her leg. 'Last time you did that, we ended up back in bed.'

A slight smile touched the corner of his mouth and he watched her with lazy amusement. 'And that's a problem?'

'No.' Not a problem at all. *He made her feel beautiful.* 'But I'm enjoying talking to you.'

'I can talk and perform at the same time,' he said silkily, and Kelly shot him a warning look, trying to ignore the immediate response of her heart.

'Try and last six seconds without thinking about sex. Try really hard.'

'If you're going to flaunt yourself in a minuscule bikini, then you are asking the impossible.'

'You bought me the bikini.' But she loved the fact that he couldn't get enough of her. 'I don't suppose I'll be fitting into this for much longer anyway.' From under the brim of her hat, Kelly sneaked a glance at him, testing the temperature of his mood, wondering if the reference to her pregnancy would upset the balance of the atmosphere.

Alekos was frowning down at his mobile. 'Excuse me. I need to make a call.' He sprang to his feet and paced to the far end of the terrace, his shorts riding low on his lean hips, his feet bare.

Unable to decide whether his sudden need to make a phone call was the result of her mentioning the baby, Kelly felt a flash of anxiety. Even after ten days of almost continuous love-making she still couldn't completely relax. Electrifying sex and generous gifts hadn't been enough to delete the dull ache of worry that gnawed away at the pit of her stomach. And her anxiety was not without foundation, was it? Alekos had made no secret of the fact he hadn't wanted children. Even if she now understood and was sympathetic to the reason, it didn't change the fact that this wasn't what he would have chosen.

A person didn't change overnight, did they?

She'd grown up watching her mother try to convert her father from wild boy to family man. It hadn't worked.

Watching Alekos, Kelly felt a flicker of unease, unable to dismiss the fact that he'd made the call after she'd brought up the subject of the baby. Was he using it as an escape from a subject he found hard to discuss? Did it mean he was still having trouble accepting the situation?

She watched him as he paced the terrace and talked, gesturing with his hands, making an instantaneous shift from Mediterranean lover to ruthless businessman while she reasoned with herself.

He was here, wasn't he? That had to count for something—a lot, actually. Of course he wasn't going to get used to the idea overnight, but he was obviously trying.

Attempting to push away the dark mist that was pressing at the edges of her happiness, Kelly glanced round the beautiful gardens that tumbled from the sunlit terrace down to the beach. The rioting, colourful Mediterranean plants attracted birds and bees, and the only sound in the air was the cheerful chirrup of the cicadas and the occasional faint splash as a swallow swooped to steal water from the swimming pool.

It was paradise.

Paradise with a cloud on the horizon.

Ending the phone call, Alekos strode back to her,

simmering with frustration. 'What do you do when two of the children in your class constantly scrap?'

'I separate them,' Kelly said instantly and he looked at her, eyes narrowed.

'You separate them?'

'Yes. I don't let them sit together. If they sit together then they focus on their interaction rather than their work. They put all their energies into being in conflict with the person next to them, rather than listening to me.'

'Genius,' Alekos breathed, dialling another number and lifting the phone to his ear. He spoke in Greek, his tone clipped and businesslike as he delivered what sounded like a volley of instructions.

Kelly waited patiently until he'd finished talking. 'What was that all about?'

'Two of my very senior executives seem unable to interact without generating major conflict.' Alekos strolled to the small table and poured some lemonade for her. 'They're both too good to lose, and I've been trying to find a way of making them work together. It hadn't occurred to me to separate them. It's a brilliant idea.'

Kelly flushed with pleasure, ridiculously pleased by his praise, and incredibly relieved that it obviously was a really pressing crisis that had driven him to take that call, nothing to do with the baby. 'So that's what you've done?'

'Yes.' Ice cubes clinked as they tumbled into the glass. 'I've moved one of them to Investor Relations. Perfect. I think you should come and work for my company. You can sort out all the people problems that drive me demented. You're very clever.' He handed her the drink and she took it gratefully, touched again by his praise.

'I'm just a schoolteacher,' she muttered. 'I teach eight-year-olds.'

'Which makes you extremely well qualified to deal with my board,' Alekos drawled, glancing at his watch. 'Go and get dressed into something slightly less provocative. I want to take you out.'

'Out?'

'Yes. If you want to talk and not have sex then we'd better go somewhere extremely public.'

He took her to Corfu town and they wandered hand in hand around the old fortress, mingling with the tourists. 'Did you always want to be a teacher?'

'Yes.' Kelly was rummaging in her bag. 'When I was small I used to line my toys up in a row and give them lessons. Alekos, I've lost my sunglasses and my new iPod. I *know* I put them in my bag. I think.'

'Your sunglasses are on your head. I have your iPod.' Visibly amused, Alekos pulled it out of his pocket and handed it to her. 'You left it in the kitchen. Maria found it.'

'The kitchen?' Kelly took it from him gratefully, trying to remember when she'd taken it to the kitchen. 'How weird.'

'It was in the fridge,' he said dryly, and she gave a helpless shrug.

'Even more weird. I suppose I must have left it there when I was pouring myself a glass of milk.'

'That sounds completely logical.' His voice was gently mocking. 'If I lose any of my possessions, the first place I look is the fridge.'

'You never lose anything because you're scarily organised. You ought to loosen up a bit. And it's mean to tease me. I'm just really tired.' Her comment wiped the indulgent smile from Alekos's face.

'We will go home and I will call the doctor.'

'I don't want to go home and I don't need a doctor,' Kelly said mildly, pushing her iPod deep into her bag to avoid losing it again. 'I'm pregnant, not ill.' Glancing at him, she noticed the sudden tension in his shoulders and sighed. It was like waiting for a bomb to go off. 'I just need a decent night's sleep.' And she needed to stop lying there worrying that he was going to change his mind and walk out any day. 'It doesn't help that you're insatiable.'

'I seem to recall *you* were the one who woke *me* at five this morning.'

Kelly turned scarlet as two women turned their heads to stare. 'Could you keep your voice down?'

'They shouldn't be listening to a private conversation.'

But Kelly knew that the truth was that wherever they went women stared. Alekos attracted female attention. Slightly uneasy about that fact, she changed the subject. 'I expect you did well at school. You're very clever.'

'I was bored stiff.'

Kelly gave a strangled laugh. 'I pity your poor teachers. I wouldn't have wanted to teach you.'

Alekos stopped and pulled her into his arms, smoothing her hair away from her face with his hand. 'You *are* teaching me,' he said huskily. 'All the time. Every day I learn something new from you. How to be patient. How to solve a problem in a non-violent way. How to find an iPod in a fridge.'

'Ha ha, very funny.' Her heart was thundering like horses' hooves in a race, because he was so indecently good-looking and all his attention was focused on her. 'You're teaching me stuff, too.'

He gave a slow, dangerous smile. 'Perhaps you'd better not list exactly what I'm teaching you while we're in a public place. That's why we came here, re-member?'

'I didn't mean *that*.' A warm, fluttery feeling settled low in her belly, a feeling that increased as he lowered his mouth to kiss her.

Alekos led her along a narrow back-street and into a tiny restaurant where he was greeted like a hero.

'My grandmother used to bring me here. It is tradi-tional Corfiot cooking.' Alekos pulled out a chair for her. 'You will enjoy it.'

'You adored your grandmother.' Kelly twisted the ring on her finger self-consciously. 'I feel so guilty that I almost sold this. I had no idea it was hers. And I didn't have a clue that it was that valuable. I almost had a heart attack when I saw that bid.'

'But not as big a heart attack as when you saw me standing at the school gates and realised that I'd bought it.'

'That's true.' Kelly wanted to ask whether he'd in-tended to give it to Marianna, but she decided that their fragile relationship didn't need any more exter-nal bombardment. 'It was a shock.'

'Why did you choose to teach in that place? You could have taught in a big school in a city.'

Kelly watched in surprise as several waiters arrived

carrying a dozen small plates of different Greek specialities. 'When did we order? Or did they just read your mind?'

'They give you whatever the kitchen has freshly prepared. If you want authentic Greek cooking, then this is the place to come. You haven't answered my question.'

'About why I chose Little Molting? I wanted to keep a low profile.'

In the process of spooning *dolmades* onto her plate, Alekos paused. 'A low profile?'

Kelly picked up her fork, wondering how honest to be. 'The whole press thing was a bit overwhelming after our wedding that didn't happen. They wouldn't leave me alone. Only because I was linked to you, of course,' she said hastily, her hair falling forward as she studied the food on her plate. 'Not because I'm interesting by myself. And, actually, I wouldn't really want all that. Can you imagine what they'd print about me in one of those celebrity magazines? "And Kelly has graciously invited us to photograph her in her beautiful home. And here we are in her kitchen where you see that, oh dear, she has forgotten to empty the bins".' Realising that Alekos hadn't said a word, her voice tailed off and she looked up at him. 'What? I'm talking too much?'

'The doctor said that the press hounded you on our wedding day.'

Kelly tucked her hair behind her ear. 'Yes, well, you not turning up at the wedding was quite exciting for them, I suppose. For reasons I've never understood, some people thrive on the misery of others. Watching someone coping with trauma appears to be a popular spectator-sport. I don't get it myself. If I see someone upset I either want to comfort them or give them privacy, not ogle them, but there you are—people are sometimes a bit disappointing, aren't they?'

'*Theé mou*, I am truly sorry for what I put you through.' His voice was hoarse and he reached across the table and caught her hand. 'I didn't think about the press or the attention that would be focused on you.'

'That's because you live your life behind high walls and you have security men who make the Incredible Hulk look puny.' Kelly stared down at the strong, bronzed fingers covering hers. She wondered if he realised that she was still wearing his ring on her right hand. Maybe he'd just forgotten; men were pretty rubbish at noticing things like that, weren't they? She tapped her fingers on the table, hoping to draw attention to it. 'Are you right-handed or left-handed?'

Alekos looked astonished by the sudden change of subject. 'Right-handed. Why?'

Because I'm trying to bring up the subject of hands, Kelly thought wildly, deciding that subtlety wasn't her strong point. 'I'm right-handed too.' She waggled her hand, making sure that the diamond flashed in his face.

'You're right-handed.' He looked at her cautiously. 'I suppose it's always useful to know these things. I really am sorry that you were subjected to so much press attention.'

Nowhere near as sorry as she was that he hadn't said anything about her wearing his ring on her right hand. Kelly put her hand back in her lap, despondent. 'It's OK—well, not completely OK, of course. I *was* very upset. It was jolly humiliating, if I'm honest. I was pretty angry with you.'

'*Pretty* angry? You should have been livid.'

'All right, I was livid,' she confessed. 'I felt like a total idiot ever thinking that someone like you could be interested in someone like me.' Maybe she was still behaving like an idiot. Maybe it was idiotic to think that this could ever work. 'Billionaires don't usually hang around with penniless students. Not in the real world.'

'Then they ought to,' Alekos drawled. 'They might be happier.'

Kelly looked at him, wanting to ask if he was happy—*wanting to ask how he was feeling about the baby now that several weeks had passed.* But broaching that subject felt like handling a priceless Ming vase: she was too afraid she might smash the whole thing to pieces if she touched it in the first place.

'If it would help, you can hit me now.' Alekos studied her across the table, clearly sensing the undercurrents but mistakenly attributing them to the past rather than the present. 'You might find it cathartic.'

'I'm non-violent,' Kelly muttered. 'I don't think it would have made me feel any better to bruise your face, then or now.'

'It might make *me* feel better.'

She looked up at him, slightly reassured by the fact that he clearly regretted the way he'd treated her. At least he hadn't *tried* to hurt her.

'I understand better now.' She pushed her fork into a piece of spicy local sausage. 'Things were really intense between us. We barely stopped kissing long enough to have a conversation. Neither of us really thought further than the moment. And I was all over you, saying stuff because I'm useless at holding it all in. I've thought about what you said—about waking up that morning and seeing the story in the magazine about me wanting children. It's no wonder you freaked out.'

Alekos drew in a deep breath. 'You don't have to make excuses for me.'

'I'm not. I'm just saying that I can understand it better now. Maybe if that magazine had come out the day before, or even the day after, we could have talked about it, and who knows?' Kelly shrugged. 'The morning of the wedding was just basically very bad timing.'

'What I did to you was unforgivable.'

'It wasn't unforgivable. It was hurtful, scary—loads of things, actually.' Thinking back to that time made her feel slightly sick. 'But it wasn't unforgivable. Especially not now I understand why you reacted that way. I shared some of the blame for just diving into a hot, intense relationship with you without discussing the really important things.'

Alekos studied her for a long moment. 'You are the most generous person I have ever met,' he said gruffly, and Kelly blushed.

'Not that generous. I said a few bad things to Vivien about you, I can promise you that.' Agonisingly conscious of him, she looked down at her plate. 'Do you forgive me for selling your ring?'

'Yes.' He replied without hesitation. 'I drove you to that.'

'If it belonged to your family, why did you let me keep it in the first place?'

'It was a gift to you.'

'Well, that was a very generous gift. I had no idea it was worth—' she lowered her voice to a whisper '—four-million dollars.'

'It is worth a great deal more than that,' Alekos said calmly. 'Try this lamb. It's cooked in herbs and it's delicious.'

'More?' Kelly's voice was a squeak and Alekos smiled.

'The ring has been passed down my father's side of the family for generations.' He toyed with the stem of his glass. 'My great-great-great-grandfather was apparently given it as a reward for saving the life of an Indian princess. Or so the legend goes.' A cynical smile touched his mouth. 'I suspect the stone may have less romantic origins, but I've never explored it further.'

'I don't even want to know how much it's worth,' Kelly said faintly, glancing cautiously over her shoulder to check the other diners weren't listening. 'As soon as we leave this place, I'm giving it back to you. It's crazy giving anything that valuable to me! I'll leave it in the fridge or something. You know I'm useless.'

'It is perfectly safe on your finger.' Amused, Alekos dismissed her concerns, but Kelly stared down at the sparkling, winking diamond, no longer able to pretend that he might have forgotten she was wearing it on the finger of her right hand.

He hadn't forgotten.

So why hadn't he suggested she move it to her left hand?

On the surface they appeared to be getting on well, but he still hadn't talked about the future, had he? He hadn't mentioned marriage.

He hadn't said 'I love you'.

And neither had she, because this time she was terrified of saying the wrong thing. Of spilling out something he didn't want to hear. Every time they made love she had to clamp her mouth shut, terrified that the words might fly out by themselves in an unguarded moment of ecstasy.

Her appetite gone, Kelly put her fork down and took a sip of water.

It was early days, she told herself firmly. It was going to take time to rebuild what they had. And, anyway, they were building something new. Something better. Something deeper and more enduring.

That wasn't something that could be rushed. He was right to wait. She had to give it time.

But telling herself that did nothing to alleviate the sick feeling in the pit of her stomach.

Chapter 9

'We're *flying to Italy for one evening?*' Kelly decided that she'd never be able to be as cool as he was about foreign travel. 'Where, exactly?'

'Venice. We're attending a reception at a gallery.' Alekos didn't quite meet her eyes and she had a distinct feeling that there was something he wasn't telling her.

'And they like you because you're rich and you spend money? Can we go on a gondola?' She was talking to his shoulders because he'd already walked into his dressing room.

'That's for tourists.'

'*I'm* a tourist.' Bouncing off the bed, Kelly followed him into the dressing room. 'I've always wanted to go on a gondola.'

Selecting a suit and a fresh white shirt, Alekos gave a tense smile. 'All right. I'll take you on a gondola tomorrow before we come home. Tonight is a very smart gathering. You need to dress up.'

Kelly rested her hand over her stomach self-consciously. 'I'll have to wear something baggy; my tummy is sticking out. It must be too much Greek food.'

'Or it could be our baby,' Alekos said softly, placing his hand over hers. For a moment his eyes lingered on hers and then he lowered his head and kissed her on the mouth. 'I bought you a dress.' Reaching into the wardrobe, he retrieved a large box decorated with a subtle, tasteful logo. 'I hope you like it.'

'You mean you hope it covers my fat tummy. At least I have an excuse—the worst thing is when someone asks you when the baby is coming and you have to tell them you're not pregnant.' Light-headed, thrilled by his unexpected warmth towards the baby, Kelly chatted away. 'It's almost worth being pregnant for ever just so that you have an excuse when your clothes are too tight. Oh.' She removed the dress from the tissue paper and stared at it in awe. 'It's stunning. Gold. Long.'

'Is it all right?'

Kelly wondered why he was asking her that when he'd bought her clothes before without ever asking her opinion. Why be worried about this one? Unless it really was a very important evening. 'The dress is perfect.'

'I hope you don't trip over the hem.'

'Me too. With any luck there won't be any stairs,' she said hopefully, fingering the fabric with deference. 'Where did you buy it?'

Alekos turned away from her and delved inside the

pocket of his suit, searching for something. 'It was made especially by an Athenian designer,' he said vaguely. 'I gave her your measurements.'

Was it her imagination or was he suddenly a little tenser than he'd been a few moments before? Picking up an atmosphere but not understanding it, Kelly was worried she hadn't been enthusiastic enough. Perhaps he thought she was being ungrateful.

'I love it. Honestly, it's gorgeous. I've never had anything made especially for me before.' She delved in the box and pulled out a pair of shoes made from the same fabric. Eyeing the heels, she gave a faltering smile. 'Will there be a lot of valuable items on display for me to crash into?'

'You won't be crashing anywhere tonight, *agape mou.*' Relaxed again, Alekos strolled towards the shower. 'Your stylist will be here in half an hour, so why don't you grab some rest while you can?'

'My stylist.' Kelly grinned to herself. 'I'm not sure why that sounds so good. I ought to be able to style myself, but it's awfully nice to know that there will be someone else to blame if you end up looking a total mess. Are we coming home tonight?'

'No. We're booked into a suite at the Cipriani.'

'The Cipriani? I've heard of that,' Kelly squeaked. 'Wow. Lots of famous people stay there: George Clooney, Tom Cruise, Alekos Zagorakis…'

'And Kelly,' Alekos finished, and she gave a weak smile.

'And Kelly. I just hope George Clooney doesn't feel upstaged by me being there. Poor him. He doesn't stand a chance, does he?'

* * *

As the limousine pulled up to the end of a long red carpet, Kelly shrank. 'You didn't say anything about a red carpet, cameras and a million people staring. Alekos, I can't walk in these shoes in public.'

'If I'd mentioned it, you just would have worried.' Alekos took her hand and gave it a squeeze. 'I'm with you this time. You just smile and look aloof.'

'It's hard to look aloof when you're nose is splattered on the floor, which is where mine will be if I have to walk the length of that carpet in front of an audience!'

'I'll be holding your hand.'

'Can I take my shoes off?'

'Not unless you want to attract extra attention. Smile,' Alekos instructed as the car door was opened from the outside and a burst of light filled the car. 'Leave the rest to me.'

Kelly stepped gingerly out of the car and was immediately blinded by flashbulbs. Her lips fixed in a rigid smile, she took one look at the yelling crowd, and would have shot back into the car but Alekos's fingers handcuffed her wrists.

'Walk. Incline your head. Lift your chin slightly— better.' He issued a stream of instructions and encouragement, his hand holding hers tightly as he walked her down the red carpet and into the gallery. 'Now you can relax.'

'Are you kidding?' Kelly stared nervously at the priceless artefacts. 'I won't relax until I leave knowing I didn't break anything.'

'If you do break something, no one will dare comment,' Alekos said smoothly. 'I'm an extremely generous benefactor. And, no, before you ask, that doesn't give me warm, fuzzy feelings.'

'I don't think even I'd get warm, fuzzy feelings about a painting,' Kelly confessed, craning her neck as she looked at the art on the walls. 'Why do you support a museum in Venice? Why not the museum in Athens?'

'I do support the museum in Athens. Come with me, there is someone I want you to meet.' Supplying her with a drink, Alekos led her through the elegant throng of people towards a man who stood admiring a painting. 'Constantine.'

The man turned and Kelly saw that he was elderly. His white hair was swept back from a face that was still handsome, despite his years. 'Alekos.' His expression brightened and there was a brief exchange of rapid Greek before Alekos drew Kelly forward and introduced her.

'Ah.' Constantine smiled at her, a knowing look in his eyes. 'So we are surrounded by priceless works of art but still Alekos manages to arrive with something more dazzling on his arm.' He lifted her hand to his lips. 'Even the gold of the Renaissance doesn't shine quite so brightly as a woman in love. Good, I'm pleased. And not before time, Alekos Zagorakis.'

Kelly felt Alekos stiffen beside her and suddenly she wanted to put her hand over the other man's mouth to silence him.

She'd been walking on eggshells for weeks, and now this man was stomping over their fragile relationship with hobnail boots.

'I love this painting,' she blurted out in a high voice. 'Is it a—?' Suddenly her brain emptied; she couldn't think of a single Italian artist. Panic had wiped her mind clean. 'Canaletto?'

Constantine looked at her curiously and then shifted his gaze to the information plate next to the painting that clearly said *Bellini*.

Kelly gave a weak smile. 'Bellini—of course. I wonder if they have any postcards that I can buy for the children…' Gabbling nervously, it took her a moment to realise she'd inadvertently said totally the wrong thing.

'Children? You have children?' Constantine glanced from her to Alekos, who was standing as frozen as a statue. 'This is good news. Is there a reason for me to congratulate you?'

Horrified, Kelly sneaked a look at Alekos, whose face was a study in masculine tension.

'No,' he said shortly. 'You have no reason to congratulate me.'

'I meant the children that I teach. I'm a teacher.' But Kelly's legs were shaking and she put her hand against the wall to support herself.

Constantine slapped Alekos on the shoulder. 'So you're not a father yet?'

'No.' Alekos's voice was hoarse. 'I'm not a father.'

Kelly felt as though he'd punched her.

She felt hideously, horribly sick. Had he really said that?

He still wasn't telling anyone. He was still denying the existence of the baby.

Not trusting herself to speak, Kelly wished she could drink the champagne that was circulating, but she had to settle for orange juice which proved absolutely useless for numbing pain. Alekos had smoothly changed the subject, but Kelly was so upset she couldn't even bring herself to look at him. Her hands shook so much, she sloshed orange onto the floor. Normally she would have been mortified by her clumsiness, but tonight she didn't even care.

I'm not a father. He'd actually said those words.

I'm not a father.

What was she doing with him? She was a complete and utter fool, trying to shape this relationship into something that looked normal.

She was kidding herself if she ever thought he was going to suddenly come round to having children. And just because she was sympathetic to his reasons didn't mean she was willing to allow her child to have the same dysfunctional relationship with him that she'd had with her father. No way was she going to have her child waiting on a doorstep for a father who just wasn't interested.

I'm not a father.

'Alekos!' A woman with sloe eyes and an impossibly slender frame joined their group, kissing first Alekos and then Constantine. 'Isn't this a terrible crush? Still, it's good to do one's bit for the arts.' Her eyes fastened on Kelly's dress and then widened. 'Is that—?'

'Tatiana, this is Kelly.' Alekos interrupted the woman swiftly but Kelly stared at her numbly, wondering why her dress was causing such a stir.

Why was everyone so shallow? Yes it was pretty, and she liked having something special to wear as much as the next girl, but no dress, however gorgeous, could make up for a completely deficient relationship.

I'm not a father.

'Why are you staring at my dress?'

Tatiana laughed, a sound like glass shattering. 'It's by Marianna, isn't it? Lucky you. She only designs for the favoured few. Completely impossible to get hold of any of her pieces.' She gave Alekos a knowing smile. 'Unless you have a particular place in her heart, of course.'

By Marianna.

Marianna?

Kelly stared at the woman. Then she looked down at the gold dress, remembering how tense Alekos had been when he'd given it to her.

No wonder, she thought numbly. No wonder he'd been behaving oddly.

He must have been terrified that she'd find out.

What sort of insensitive brute dressed his current girlfriend in his ex's creations?

The same insensitive brute who still denied the existence of their baby. The same insensitive brute who hadn't told her to move her ring to the other hand.

Her eyes scalded by tears, Kelly stared hard at the Bellini on the wall, wondering if Renaissance man had been any more considerate than modern man.

Fisting her hand into the gold dress, she pulled it off the ground and swept towards the exit, brushing against a fine Renaissance sculpture in her attempt to get away as fast as possible.

As she ran back down the red carpet, her eyes stung and there was a solid lump lodged in her throat.

She'd expected something to shatter into a million pieces that night. She just hadn't expected it to be her heart.

* * *

The hotel suite was like a glass capsule, suspended mid-air over the lagoon, but if Alekos had expected a display of Kelly's normal exuberant enthusiasm then he was disappointed.

He'd caught up with her at the end of the red carpet and bundled her into the back of his waiting limousine, concerned that she hadn't appeared to be thinking about where she was going or what she was doing.

Once they'd arrived at the hotel, she'd stalked into the room ahead of him, tugged off her shoes and dropped them on the floor without giving him a backward glance. Now she had her hands behind her back, wriggling and writhing in an attempt to undo the invisible zip, clearly determined not to ask for his help.

She was seething; furiously angry.

Alekos strolled across to her and put his hands on her back, but she knocked him away.

'Don't touch me.' Her voice was shaking. 'On second thoughts, unzip this stupid dress so that I can take it off. I don't want to be wearing something made by one of your ex-girlfriends.'

Alekos took a deep breath. 'It did occur to me that you would be upset that the dress was by Marianna, which is why I didn't tell you.'

'It would have been better if you hadn't given me a dress by her in the first place!'

'I knew that red-carpet display would unnerve you.' He slid the zip down from neck to hem, feeling his body tighten as his eyes lingered on the smooth lines of her bare back. 'I thought it would help if you liked the way you looked. Her clothes are highly sought-after, and I thought it would give you confidence to wear one of her unique creations.'

'Confidence?' She whirled round, her hair tumbling down from the elegant clip that had restrained it all evening. 'You think it gives me confidence to be told in public that I'm wearing a dress designed by your ex-girlfriend?'

'I did not know that Tatiana was going to make the connection.'

'Oh, well, that makes it fine, then!' Her voice thick with tears, Kelly yanked at the dress and pushed it off her body as if it were infectious. 'I see the label now.' She snatched the dress off the floor and stared at the elegant 'By Marianna' that had been discreetly hand-sewn onto a seam of the dress. 'I'm a complete and utter fool.'

Dragging his eyes from the generous curve of her creamy breasts, Alekos tried to focus. 'You are not a fool.' He breathed unsteadily but Kelly pushed her fists into her cheeks, her face crumpling as she struggled for control.

'Just get away from me. Only you can turn the most romantic city on earth into a hell hole.' Still dressed only in her underwear, Kelly stalked over to the window, hugging herself with her arms as she looked over the lagoon. 'That place is probably littered with the dead bodies of women who have thrown themselves in after spending a night with men like you.'

Raising his eyes to the ceiling, Alekos walked across to her. 'Marianna makes unique, elegant evening-dresses. She has a four-year waiting list because she is the best, and I wanted to buy you the best.'

Her shoulders stiffened a little more and she didn't turn. 'It was hideously insensitive.'

'I am with you, not her.'

'No, you're not—you're not with me, Alekos. Not really. We've just been going through the motions, haven't we?' She turned then, her face wet with tears, her mascara streaking under her eyes.

It occurred to Alekos that he'd never seen a woman cry properly before with no thought to her appearance. Instead of sniffing delicately, Kelly rubbed her face with her hand, smearing tears and mascara together. Alekos, who had never before been moved by tears, had never felt more uncomfortable in his life.

'We are *not* going through the motions.'

'Yes, we are. Have you ever said "I love you"? No, of course not, for the simple reason that you *don't* love me! I started off as someone to have sex with and ended up as someone having your baby—' Her voice hitched. 'And it's a *mess*. The whole situation is a horrid, tangled mess. And it's not supposed to be like this. It just isn't!' She started to sob but when Alekos put his hands on her shoulders she pushed him away roughly.

'You did it again. When Constantine asked you if you were a father, you said no!' Her face was wet, her eyes were red and swollen, but Alekos stood with his hands frozen to his sides, knowing that if he touched her she'd flip.

'Kelly…'

'No.' Her hair flew around her face as she shook her head. 'No more *excuses*. Do you know what, Alekos? I just can't do this. I can't carry on living on a knife edge, wondering whether this is going to be the day you tell me you can't do this any more. I don't want our child growing up wondering whether you're going to be there or not, feeling like he's done something wrong. You can't be there one minute and not the next, because I know how it feels to be standing on a doorstep waiting for a dad that never turns up!'

Transfixed into stillness by that revealing statement, Alekos stood watching her, waiting for Kelly to spill her guts as she always did and elaborate on the true reason behind her explosive reaction to his clumsy behaviour.

But tonight she just turned away from him and stared over the lagoon.

'I want to go h-home,' she sobbed. 'I want to go home to Little Molting. We'll sort the details out later.'

'You stood on a doorstep waiting? Is that what happened to you?' His voice was soft as he prompted her. 'Did your dad leave you waiting for him?'

She kept her back to him, her shoulders stiff. 'I don't want to talk about it.'

Alekos hung onto his own temper with difficulty. '*Theé mou*, you talk about everything else! There is not a single thing going on in your head that doesn't come out of your mouth, but this—' he gestured with a slice of his hand '—this really important thing, you don't mention to me. Why not?'

It was a moment before she answered. 'Because talking about it doesn't help,' she muttered. 'It doesn't make me feel nice.'

'Kelly.' Struggling to get it right, Alekos drew his hand over the back of his neck. 'Right this minute I'm not feeling nice, and I don't think you are either, so it would be great if you could just not pick this particular moment to clam up. Tell me about your father. I want to know. It's important.'

She rubbed her hand across her cheek and sniffed. 'My mum spent half her life trying to turn him into what she wanted him to be.'

'And what was that?'

'A husband. A father.' Her voice thick with tears, she kept wiping her eyes with her hand. 'But he didn't want children. Mum thought he'd come round to the idea, but he never did; that wasn't what happened. Occasionally his conscience would prick him and he'd phone to say he was coming to see me.' Her voice split. 'And I'd boast to all my friends that my dad was going to take me out. I'd pack my bag and wait by the door. And then he wouldn't turn up. That makes you feel pretty lousy, I can tell you. As childhoods went, it was no fairy tale.'

And she'd always wanted the fairy tale.

Thinking about his contribution to slashing those dreams, Alekos pressed his fingers to the bridge of his nose and tried to think clearly. 'Why didn't you tell me any of this before now?'

'Because it has nothing to do with us.'

'It has everything to do with us,' he said thickly. 'It explains a great deal about why you find it so hard to trust me. It explains why you keep giving me nervous looks. Why you keep waiting for me to fail.'

'The reason I keep giving you nervous looks is because I know this isn't what you wanted. And I know that this sort of situation doesn't have a happy ending. We could keep it going for a while—maybe we'd split up and then get back together, who knows—but that isn't what I want, Alekos. I don't believe in the fairy tale any more,' she said in a faltering voice. 'But I do believe I deserve better than that. And so does my baby.' Without looking at him, she walked into the bedroom and closed the door.

Staring at that door, Alekos knew the gesture was symbolic.

She'd shut him out of her life.

Kelly dialled Vivien's number for the fourteenth time, left a fourteenth message and then ended the call.

She desperately needed to talk to someone, but her friend just wasn't answering the phone.

Scrabbling for a tissue, Kelly blew her nose. She had to stop crying. This was ridiculous; how much water could one person safely lose in twenty-four hours?

She'd been in no state to travel anywhere on her own so she'd agreed to travel back to Corfu and then back to London from there. And she'd cried for the whole duration of the flight. If the baby hadn't already scared Alekos off, then her tears would have done the trick, Kelly thought numbly, remembering Alekos's taut silence as he'd handed her tissue after tissue.

When he wasn't mopping up her tears, he'd worked, occasionally lifting his eyes from his emails to check on her.

Check that she wasn't about to go into meltdown.

But he hadn't attempted to resume the conversation they'd had the night before. He obviously thought she'd totally lost it, Kelly thought gloomily, remembering the look in his eyes as he'd watched her.

When she'd reminded him in a stiff voice that she wanted to return to England on the first available flight, he'd agreed to make arrangements, but the moment they'd arrived back at the villa he'd disappeared, presumably to his office to bury himself in work.

And now she was back in the master-bedroom suite, trying not to look at the enormous bed which dominated the beautiful room.

Switching off her brain, Kelly took a shower, dried her hair and then walked into her dressing room. She pulled on a pair of shorts and a simple tee-shirt and then tugged out her suitcase.

For a moment she stood, just looking at her clothes.

What use were any of those in Little Molting? She couldn't teach the children wearing pale-blue linen, could she?

And she couldn't wear any of the beautiful shoes unless Alekos was next to her, holding her arm.

Trying not to think about that, she walked back to the bedroom and instantly saw the note on the bed. Walking across the room, she picked it up, assuming it was her flight details: *meet me on the beach in ten minutes. Bring the ring.*

Of course. The ring.

Gritting her teeth against the tears that threatened, Kelly scrunched the note up and threw it in the bin. Great; so he wanted to make sure she didn't run off with his precious ring a second time.

She looked down at her hand, at the ring that had been with her on the bumpy journey that was her relationship with Alekos. The thought of parting with it just felt hideously sad.

Tugging it off her finger, she weighed it in her palm for a moment and bit her lip.

She had no idea why he wanted to meet her on the

beach, but if that was what he wanted then that was what she'd do.

She'd deliver the ring to him in person for a final time.

Then she'd go back to her old life and try to learn to live without him.

Kelly walked slowly down the path, trying not to think about how perfect it would have been to bring up a child here, among the olive groves and the tumbling bougainvillea.

She felt as though someone had punched a hole through her insides. *As though she'd lost something that she'd never find anywhere else.*

Pausing for a moment, she closed her eyes. She just had to get through the next five minutes and that was it. She could go away and she'd never have to face him again.

Determined to be as dignified as possible, she walked onto the beach and stopped.

In front of her was a semi-circle of chairs, and in front of the chairs someone with flair and imagination had created an arch of flowers, a riot of colour that clung to the invisible wire-frame and created a door facing the sea.

It looked like a movie set for a very romantic wedding.

Which didn't make sense at all.

'Kelly?' Vivien's voice came from across the sand and then her friend was running towards her, her hair flying, her long dress tangling around her slim legs.

Laughing and crying at the same time, Kelly hugged her. 'I've been phoning you and phoning you—what on earth are you *wearing*?' She stood back from her friend and stared down at the dress in amazement. 'You look fantastic. Very glamorous. But—?'

'I'm your bridesmaid,' Vivien squeaked. 'He said it had to be a surprise so I switched my phone off, because you know I'm utterly useless at keeping secrets, and I knew if I spoke to you I'd give it away. Are you pleased?'

Kelly was confused. 'I—you look lovely, Vivien, but I—I don't need a bridesmaid. I'm not getting married.'

'What? Of course you are! Alekos flew me over here especially for your wedding. I had the whole private-jet experience.' Vivien grinned. 'I won't tell you how many mojitos I drank, but my head is killing me. Can we just get on with this?'

'You spoke your lines too early,' Alekos drawled from behind them. 'I was supposed to go first. She doesn't know anything about this.'

'What?' Vivien gaped at him. 'When you said it was a surprise, I assumed you meant that me being a bridesmaid was a surprise—not the whole wedding.'

'Things don't always go according to plan, and that is especially true of my relationship with Kelly.' Unusually hesitant, Alekos took Kelly's hand in his. 'Last night, in Venice, I was going to ask you to marry me. That's why I took you there.'

Vivien gave a whimper and pressed her hand against her chest. 'Oh my.'

'Vivien.' Alekos was still looking at Kelly. 'If you open your mouth again before I give you permission, you will never travel on my private jet again.'

'Mmm.' Vivien made the sound through sealed lips, but Kelly was staring at Alekos.

'Y-you were going to ask me to marry you?' She shook her head. 'No! You were tense and edgy about the whole dress thing, and then when Constantine asked if you were a father you said no—you can't talk your way out of this one, Alekos.'

'I was tense and edgy because I was going to ask you to marry me and I was afraid you would turn me down,' he said huskily. 'After the last time, why would you trust me? I was gearing up to it for days. I took you to what I thought was one of the most romantic places on earth.'

'But—'

'All evening I was planning how to ask you, where would be best.'

'But Constantine?'

'Asked me if I was a father. I said no, because to me being a father is so much more than just creating a child. That's what your dad did, but he wasn't a father, was he?' His voice hoarse, he stroked his hands over her cheeks and cupped her face. 'Being a father is about loving your child more than you love yourself, putting their welfare before your own, protecting them from a very hard world and making sure that they know that, whatever happens, you're there for them. And I can tell you that I'll do all those things, but it would mean more if I showed you. And that's going to take time.'

Kelly couldn't breathe. 'Time?'

'Let's start with fifty years or so.' His eyes scanned her face. 'We'll have to have quite a few children so that I get plenty of practice—at least four. And you can tell me how I'm doing. Maybe after fifty years and four children if someone asks if I'm a father I'll feel able to say yes.'

Kelly swallowed. 'I thought the whole idea scared you.'

'I didn't say I wasn't scared. I am. But I'm still standing here,' Alekos said softly. 'And I'm still holding your hand. And talking of hands...' He slid the ring off Kelly's hand and transferred it to the other hand.

Kelly felt her eyes mist. 'Alekos...'

'I love you, *agape mou*. I love you because you are generous, kind, funny and the sexiest woman I know. I love the fact you have to hold my arm because you can't walk in high heels; I love the fact you hate bits in your lemonade; I even love the fact that you drop your belongings everywhere.' He smoothed her hair away from her face. 'And I love the fact you would walk away from this relationship if it meant protecting our baby. But you don't have to do that, Kelly. We'll protect him—or her—together.'

Terrified to believe what was happening, Kelly stared down at the ring on her finger. 'You love me?'

'There is no question about that,' he said shakily. 'The only question is whether you can believe me, because if you're always going to doubt me then this will never work. I'd like to think I'll never say the wrong thing to you, but I'm a man, so there's a fairly strong chance that at some point I'm going to get it wrong— like last night in Venice.' He spread his hands in a gesture of mute apology. 'I can see why you interpreted what I said that way, but—'

'You hadn't said you loved me,' Kelly muttered. 'You hadn't told me that. I was dying for you to tell me to move the ring back to my other hand, but you never did.'

A muscle flickered in his jaw. 'Kelly, four years ago I left you on your wedding day. That is a hard thing to forgive—we needed time, you know we did. I was afraid that if I asked you too soon you'd just refuse. I was *terrified* that you'd refuse. I was waiting.'

Kelly thought about the way their relationship had deepened over the past couple of months. 'I kept wanting you to ask. When you didn't, I assumed it was because you didn't love me.'

'I wanted you to be secure in the knowledge that I love you.'

'Alekos…'

'You have to know that, just because the wrong thing may have come out of my mouth, doesn't mean the right thing isn't in my heart.' Alekos lowered his head and kissed her, and for a long moment no one spoke.

Then Vivien cleared her throat. 'All right. Enough of this. It was pretty obvious to me that he loved you, Kel,' she said bluntly. 'I mean, you don't have any money of your own, you're rubbish at organisation, and although you can look pretty when you make an effort you're no one's idea of a trophy wife because you haven't got that haughty look, and you fall over in high heels, so basically you don't have much going for you.'

'Thanks.'

'Which means it has to be love,' Vivien said airily. 'So can we get on with this before the bridesmaid gets sunburn?'

Half-laughing, half-crying, Kelly looked at Alekos. 'You want to get married right here? Now? I can't believe that you've arranged this on the beach—the flowers, the chairs.'

'I wanted to give you the fairy tale,' he said huskily. 'And, yes, we're doing it right now. I'm not going to change my mind, Kelly. I know what I want. And I think I know what you want. Neither of us need a crowd. If you say yes, then I have two people waiting in the villa—my head of legal, Dmitri, who also happens to be a close friend, and a man who is going to marry us.'

Caught in a whirlwind of happiness, Kelly gave a faltering smile. 'I can't get married wearing shorts.'

'Told you!' Vivien said triumphantly and she gestured to a pile of bags folded over a chair. 'Luckily for you, he's bought you a dress.'

Wondering if it was by Marianna, Kelly tensed, and Alekos gave a humourless laugh, reading her mind.

'No,' he said quietly. 'It isn't. In the name of honesty, I have to admit that I did order one, but that was before I knew it would upset you.' He breathed. 'I had ten different ones delivered to the villa this morning. You can choose something different.'

'Ten?' She stared at the pile on the chair. 'Ten.'

'I wanted you to have the choice.' A flicker of a smile touched his mouth. 'And I think you're supposed to surprise me.'

Touched by the thought behind the gesture, Kelly lifted her hand to his cheek. 'I love you. Thank you.' Tears spilled out of her eyes and Vivien gave a squeak of horror.

'Don't cry! You look hideous when you cry, and I'm supposed to do your make-up. There's not a lot I can do with super-red eyes. Go for a walk for half an hour, Alekos, so that I can get her into this dress. You're not supposed to see the bride—it's bad luck.'

'I could go to the villa,' Kelly protested, but Alekos shook his head.

'I'm not taking any chances,' he said huskily, lowering his mouth to hers again. 'I love you and I'm marrying you right now. I'd marry you in shorts.'

'Alekos Zagorakis, she is not wearing shorts! She has to drool over these wedding photos for the rest of her life, and no one can drool over a pair of shorts.' Outraged, Vivien gave him a push. 'All right, compromise—go and fetch your best man or whoever he is and come back in ten minutes.'

Ten minutes later, Kelly was standing under the arch of flowers, wearing the most beautiful dress she'd ever seen, gazing up at the only man she'd ever loved.

Vivien was making eyes at Dmitri.

'I have a feeling that neither your bridesmaid nor my best man are concentrating,' Alekos drawled, pulling Kelly against him, ignoring the disapproval of the man who was marrying them. 'We might have to do this without help.'

Kelly clutched the bunch of flowers that Vivien had pressed into her hands and smiled up at Alekos. 'I can't believe we're doing this at all. I didn't think it was going to end this way.'

'Does it feel like the fairy tale? Perhaps I should have laid on a couple of white horses and a carriage.'

She laughed. 'You'd never get a carriage down to this beach.' Standing on tiptoe, she kissed him. 'You got the important bits right.'

'We belong together,' he said huskily. 'For ever.'

Kelly smiled against his mouth. 'That sounds like the fairy tale to me.'

* * * * *